BOOK TWO OF THE MACHINISTS

# SPLINTER

## CRAIG ANDREWS

# ALSO BY CRAIG ANDREWS

## FRACTURE

## SPLINTER

## MARTYR
(forthcoming)

For exclusive content follow Craig
Andrews on Facebook or sign up
for his Mailing List.

https://www.facebook.com/craigandrewsauthor

http://eepurl.com/IEjIr

For my Mom, who's the strongest, most compassionate, hardest working person I've ever met. And for my Dad, who taught me what it means to be a man, a father, and a geek. You are *my* heroes.

# CHAPTER 1

**F**OUR DAYS, ALLYN THOUGHT. *FOUR days since I became a murderer.*

His stomach twisted at the thought as the memory flooded back. He could see Lukas clearly, as if he were standing in the small cabin bedroom with him. Red coils of electricity wrapped around Lukas's golden skin, shaking his rigid frame violently. Steam rose from his blistering body, and Allyn closed his eyes, pleading for the image to disappear. It didn't—it never did. He gagged, drowning in the putrid scent of burning flesh, like a shipwreck survivor in the middle of the vast sea of regret. Everywhere he went, he could see it. Smell it. Taste it. The vision had become a waking nightmare—and sleep was worse.

The springs of the old twin mattress groaned as he rolled out of bed to open the small single-paned window nearby. A bitter winter breeze slapped away Allyn's nausea and dried his flushed face. He leaned his forehead against the fogging window, breathing raggedly—only the cold helped him escape the nightmare. He closed his eyes, relishing the short reprieve.

Liam's scream cut through the early morning like a siren.

Allyn snapped open his eyes and whipped his head around

to look at the door behind him. Liam had grown quiet—his scream muffled and cut short. It could mean only one thing. They had been found.

Allyn turned back to the window, peering into the night. Thick fog blanketed the gravel driveway, mixing with the freshly fallen snow so that it was difficult to tell where one ended and the other began. Hidden amid the fog, the evergreens were little more than shadows, still and unimposing. A thin layer of ice covered the windshield of the old Cadillac Jaxon had bought after fleeing the manor, but the property was otherwise undisturbed. Nothing was amiss.

*Then why the scream?*

Allyn made for the door. The cabin was quiet, and though he was mindful of his footfalls, the floor squeaked, piercing the silence. If the police had arrived, he would have heard them. *Wouldn't I?* The door would have come crashing down. There would have been shouts of alarm and orders to freeze. Something was off, and Allyn was beginning to think it had nothing to do with being found.

He grabbed the tarnished doorknob and slowly opened the door. The dry hinges squealed. Allyn stopped and waited. When he didn't hear anything, he drew close to the door and peeked through the crack. The cabin was still. Moonlight reflecting off the snow outside illuminated the cabin through the living room's floor-to-ceiling windows with a soft white light. The couches that had been pushed to the edges of the room to create more sleeping space were empty. So were the large rug in the center of the room and the area in front of the brick fireplace. Allyn didn't see *anyone*.

*That's odd.* The cabin was bursting with occupants, and magi should have been strewn about under blankets and in sleeping bags, on the couches and rugs, and in front of the fire. One or two missing would be normal. Restless sleepers rose throughout the night to walk around and stretch aching bodies, while others would be up to relieve themselves or to grab a drink of water. *But everybody?*

The floor creaked.

Allyn drew closer to the doorframe. *Was that a shadow in the—*

The edge of the door smashed into the center of his forehead. Dazed, Allyn staggered back, one hand covering his face.

Four dark figures rushed into the room. They were on him in a blink, wrestling him to the ground and binding his hands and feet. Stunned, Allyn didn't fight back. Blood trickled from his forehead, catching in his eyebrow, as the figures pulled him to his feet and ushered him out of the room.

Comprehension returned with each step. The cabin was being attacked. Allyn dared a glance to either side, but the firm hand holding his neck kept his gaze on the back of the slender magi in front of him.

They ushered him outside. The snow bit the bottoms of his bare feet, and the icy air took care of his remaining wariness. Dim starlight revealed a scar that ran from the corner of the procession leader's eye down to her jaw. Allyn knew that scar.

"Ren?" Allyn asked. He hadn't had many interactions with the woman, but she had been a member of his squad when they reclaimed the McCollum Manor. She ignored him, but the way her body had tensed when he'd identified her told him he was correct. "What are you doing? Where are you taking me?"

"Quiet," the man with the firm hand said.

*I know that voice.* Allyn instinctively turned to look at him, but the man's fingers tightened around his neck and held his head in place. The magi at his sides slunk back, falling into step with the man behind him so he could no longer see them.

Ren led them into the forest, following one of the magi

9

trails. Boredom plagued the younger magi, and they had taken to hiking the hills surrounding the cabin. Kendyl enjoyed being their guide and revisiting scenery she had loved as a child.

Allyn probed the oppressive night, seeking an escape route. Whatever Ren and the rest of the magi were planning, they had taken to force, and he wanted no part of that. But even if he could get free, the dense forest was black, and the snow deep. The binding around his feet allowed him to walk, but he couldn't run.

*Stupid*, he thought. *You were taken in your own room.*

They crested the hill then continued down the hillside into a clear-cut area. Young saplings covered the hillside, mixing with dead trees and discarded timber like flowers atop a grave. The moon had risen high, lighting the edges of the thin clouds above like a fire burning the edges of paper.

*Fire.* Allyn cursed to himself. The four people around him were magi who could wield. He could wield, too, even if it didn't come naturally yet. His first instincts were to punch, kick, fight, or run. He hadn't lived with his abilities long enough. And if he did wield... the scent of burning flesh returned.

Allyn began his calming exercise, focusing on the freezing elements when he saw them. A group of people dressed in black stood in a circle in the center of the clearing. Jaxon waited atop a fallen log, his powerful frame bulging under his sleeveless black vest. The wind kicked up, blowing across his branded arms, but Jaxon remained still, unfazed. His large expressionless eyes looked like tiny moons watching Allyn.

The circle opened, allowing Allyn's procession to enter. Liam was on his back at the center of the circle with his legs tied to a stake in the ground. His arms were outstretched, palms facing the earth, and tied to two stakes of their own. He saw Allyn and smiled.

Allyn tried to speak, but nothing came out. He was

confused beyond words. The sight of his friend smiling eased his nerves, but there was something else in Liam's eyes—fear. *What would make a man fearful yet happy?*

Ren led Allyn to the center of the circle and began to undo the binds at his hands. Allyn looked around. Familiar faces watched him—Mason, Rory, Andrew, Topher, and others. All magi. No clerics. *Where are Nyla and Leira? Where's Kendyl?*

"Lay down," Ren said as the bonds tying his hands slackened.

"What?"

She pointed at the cleared space beside Liam, where three more stakes had been driven into the ground. Liam watched him with the same befuddled smile. Instinct pleaded with Allyn to run. Curiosity urged him to stay. His body coiled like a spooked steer in the stockades, and he took a hesitant step backward, ready to bolt.

They were on him in a second. Two of the guards from his procession took him by the arms and dragged him forward. One swept Allyn's feet from under him, and he went down hard. The magi who'd tripped him—Allyn never got a good look at his face—straddled his chest, driving his knees into Allyn's arms and pinning them to the ground while the other magi bound them to the stakes.

Allyn fought. Shifting and screaming, writhing and turning, he bucked like a bull trying to toss a cowboy. The magi on his chest rocked forward, and his knees slipped under the muscle and settled on a nerve cluster, sending enough pain shooting through Allyn's body to paralyze him. Ren and the others quickly tied his wrist to the stake and moved to the other. With his second hand fastened and immobile, they moved to his feet.

The pressure on Allyn's chest and arms relaxed as the man rocked backward. With the moon directly behind his head, Allyn couldn't see his face, but the man gave Allyn a gentle slap across the cheek that said, "Good try." Finished with his hands and feet, the three magi withdrew, disappearing into the mass of people.

"It's okay," Liam said softly. He looked at Allyn as though he were thankful to experience this with him.

Heavy footsteps drew closer, and Jaxon appeared. He stepped between Allyn and Liam, walking toward the bottom of the circle, his back to Allyn. Something dark rested over the crook of his arm. He stopped beside Rory. The young magi's face still bore the scars from the Reclaiming, a constant reminder that, if not for Liam, he would have died that night.

Jaxon held out the dark object, and Rory wielded fire around its tip. After a few moments, Jaxon moved to the next magi, then the next, working his way around the circle. By the time he was a quarter of the way around, Allyn realized what was in Jaxon's hands. He sank deeper into the ground, his uneasiness blossoming into panic. He didn't know who had grabbed it or when—most of the ancient magi artifacts had burned with the manor—but there was little doubt in his mind as to what it was—a brand.

*It's an initiation.* They weren't doing this out of spite or cruelty. They were doing this because they deemed Allyn and Liam worthy. Because he and Liam were like *them*.

All Liam had ever wanted was to fit in. And the Branding was the symbol of that acceptance. It was barbaric, if a bit poetic, and Allyn had never signed up for it.

Jaxon worked his way around the circle until he finished where he began. He handed the brand to Rory, and they stepped forward with two other magi that Liam had saved during Lukas's assault on the manor. Rory walked with a limp—his knee hadn't healed completely since the Reclaiming—but he strode purposefully toward Liam.

Liam shifted uncomfortably as they approached, the orange tip of the brand reflecting in his glassy eyes. Jaxon walked around Liam and knelt over him, gently taking his head in his hands.

One of the other magi placed a cork in Liam's mouth. "Bite down on this," he whispered. "It'll help."

Rory waved the brand in front of Liam's face, drawing jagged and curving vertical lines in the air. Allyn recognized it as the magi symbol for fire. Heat radiated from the tip of the brand, distorting the air. Liam gulped.

Jaxon drew closer, his lips beside Liam's ear. "Ready?" he whispered.

Liam gave him a terrified nod.

"From our collective fire, we deem you *fieri*," Jaxon announced.

The collective murmur among the magi was interrupted as Rory drove the brand into Liam's upper arm. It hissed, and smoke curled into the air.

Allyn nearly vomited.

Liam screamed, his chest arching toward the sky, the veins in his neck bulging. Jaxon spoke to Liam, but his words were too soft for Allyn to make out. The other two magi held Liam still as Rory rolled the brand from one side to the other, making sure to get good contact around Liam's skinny arm.

When Rory finally pulled away, a bloody, black and red wound remained. Liam's screams subsided and were replaced by short, ragged breaths. He stretched his neck to the side in an attempt to see the wound, but the bonds held his arms in place, and Jaxon held Liam's head still.

"Not yet," Jaxon said.

Rory stepped around to Liam's other arm.

*Two brands*, Allyn remembered. *I have to go through this twice.* Apprehension settled in his chest, stoking his fear like a coal burner.

Rory picked the same spot on Liam's opposite arm, so that the two brands would mirror each other. Allyn tried to drown out the sights, sounds, and smells by focusing on his physical discomfort. A fist-sized rock was digging into Allyn's lower back, just below his kidney. He pushed against its weathered edges, and sharp pain shot through him. He focused on that, pushing harder. The pain took his breath away.

Liam laughed. The sound sliced through Allyn's distraction, leaving him with only a dull ache where he had sought solace. It was a pained, relieved laugh. Tears slid down the side of Liam's face, and more threatened to follow. Jaxon smiled at him, patting him gently on the cheek, as the two magi undid the binds at his arms.

Liam sat up and inspected the blistered brands with a grimace. They almost seemed to glow from within. Blood trickled down his right arm, disappearing under his elbow and dripping onto the white snow. Liam looked at Allyn, prideful, and Allyn tried to smile back, but his body wouldn't cooperate. His mouth was beginning to salivate, his throat constricting. He tried to take slow, deep breaths to relax, but even that proved difficult.

He'd gone to battle and seen magi die around him. He'd even killed, but his body had never betrayed him like this. *What's different? The anticipation? The binds? The promise of pain?*

Rory wielded more fire, reheating the brand until it glowed orange, then passed it to Liam, who had gotten to his feet. Rory and the other two magi returned to the circle. Mason and Ren advanced.

Allyn wanted to laugh. He barely knew Ren, and he didn't like Mason. He was the bully on the playground who pretended to be friendly from time to time. Allyn didn't have the temperament to deal with his arrogant, self-indulgent, abrasive personality. And yet, here he was, initiating Allyn into the magi ranks.

*Who's left?* The question reverberated through Allyn with a spike of remorse. While living with the McCollum Family, he'd grown closest to Liam and Nyla and developed a mutual respect for Graeme and Jaxon, but he knew little of the rest.

He knew dozens of other faces and even a few names, but they were little more than that. He'd never gone out of his way to meet the other magi. They had intimidated him, and he hadn't expected to stay with the Family for long.

His purpose had been simple: rescue his sister. But things had grown complicated, and he had remained with the Family, even rising to a prominent figure within their ranks. Thinking about it made Allyn uncomfortable. He didn't know the magi around him. Still, they were inviting him to join their Family, welcoming him with smiles and respect.

*I can do this.* Allyn steeled himself and met Liam's eye. He stood above Allyn, holding the glowing brand in both hands, blood seeping from his wounds. Something about Liam felt different. He looked stronger, more confident. He looked like a leader.

Allyn gave him a slight nod, and Liam drove the brand down onto Allyn's arm.

# CHAPTER 2

"**S**HE'S GETTING WORSE." JOYCE WATCHED as the nineteen-year-old girl rocked back and forth against the wall.

Canary—a nickname given to her because of her yellow-and-black-streaked hair—had her knees pulled tight against her chest and her hands clamped over her ears. A steady stream of incoherent ramblings poured from her mouth.

Jaxon knelt in front of her, dropping his head to the side in an attempt to make eye contact. Canary didn't look up, and the ramblings didn't stop.

"Stress?" he asked.

"Undoubtedly," Joyce said. "She grew irritable the first day and struggled to keep on task. We were all emotional, so I didn't think much of it. The second day, she complained of noises that didn't affect any others. I thought she was over stimulated, so I kept her workload as light as possible. But by the time we arrived here, she just shut down."

"And now this."

"And now this," Joyce repeated. Her voice was even, but worry creased the edges of her eyes.

"We've all been through a lot," Jaxon said, standing.

"Allow her time to cope. If that's not enough, talk with Leira or Vincent and keep her under. Her mind needs time to heal."

Joyce nodded, though she didn't look as though she approved.

"Speak," Jaxon said, the word coming out rougher than he intended.

"This is outside my realm of expertise," she said. "I treat cuts and scrapes, even burns and stitches on occasion, but this..." She looked back at Canary. The poor girl didn't seem to realize anyone was in the room with her. "I don't know the first thing about treating a mental breakdown."

"Do what you can," Jaxon said. *We're all in over our heads.* He stepped out of the room and closed the door behind him, relieved to escape Canary's ramblings. Deep down, he knew mental illness wasn't contagious, but that didn't make it any more comfortable to be around. The idea that he was only one trigger away from madness was a truly terrifying thought.

He stepped into the main living space. The inside of the cabin was larger than one might have expected based on its deceptively small exterior. Complete with a full kitchen containing an eat-in bar and dining and living rooms, the main living quarters consisted of one giant great room centered around a stone fireplace, where a fire burned day and night. Furnished with two ancient couches and a slab from a great redwood serving as the dining room table, the cabin was filled with eclectic designs that didn't complement each other. A floating staircase led upstairs to a loft, where Allyn and Kendyl had played as kids. Now it slept the bulk of their number. Privacy was a thing of the past.

Even then, the cabin was still too small for their number. But they worked to make do. The cabin echoed with the sounds of hammers and saws, and it smelled of sweat and fresh-cut timber. A team of young magi were using the rusty tools Jaxon had found in the garage to build bunks along the long wall of the living space. Jaxon didn't believe they would necessarily be using the bunks—he hoped to leave any day—but staying productive would keep their spirits up.

"Jaxon."

Jaxon turned to find Erik, the building team's leader, waiting anxiously. He had removed his shirt, exposing his sweat-slick olive skin and well-defined frame. Having been his instructor for years, Jaxon knew the young magi well. He'd been there when Erik had wielded for the first time, and after only a year, he was one of the Family's quickest learners.

"We have a problem," Erik said.

Jaxon stifled a groan. When Erik didn't immediately come out with it, Jaxon gave him an irritated go-ahead gesture.

"We're running out of lumber," Erik said.

If it hadn't been for a series of similar complaints over the last couple days, Jaxon wouldn't have believed what he was hearing. "You're in the middle of a forest. Go cut down more."

"We can't."

Jaxon resisted the urge to pinch his forehead. "Why not?"

"The ax handle broke," Erik said.

"And are you, or are you not, a magi?"

"I would blast them down, but..."

"But what, Erik?"

"You ordered us not to perform any magic."

Jaxon exhaled his frustration in a long breath. He *had* issued that order. The cabin was secluded and barely visible from the mountain highway, but they were a house full of wanted people who had lived in the shadows for centuries, and he didn't want to attract any unwanted attention. Their days were already numbered.

"You're right," Jaxon said. "I apologize for being short. In this, I grant you permission, but do so away from the road, and set up sentries to be sure no errant hiker stumbles on you."

"Okay," Erik said. "Thank you, Jaxon."

Before Jaxon had a chance to respond, Erik was assembling a small squad, ready to move forward. Jaxon swelled with satisfaction—the young man's eagerness was one of the traits that had endeared Erik to him.

Leira appeared out of their shared bedroom, his phone in her hand. "Jaxon?"

Jaxon stiffened. *What now?*

She held up the phone.

*Who would be calling?* What remained of the Family was at the cabin. *Unless it's another Family prepared to offer aid?*

"I'll take it outside," he said, moving toward the door, which opened onto a covered wraparound porch.

A waist-high railing, painted a faded red that was flaking away, ran the length of it and overlooked the front of the property, where the gravel driveway and evergreen trees were heavy with fresh snow. To his left, trails led to the clearing where he had performed the Brandings. The hills to his right fell away and wrapped around into a deep valley behind the cabin. Leira emerged, holding the phone in front of her as if it were soiled clothing.

"Everything all right?" Jaxon asked.

"It's your Family," she said.

Jaxon hesitated. *My Family.* They must have received word of the fall of the McCollum Manor. *Are they planning to offer asylum?* He took the phone. "This is Jaxon."

"I should be relieved to hear your voice." Talisa Green was a sharp woman with a nasally voice. Smart, driven, and set in her ways, she was not a woman Jaxon wanted to cross. She scared him more now than she had when he was a child.

"Hi, Mother."

"It's true then," she said. "Graeme is dead."

Jaxon glanced at Leira. She wore a slightly puzzled expression, but she touched his shoulder, offering her silent support. She had likely also expected the call—though she was probably put off by the timing.

"Yes," Jaxon said.

"Leira has never shown much interest in leading the Family, and even if the rumors of Liam's *ailments* are exaggerated, he's too young. So I suppose then that that means you're the McCollum Family's acting grand mage." She hadn't asked a question, but the dead air following her statement suggested she expected an answer.

Jaxon kept it short. "It does."

Talisa sighed deeply. "Your father isn't going to be pleased. He wants you home."

"You know I can't do that."

Leira's face reflected full-blown confusion. "Do what?" she mouthed.

Jaxon held up a finger. The conversation was awkward enough—he didn't need her involved, too.

"They're not your responsibility, Jaxon," his mother said.

"I'm not going to argue about this," he said. "I'm here. And I have accepted the responsibility."

"Jaxon—"

"No." Jaxon exhaled sharply, reining in his anger. "I have lived with this Family for nearly as long as I lived with my own, and I will not leave it to splinter further. If you and Father wish me home so badly, then I will return with the condition that the McCollum Family returns with me."

Her answer was quick. "No."

"No?"

"No," Talisa said with the full weight of authority. "The McCollum Family is on the brink of collapse and has gone to war with a rival Family without the permission of the Forum."

"Mother—"

"I will not have this Family drug into it."

"It already has been," Jaxon said. "I was part of it."

"Which is why we want you home."

"You have my conditions."

"And you have our answer."

Jaxon turned away from Leira, moving farther down the porch. "This is madness. The McCollum Family is one of the oldest Families in the Order. How can you reject their plea for help? How can you deny *my* request?"

"Jaxon," Talisa said, her voice taking on a motherly tone, which he instantly distrusted. "It's better this way. The Family will splinter, but other Families will absorb them. Their bloodlines will continue."

Jaxon set his jaw. "This is your will?"

"It's the will of the Forum and Arch Mage Westarra himself."

"Why?"

"They have nothing to offer."

"That's not true," Jaxon said. "If I had been made aware of the session, as I should have been, I could have—"

"The McCollum Family no longer exists in the eyes of the Forum," Talisa said. "Arch Mage Westarra had no reason to invite a delegate from the Family. Furthermore, any further requests for aid will be denied—by any Family."

Jaxon tapped the phone against his forehead, thinking.

"We expect you home within the week," Talisa continued. "Tidy up your replacement and be gone. If not, we will be forced to remove you."

The call went dead.

Jaxon felt Leira approach. "I'm being torn in two," he said softly.

"What happened?" She rubbed the back of his neck with her thumb and index finger.

He could feel her concern and wished he had the strength to tell her that it was going to be all right. Thankfully, she didn't say anything more. She knew what was at stake. She knew the strain he was under. The weight of two Families bore down on his broad shoulders, and no matter which side he chose, he would hurt people he cared for deeply. There was no right answer. He'd failed.

Jaxon imagined slamming the phone into one of the nearby wooden beams that supported the overhang. It somehow felt *right*.

"Jaxon!"

He blinked, looking down. The phone was shattered in his hands. Broken bits of plastic and glass covered the railing.

"I..." he stammered.

Leira reached for him tentatively, her expression equal bits of shock, concern, and fear.

"I'm fine," he said sharply.

She pulled her hand back and brought her fist to her lips. Behind her, a few surprised onlookers watched from the cabin doorway.

Jaxon flushed. He was the anointed grand mage of the McCollum Family and heir to the same position in his own Family, yet here he was, behaving like a pubescent teenager. No worthwhile magi, let alone a grand mage, lashed out and smashed objects in anger.

Embarrassment turned to frustration, then anger, mixing with his already present fury. It was his responsibility to keep it together so others didn't have to. Having failed at that, he could see the vanishing trust in the eyes of the watchful magi. Leira must have seen it, too—she turned and told them to go back inside. When she returned, she opened her mouth to say something.

Jaxon cut her off with a dismissive wave. "I'm fine. I need space."

"Jaxon..." Leira took his hand. He could feel her pulse racing through her fingertips. She shared in his terrified feelings. "Let me in."

Jaxon shook his head. She didn't know what she was asking. He'd come to the McCollum Family as a boy in a man's body. Like Liam, he'd grown up in a solitary world, one chosen for him, and had been groomed and trained for a singular purpose. His upbringing hadn't left many opportunities for friendships, but in the years he'd spent with Graeme as his mentor, he'd grown closer to his children than he had anyone else. Liam had become his younger brother, someone to watch over and protect, someone to guide and counsel. Jaxon had taken great pride in watching Liam grow and begin to fulfill his potential.

Leira had become something else. He didn't know if he could call it love, but he did know that he'd never felt the same way about anyone else as he did her. She was smart, beautiful, and strong. He could lean on her. And she had a way of seeing him as nobody else did. They were... compatible, if nothing else. But his time with the McCollum Family had always been finite. He hadn't let himself fall for her, not completely. He couldn't stay, and he doubted she would follow. That was not who Leira was. To open up, to let her in, would only make the pain of his inevitable decision cut that much deeper.

"I can't."

"Why?" She had inherited her father's stubbornness.

*How did Graeme hold it together? Was it a stubbornness to succeed?* Jaxon was under only a fraction of the pressure Graeme had experienced. A splinter. Rebellion. Death. Graeme had been a pillar of strength through it all, unflinching and unwavering. He had held on until the end, and because of him, his Family survived. His children lived. And because Jaxon was too weak, he had put that all into jeopardy. His anger boiled again.

"Nobody expects you to do this alone." Leira's words cut at the heart of his self-deprecation. Of course he was supposed to do this alone. That was what the position entailed. That was what leadership meant—a leader had to be the example he wanted the rest to strive toward.

"We all need help sometimes, Jaxon. And it can take on many different forms—everyone needs something different.

So whatever you need, I'm here." She squeezed his hand, her eyes pleading with him.

Jaxon took a deep breath. Whether he wanted to admit it or not, they were in this together. "Let's take a walk."

---

A short time later, Jaxon found himself walking with Leira down the narrow mountain road adjacent to the cabin. The peaceful trickle of a slow-moving creek somewhere in the sparse wood off the road accompanied the soft crunch of their steps. Clumps of grass grew between the cracks of the crumbling asphalt, their green tips barely visible above the accumulating snow. Frozen branches overhead glistened like crystalline wonders in the soft glow of the winter afternoon. More tiny flakes fell, covering their tracks and melting against Jaxon's bare arms. Most young magi assumed he simply ignored the cold. They didn't know that as long as they kept their chests warm, their limbs would be, as well.

Leira was bundled under a black coat held together by a series of silver buckles. Her chin-length black hair was hidden under its hood. She glanced at him from time to time, occasionally offering a smile, which he returned.

Nothing centered him like the outdoors. *I need to do this more often,* Jaxon thought, remembering that Graeme had often walked in the woods surrounding the manor. He'd even cultivated an outdoor office there, a private sanctuary of sorts. Jaxon had been so caught up in managing the Family's struggles that he'd forgotten to take care of his own.

*Yes,* he decided, *I will make a habit of this.*

"Do you remember the night Lukas left?" Leira's voice was quiet and hesitant, as if she were afraid to interrupt their private retreat.

"Of course." *How could I forget?* Lukas had splintered the McCollum Family, leaving with nearly a third of its members, then continued to spread his vitriol, verbally assaulting their most sacred traditions in an attempt to recruit from Families unsympathetic to Graeme's philosophies. He sought the youngest and most ambitious magi, those with a chips on their shoulders. Those who felt they had something to prove—and they flocked to his message. Lukas had done more than decimate the McCollum Family's strength; he had destroyed their reputation. The Families avoided them as if their presumed weakness was contagious, and even after Lukas's downfall—and Graeme's death—the Family still hadn't recovered.

"I found my father in his study. It was dark, and he stood at the window, watching as Lukas led his followers away. To this day, I don't know what hurt him more—their departure or their excitement in doing so."

Jaxon remembered the evening clearly. It had been a blistering-hot late-August evening, and tempers between Graeme and Lukas had flared for the final time. They had fled at dusk when the sky was an angry mix of reds, oranges, and yellows. Lukas had turned the somber event into a celebration, throwing balls of fire into the air like fireworks. His followers danced, cheered, and made a mockery of those who had remained. Lukas enjoyed rubbing Graeme's nose in it.

"A piece of him left with Lukas that day," Leira said. "He became somber, bitter, and distrustful. He ceased being my father, instead becoming more interested in being my leader. And I *hated* him for it."

Jaxon looked at her in surprise. Leira had barely spoken of her father since his death, but when she had, she'd never spoken ill. Her honesty made him uneasy.

"I don't want to see you make the same mistake."

"I'm not contending with a splinter," Jaxon said.

"That's not what destroyed my father. His downfall wasn't circumstance—it was how he responded to it."

"Your father was the strongest man I've ever known."

"That's where he failed," Leira said. "He tried to shoulder the burden himself. Tried to turn himself into the manor and shelter us inside, but it was too much to bear. It wasn't a coincidence that my father died the same night the manor was destroyed. They were too intertwined. One couldn't exist without the other."

"The Family needs a strong leader."

"Strength comes from a strong foundation, Jaxon. You don't have to be the walls and the roof, too."

Her words echoed something Graeme used to say. *"You're only as strong as your support structure."*

*But who had been Graeme's support structure? Who held him up when he would have otherwise fallen? His Family? Me?* If that were the case, then Jaxon had been a lousy pillar of support—he'd often used Graeme's moments of council to question some of his deepest philosophies. Had he hoped for Jaxon to share in his burdens?

"You want to play a larger part," Jaxon said.

Leira stopped and turned to face him. "I want to play *a* part, Jaxon. This is my Family, too."

He studied the conviction in her eyes. It stirred something inside him—her conviction was one of the things he treasured most about her, even if it could be frustrating. "I'm not trying to shut you out."

"I know." Leira turned from him and walked into the sparse forest. She found a fallen tree, then sat down, and waited for him to join her.

He stood there for a moment, feeling awkward. The way her eyes bore through him, into his soul, made him self-conscious. But the way he cherished it terrified him even more. Hesitantly, he made his way to the fallen tree and sat next to her.

Leira slid closer until her leg touched his. "Will you tell me what happened back there?"

Jaxon exhaled, his breath billowing into the air. "I don't

know," he said honestly. "The anger came so fast. It's just too much, and I got lost in it."

"What's all too much?"

Jaxon shot her an irritated look.

"Don't look at me like that," she said. "Pulling words and feelings out of you is like pulling stars from the sky—damn near impossible and probably not worth the effort. The other half the time, your face is as hard as granite. So if you don't tell me what's going on, I have no way of knowing."

"I don't try to be difficult," Jaxon said.

"I know. It just comes naturally." Leira smirked and prodded him with an elbow. "So tell me. What happened with the call?"

Jaxon drew a deep breath. "My Family is unhappy that I'm the interim grand mage for your Family. They want me to anoint another and return home."

Leira's eyes fell from his, but her face remained placid. The news shouldn't have come as a shock. She had been privy to his half of the conversation and should have come to the conclusion herself. "What will you do?"

"What choice do I have?" Jaxon asked. "They're *my* Family. I can't leave them any more than you can leave yours."

"I see," Leira said softly.

"But that's not the worst of it," Jaxon said. "The Forum held a session without a McCollum delegate."

Leira looked up from the ground, meeting his eyes. "But—"

"They've disbanded us, Leira. This Family no longer exists in the eyes of the Forum."

Leira stood, covering her gaping mouth with her hand. "They can't! We... I... they can't!"

"It's done."

Leira turned her back to him, her body tensing. She shook her head. "No."

"Leira—"

She spun on him, cold fury in her eyes. "No. They have no authority to do this."

Jaxon raised an eyebrow. "It's the Arch Mage, Leira. And he has the consent of the Forum—they have the only authority."

"No," Leira said again. "The Forum can no more destroy a Family than they can create one. We are held together by the bonds that brought us together in the first place, and I will not see them broken. I won't let this Family splinter."

Jaxon stood and stepped toward Leira, reaching out a compassionate hand. She recoiled.

"What do you mean to do?" Jaxon asked.

"They must have given a reason." She said it as much to herself as she did him.

"Their charge," Jaxon said slowly, "is an act of war against a magi Family without the consent of the Forum."

"If the Forum had acted in the first place, we wouldn't have been forced to..." She bit her bottom lip angrily.

Jaxon held up a hand. "But," he said, letting the word hang in the air for a long second, "I believe their true reason remains unspoken. My mother said something I can't seem to shake free from. She said the members of the Family would be absorbed by the other Families, that their magi bloodlines would continue. Only the McCollum Family name would cease to exist."

"I don't understand."

"They want us," Jaxon said. "But they don't want our Family."

"Why?"

"Because we're weak. We have nothing to offer and would be a drain on any Family that took us in."

"But that's not true," Leira said. "We have Liam. And Allyn. We know about a new kind of magi."

"I know."

"We have to speak to the Forum."

"That's not going to happen," Jaxon said. "They won't assemble for us. Remember, we no longer exist in their eyes."

"Then what do we do?"

"We force them to look at us."

"How?"

"We show them our strength."

# CHAPTER 3

ALLYN HELD HIS BREATH AS Kendyl removed his bandage. Her dark hair was pulled back in a quick ponytail, and a couple of strands hung loose to frame her face. She wore the black magi compression armor, though hers was untarnished—unlike his, hers had never seen battle. It had never seen death.

Allyn grimaced. The bandage had a way of sticking to the wound, so that when Kendyl pulled the strip away, it tugged painfully on his blistered skin.

Kendyl sighed, her eyes darting to his before returning to the wound. "Why don't you just have Nyla or Leira heal this?"

The brand looked worse than it had the last time she'd changed the dressing. The skin around the edges was dry and leathery, and the angry-red center looked wet, even though she hadn't yet applied the salve. Small crimson droplets spattered the inside of the bandage, but the wound didn't bleed in the open air, though it did seep when he moved his arm to look at it. Liam hadn't cauterized the edges of the brand as thoroughly as Rory had his.

"That's not how the ceremony works," Allyn said. "It has to heal on its own. It's a magi rite of passage."

"It's barbaric." The heat in her voice surprised him.

"I think it's kind of beautiful."

Shaking her head, Kendyl grabbed the bottle of water off the windowsill. She poured some over the top of his arm, just below the shoulder so that the cool liquid trickled down over the brand.

Allyn grimaced as the water washed over the wound and dripped from his elbow onto the bed. Kendyl's room, like his, was full of childhood relics. A princess pillowcase accompanied the pink frilly comforter that covered her bed, and the door was covered in faded Barbie stickers. They had found old toys hidden under the bed and inside the small closet. Kendyl displayed them on the windowsill. She wasn't embarrassed; she was proud.

When they had first moved in, she had attempted to give the room to someone more valuable, but Jaxon hadn't allowed it. The McCollum Family were guests in the cabin, and as the host and hostess, Allyn and Kendyl had the privilege of their own rooms.

"You confuse me sometimes, Kendyl. I know you like tattoos and piercings. How are these any different?"

Her hand went to her hip, gently rubbing her pants, as if she had a tattoo hidden beneath. "A tattoo is voluntary."

"So was this."

Kendyl's expression told him she didn't believe him.

"Jaxon said they don't always do it that way—that they only tied me to the ground so they could get a clean burn—a good brand."

"They didn't think you could handle it."

"What's gotten into you?" Allyn asked. "You've been on edge all day."

Kendyl spooned out the antibiotic ointment and dabbed it on with her fingers. "You don't even like body art."

*What does that have to do with anything?* This was the third time she had helped him clean his brands, and each time, she'd grown more agitated. Allyn appreciated her help, but if it was going to come with an assortment of verbal barbs, he would just as soon go to Joyce. Kendyl was acting like a...

"You're jealous!" Allyn couldn't believe it—Kendyl didn't get jealous. "They dragged me out of my room in the middle of the night. No warning. Nothing. I didn't have much of a choice."

"You just said you did."

Allyn hesitated. Kendyl didn't have much of a temper—he'd inherited that trait—but what little she did have, she reserved for him. "I don't know what to say, Kendyl. I didn't ask for these, and you're right—given the choice, I'm not sure I would have wanted them. But *the Family* feels I earned them, and that means something to me."

She exhaled long and slow then reapplied the bandage. "It's not about the brands." Her voice was quiet, almost as if she were talking to herself.

"But you said—"

"You're about as perceptive as a rock sometimes. You know that? Honestly, Allyn, how were you ever a successful attorney?"

"My clients *wanted* to talk. They didn't say one thing and mean another."

Kendyl laughed.

"What?"

"Nothing."

"Don't play that game. Something is bothering you, and you obviously want to talk about—"

"I don't know what I'm doing here! Okay?" The words came out of her mouth so quickly that Allyn struggled to keep up. "While you're out there saving the day and getting brands and whatever else, I'm here, twiddling my thumbs, trying to find a way to be helpful. But I'm not. I'm useless."

"Kendyl..."

"Don't look at me like that," she said.

*Like what? I'm not smiling, am I?* He had a tendency to smirk when he was uncomfortable. "Do you want to leave?"

"No." Kendyl took a deep breath. "I know I'm here for a reason." Her tone had become softer. "I just need to find out what that reason is."

"Whatever it is, I'll help you find it."

"I don't think it's something you can help me with."

Allyn didn't know what to say, so he remained silent. The floor squeaked behind them, and Allyn turned to find Jaxon standing at the door, mouth agape, his hand raised as if he were about to knock. He looked uncomfortable, as though he had been standing there for a while, unsure of how or when to interrupt.

"I need to speak with you," Jaxon said, his eyes darting to Kendyl. He had definitely been standing there for a while.

"Okay," Allyn said, looking at Kendyl, feeling their conversation was coming to a premature end.

"It's okay," she said.

Allyn gave her a small smile and withdrew into the hall.

Jaxon leaned in close. "Is everything okay?"

"To be honest," Allyn said, "I don't really know."

Jaxon nodded knowingly. "We've got other problems." He gestured to his room across the hall and pushed open the door for Allyn to enter. As the new grand mage of the McCollum Family, Jaxon had been granted the privacy of one of the bedrooms. Lightly furnished with a twin bed and a rickety bedside table that Jaxon used as a desk, the small room housed the few artifacts they had rescued from the manor.

"Sit." Jaxon motioned toward a small chair in the corner.

Allyn sat.

"I spoke with my Family today," Jaxon said, leaning against the wall and crossing his arms. "And... I've been summoned back."

"Summoned back?"

"My time with the McCollum Family was to be spent shadowing Graeme, studying his leadership. Now that Graeme is gone, they feel that my time here should end."

Allyn fumbled for words. Jaxon was the de-facto leader of their Family. Ever present. Strong. Reliable. His strength held this fragile Family together. "You can't. This is where you're needed most."

"I have other responsibilities than this Family. But I will leave at a time of *my* choosing."

"When is that?"

Jaxon looked at the brands in the holder near the door. Three in all, they were the black color of pure iron, with a handle on one end and an elemental design on the other. Allyn's wounds burned at the sight. Lifting one of the brands out of the holder, Jaxon peered at its head, then at Allyn, and back at the firebrand. His face grew determined. "When I'm sure the McCollum Family is strong enough."

"You mean to find another grand mage."

Jaxon nodded.

"Who?"

"It's Liam's position by rights."

That wasn't entirely true. While the line of grand mages usually traced the hereditary line, it wasn't an absolute. Like the medieval line of kings before it, the tradition said that when the heir was too sickly to rule or there was no suitable heir at all, Families could anoint one of their choosing. And even then, a suitable heir had to be ratified by the Family in a form of monarchal democracy.

"Do you think they'll follow him?"

"In time." Jaxon returned the brand to its place. "His powers grow every day, and his influence with them. Liam is the first of his kind, and I mean to make the McCollum Family the first of its kind, too. This will be the Family that the other machinists flock to. And they'll want one of their kind to lead it."

34

"How are you going to find more?"

Allyn and Liam remained the only machinists discovered inside the McCollum Family.

"You believe that the machinists lie within the ranks of the non-wielders, correct?"

"Yes."

"Well, I'm seeking them out. Here at the McCollum Family, we're offering a fresh start, free of judgments and condescension. Once they're here, we'll show them what we've discovered with you and Liam."

It was a gamble. If he and Liam were correct, they could populate the machinist numbers through the non-wielders, and their Family would grow stronger. However, if the non-wielders were unable to develop machinist abilities or were unwilling to try, the McCollum Family would be left with the burden—a burden they could ill afford to take on.

"Why not come out with our discovery and use that to regain influence? That's what Graeme had intended."

Jaxon grimaced. "That was before his death and the loss of the manor. Before we were wanted by every police officer and detective in the Northwest. I've sought an audience with the Forum, but we're alone for now."

Allyn shook his head. That didn't seem like the magi way. The Families had come together out of necessity, for protection, because the magi race would have dissolved into oblivion if they had not. It felt odd that no other magi Family was willing to come to the McCollum Family's aid in its time of crisis.

"When we're strong enough, the other Families will listen," Jaxon said. "But first, we need to grow into the first machinist Family and show our strength."

"How will we do that?"

"By growing our numbers and reclaiming what is rightfully ours. We're going to take back the library and all of its contents."

Liam missed his library. He missed his ergonomic workstation and the way it kept his body from aching after a long day's work. He missed the steady artificial light, the feel of the abnormally dry air, and the constant hum of the air purifiers. He missed the smell of aging paper and leather. He missed the silence. He even missed the occasional loneliness. But above all, he missed having a place that was *his*.

Since moving to the cabin, he'd tried working at the giant redwood table, but had been quickly forced to move when his computer battery had died, and there wasn't a convenient power outlet nearby. He'd tried working on the front porch, but in the cold mountain air, his fingers had grown stiff, and he'd been unable to concentrate on anything but keeping his teeth from chattering. He'd even attempted to work in Allyn's and Jaxon's rooms, but anytime he'd worked himself into a groove, they had kicked him out.

So he had resigned himself to the dark, noisy, uncomfortable corner of the loft where he slept. He sat with a pillow against the wall and his computer on his lap. His legs would eventually grow stiff and fall asleep. His back would ache and spasm. And the single dim light would strain his eyes enough to give him a headache. It wasn't ideal. Then again, nothing about their current situation was.

Liam picked up the thin black book and flipped to the page he was currently transcribing.

*Unto each, they sacrificed their soul.*

Liam quietly read the words aloud, typing them into his open document, then checked again for accuracy. He hadn't made any mistakes, and satisfied, he continued.

*Given freely, their heat, their water, and their blood. Their very lives. Seven in all, they sacrificed.*

He'd been at it for the better part of the morning after nearly all of the previous day. The thin book he'd recovered—

Allyn liked to tease him, saying that he'd stolen it—from the Hyland Estate was the only book he still had in his possession, and as far as he knew, it was the only one of its kind. It was too important to wait. Their situation was too precarious. The book *needed* to be preserved.

*Even now, the cold iron glows with their lifeblood. White hot, it will burn for generations so that we may continue. Let it not be forgotten of the sacrifice of the seven.*

The passage ended.

Liam closed the book and rubbed his eyes. He was little more than three-quarters of the way done, and under normal circumstances, he would have been only a couple hours away from completing the transcription. But this particular work was more difficult than most. He was used to faded or damaged texts, and in many cases, he'd been forced to guess or leave the transcription incomplete. This was something else.

The book was written in a series of first-hand accounts of a single event. What made it particularly difficult was the inclusion of early modern letters, abbreviations, and the lack of standardized spelling. He made an effort to leave the text as unaltered as possible, but he'd been forced to adapt the long *S* into the modern short *S* simply because he had no way to type it into his document as written. More than that, it was nearly impossible to read.

Many words like *crosse* or *newe* used additional silent letters that he was unaccustomed to, while others used vowels interchangeably or based on their position in the word. Even the word *the* was abbreviated strangely. He wasn't transcribing—he was adapting, translating, and it gave him a headache.

Even so, the very things that made the book difficult to transcribe helped him date it. The English language didn't have standardized spelling until the mid-seventeenth century, so the book must have predated that. By how much, he had no idea. His next step was to cross-reference many of the names and locations to get a better sense of the era. Unfortunately, without the books in his library, he didn't have many sources.

His mind wandered to the library again. Had it survived the collapse of the manor? Had it been discovered? His body ached at the thought of dirty police hands mishandling his books. He loathed to imagine the secure concrete facility where the books and artifacts would be stored and catalogued, far removed from the hands of the people who could use them, who *needed* them.

But for the time being, the library was out of his reach. So his focus needed to remain on the computer on his lap. Every book he'd been able to transcribe lived a digital life on its hard drive. He needed to back them up, store them, and maybe even send them to other Families for safekeeping. As long as the remaining McCollum books lived solely on his computer, they were at risk.

He hit Save—just to be safe.

Liam's computer chimed, and it took him a moment to realize why. *An email.* He saved the document one last time and quickly pulled up his browser. He'd received a Google Alert. Concerned about being on the wrong side of a statewide manhunt, Allyn and Jaxon had asked Liam to track any news that named Allyn or Kendyl by name. Liam clicked on the link. The YouTube video was poor in quality, with a grainy picture and washed-out color, but Liam knew instantly what it was. By the time it ended, he was covered in cold sweat.

# CHAPTER 4

ALLYN HUDDLED WITH JAXON AND Leira in a semicircle around Liam, who had pulled up a chair in front of the rickety bedside table Jaxon used as a desk. The room was tight with the four of them, and because Liam had insisted they close the door, it was also growing hot.

The video, which had no sound, had been taken from the dash-mounted camera of a vehicle driving down a lonely, narrow road devoid of streetlamps. The faded yellow center line was nearly impossible to make out, and sometimes, it disappeared entirely under a thin fog. Thick, uncultivated trees lined the road to one side, while the other was a wall of exposed rock with leafy foliage growing through the cracks.

Allyn leaned in closer, his insides twisting into a knot, nearly overwhelmed by a powerful wave of dread and familiarity.

As the car rounded a tight corner, flashing blue and red lights reflected off the guardrail. *It's a squad car.* The car straightened, and a new light streaked toward the camera. There was a bright flash, and Allyn lost all sense of direction. The world flipped and spun as if the video had been taken from the inside of a carnival ride, then finally, the vehicle lurched and came to a rest on its side. A single headlight shined across the narrow road toward the trees, and only a few feet beyond the tree line, the ground fell away abruptly.

"That's where Lukas ambushed us," Allyn said. He felt three pairs of eyes turn to him. "But that isn't how the attack happened. I—"

A dark figure stepped into the frame. Dressed all in black and moving with lithe, snake-like movements, the man moved in front of the headlight. His already-pale skin was washed out in the poor video quality. It wasn't Lukas.

"Who is that?" Allyn asked.

Nobody answered.

Bright-orange balls of flame—little more than white circles of dancing light on the monitor—formed in the man's hands. Something streaked toward him. He met it in the air with one of the balls of light. There was a bright flash, and when the image reappeared, the magi was on the ground, dazed. Struggling to regain his wits, he shuffled backward as another man stepped into frame. This man was dressed in full white battle attire, and he moved with a quiet confidence.

"Graeme," Allyn said.

Liam shifted in his seat. Allyn wondered what the young man was thinking. His father had only been gone for four days, and Liam hadn't had a chance to heal. Allyn remembered the anguish of seeing pictures and videos of his mother in the weeks and months following her passing. He even sometimes choked up to this day, years later—some wounds never healed entirely. And Liam wasn't watching a video of a birthday or Christmas morning. This was his father fighting for his life.

Graeme knelt over the other man, seeming to talk to him. Allyn found himself straining his ears in an attempt to hear what they were saying, though the video had no sound.

Graeme and the fallen magi went on like that for nearly half a minute. Graeme visibly grew increasingly agitated as the conversation wore on, until finally, he stood, wielded, and—

Allyn looked away, his skin suddenly clammy. He knew what came next—more death. *When will it end?* By the time he looked back up, Liam had paused the video. Graeme stood, staring straight at the camera. To those who already knew him, he was unmistakable.

"Where did you find this?" Allyn asked.

"It's everywhere." Liam punched the Escape button, and the video shrank to a small window on the monitor.

Allyn laughed bitterly. *YouTube?*

Circling the total views, Liam said, "It's been viewed over fifty thousand times since this morning."

That sucked the air out of Allyn's lungs. *Fifty thousand views?* Fifty thousand fresh eyes were watching something play out among a race of people they hadn't previously known existed.

Allyn rubbed the back of his neck. "Who uploaded it? The police?"

Liam shook his head. "I don't think so. Look at this." He circled the name of the YouTube user who had uploaded the video.

"J.P. Niall," Allyn read. "Am I supposed to know who that is?" He looked to the rest of them, hoping to see an expression of recognition.

Jaxon narrowed his eyes but didn't look away from the screen. "I doubt any of us do."

"I don't know why," Liam said, "but I feel like I've seen it before. It's... familiar."

"Another magi maybe?" Allyn asked.

"There isn't a Niall Family," Jaxon said.

"Was there ever?" Allyn asked. "Whoever uploaded the video could have referenced an old Family name, something only we would recognize, to get our attention."

"Who would want to do that?" Leira asked bitterly. "We've been disavowed."

"Then maybe they're not trying to help..." Allyn said.

41

"Lukas is dead," Liam said.

*Lukas.* Allyn couldn't prevent the nightmare from returning. His throat constricted against the sudden smell of burnt hair—and he couldn't tell if he was going to retch or suffocate. He stepped away from the group, looking for space. When he didn't find it, he closed his eyes and forced himself to take long, steady breaths, counting each one.

*One.*

"The Hyland Family is still out there," Jaxon said.

*Two.*

"Darian?" Leira said. "I thought he was dead."

*Three.* Allyn opened his eyes and turned back to the group. None of them so much as gave him a puzzled look. They probably thought he'd moved away to think.

*Four.*

"His body was never recovered," Jaxon said.

The implications hung in the air. The heir-apparent to Lukas's movement might not only be alive; he might be active. That complicated matters.

With a dry tongue, Allyn licked his lips. "We're missing something. It's police footage, and only they should have access to it. If Darian uploaded it, how did he get ahold of it?"

"Someone could have removed the dash camera before the police arrived," Liam said. "Or... it could be a police trap to lure us out." He added the last bit with a crooked smile as if to suggest he didn't believe it.

"That doesn't feel right, either," Allyn said. "It's too convoluted. Too unconventional. The police wouldn't dump evidence straight onto YouTube. They would release it through official channels—TV, news websites, that sort of thing."

"That's not true," Liam said. "I've seen requests for help on social media."

Allyn looked at Liam, bemused. *When did he become the*

42

*expert on police procedure?* "You're right. But this is different. This isn't a picture of a missing teenager floating across social media. This was uploaded straight onto YouTube without even a description. Don't you think if this was the police looking for help, they'd include some sort of contact information? At least an email or a number to call if you have any information?"

"I suppose," Liam said, though the tone of his voice suggested he still wasn't convinced.

"Either way," Leira cut in, "the longer we sit here talking about it, the more people are watching it. Can you take it down?"

Allyn agreed with her. Unlike most of the videos on YouTube, this one had an air of brutal authenticity, which was probably the reason it was drawing so many viewers. Because it was taken from the dash cam of a police car, a small number of viewers had no doubt already accepted it as genuine and had been convinced that real-world magic existed faster than Allyn would have expected them to. Faster than he had. If there were enough believers in the audience, the questions would reach a tipping point. People would come looking, and the magi's ability to hide in their shrinking world would disappear.

A few comments poked fun at the video's "poor special effects work," but those were few and far between. To most, the video was entertainment, and they were impressed with the quality of the work. Most importantly, regardless of whether the police had released the video or not, it was still evidence, and it was only a matter of time before someone within the department made the connection. The video had to come down.

"I'm not sure that's possible," Liam said.

"Why?" Leira asked.

"Well, on a normal video, yes, I could do it. But with something that's gone viral like this..." Liam winced. "It's been linked to and embedded onto thousands of other sites and social media pages. It's spread too far. And it's not slowing down." As if to drive his point home, Liam refreshed the page. In the time they had gathered to watch it, the video had been viewed more than fifteen hundred more times and shared more than one hundred times.

"What happens if you remove the original video?" Allyn asked. "Remove it, and the rest will disappear too, right?"

"The ones that link back to this original video will," Liam said. "But people try and capitalize off viral videos, piggyback off their viewers. These other videos"—he dragged the cursor over the Suggested Videos link on the right side of the screen—"aren't simply embedded or linked to the original. They're copies, recreations, videos of people watching the video."

"What are you saying?" Allyn asked.

"I'd have to go in and remove them one by one."

"How many are there?" Leira asked.

"Best guess? Hundreds."

"So you're saying it can't be done," Allyn said.

"No," Liam said. "It can be done, but it will take a very long time. And what happens when every video involving real-world magic mysteriously vanishes from the Internet? Won't people notice that, too?"

Allyn pinched the bridge of his nose. "Then what do we do?"

"I can remove the original video," Liam said. "That will slow the process down and make it harder to find the others, but it won't stop the spread."

"Do it."

"Wait." Jaxon knelt beside Liam. Allyn realized that the man had been quiet for several minutes. "Can you trace it? Find out where it originated from?"

"Probably."

"Give it a try."

"Now?"

Jaxon nodded.

Liam minimized the screen and set to work.

"What are you thinking?" Allyn asked.

"Whoever posted this video is obviously trying to capture our attention," Jaxon said. "We should find out why."

"Even if it's the police?"

"We need to know who we're contending with," Jaxon said matter-of-factly. He turned back to Liam and watched as the young magi toggled through multiple screens, his hands a blur. The room remained quiet for several minutes. The others were probably like Allyn, afraid to interrupt, fearing they might break Liam's rhythm and slow down the process.

"Almost there," Liam said, never breaking stride. Liam's abilities had grown with his confidence. He'd always had skill with electronics—that much had been clear during Allyn's first encounter with him—but Allyn believed there was little Liam *couldn't* accomplish anymore. The only binds that held him back were of his own making—his limits were truly the limits of his imagination. Unfortunately, on the surface, Liam's abilities looked like nothing more than skill—even Allyn had trouble distinguishing between the two—and that was how they'd gone unnoticed for so long to begin with. When the time came, how would they convince the other Families that these newfound abilities were real? Allyn's magic was obvious magic, but Liam's...

"Done." Liam leaned back in his chair and placed his hands on the top of his head.

"Who is it?" Jaxon asked, leaning over Liam's shoulder. "Is it Darian?"

"I don't know," Liam said. "All I could pull was an address, but the video didn't originate from the Hyland Estate."

"Where did it originate from?"

"Here." Liam pointed at the address hidden among the rest of the computer code.

"There's no way..." Allyn said. "There has to be some kind of mistake."

"No," Liam said. "I traced the IP address back to the Internet provider, then cross-referenced it with their user database until I found a match. That video was uploaded by that user from that address."

Allyn shook his head. "That's not possible."

"What's wrong?" Jaxon asked.

"That's *my* address," Allyn said. "*That's my condo.*"

# CHAPTER 5

SPECIAL AGENT RICHARD MADDOX STROLLED through the charred remains of the manor. Much of the white stone, blackened by smoke and flame, still stood, but the roof had collapsed, leaving the smoke-stained walls standing like ghosts, lost and alone. The fragile remains of half-burned belongings crunched under his feet, covering his polished black boots in gray ash and soot. The smell of smoke hung in the air, oppressive and clingy. He and his partner had spent the last two days at the manor, and Maddox hadn't been able to get the disgusting scent off himself either time. He was beginning to think that he would forever smell like a campfire.

The sun slipped past the trees behind him, and long shadows stretched over the grounds, peeking through the manor's ruins like timid fingers. Large stadium-like lights had been erected around the perimeter of the manor so that the arson unit and other crime scene investigators could work into the night. So far, they had turned up very little. An accelerant had been used on the walls, and the manor had gone up in flames in an instant. But according to the reports of the officers on location, the manor had been clear when they'd arrived. A large number of people had returned—and died—at nearly the same time the manor had been torched. None of it made sense.

His standard missing persons case was rapidly growing more complex. What had Allyn Kaplan, a young, well-to-do attorney with no family, been doing there? Why had he kidnapped his twin sister to begin with? The officers who found Kendyl had said that she was bound and gagged, but they also said that Allyn had surrendered himself peacefully.

Most kidnapping cases came down to one of three things: power, money, or sex.

Maddox had eliminated sex from the equation immediately. Neither Allyn nor Kendyl had a history of sexual harassment or abuse. Money seemed easy to eliminate, as well. By all accounts, Kaplan was an up-and-coming lawyer at one of the most prestigious law firms in the Northwest. According to the partners at Clarke, Poole, and Associates, Kaplan was making well into six figures per year with an impressive benefits package. And while most recent graduates were buried under student debt, an inheritance from his mother had paid for most of Allyn's education. On the other hand, Kendyl was dead broke. The part-time barista at a trendy northeast coffee shop spent more money on her private art studio than she did on rent. If money had been the motive, *she* would have kidnapped *him*.

That left power. Maddox struggled to justify that too, but other elements seemed to click into place. Theresa Kaplan had died when her children were just teenagers, and without any other family to go to, Allyn had taken charge. He had a history of thriving while in power. That was one of the attributes the partners at Allyn's firm had loved about him— he didn't get nervous or rattled. If he saw a problem, he found a way to fix it. Perhaps a conflict between the Kaplan siblings had caused Allyn to assert the same authority he'd acted upon earlier in life. That didn't feel right, either. Allyn had taken on a parental role, and while parents are prone to acting irrationally, they don't kidnap their misbehaving children.

*It's not your job to convict him*, Maddox reminded himself. *It's your job to catch the son of a bitch. Let the lawyers deal with the rest.*

Maddox arrived at what his partner referred to as the "museum." The area around it had been dug away, exposing the long rectangular structure below. From the outside, it was hardly remarkable, little more than an enclosed concrete basement with high ceilings and a sliding door with a digital passcode. But inside, it was something to behold: a private collection of ancient weapons, armor, paintings, sculptures, clothing, books, and more. Items lined the walls and filled displays evenly spaced throughout the room. It made Maddox contemplate what other wonders had been destroyed along with the manor. The museum would have housed the true marvels, but the manor had no doubt displayed other majestic pieces of history.

A hollow path, maybe ten feet wide, circled the museum like a moat. Maddox whipped his leg around the ladder and quickly descended the fifteen or so feet to the ground. The area around the museum had been cleaned away, and sheets of plywood created a makeshift path atop the moist ground. Below the smoldering wreckage, the air was clean and smelled of wet soil. Maddox took a deep breath then spat as the scent of smoke again tickled his nostrils. No matter where he was or how little time he spent in the rubble, he couldn't get away from that smell. It stuck to him, latched onto his clothes, and didn't let go.

*No wonder I get the distinct impression this case is going to be a clusterfuck.*

Maddox rounded the north side of the structure, coming to a sliding-glass partition that was nearly as wide as the structure itself. Maddox punched in the new code—he'd heard reprogramming the door had been a nightmare—and entered. Without a proper decontamination chamber outside the partition, the museum wasn't exactly a clean room, but the crisp air smelled sterile and was a cool sixty-five degrees Fahrenheit—the optimum temperature for preserving aging texts. Or so he'd been told. The door slid closed behind him.

Nolan was already inside, sitting at a table, going through one of the museum's books. He had the look of a man who would have a fine career as a special agent. Tall and broad in the shoulders with a thick chest, Agent Nolan was larger than most men—though still shorter and skinnier than Maddox himself—but he had the square jaw, blond hair, and blue eyes of the boy next door. He was personable, quick to smile, and instantly trustworthy. Maddox wasn't sure if he liked him.

He looked up as Maddox strolled toward him. His dark jacket had been thrown over the table beside him, and his starched white shirt was coming un-tucked in the back, exposing a little skin just above his belt. Maddox would have to talk to him about that. Their authority came from their office, and their dress was an extension of that. To slack there undermined that authority, damaged their credibility, and diminished their power. They needed to be in uniform at all times. No exception.

*This is coming from the man who smells like a cheap cigar?*

"How was dinner?" Nolan asked.

"It was dinner," Maddox lied. He'd stepped away, using food as an excuse, just to get some time away from Nolan. The man never shut up. Even while he read, he talked—Maddox hadn't even known that was possible—and Maddox found himself fantasizing about using his fist to plug the young agent's hole. *It's unfortunate the bureau frowns on violence between agents.* "What are you reading?"

Nolan looked at the text reverently. The thing was ancient. Its wooden cover was wrapped in leather and ornamented with metal corner pieces and a raised medallion in the center.

The parchment had yellowed with age, and the deteriorated black ink was difficult to read. The images inside, though, were striking. The gold pictures sparkled and shined when Nolan turned the page with a latex-covered finger.

"I'm not sure," Nolan said, scanning the next page. "The script is elegant and hand-written, but it's written in another language, so I have no idea what it says. The pictures are interesting, though."

Maddox peered over Nolan's shoulder. Each page had two or three images, each bracketed by flowing text that reminded Maddox of a history book. But each image, while lifelike, lacked the detail and perspective of modern art. Nolan had stopped on a page with three images of battle. Bloodied bodies were strewn about the landscape, while dark figures dressed in black robes and demonic masks held torches to the dead.

"It looks like a purge," Maddox said. "From the Plague maybe?"

"I don't think so," Nolan said. "It looks like a battle. And I've seen other art similar to this in the museum."

Nolan had spent nearly every available moment in the museum. He was drawn to its contents in a way that he'd been unable to articulate. It grated on Maddox. They had a job to do. Kendyl Kaplan was still missing, and her kidnapper was still at large. Until those two issues were solved, Maddox didn't give a damn about art or any of the other personal effects within the manor. He *had* allowed Nolan a little time every day to sift through its contents, though. Something had drawn Kaplan to the manor, and maybe the reason could be found in one of the books.

"Oh," Nolan said, "Vaughn brought some coffee." He pointed at a pair of cups at the end of the table. "It's probably cold by now, but..." He shrugged.

Maddox walked to the end of the table and grabbed the cup. He pulled off the lid and shook his head in dissatisfaction. It wasn't coffee. It was an overly sweetened, caramel-swirled, whipped-cream-topped desert drink posing as coffee. Coffee was coffee. Black. It grated on him when people tried to make something into something it wasn't. He placed the cup back on the table.

"Where are we with forensics?" Maddox asked.

"They came back negative."

"Negative? On everything?"

"That's what the lab said."

"That's not possible. We recovered twelve bodies, and we didn't find a match with any of them?"

Nolan shook his head.

"No DNA? Dental? Nothing?"

"Nothing." Nolan closed the book and slid it across the table. "Something's going on here. Something we're missing. How is it that a two-hundred-year-old manor exists without so much as an address? This private museum alone is worth millions, and it was built inside a climate-controlled environment that would have cost another million to construct. Where does the money come from? Who are these people?"

"The manor *did* have an address," Maddox said. "Though it wasn't easy to find. It's owned by a real estate company called First Family LLC."

"A real estate company?" Nolan repeated. "Who's the controlling party?"

"I'm working on that."

"It should be on their yearly tax documents."

"It would be," Maddox said, "if they'd filed any."

"Bank accounts?"

"All off-shore."

"Of course," Nolan said. "Someone is taking extraordinary measures to stay hidden."

"I know it's odd," Maddox said, "but answering those questions isn't our job. Finding Kaplan is."

"He's an enigma, too," Nolan said. "He doesn't fit the profile."

"I'm struggling with that, too. All I can say is that, at this point, the profile goes out the window. We have multiple witnesses placing him at the scene of the crime, which he fled once the police were called. He was found here weeks later, with his sister bound and gagged, only to escape once he was in transit, leaving three police officers dead. That's proof enough for me."

"I'm telling you—we're missing something," Nolan said. "Something important. And it has to do with all of this."

"You'll learn that the world doesn't always fit neatly into a little box, Agent Nolan. There will never be a time where you get all the answers or solve all of the mysteries, and that means you're going to make mistakes. You're going to have to learn to live with that, because what matters is that we make sure this sort of thing doesn't go unpunished. It's not our responsibility to convict criminals or hand down punishments. We just deliver them to the people who do."

Nolan looked as though he were about to respond, but Maddox's phone cut him short.

Maddox frowned at the incoming number. "Maddox," he said, answering the call.

"What the hell kind of clusterfuck are you running down there?" The voice on the other end was screaming, forcing Maddox to hold the phone away from his ear.

Maddox set his jaw. He didn't care if it was Special Agent in Charge Kathleen Hanigan or not—he *loathed* being yelled at. "Sir?" he said, only barely restraining his anger.

"You have a leak, Agent Maddox," Hanigan said, her voice only slightly less agitated than it had been before.

Maddox imagined Agent Hanigan behind her wide, L-shaped mahogany desk, her sharp face punctuated by her square, black-rimmed glasses. Some said her scowl alone could wilt a perpetrator into talking. It was bullshit, of course, but the rumor was so old and so prevalent that

Maddox secretly wondered if Hanigan had begun to believe it, too.

"I don't understand, sir."

"Your evidence is on the fucking Internet!"

Maddox hung up.

Nolan's eyes went wide. "Did you just hang up on the special agent in charge?"

"I don't appreciate being yelled at."

"But—"

"If she wants to talk to me," Maddox said tightly, "she can talk to me like an adult. I won't be scolded like a troublesome child."

Maddox's phone rang again. He declined the call.

"Are you insane?" Nolan asked. "You're going to get us thrown off the case."

"Doubtful."

Nolan licked his lips nervously. "I don't appreciate being thrown into the middle of this."

"You're not. This is between her and me."

Nolan shook his head and gave Maddox an irritated smile. "I will admit, you've got a swinging set on you, Maddox."

Maddox waited for the third call, but it didn't come. Instead, Nolan's phone rang.

"So much for it being between you and her," Nolan said, pulling the phone out of his jacket pocket. He held the phone out for Maddox.

"No," Maddox said. "She's calling *you*."

"Looking for you!"

Maddox shrugged. "You better answer it. Ignoring it is only going to piss her off more."

Nolan gulped. The phone rang again. A couple more, and it would go to voicemail.

"If you're hoping that I'm going to swoop in and save you," Maddox said, "then you're going to be disappointed."

Nolan locked eyes with Maddox and took a deep breath

before answering the phone. "Nolan," he said, his voice surprisingly less flustered than he appeared. "Yes, sir. He's right here, sir." Nolan held the phone out to Maddox.

He shook his head and clasped his hands behind his back.

"She wants to talk to you," Nolan said.

Maddox remained silent.

"Quit playing games and answer the damn phone, Maddox."

"Ask her if she's done yelling."

"I'm not going to ask the special agent in charge if she's done yelling."

"Then I'm unavailable to talk."

"Maddox—"

"No."

Nolan shook his head irritably. "I'm going to kill you when this is over." He put the phone back to his ear. "I'm sorry, Special Agent Hanigan, Agent Maddox is apparently unavailable. What can I help you with?" He winced, yanking the phone away from his ear as the voice on the other end erupted again. "I understand," he said, cutting in. "I understand. It will be handled. But, sir? Sir? What evidence?"

Nolan's eyebrows rose as he bent down to pull his laptop out of his briefcase. With the phone pressed between his shoulder and his ear, he opened the computer. "I'm pulling it up now."

While Nolan typed furiously, Maddox circled so he could see what the young agent was looking at. He'd logged on to the Internet and pulled up a video. Maddox cursed and stepped away from the table. Exasperated, he placed his hands on the top of his clean-shaven head. He didn't need to see the rest. It was a video taken from the night Kaplan escaped custody—a video that was supposed to be in police possession.

*A leak.* Someone under his responsibility was releasing evidence.

"Let me call you back, sir." Nolan hung up before the receiver rang with more shouts.

Maddox turned and looked at the young agent, amused. "Did you just hang up on the special agent in charge?"

"Shut it," Nolan said. "We're in deep shit."

# CHAPTER 6

THE CABIN'S ISOLATED LOCATION WAS both its greatest asset and its greatest liability. Just under one hundred miles east of Portland, it took them two hours to venture from it to the outskirts of the city. A thick blanket of dark clouds hung over downtown, casting the buildings and citizens under a perpetual gloom and a steady drizzle. The city had entered the dark winter, and Allyn wondered what they were walking into.

Jaxon drove, silent and focused, his eyes glued to the road. If he was nervous or had any reservations about their plan, he hid it well. Leira was at his side, watching their surroundings like someone who didn't get out much—wide-eyed and lips parted. She occasionally shot Jaxon concerned glances from the corner of her eye. She'd advocated waiting, not wanting to rush into a trap, but when it became apparent that Jaxon was set on investigating, she'd changed tactics and pleaded with him to take a larger squad. But Jaxon said that he preferred the stealth and quickness of a small force to the strength of a large one.

Nyla, who sat in the backseat with Allyn, was the only other occupant in the car. Her silver hair was pulled into a tight ponytail and tucked into the neck of her compression armor. She smiled at him before returning her gaze to the world outside. The small gesture stirred something inside him. Nyla was beautiful, and she was growing more playful every day as the wound left from Baylis's death slowly healed. It was a slow process as she wasn't simply mourning the loss of a loved one; a piece of her had died with him. Allyn wondered if she would ever fully get over him.

Allyn's phone vibrated against his leg. He pulled it out of his pocket and opened it to find a text from Liam. *Are you there yet?* Liam had taken Jaxon's decision to leave him behind as a slight against his ability. Even with his increasing talents and influence, Liam still hadn't outgrown his insecurities. Jaxon had tried to explain that the Family needed him to stay behind because a McCollum should always be with McCollum Family in case tragedy struck, but Liam had grown irritated and refused to listen. Allyn wished he could explain that this was another step in Jaxon's plan to groom him to lead and that the Family needed to grow accustomed to seeing Liam in a leadership role, but Jaxon had advised against telling him. He wanted Liam to grow comfortable with his increasing influence organically. Telling him of Jaxon's plan might stunt his growth.

Besides, one of the benefits to Liam's abilities was that he could use them anywhere. As long as Liam had access to the Internet and a computer, he could do whatever they needed him to, and probably quicker without the inherent distractions of being in the field.

*Almost*, Allyn wrote. *Just got to Portland.*

*Keep me posted.*

*Will do.* Allyn grinned as he slid the phone back into his pocket.

"What?" Nyla asked.

"Liam," Allyn said. "He wants to be kept in the loop."

Jaxon watched him from the rear-view mirror for a moment, then returned his attention to the road. They followed I-84 West, past the Lloyd Center Mall, then merged with I-5 North and rounded past the Moda Center. Across the river, the tops of the downtown skyscrapers were hidden in the low-hanging clouds, and the windows of the upper floors shone through like dim stars. It was only late afternoon, but it felt like twilight, and even the streetlamps and headlights had trouble piercing the gloom.

Traffic slowed to a crawl through the city, painting the interstate red with brake lights, and crossing the Freemont Bridge into downtown took another twenty minutes. From there, Allyn guided Jaxon through side streets, bypassing the deadlocked traffic into northwest Portland, where his condo was located.

He'd been too preoccupied with trying to figure out how the video had originated from his condo to give much thought to returning home. So when Jaxon turned into the complex, a sudden wave of melancholy washed over Allyn. This was his home. His *first* home. He'd found it. Bought it. Furnished it. Much like his first car had represented his transition from childhood into adolescence, buying his first home had been his transition into adulthood. It meant he'd established himself. Achieved a level of success. Grown up. And he'd done it at twenty-six.

The complex looked much like it had before. Conjoined complexes painted muted reds, blues, or greens lined both sides of the private street. Construction still continued, but in the weeks since Allyn had left, more homes had been built and sold. The community was filled with other young, successful businessmen—the kind of people Allyn had worked to associate himself with.

Jaxon drove slowly, his eyes darting from one side of the road to the other, searching for anything out of the ordinary. The community was quiet, and the driveways were empty—long hours were the mark of young businessmen. Jaxon pulled into the vacant visitors lot, parking so that the car faced Allyn's unit across the street. His condo, like the others, was quiet, its windows dark. The clear tarp draped over the broken sliding-glass door swayed in the breeze, and the bottom billowed inward, allowing the rain to blow inside.

Even though Allyn had chosen family over his old life and had willingly left the condo and all his possessions behind, he was still angry to see it neglected. He imagined pools of standing water warping his hardwood floors and saturating his carpet, filling the condo with the musky smell of mold and decay. He imagined the hollow sounds of wind blowing through the halls and the soft rustle of the tarp shifting against the broken door. He imagined the cold suffocating what had once been his warm, inviting home. But above all, he imagined how much it would cost to repair.

*You left that life behind*, Allyn reminded himself. But being back stirred something inside him. It was one thing to step away when he didn't have to face what he was stepping away from. It was quite another when he had to see it, remember the sacrifices, hard work, and long hours that had gone into it. It had only been a few weeks, but he felt the pangs of nostalgia. This wasn't just a collection of belongings. This was the fruit of thousands of early mornings and late nights. This was his life. This was his *home*.

Or it had been.

Jaxon shut off the car. "Wait here," he said, keeping his eyes straight ahead. "Watch for anything unusual. Leira and I will walk the perimeter and see if we can get an idea of what waits for us inside."

Allyn nodded, and Jaxon stepped out of the car. He pulled his fashionable, gray coat tight—it was the first time Allyn had seen Jaxon wear a coat—and hunched his shoulders as if he were trying to hide from the rain. It was an act, of course. Jaxon never let the elements get to him, but Allyn was surprised how authentic it looked. Jaxon looked... normal. He circled the back of the car, to where Leira was waiting, her heart-shaped face and chin-length black hair hidden under a black hood. He took her hand, and together, they walked along the sidewalk toward the main office as if they were a young couple looking to view a home.

Nyla undid her seatbelt and turned sideways, leaning against the door and pulling her legs onto the bench seat. Her feet touched Allyn's thigh. "So this is where you lived?" A hint of amusement lurked in her voice.

"You say that like you didn't already know," Allyn said. "You were here the night Lukas came for me." *The night it all began.*

Nyla shrugged. "It looks different than I remember it."

"How so?"

Jaxon and Leira disappeared from view.

"It's so..." Nyla trailed off, searching for the words. "Uninspiring." She pushed him playfully with the bottom of her foot.

"It may not be a century-old manor," Allyn said with a sarcastic smirk, "but it was mine."

"You miss it."

Allyn nodded.

"Would you go back if you could?"

Allyn turned to her. Intensity hid behind those blue eyes of hers, and it gave him pause. He didn't have an answer. He'd left that life behind for answers. For help. He had gotten those answers, and he'd gotten Kendyl back. So what was keeping him from returning? Kendyl? She'd been the one who wanted to stay with the McCollum Family; it had been new and exciting, a fresh start where she was something special. But her feelings had soured, and she'd already voiced her displeasure. If he returned to his old life, he thought she might follow. *Then why do I stay?*

*The police.*

Even if he wanted to, he had no way to clear his name—he didn't have the evidence. And if he did come forward, his defense would rely on a Family of people who worked to remain hidden.

But that wasn't the question. She'd asked: what if he could? *I don't know. What does that mean?*

"I can't," Allyn said. "So it doesn't matter."

Nyla blinked, and her playful expression slipped from her face.

The conversation died there, and an uncomfortable silence replaced their lighthearted banter. Nyla swung her legs back onto the floor so that she was facing forward again. She refused to look at him. Allyn wanted to tell her that it wasn't personal. The fact that the decision was so difficult meant that he'd built strong relationships with her, Liam, and the other members of the McCollum Family. He couldn't easily walk away from that. But he didn't know how to tell her.

The minutes ticked by painfully slowly as the twilight became darkness, until eventually, Jaxon and Leira reappeared. Leira strode in front of Allyn's condo, alone, casually glancing at the dark windows as if she were trying to peer inside. Jaxon appeared a moment later, walking toward Leira from the back of the unit. He said something to her. Then they stepped up to the front door and knocked.

"Here we go," Allyn said. The knock was their signal that Jaxon and Leira hadn't found any reason to call off the mission.

Without a word, Nyla opened her door and stepped out. She was halfway across the street by the time Allyn emerged from the car. Lacking the cold bite of the mountain air, the temperature was warmer than he expected, and a thin layer of fog clung to the pavement, giving the scene an eerie, dreamlike quality. Allyn walked casually, his hands in his pockets. Jaxon and Leira may not have found anything amiss, but that didn't mean they were free from prying eyes. He wore, as he always seemed to these days, a black compression armor top and a pair of jeans over a matching pair of compression armor bottoms.

"Anyone home?" Allyn asked as he approached.

Jaxon shook his head. "The door is locked, too."

Allyn did a final check of his surroundings, and still not seeing anything concerning, he pulled his keys from his pocket and unlocked the door. It opened into darkness. Immediately in front of him was the stairwell that led up to the second level, where the living room, kitchen, and dining rooms were. Directly to his left was another door leading to the garage. Jaxon walked past him, ascending the stairs in a crouch. The air distorted around his hands. He had them wrapped in air, prepared for a fight. Leira and Nyla were inside a moment later, only a step behind Jaxon.

Allyn followed. Once inside, he wielded, and on command, red coils of electricity shot around his arms. They were in constant motion, writhing around each other, hissing, crackling, and sparking as they collided. They didn't burn or harm him in any way, but they made his arms tingle as though they were in close proximity to a great power. The wave of nausea struck him like a blow to the stomach. He stumbled on the stairs, letting the coils singe the carpet.

"Are you all right?" Nyla had stopped a few steps above him and looked down at him, concerned.

"I'm fine." Allyn stood, feigning strength. "I tripped." He kicked the door closed behind him—the electric coils illuminated the narrow hall in a bloody light. "Let's go."

Jaxon ascended the last of the stairs and stopped on the landing. He gave Leira a curt nod, and she raised her hand, narrowing her eyes, searching the condo for other occupants. The strongest clerics had the ability to sense another person's presence, though the ability was limited by proximity. The closer the cleric was to the person, the more likely they were to feel them. If they were too far away, the ability was less accurate. If someone was within the confines of the condo, Leira would know.

"We're clear," she said.

Jaxon stepped onto the second-level landing and disappeared around the corner into the main living space of the condo. The rest followed.

The condo was dark. The only light inside came from the streetlamp outside the kitchen window, and the half-drawn blinds obscured even that. Allyn's breath caught in his throat, and the electric coils dissipated. He'd known what to expect, but he wasn't prepared for the torrent of emotion that nearly overwhelmed him. Fear. Anxiety. Surprise. They swirled inside him, battling with relief and poise. Returning put into perspective how much had changed. He was no longer Allyn Kaplan, the first-year associate who had been mysteriously and brutally beaten inside his own home. He was Allyn Kaplan, the machinist who had led the McCollum Family in destroying their greatest adversary.

The condo looked much as it had the night of the attack. The dining room table lay crushed on the maple hardwood floor, covered in shattered glass from the sliding-glass door. The clear tarp rustled under the gentle breeze, billowing inside, and rainwater glistened in the orange light of the streetlamp. Allyn walked across the living room to grab a table leg that rested in front of the couch. In a final, desperate move, he'd hurled it at Lukas, only to see it veer unnaturally into the wall beside him. Lukas must have hit it with a small blast of air. Allyn traced the dent in the wall with his fingers. The table leg had struck soundly, and the white paint was cracked and flaking away.

"We need to find your computer," Jaxon said from the kitchen. His face was half-hidden in shadow.

"It's upstairs." Allyn dropped the table leg and turned to lead them to the third level. The second stairwell was directly above the first, hidden behind the wall the television was mounted on. Allyn slowed to a halt as he approached. At eye level, against the wall at the base of the stairs was a red stain. Allyn thoughtfully rubbed the back of his head. His memories were so strong. Lukas, a human pit bull, stalking him. Blasting him into the wall. Terror. Darkness.

The same Lukas who had died by his hand. The same Lukas who—

Nyla gently laid a hand on his arm. "It's over now."

She was right. Lukas was dead. He couldn't hurt Allyn, or anyone else, ever again. What Allyn had done to stop him was justified. *Then why does it make me sick?*

The third level of the condo hadn't been damaged during the battle, but there were signs other people had been inside. Dirty footsteps soiled the light carpet, tracking to and from his bedroom, where the police had likely searched for evidence. *Did they take anything?* Entering the spare room that he'd used as a home office, Allyn got his answer. He stopped in the center of the room, focused on the desk in front of the small window.

"What is it?" Jaxon asked.

"It's gone." Allyn walked around the desk. The monitor, the tower, even the paperwork he'd had on the desk—it was all missing. "The police took it."

"Then how...?" Nyla's question hung in the air ominously.

Allyn met Jaxon's eye. *Liam is never wrong,* Jaxon seemed to say.

*How could the video have originated here if the computer is gone?* The video couldn't have been uploaded before the computer was taken. It hadn't been online for more than a few hours. Allyn pinched his forehead. *What the hell is going on?*

"Jaxon," Leira called from another room. "In here."

Jaxon's eyes widened in alarm, and he rushed out of the room. Allyn followed, finding Jaxon and Leira in his bedroom.

In front of them, on the foot of his bed, was a laptop. It was open, displaying the video from the ambush.

Allyn felt three sets of eyes on him. "That's not mine."

The video began again.

Allyn sat down and pulled the computer onto his lap. He stopped the video and minimized the screen. The desktop was empty, save for a single unnamed folder, which opened into two or three dozen subfolders. The top one was titled "Moscow, Russia." *Dresden, Germany. Nuremberg, Germany. Bucharest, Romania. Lisbon, Portugal. Macau, China.* He read through each of them until he came across one that piqued his interest. *Portland, Oregon.*

"What are they?" Leira asked.

Allyn opened the folder and took in a sharp breath.

"What is it?" Jaxon asked.

Allyn shook his head, staring on in horror.

"Allyn?" Nyla asked.

*This isn't real.* He scanned the subfolder's contents. *This can't be real.*

Nyla dropped onto the bed beside him. She ignored the computer, looking at him.

"It's me." Allyn pointed at the contents within the Portland subfolder. "It's all me."

He double-clicked on the first item. It was a newspaper article taken from the *Oregonian*—the same one Graeme had shown him during his first days at the McCollum Manor. It described the strange circumstances of Kendyl's disappearance and named him as a person of interest. The second item was another newspaper article, this one taken from the *Columbian.* The writer of this article had a police statement regarding the condition of Allyn's condo. It, too, was considered a crime scene. It still hadn't named Allyn as a suspect. There were other newspaper articles, photographs, and work and college records, some dating back to his childhood. Whoever was behind the video was building a timeline of his life. A biography.

"I don't like this," Jaxon said.

Allyn clicked on another subfolder. Though it had fewer contents than the previous one, this folder also tracked a single person—a raven-haired girl. He clicked on another subfolder. Then another. Each contained files regarding a different person.

"Destroy it," Jaxon said.

Allyn looked up with a start. "What? No!"

"If we destroy it, we'll lose our only lead," Leira said.

"It's not worth the risk." Jaxon reached for the computer.

Allyn slid it aside, placing himself between it and Jaxon. "What risk?"

"Someone could track it back to us the same way we tracked it here."

"Liam tracked the Internet carrier," Allyn said. "Not the computer. The only way we found it is because they logged on to my Wi-Fi."

"Allyn—"

"Someone wanted us to find it."

"That's what concerns me."

"I think they're looking for me." Allyn looked at the computer. "For us. Each one of these folders is a different person. It's not only me they're searching for."

"Who?"

"If we don't take the computer, we'll never know." He minimized the screen, showing them the blank desktop. "There's nothing else on here. No other pictures. No videos. No school papers. This computer has one purpose—to get our attention."

"If there's nothing on it, how will it lead us to who's behind it?" Nyla asked.

"Just because there's nothing on here now doesn't mean

nothing ever was," Allyn said. "If there was, Liam can find it. It might lead us to another clue."

"I don't like it," Jaxon said. "But I like being in this place even less. Grab the computer, and let's go."

Allyn slapped the computer shut and tucked it under his arm. Jaxon was out the door before he looked up. He thought about grabbing other belongings—the compression armor was constricting and not particularly warm—but without a way to carry any of it, he decided against it.

Jaxon, Leira, and Nyla were already on the next set of stairs by the time Allyn made it to the living room. He was alone. He didn't consider himself a sentimental person, but faced with leaving his condo for possibly the final time, he found himself unable to move. Overlooking the recent damage, he remembered the condo for what it had been. He remembered the fun times. The late nights with friends. Drinks and games with coworkers. The occasional dinner with Kendyl. The quiet nights alone. It wasn't the memories that got to him, but the idea that he would never be able to recreate them again. His life had changed from a quiet, private life to a communal one. He wasn't making decisions for himself anymore; he was making decisions for the Family. And it left him feeling as if he were in a perpetual state of running. Running from Lukas. Running from the police. Running from who he'd used to be. Running from who he needed to become.

Suppressing a frown, Allyn took a final look and left.

Jaxon pulled the car around and parked in the center of the street, leaving the engine running. Another car approached slowly, but it was still a few units down, so Allyn stepped into the street, ducking his head and holding the computer against his chest. Rain pelted him, streaking off his compression armor and soaking his pants in an instant. The approaching car, a newer Chevy Impala, stopped as Allyn neared Jaxon's black sedan. The other car was white with blacked-out windows, but Allyn could see two men through the windshield. The driver was a mammoth of a man with a bald head on broad shoulders. He had a neatly trimmed goatee and large, deep-set eyes. The passenger was about Allyn's build, though he appeared more solid, with styled hair and a movie-star face. Both men were watching him.

"Allyn," Jaxon said from the driver's seat, his voice tight, "get in."

Red and blue lights flared to life.

# CHAPTER 7

"**G**o! Go! Go!" ALLYN SHOUTED, diving into the car.

Jaxon stomped on the gas, and his black Lincoln Town Car lurched forward, tires squealing. Sirens blared behind them, and the darkness became a violent mixture of red and blue lights as the white Impala flipped a U-turn in pursuit. They tore through the community, Jaxon's sedan maintaining the half-block head start.

Allyn grabbed the seatbelt. It was stuck. He yanked harder. *Locked.* "Shit!"

Jaxon swerved to the left, narrowly missing a pickup backing out of a driveway. The force threw Allyn against the door, smacking his head into the window. Dazed, he was even less prepared when Jaxon slammed on the brakes and turned out of the neighborhood. Allyn flew across the backseat and crashed into Nyla, his feet in the rear window, head in the floorboard.

"Get buckled!" Nyla shoved him back toward his seat.

Frantic, Allyn righted himself and fell into his seat. He pulled the seatbelt across his body and snapped it locked.

"Ideas?" Jaxon shouted.

"Uh..." *Where are we?* Large craftsman and Tudor-style homes with Subarus and hybrid vehicles parked in their driveways lined both sides of the street. White lights lit the trees along the road, making the narrow street look like a runway. They were racing toward a stop sign. Jaxon sped through the intersection, and Allyn glimpsed a busy street lined with small shops and more lights. He suddenly knew where they were.

And they were going the wrong way. "Right!" Allyn yelled. "Go right!"

"Where?"

"Anywhere!"

The car jerked right. Allyn stiffened, grabbing onto the seat and the side of the door, screaming.

Jaxon accelerated through the drift, counter-steering to the left, and stabbed the gas, bringing the car back under control in time to avoid the cars parked along the street.

Allyn's jaw fell open. *Where did Jaxon learn to drive like that?*

"Now where?"

"Another right!"

"That's the way we came."

"Do it!"

Jaxon took another corner with expert precision. This time, Allyn was a little more prepared, but he still held on, expecting the screech of metal on metal. When it didn't come, he looked out the back window. The Impala slid around the corner, red and blue lights still flashing. It was now over a full block behind them, but somewhere in the distance, Allyn heard more sirens.

"We need to lose them," Allyn said. "The longer this plays out, the more cops we'll have on our ass."

"Where are you taking us?"

"Out of the city."

They were heading north, toward the highway, but Allyn had no intention of taking them *there*. The moment they got on the highway, they were done, but hidden within the suburban sprawl, they had a chance of escape. They had to make it into the West Hills, where they could lose their pursuers somewhere in the winding roads and dense forests. But they had to get there first.

The buildings whipped by in a blur. Allyn liked to think Northwest Portland was divided into three sectors. The high-end shops and restaurants, the private coffee shops and local breweries of Northwest Twenty-First and Twenty-Third, then the residential area to the north and west. Jaxon had them in the third sector, the business sector, where there was a strange mixture of warehouses, office buildings, and storefronts. The roads were wide enough to accommodate dual-axle semis, and thankfully, business was closed for the day, and the foot traffic was minimal.

Everett. Flanders. Glisan. They tore past the streets in a flash. Hoyt. Irving. Johnson. They were getting close. Allyn turned to look behind them again—

Headlights. Tires squealed. *Bang!*

The truck hit them on the passenger side.

The Town Car lurched violently. Nyla's window shattered, and glass peppered Allyn's face. The world spun. Something silver and heavy flew past Allyn's head, slamming into the window behind him. There was a second bang as the car clipped something hard then whipped back around in the opposite direction. It teetered on two wheels, threatening to flip over, then fell back onto its tires with a *crash* of finality.

Allyn's heart thundered, and his knuckles were white from gripping the side of the door and seat. The world had gone silent. He could see the white Impala racing toward them, lights still flashing, but he couldn't hear the sirens anymore. In that moment, the car almost seemed to be coming to their aid.

Trembling, Allyn held his hands in front of him. He was cut, scraped, and bruised, but he didn't think he was seriously hurt. Nyla was limp, and blood poured down the side of her face.

"Nyla!" Allyn reached for her. His breath caught as pain shot through his chest. The seatbelt cut into him. He was leaning back in the seat, letting the seatbelt relax, when the car roared back to life. Anger. Pain. Squealing. Allyn was pinned against his seat as the car sped up, rushing down the street like an athlete attempting to walk off an injury. The night had grown darker. *No*, Allyn realized—their car now only had one headlight.

The sirens returned. The Impala was heading straight toward them.

Jaxon floored it. Though hesitant and not as powerful as before, the car zipped forward. Jaxon wore a determined expression, his hands tightening over the steering wheel as the two cars sped toward each other. Half a block away, the Impala slid to a halt, and its back end swung around to block a large portion of the street. As if he had expected it, Jaxon veered right, toward the parking lot of a nearby business. A shower of sparks accompanied a sharp scraping noise against the undercarriage as they hit the driveway and nearly launched into the air. Nyla swayed against the seatbelt, her head bobbing violently from side to side.

The two men in the Impala watched in surprise as the Town Car shot through the parking lot. There was another shower of sparks as Jaxon pulled onto the street. He had them traveling toward Twenty-First, toward the traffic and crowds. Already, the road was growing more congested.

The distant sirens drew closer.

"We're not going to make it far," Jaxon said.

They didn't have many options. The Impala was only a block or two behind them again, and Allyn didn't believe their car would last much longer. It hissed and squealed, and the rear tire sounded as if it might fall off. But they couldn't ditch it and try and escape on foot, either. Not with Nyla unconscious. Not unless they put some distance between them and the Impala.

"Punch it." Allyn hated himself for saying it. It was risky. There were people everywhere, and shoppers in the Northwest acted as if they were exempt from traffic laws and impervious to accidents. They wouldn't see them coming. But if Jaxon could get past Twenty-Third, they stood a chance of escaping. From there, the traffic would thin out again, and they would be in the residential area. *What then?* "Use the horn and punch it." *Get there first, and we'll figure it out.*

Jaxon let out a pained breath and laid on the horn.

Almost as loud as a bullhorn, the racket made the pedestrians on the sidewalk jump in surprise. The Impala, as if understanding what Jaxon was planning, began chirping its sirens, drawing more attention to the speeding cars. Jaxon barreled through Twenty-First without incident then swerved past a car on Twenty-Second, continuing forward unscathed and distancing the Town Car from the Impala.

They raced toward the Twenty-Third intersection at freeway speeds. They were committed, and Jaxon couldn't slow down in time, even if he wanted to.

Allyn's stomach dropped when he saw a family about to step into the crosswalk. Bundled under thick coats and hidden under an umbrella, the two young children were oblivious to the oncoming car. Jaxon gave a series of sharp horn blasts then held one long, continuous one.

The child in the crosswalk froze—a young girl, maybe six years old, wearing a pink coat with her hood drawn up. Her eyes were wide with terror as the black monster barreled toward her. *Get out of the way*, Allyn thought. *Please! Move!*

Jaxon screamed and slammed on the brakes. The tires locked up and slid on the wet pavement, screeching and billowing smoke. In a single swoop of his arm, the girl's father snatched her out of the crosswalk. Still screaming, Jaxon stabbed the gas, accelerating into the intersection, clipping the front of a red Mercedes. A shower of sparks exploded against Allyn's door, and Jaxon nearly lost control. He slid beyond the intersection, bouncing off a parked car before finally righting the vehicle.

*Crash!*

Allyn looked behind them. Steam bloomed from the hood of the Mercedes, obscuring the white Impala that had slammed into it. Jaxon must have hit the Mercedes hard enough to block the intersection.

*We did it*, Allyn thought. *It worked!* The driver stepped out of the Mercedes just before Jaxon turned down a side street. Somewhere, buried under his relief, Allyn felt bad for the other driver.

"See that traffic signal up ahead?" Allyn asked. "That's Lovejoy. Turn left onto it and follow it up the hill."

Jaxon nodded and slowed to a more reasonable speed. The sirens had grown faint, but Allyn still didn't want to attract more attention. *Though a Town Car with a shattered headlight isn't exactly inconspicuous.*

Turning his attention to Nyla, Allyn felt concern quickly replace exultation. She was slumped against the seatbelt, blood dripping from her face. Leira unbuckled and climbed between the front seats to get into the back with them. She took Nyla's hand in hers, and white pulses of energy immediately rippled up Nyla's arm, disappearing under her navy compression armor. When they reached the top of her head and the tips of her fingers, they reversed course, returning back through Nyla's body to Leira's hand. With each returning ripple, Leira would learn more about Nyla's condition.

Leira's expression softened. "She's got a bump on the head and some moderate bruising, but other than that, she's fine."

"Can you wake her?" Jaxon asked.

"In a moment," Leira said. The waves of energy took on a

new intensity. The white light grew brighter, causing Nyla's skin to glow, and shot through her with greater urgency. Nyla stirred. Allyn knew that somewhere under the mess of silver hair, the cut on Nyla's scalp was healing, and another was simultaneously forming on Leira's head. Because they were mostly minor wounds, Leira had healed them only enough to stop the bleeding. She shouldered the pain with Nyla without taking it all on herself.

As the ripples dimmed and dissipated, Nyla regained consciousness. "What happened?" Her voice was strained and groggy, as if she'd been woken up in the dead of night.

"We escaped."

"And me?"

"We were in an accident," Leira said. "You're okay now."

"Thank you." Nyla gave Leira a small smile and sat up to scan their surroundings. "Where are we?"

"We're—"

The engine sputtered.

Jaxon frowned at the dash, obviously confused. The car sputtered again, and the headlights flickered. Half a block later, the engine died, leaving them coasting.

"What's wrong?" Leira asked.

"I don't know," Jaxon said. The dash lights had gone completely dark.

"Are we out of gas?" Allyn asked.

"No." Jaxon turned the key. Nothing. He did it again, pumping the gas. Still nothing. Not even a click. "Come on," he urged the car.

"Find somewhere to pull over," Allyn said.

That was easier said than done. The neighborhood was full of older homes without garages. Cars lined both sides of the street, not an empty space among them.

Still coasting, Jaxon continued to try to start the car. Eventually, the car came to rest in the middle of a four-way intersection. Jaxon cursed, slamming his hands on the steering wheel in frustration. He turned to the three of them, fury in his eyes. "Out."

Allyn hesitated. Jaxon's anger made him uncomfortable. The man was usually so practiced in hiding his emotions. Nyla and Leira attempted to exit the passenger side, but the door wouldn't open. They turned to him, wearing the same impatient expression.

Allyn popped open the door and jumped out. Seeing the car from the outside, he was amazed it had gone as far as it had. The driver's door was caved in, and a long red dent trailed behind it like a tail from a meteor. The rear bumper hung on the ground, and the vehicle was leaking a green, oily fluid that smelled like sweet candy. But the real damage was on the passenger side. The truck had hit them just behind Nyla's door, and the impact had crumpled it, wedging it shut. Nyla's window was shattered, and the rear tire leaned inward. Smoke escaped from somewhere inside the assembly.

"Stand back," Jaxon said. He was behind the car, trying to pop the trunk. Allyn barely had time to move before the trunk lid blasted open. Jaxon grabbed an emergency kit and threw it to Allyn, snatched a gallon of water, and slammed the trunk lid closed. Jaxon turned to Allyn and exhaled sharply. "I saw a couple houses under construction several blocks back. We can hide there until things calm down."

A car pulled up to the stop sign behind them. Allyn cursed under his breath, watching as the car turned toward them.

The driver came to a stop beside Allyn and rolled down his window. The slender man with thinning dark hair and glasses wore a concerned expression. "Is everything all right?" he asked.

"Yeah," Allyn said. "We've got a tow truck on the way."

"Are you sure?" the driver asked. "I can wait until they arrive."

"That's okay. They should be here any minute. I appreciate the offer, though."

The driver looked at him skeptically but gave him a small smile and nodded. "All right then. Have a good night."

"Thank you. You, too."

After the driver pulled away, Allyn turned to Jaxon. "We need to go."

They hastily made for the sidewalk where century-old maple trees lined the street in the small patches of grass between it and footpath. Their thick, twisting branches blocked the light from the streetlamps, keeping Allyn and his company in the shadows.

Allyn stopped abruptly, cursing.

"What's wrong?" Nyla asked.

"The computer," Allyn said, grimacing. "It's in the car." He looked back at the old Lincoln. It was almost three blocks away and nearly out of sight. The computer had nearly got them caught once. Was it worth the risk again? They still hadn't learned who was behind the video. *And those folders. Who are those other people? Magi? Machinists?* He had to know.

Allyn turned back to Jaxon and met his gaze. "It's worth it."

Without waiting for a response, Allyn broke into a run, racing back to the car. By the time he reached the end of the sidewalk, no one had stopped to inspect the Town Car. Waiting for another car to pass, Allyn fought every urge he had to run, instead casually strolling across the street and calmly opening the back door. The computer was on the floorboard, half-hidden under the driver's seat. Allyn grabbed it and crossed the street again with his same nonchalant pace.

When he returned, Jaxon and the rest were gone. *Where did they—*

"Get it?" Jaxon emerged from the other side of a weathered cedar fence.

Allyn held up the computer.

"Good," Jaxon said. "This way. We found a place to hide out."

Jaxon had chosen a new house still under construction. With a stone and vinyl siding exterior, the modern and elegant house didn't fit in with the style of the neighborhood.

The temporary front door, a plain white door without a knob, swung open without resistance, and Jaxon ushered them inside, keeping a watchful eye on their surroundings. Nails and pieces of scrap wood covered the unfinished floors, and the walls were framed and sheet rocked but weren't mudded or painted. The air smelled sweet, and their footsteps echoed as they made their way into what would eventually become the living room.

Exposed wires hung out of open electrical sockets, and empty snack bags and soda cans littered the floor, mixing with sawdust and footprints from the day before. It wasn't an ideal hideout, but it would keep them dry.

Perhaps it was the loss of the car, or maybe it was the exhaustion from again having to run, but once they were situated, a gloom like an Oregon winter fell upon them. They didn't talk. They didn't plan. They didn't do *anything*. Jaxon found a place upstairs where he could keep a lookout, and after checking on Nyla's condition, Leira joined him.

Allyn sat in the living room, leaning against a gas fireplace. He wished he could turn it on and feel the warmth on his back—his damp clothes would never dry in the cold, moist air. Nyla sat across the room from him. She had her eyes closed, and her breathing was steady. He couldn't tell if she was sleeping or just resting. He slid the computer in front of him. Unlike the rest of them, he was still burning with curiosity. He opened it, and his insides tore apart when he saw the screen.

A large crack ran from one corner of the monitor to the other. He laughed bitterly. Laughing kept him from crying. From taking the computer and throwing it out the window.

From jumping and stomping on it like an angry Yosemite Sam. It kept him from walking out the door and turning himself in. From walking away and disappearing.

He pushed the power button, knowing deep down that it was pointless, and was shocked when the monitor glowed with life. Hope flared briefly in his chest, warming him to his bones, and was almost immediately dashed when the screen dimmed and went black. It took him a moment to realize the computer had gone into power-saving mode. The battery was dead.

He slammed the laptop closed and slid it out of his immediate reach.

*What do I have to do?* Sometimes, he felt like the world's punching bag, always taking its blows and unable to fight back. Whatever he touched, whatever he did, he only made things worse. He was a fraud, someone who jumped at random noises and saw ghosts of death and misdeeds everywhere he turned. He didn't belong. The McCollum Family was better off without him. *Why can't they see that?*

*Stop*, he told himself. *Just stop. Complaining is only good for one thing—identifying the problem. You're dwelling on it. Move on.*

Carrying on a one-sided conversation was crossing farther into Crazy Town than he was willing to venture, so he didn't respond, but he did lean forward and slide the computer back in front of him. He couldn't stop himself from jumping at shadows or becoming nauseated at the smell of burning meat. He couldn't answer who had uploaded the video or why. And he didn't know what to do about the McCollum Family or the police.

But he could push forward. He could keep trying. Because when it came right down to it, he had only two options. Give up or keep going—and he wasn't the giving-up type.

He ran a finger around the edge of the computer, touching the various ports, until he came to a small rectangular one with five small prongs. Not a USB, HDMI, or Ethernet port, this was for the AC power adapter. If the computer's battery was dead... Allyn wielded, projecting the energy into his hand. He tried to hold back and keep the power as low as possible. The computer wouldn't be able to withstand more than one hundred watts.

The red coils didn't dim, but there were fewer of them; only one or two circled from his hand to his fingertips in a figure-eight pattern. He extended his index finger and pressed it against the five prongs of the AC power port. A click was followed by a high-pitch spinning noise. Allyn nearly withdrew, but the light on the front of the computer glowed to life, and then the monitor a second later.

The monitor flickered, and Allyn smelled something burning. It reminded him of the smell an old baseboard heater made when it was full of dust and hadn't been turned on since the previous winter. Something popped. The monitor sparked. Allyn jumped, cutting off the power as if he were unplugging it from a wall. Smoke curled out from the thin vent along the backside of the computer.

He pushed the power button. Nothing. He tried again. Still nothing.

He inspected the port. The silver casing was blackened where it had been burned, and the copper-colored prongs were melted. He didn't know how much power he had supplied, but it had obviously been a lot more than the port could handle.

He shook his head, cursing himself. *What was I thinking?*

Just because he *could* do something, didn't mean he should. He should have waited. He didn't have enough control of his abilities yet to try something as precise as that. Liam surely had a power adapter that would have worked with the computer—now even if he did, Allyn had ruined their chances at recovering anything.

Oddly enough, though, a part of him was satisfied that he

had made an attempt. Being proactive felt good. And maybe Liam *could* still do something with the computer. Instead of wallowing in his failure, Allyn focused on what he would do differently next time. He could learn to limit the amount of power he projected.

He heard the first sirens a short time later. Their car had been found. If they weren't already, the police would soon be combing the area and talking with neighbors. Roadblocks and barricades might be set up. They would search backyards and parked cars, bars and restaurants. *But will they search the unfinished homes half a mile away?*

If the way things had been going were any indication, Allyn wouldn't have been surprised if they did.

# CHAPTER 8

MADDOX APPROACHED THE REMAINS OF the black Continental. From what he could tell, it was a mid-nineties model, long, boxy, and *ordinary*, the kind of car that would blend in anywhere. When he got a look inside, though, the modifications became apparent. The blacked-out windows were made of reinforced glass, not quite police grade, but nearly half an inch thick. The rear passenger-side window had shattered only because it had taken a direct hit from a small four-wheel-drive pickup with an aftermarket front winch attached to its bumper.

Maddox slid on the second of his latex gloves and ducked inside the vehicle. An additional bench seat similar to that of a limousine had been added behind the driver and passenger seats, allowing for three extra occupants. Something wet dotted the carpeted floorboard. He borrowed a flashlight from a nearby officer then dabbed a gloved finger in the spot and held it in front of the light.

*Blood.*

Maddox returned the flashlight to the officer, strode toward the nearest squad car, and removed the evidence collection kit from the trunk. Inside were plastic evidence bags, sterile cotton swabs, cuticle sticks, combs, tweezers, and transfer pipettes. He returned to the Continental, opened the kit, removed the cotton swabs and two evidence bags, then set to work. He started with the bloodstain. Since it was still wet, he was able to soak it up with a cotton swab instead of cutting out a section of carpet. He bagged it, tagged it, photographed the area he'd taken it from, then moved on.

In the span of only a few minutes, Maddox had filled the evidence bags with blood samples and two different strands of hair—one black, maybe nine inches in length, and another longer, lighter-colored strand.

"What color do you think this is?" Maddox asked, holding the second hair strand in front of his face with a pair of tweezers.

Nolan drew closer, squinting in the soft light as he looked at the hair sample. "Blond?"

"Blond?" Maddox asked. "No. White, maybe?"

"I meant platinum blond."

*What the hell is platinum blond?* "Silver?"

"I'll go with that."

*Silver hair?* Maddox could always count on Portlanders to find a way to be strange. Tattoos. Piercings. Hair color. He'd seen worse. *But still...* "Who walks around with silver hair?"

"I don't know," Nolan said. "But it should make them easy to spot."

Maddox dropped the hair sample into another evidence bag and took a deep breath. It had been a long night, and it wasn't even close to being over. They still needed to dust for prints and get the samples to the lab. Then came the paperwork and reports. Part of him wondered if it was worth the effort. What new leads would fresh DNA provide? The dozens of samples collected from the manor hadn't led to anything. No matches. No dental records. It was more than odd, more than abnormal. It was impossible.

That didn't mean he could stray from procedure. He sealed the evidence bag and stepped away from the car, surveying the scene. Police cars surrounded them, blocking off the street from all directions. Officers leaned against their vehicles—talking, laughing, and joking—their faces clearly visible even in the night.

"What's going on through that giant head of yours?" Nolan asked.

"Kaplan has help," Maddox said. "We need to put a face to his accomplices."

The first step to tracking any suspect was to build a list of known associates—friends, family, coworkers, neighbors, anyone who might have a connection with the suspect—and expand the search from there. But Kaplan's few friends had refused to believe that he'd had anything to do with his sister's disappearance. They were loyal, devoted even, and fervent in their defense of him.

Adding to the problem, Kaplan's sister was his only remaining family. His mother was deceased, and his father had walked out on them years ago. Wherever Kaplan had disappeared to, he hadn't sought asylum with family. Even his coworkers had distanced themselves from him, and they were lawyers who weren't about to talk. The list had stopped growing before it had ever begun.

Time to change tactics. If they knew who had been in the car with him, they could build a new network of known associates. They had the DNA, the prints, and the car. But it wouldn't be enough. It hadn't been enough at the manor, and it wouldn't be enough now.

A camera flashed.

Maddox turned back to the car. With his business complete, a plain-clothes officer had stepped in. He was taking pictures of the interior of the vehicle, cataloguing the scene before he began dusting for prints. The camera flashed again.

*The camera—pictures!*

If they hit on the DNA, they could identify Kaplan's help,

and he would have driver's license photographs, social media pictures, high school photos—whatever he wanted—to send to every news program, newspaper, and concerned-citizens group in the Northwest. He could let the public run the investigation for him. But if they didn't get a hit, they would remain at square one. And they were running out of time.

"Maddox?"

He blinked.

Nolan was watching him, as if Maddox had been ignoring him.

"We're doing this backward," Maddox said. "We don't know where they're going, but we know where they were."

"I'm not following."

"Every bridge in Portland is monitored by a series of traffic cameras," Maddox said. "We know Kaplan left his house roughly two hours ago, and we know what they arrived in. A black, mid-nineties Continental may not stick out like a Ferrari, but it's not a Honda Civic, either. Track them back far enough, and it'll lead us to where they came from."

"That's a lot of cars," Nolan said. "We're talking evening traffic."

"Slow-moving traffic," Maddox corrected. "It'll make them easier to spot."

"I don't know."

"I'm not asking you to know," Maddox said. "I'm telling you what we're doing."

---

Allyn awoke cold and stiff and curled into a ball to preserve his body heat. His aching joints popped as he stretched and rolled onto his side. He ran his hands through his hair, feeling more of it than he was accustomed to, and brushed off the sawdust that clung to the side of his face. Already, the dark figure that had stirred him awake was looming over Nyla.

"It's time," Jaxon said after Nyla's eyes popped open. She was instantly alert. It was still dark outside, and rain tapped steadily on the unfinished roof.

"What's going on?" Allyn asked.

"We're leaving." Jaxon's voice lacked urgency, suggesting it was by choice, not necessity.

Allyn stood with a groan. He'd been restless over the previous couple of hours. He'd slept—though he supposed it was more of a series of short naps than a restful block—and it left him feeling heavy and slow. Before he could ask where they were headed, the front door opened and Leira entered, followed by another slender figure.

Liam brushed aside the hair on his forehead and strode toward Allyn with a broad smile. "You found it? Let me see it."

"Found what?"

"The computer!" Liam scanned the room. "Where is it? Is that it?" He pointed toward the silver laptop sitting on the counter. He brushed past Allyn toward it.

Jaxon reached it first and slid the computer under his arm. "Not until we're in the car."

"Oh," Liam said, failing to mask his disappointment. "Right. Of course."

The car, an early-nineties full-size Cadillac, was parked beside another vehicle in the middle of the street with its emergency lights flashing. They had bought it as a way to transport the remaining members of the McCollum Family to the cabin. It was meant to blend in, but compared to the Mercedes and BMWs populating nearby driveways, it probably had the opposite effect. They needed to move quickly.

Allyn felt a spike of annoyance when he saw Mason behind the wheel. The short man aggravated him. His shrill little voice irritated him. Most of all, Mason's distrusting attitude galled him. If Allyn had wanted to betray the Family's trust, he would have done so. He'd had multiple opportunities.

And yet, just a few short hours ago, he'd questioned why he remained with the Family. The revelation irked him more than anything. *Sometimes nothing's worse than admitting you're wrong, and that the person you can't stand is right.*

Though larger than the Continental, the Cadillac lacked the additional bench seat, and four of them had to sit almost on top of one another. Fortunately, Jaxon rode up front with Mason, leaving Allyn sandwiched between the slender women and the scrawny Liam. It was far from comfortable, but it was still better than being cuffed in the back of a squad car.

Once the car was moving, Jaxon handed Liam the computer.

Allyn started to warn Liam of the computer's condition, but Liam was too quick. He opened the computer and saw the crack across the monitor. Frowning, he pushed the power button. Nothing happened. He turned to Allyn, his mouth agape.

"We were in an accident," Allyn said. "It almost took my head off."

Liam looked back at the computer in disbelief.

"I saw a little of what was on it," Allyn said. "Folders, maybe two dozen of them, each named after a specific city." He hesitated. "One was named 'Portland, Oregon.'"

"What was in it?"

"Me," Allyn said simply. "Photographs, school records, information about where I worked, where I lived. Newspaper articles about me and about Kendyl's disappearance. It's like they were building a profile. A biography."

"And the other folders?"

"Were the same," Allyn said. "From what I could tell, anyway. But they were from all over the world. Europe. Asia. South America. I only glanced at a few."

Liam ground his teeth. Allyn understood, and he couldn't help but feel responsible. If he'd fled his condo a little faster or read the files in the car, they might not have been spotted, and the computer would still be intact.

"I might be able to recover the files," Liam said. "It looks like only the monitor was damaged. If that's the case, then we can transfer the files from this computer to mine, or if need-be, pull the hard drive and install it in another computer. But I hope that's not the case—laptops aren't really designed to be disassembled."

Allyn felt a surge of excitement. "You can do that?"

Liam shrugged. "Of course."

"That would be..." Allyn trailed off, remembering his failed attempt to power the computer. "There's something else." He pointed at the damaged power port.

"What happened?" Liam asked, eyes wide. He traced the blackened port with a finger.

"The battery died," Allyn said. "I tried to power it back up."

"You what?"

"Don't look at me like that. I was curious."

Liam shook his head.

"Do you think I ruined it?" Allyn asked.

"It depends on how much power you used. You could have melted the circuits together. We won't know until I start the transfer."

"I'm sorry, Liam," Allyn said. "It worked for a second."

Liam pursed his lips, clearly disappointed.

"If you are still able to transfer the files," Allyn began. He thought about how to explain. "The desktop was empty, except for that one master folder, but even before the accident, the computer was pretty beaten up. I have a hard time believing that the one folder was the only thing ever on the computer."

"You think someone wiped the hard drive?"

"Yeah," Allyn said.

Liam sat back, a contemplative look on his face. "Then we found only what they wanted us to find."

"Exactly," Allyn said. "But I'm just as interested in what they *didn't* want us to find. It might tell us whose computer it was and lead us to who's behind all of this."

"Unless the computer was stolen."

"I hadn't thought about that." Allyn's budding enthusiasm soured a bit. "But then again, if it was stolen, why go through the trouble to wipe the hard drive?"

"I don't know," Liam said slowly. "I can still try to recover the lost files, but it's going to depend on how they wiped the hard drive. If they did a quick delete, then there will be fragments and archived information, but if they did it right, we'll be lucky to find anything more than crumbs."

"And if it was stolen, the information will lead us nowhere."

"True."

Allyn shrugged. "Anything is better than what we have at the moment."

Liam nodded and sat up a little straighter. Allyn had given him a project, and more than that, they still had hope. Allyn felt a little better, too. The tension in his shoulders was melting away. If anyone could salvage the computer and recover its information, Liam could.

As Allyn's pressure and anxiety eased, the lack of sleep threatened to catch up to him. He leaned his head on the window and looked out. It was the darkest kind of night, where the moon and the stars were hidden behind a thick mass of clouds, and even the streetlamps were off or burned out. They followed the river; its slow moving water looked like shadowed glass. Their car was the only car on the otherwise lonely highway.

Allyn pulled away from the window abruptly. The river was on the wrong side of the road. "Where are we going?" he asked.

Jaxon shifted in his seat but remained silent. The rest of the car's occupants watched him but didn't pipe in with additional questions. Allyn didn't like it. Jaxon was the acting grand mage, but his time in that position was limited, and he'd made a point of including Liam and Allyn, along with Leira and Nyla, in his decisions. Wherever they were going, whatever they were doing, it was for Jaxon, not the Family.

They rode in silence for a time, continuing to follow the river until, eventually, Mason turned off the highway onto an old two-lane logging road. The winding road led them deep into the forest, and Allyn quickly lost all sense of direction. Mason turned onto a narrower lane, where a steep cliff was slowly overtaking the asphalt, then from it to another, always going uphill and deeper into the wilderness. The paranoid part of Allyn felt like an abused pet unknowingly being driven into the woods to be abandoned, but the rational part watched his surroundings, a realization brewing. The deeper and deeper Mason drove, the clearer and clearer their destination became.

Allyn caught Liam's eye. "The manor?" he mouthed silently.

Liam's eyes grew wide, and he watched their surroundings with renewed interest. He looked unsure for a moment. Then as they continued around a bend, recognition struck. He nodded.

*Why?* The manor was under police control, likely monitored around the clock. Allyn stirred uncomfortably—his fear of abandonment had been replaced by fear of betrayal. Jaxon had made it clear they would eventually look to strike and recover the artifacts in the library. But they weren't prepared. To try before they were ready was too risky. They might as well walk into the nearest police station and turn themselves in.

Mason slowed, turning onto a gravel road, and stopped short of a faded yellow gate.

*Are we approaching the manor from behind?*

"Wait here." Jaxon opened the door and stepped outside.

Allyn decided the order was directed at Mason, and not

everyone in the car. He stepped out of the car to follow. Jaxon had already ducked under the gate and was ascending the steep hill. Allyn jogged to catch up, hearing more footsteps crunching on the gravel behind him. Fallen limbs, walnuts, and slick leaves covered the decaying road, while thick blackberry bushes lined either side and wrapped around deep-rooted tree trunks, suffocating them.

Mason shut off the car's headlights, and the world went black. Without the moon or starlight, Allyn was trapped in an expanse of pure darkness; and if it weren't for Jaxon's shuffling footsteps, Allyn would have quickly been lost.

Allyn took short, tentative steps and held out his arms as if he were walking through a strange house in the middle of the night. Liam tripped somewhere behind him, falling with a grunt, before climbing back to his feet to the sound of cracking twigs and ruffling leaves. Allyn's eyes took several minutes to adjust, but when the fuzzy outline of Jaxon's bulky frame resolved, Allyn hastened his steps to take position at his side. If Jaxon was irritated that Allyn and Liam had followed, he masked it behind a determined expression.

"What are we doing here, Jaxon?"

"Searching for answers."

His leg muscles burning, Allyn continued to follow Jaxon up the hillside, until finally, the landscape leveled off onto a panoramic vista. The trees had been cleared away from what Allyn believed was the southeast side of the hill, giving them a clear vantage into the world beyond. The manor wasn't immediately visible, but Allyn had little doubt that it was near. Lights from Portland's neighboring cities shined in the distance, reflecting off the dark clouds and casting a soft light onto the hillside.

Jaxon crossed his arms and stared into the distance. Not the horizon. He was looking at something closer. Below them, perhaps a few miles away on the next hillside, partially hidden by thick pine trees, was a series of circular lights illuminating a construction site. Allyn took a step forward.

Inside the circular array of lights were tractors, trailers, SUVs, and other earth-moving equipment. Even from a distance, Allyn could make out small shadows moving among them, marching around the site like an army of ants. At the site's center was a blackened scar resembling little more than a shadow in the night. The tractor was clearing part of it away, scooping and dumping debris into a nearby container.

"No," Liam said softly.

It wasn't a construction site. It was the manor.

"Tell me what we're up against," Jaxon said.

Allyn attempted to swallow the tension in his throat. He'd expected police escalation, especially after Jaxon had told him of his plan to retake the library, but he hadn't expected it so soon. If they were cleaning up the site, the investigation had reached a point where the police no longer needed the manor rubble. They had gathered enough evidence to move forward.

"Who were those men?"

Allyn could see them as clearly as he could see Jaxon or Liam. The one behind the wheel was huge, larger than even Jaxon, with a clean-shaven head and a goatee. The other had a square face and styled hair. They wore dark suits over starched white shirts, black ties, and grim expressions. And they had watched him as if they knew him.

"They were FBI," Allyn said.

"What does that mean?" Jaxon asked.

"It means things have escalated."

# CHAPTER 9

SOMETHING WAS OFF. KENDYL STEPPED back, observing the canvas, the tip of the paintbrush in her mouth. It wasn't the color—the forest greens, magentas, and golden yellows matched the landscape and sunrise beyond. *As much as possible anyway.* There were more colors in the sunrise than she could capture with paint. Kendyl squinted, and the landscape became a blurry mess of vague shapes: the hills, circles and ovals; the trees, jagged vertical lines; and the horizon, a curving horizontal line interrupted by the semicircle of the rising sun.

She frowned. The framing was correct, too. *Maybe it's your imagination.* But she knew it wasn't. Though unable to pinpoint the issue, she knew there was one. Something about the painting made her physically uncomfortable. Squeamish. Shaky even. She imagined the feeling to be similar to having a fear of heights and being forced to look over the edge of a skyscraper. It made her ill. The world had a natural artistic balance—the way shapes and sizes complemented each other and fit into the world. Everything had its place. Its purpose.

Kendyl held up a hand, thumb extended to the side, and closed one eye. She used her thumb as a guide to measure the landscape's features, comparing it to the corresponding features in her painting. The dimensions of the hills on either side of the valley were correct. Even the hill at the far end of the valley, the one that the sun was cresting over, was fine. *Then what in the name of—*

The valley was too wide. Kendyl cursed herself. In her haste to capture the rising sun, she must have made a mistake while sketching out the valley. It was the kind of thing that ruined the entire painting. If she widened the hills to compensate, the sun would become too small. But if she increased the sun's diameter, the colorful sky would need to be expanded, too. Like adding too much flour to cake batter— adding more hillside would throw off the entire painting. It would be easier to start over.

Sighing, Kendyl sat down on a nearby log. Just because the painting was a failure didn't mean she couldn't enjoy nature's artwork.

"That's beautiful."

Kendyl whipped around to see Allyn standing on the trail behind her. "You scared me," she said, her heart threatening to beat out of her chest.

"Sorry," Allyn said. "I didn't mean to."

"It's okay."

Allyn stepped up to the easel, observing the painting. Kendyl wanted to tell him to stop, that she didn't want him to look at it, but she remained silent, watching uncomfortably from the log.

"Did you do this just now?"

"Yeah."

"Amazing." He turned to Kendyl. "How do you do it?"

She shrugged. "The world's just a series of shapes and lines if you look at it properly. It's not all that difficult."

Allyn turned back to the painting. "For you, maybe. I wouldn't know where to start."

"It's just like anything, I suppose," Kendyl said. "Pick a spot and go."

"Most things have a beginning."

"Maybe that's what I like about art then. I can start wherever I want."

"Always the free spirit," Allyn said with a laugh. He strode toward Kendyl, and after brushing the snow off the log beside her, he sat down. "Why didn't you finish it?"

"I messed up," Kendyl said, grimacing.

"Really? It looks great to me."

She shrugged. She didn't want to talk about the painting. "You look tired."

Allyn laughed, then as if on cue, yawned. His brown eyes were swollen and red, with dark circles beneath them, and his skin was paler than usual, making his dark features more prominent. "I've been up all night."

"I was worried."

"I'm fine," Allyn said, throwing his arm around her and pulling her close.

Kendyl nearly gagged. He smelled of sweat and musty clothing.

"You stink," she said, wriggling out of the embrace. The forced closeness made her uncomfortable. Allyn wanted to act as if things between them weren't strained, but even if things were on the mend, she and her brother simply weren't as close as they used to be. It would take time—and even then, part of her wondered if they would ever get back what they'd had. "What took you guys so long?"

"We ran into trouble."

"I heard. Liam and Mason left hours ago. What happened?"

"They were waiting for us. The moment we left, the police arrived."

"It was a trap then?"

"I don't know."

"If it wasn't a trap," Kendyl asked, "then what were they doing there?"

"Maybe they were investigating the video, too." Allyn

96

shrugged. "There was only the one car. If it was a trap, why weren't there more officers? Why not grab us the second we walked inside?"

Kendyl cocked her head to the side, thinking. "That's a good question."

"You have paint in your hair."

"Huh?"

Allyn pointed at the hair draped over her shoulder. The bottoms of the dark strands were caked in various shades of magenta and fuchsia. Kendyl pinched them between her thumb and index finger and held them in front of her face while she flaked the dry paint off with her thumbnail. She always kept her hair tied back when she painted, but inevitably, a few strands always came loose to swirl in the paint on her palette.

"I need a haircut," she said. "You do, too."

Allyn laughed, running his hands through his hair. He normally kept it closely cropped—it required less work that way—but it had grown out, making him look like a mushroom. Even his face was gruff. Dark facial hair wrapped from ear to ear around his chin and mouth. He looked like a different man.

*He's not tired,* Kendyl thought. *He's worn down.*

"Are you sure you don't want to go back home?" Allyn asked.

Kendyl tucked the loose strand of hair behind her ear. "Where is this coming from?"

"They're coming after us, Kendyl. It wasn't the police at my condo. It was the FBI. They're closing in on us, and it's only a matter of time before they come searching here."

"They've already been here," Kendyl said.

Allyn looked as though he wanted to challenge her, but he let the comment slide. After they'd fled the fallen manor, the McCollum Family had arrived at the cabin to find footprints and tire tracks. They had even found an open window and dusty footprints inside where someone had searched the cabin. They couldn't be sure it was the police, but who else wearing large military-style boots would break into a cabin and not steal anything?

"That doesn't mean they won't come back."

"I don't understand what you're asking. Do *you* want to go?"

"I don't know."

Kendyl sat back, looking at him with a renewed intensity. He wasn't only physically beaten down; there was something else, something deeper. He was haunted by something.

"I'm afraid, Kendyl," he said. "I see him everywhere. Every time I wield. Every time I..." He sighed deeply, leaning forward to rest his elbows on his thighs.

"I don't know who you're talking about, but if you're running from something, you'll never get away from it. Whatever it is, you have to face it."

Allyn's face went as white as the snow around them, and he looked as though he were about to vomit. "I can't do it," he said, his voice little more than a whisper.

"Then I'll help you."

Allyn looked up at her. His eyes were glassy, his jaw tight. *He really is going to be sick.*

He gave her a single, sharp nod. "Then there's more you need to know. Jaxon's returning home."

"What?"

"He's grooming Liam to lead."

"He's too young."

"I think he expects me to stay—to help and advise him. At fifteen, Liam would be half the age of the youngest grand mage, and he would be leading a Family no other is willing to listen to. It's setting him up for failure."

"You can say no," Kendyl said.

Allyn stood and began pacing in front of her. "Can I? These people fought and died for us, Kendyl. We owe them more than we can ever give. Besides, Jaxon isn't concerned. He wants to turn this Family into something different. Something new. The first machinist Family. And he wants a machinist to lead it."

Kendyl frowned. A fifteen-year-old kid should be learning to drive, going on first dates, and getting his first job, not being burdened with the responsibility of running a Family. She knew firsthand what that kind of weight could do to a child.

Sometimes she wondered what kind of woman she would have become if her mother hadn't died or if their father hadn't walked out. She and Allyn had been robbed of their teenage years, forced to grow up too soon. It didn't make her angry, as it did Allyn, but she wasn't happy to see it happen to someone else.

"Do you mean it?" Allyn asked. "That you'll help me?"

"Yes."

Allyn let out a sharp breath. "Good."

Kendyl smiled, mostly at how little Allyn knew about himself. He was a natural leader. Always building a cabinet of trusted advisors, he was unwilling to walk away from anyone he thought needed his help. He might not have known he was coming to her to ask for her support, but he *had* done it. "I need you to do something for me, though."

"Of course," Allyn said. "Anything."

"I want you to train me."

Allyn raised an eyebrow. "You still think you can wield?"

"We're twins, Allyn. Whatever you can do, I should be able to do, too."

"I'm not sure it works like that," Allyn said. "What if it's like your painting? I can't do that."

"That's different. Painting is a skill that I learned and practiced over time."

"I'm just not—"

"Humor me," Kendyl said. "Please?"

Allyn met her eye, perhaps noticing her conviction for the first time.

"Okay," he said. "But not today. Today, I need some sleep."

———•••———

Liam worked. It kept his mind occupied, free from thinking about things he'd rather not think about. He'd spent thousands of hours in the library, organizing and digitizing its contents, preserving the fragile magi history. He was lost without it, and he hated to think about how his treasures were being treated—grimy police fingers flipping through disintegrating texts, destroying ink and parchment. Uncontrolled, unfiltered air aging his books by the minute. It made Liam want to cry in frustration.

Jaxon assumed Liam wanted to recover the library's contents as a way to verify some of the findings he'd unearthed in the strange book from Hyland Estate, but it was more than that, more important than that. Without proper care, the contents of the library would be destroyed, and everything they had from the days before the Fracture would disappear along with it. He couldn't let that happen.

The sun was cresting the hillside, bathing the room in a fiery orange. Jaxon had given Liam his room, and the privacy it offered, while he worked to recover the contents of the computer.

Liam rose from the edge of the bed and closed the blinds. He'd spent too much time outdoors of late, usually cold, wet, and miserable. After working in the library for so long, he'd developed odd quirks, and an aversion to natural light was one of them. He was most comfortable working under the yellow light of fluorescent bulbs while listening to the steady rhythm of filtered air blowing through vents.

Liam regarded the broken computer. Transferring files wasn't difficult. In fact, it was one of the simplest things Liam could do, but files could be lost, damaged, or even corrupted in the process. He also had no way of knowing if he'd recovered everything. And that assumed the hard drive hadn't been damaged in the wreck or by Allyn's reckless attempt to power the computer by wielding. If it had...

*No,* Liam thought. *Not now. Not this time. We're due for some kind of luck.*

He flipped the computer upside down and used a thin Phillips screwdriver to loosen the screws and pop open the compartment to expose the chrome hard drive inside. After cautiously pulling the hard drive free, he held it near the light and removed the four screws along the edges to take off the chrome casing. Then, careful to hold the exposed hard drive by the outer rim so he didn't damage the circuits or platter, Liam removed the black casing that covered the gold pins at the top. He grabbed the IDE-to-USB cable off his desk and plugged the hard drive's gold pins into the IDE port. Ready for the transfer, Liam held his breath and plugged the USB cable into his computer.

He exhaled when he heard the hard drive start spinning then smiled when the icon appeared on his desktop. *It worked.*

Liam double-clicked on the new icon and opened the contents of the foreign hard drive. Resisting the temptation to dig into them, he selected everything and dragged them into the folder he'd set up on his hard drive. The transfer began.

Liam sat down on the bed, leaned back, and rested his head on the wall. Depending on how much information was on the hard drive, the transfer might take hours. He grabbed the book from the Hyland Estate, then stopped and stared at the thin volume with a sour expression. It was the only book he had left. It could be a rare account of an ancient event, or it could be a work of fiction, but without the other contents of the library, he couldn't be sure. One thing was certain— as the last magi tome in Liam's possession, it needed to be preserved. It needed to be cherished. Every time he opened it, the pages deteriorated a little more and the spine fell apart further. If he wasn't careful, he would lose it, too.

Liam sighed. It wasn't a book he could read for enjoyment. Not until he was finished transcribing it. He returned the book to the nightstand and, shortly thereafter, fell asleep to the steady hum of the spinning hard drive.

# CHAPTER 10

"WE LOST THEM," NOLAN SAID. He leaned back in his chair, closed his eyes, and ran his hands through his hair. White flakes of dried hair gel fell, accumulating on the black leather chair.

Maddox pulled off his glasses and looked up from the case file. They were in the main level of the Portland FBI Field Office. Agents wearing black suits with black ties, short hair, and grim expressions worked at desks around them, hidden behind the half walls and glass partitions of cubicles. Maddox preferred working there. The steady rhythm of fingers tapping keyboards and the low murmur of conversation centered him. The ringing telephones and even the rattle of the central air system shook loose ideas like fruit from a tree. Other agents liked to talk about home, but the field office *was* Maddox's home—he'd spent far more time here in his thirteen-year career than he had anywhere else, including his house.

"Where?" Maddox asked.

"Somewhere after the I205, I84 interchange." Nolan leaned forward, sliding his computer over so Maddox would have a better view. The screen displayed a series of traffic cameras, each occupying a small window.

Nolan clicked on one, maximizing the image. "We picked them up heading south across the Freemont Bridge then backtracked them to I5 North, where they were stuck in traffic."

"That area is always a parking lot," Maddox said.

"Yeah." Nolan rubbed his eyes. The man looked exhausted. His eyes, normally lively and alert, were red from strain and lack of sleep. Nothing could prepare young agents for the stress of working on real cases or the weight of responsibility that came with it. They began like bullets fired from a low-caliber gun, quick and hot, but they flamed out quickly, crashing to the ground like everything else. The agents who lasted, agents like Maddox, were like guided missiles—they didn't burn out until they hit their targets.

Nolan pulled up another camera view. "Here they are merging from I84 onto I5, and here, we picked them up again using a traffic camera mounted to the overpass in the Hollywood District, but that's where we lose them. Away from the heart of the city, the cameras just aren't as numerous."

"What happens if you go back farther?"

"We tried that. Here's the problem." Nolan clicked on another window. It was black. "The camera is down for repair." He clicked on another. "And here's the one from the I205, I84 interchange." The image was blurry, obscured by a raindrop in the center of the screen.

Maddox cursed. "Don't they have crews that clean that sort of thing?"

"They do," Nolan said. "This is the footage from last night. The problem has since been taken care of."

"Of course it has," Maddox said bitterly. "What if we go back farther?"

"We tried that, too," Nolan said. "But we're talking about hundreds of cameras, extending over hundreds of miles, and a Lincoln Continental may not be the most popular car out there, but there are more than you think. And contrary to popular belief, these cameras aren't powerful enough to capture license plates. So without being able to trace them back step by step, we don't have a frame of reference, and the variables become overwhelming. It took me all night just to get this far."

Maddox ran his hand over his bare scalp, feeling more prickly hair than he liked. He'd need to shave it again soon. "So what do we know?"

Nolan shrugged. "They traveled west on I84, likely coming from the I205 area. Gresham, maybe?"

"Or Hood River. Pendleton. Hell, they could be coming from Vancouver or Battleground, for all we know." Maddox exhaled sharply, collecting himself. "What about the plates?"

"Registered to the same First Family Corporation."

Maddox wasn't surprised. Nothing else in the manor had any ties to any single person—why would the car? "Before you get too discouraged," Maddox said, "we did catch one break. We finally got a hit on Kaplan's father." Joseph Kaplan had been the only missing piece to their list of known friends and family. He'd disappeared from the grid three years ago.

"Where?"

"You're not going to believe it."

"I've never known you to be dramatic, Agent Maddox."

"Maybe you're rubbing off on me."

"Then you're a lucky man."

Maddox barked a laugh. "I guess that's one way to look at it."

"All right, enough already," Nolan said with a smile. "Quit stalling and come out with it."

"The Salem Pen."

Nolan raised an eyebrow. "For what?"

Maddox handed Nolan the file he'd had in his hands. "It's all in here."

"Why didn't this come up during our initial search?" Nolan began thumbing through the file.

Maddox shrugged. "Who knows?"

"The Pen is only an hour drive from here."

"I know."

"I take it we're going then?"

"Get your coat."

———————————

Agent Maddox felt as though he were looking at an older version of Allyn Kaplan. Joseph Kaplan was thicker than his son was, though much of his broad frame had gone soft with age. Gray peppered his dark hair and closely trimmed beard, and his black-rimmed glasses enhanced his already-large brown eyes. He sat with his elbows on the table, his shoulders slumped, the orange jumpsuit somewhat spoiling the comparison.

Agent Nolan stirred in his seat beside Maddox. The young agent had been a different man since entering the prison. His jovial, sometimes-sarcastic attitude had become subdued and almost depressed. His voice was soft, almost a whisper, and he wore a perpetual frown. Maddox bit back a smile. The reaction wasn't uncommon during a new agent's first few visits to the pen, but Maddox had never understood it. The visits were part of the job. They were in the business of putting criminals in prison, and sometimes that meant going there themselves. One of his previous partners—*Either Bradley or Jacobson, or maybe Livingston*—had once told him that it was unnerving to believe they were only one bad decision from occupying a cell down the block. Maddox didn't understand that, either—worry, like regret, was pointless.

"Thank you for sitting down with us," Maddox said, clasping his hands on the table. They sat in the middle of an empty visiting area, a dozen unoccupied tables surrounding them. Steel bars covered the windows along the far wall, and an overweight guard watched from the door.

"You said it had to do with my kids." The older Kaplan's

voice was deep and raspy. Like his weathered face, it was likely the result of spending too many evenings inside smoky bars.

"When was the last time you saw your children, Mr. Kaplan?" Maddox asked.

"About a month ago. Why?"

"Allyn and Kendyl were *here*?" Nolan asked, surprised.

"Allyn and Kendyl?" Kaplan asked, his eyes narrowing. He exhaled slowly, looking at the floor. "I haven't seen them in... twelve, maybe thirteen, years."

"Then who...?"

"I remarried," Kaplan said. "I'm sorry, what did you say this was about again?"

"We're investigating a disappearance," Maddox said.

"And Allyn and Kendyl are involved?"

"What can you tell us about them?" Nolan asked.

"It's been a long time," Kaplan said, leaning back in his chair and running his fingers through his hair. He seemed to be doing everything possible to avoid looking at them, and maybe it was Maddox's imagination, but Kaplan's eyes were growing glassy. "They were just kids when I left. And even before then, I wasn't... I wasn't around much. If this is about Allyn and Kendyl, I'm not sure how much help I can be."

"Where were you?" Maddox asked.

"Hmmm?"

"You said you weren't around. Where were you?"

Kaplan rubbed his hands together as if he were trying to wash them. "I was... I *am*... I've been sober for six-hundred ninety-seven days. I was drunk." Then as if he were coming to a deep realization, he repeated, "I was drunk. Some men come home from work and play with their children or watch TV for an hour or two to decompress. I came home and found joy in the bottle. As you can imagine, it didn't win me any father or husband of the year awards."

"Did you and your wife fight?" Maddox asked.

"About what?"

"Anything."

"Of course."

"In front of your children?"

"Don't judge me, Agent Maddox," Kaplan said heatedly. "I accept the choices I made and where they've brought me, but that doesn't mean I'm proud of them."

"You didn't answer the question."

"Have you ever fought addiction, Agent Maddox?"

"No."

"It's a strange thing. When you can stop, you don't want to, and when you want to stop, you can't."

"Poetic."

"Did you write that?" Nolan asked. He didn't seem to share Maddox's distaste for empty words.

"No," Kaplan said. "I read it in a book named *Candy*. But it's the best description of addiction I've ever heard. I didn't set out to live this life, to leave my wife and children behind. But when it got to the end, I couldn't stop."

"Your wife gave you an ultimatum," Nolan said. "The bottle or them."

Kaplan nodded and looked away, his breathing becoming shallow.

*And you chose the bottle, you piece of shit.*

"Kendyl is missing, Mr. Kaplan," Nolan said.

Maddox glared at Nolan. The young agent was supposed to be following his lead, not taking control of the conversation.

"We tracked her to a mansion in the hills outside of Portland," Nolan continued, ignoring or oblivious to Maddox's disapproval. "But before we could get her to safety, our officers were ambushed, and she disappeared again."

Kaplan swallowed a lump in his throat. His eyes *were* tearing up.

"I'm sorry, Mr. Kaplan," Nolan said. "I know this must be difficult, but is there anything you can remember about

Allyn that might give us a hint about his motive or his whereabouts?"

"Allyn is missing, too?"

"We believe he's behind her disappearance."

"Allyn? No." Kaplan shook his head. "No, that's not possible. He could be an argumentative little shit sometimes, but he wasn't violent."

"We have reason to believe otherwise."

*There's an understatement.* Allyn Kaplan had been involved in the deaths of three officers and had nearly gotten Maddox and Nolan killed in the high-speed chase through northwest Portland.

"He would never hurt his sister," Kaplan said. "They were inseparable."

"We have witnesses placing him at the scene of the crime," Maddox said.

"Then someone made a mistake."

Maddox opened the folder on the table and pulled out a series of photographs. It was time to stop dancing around the issue. He tossed the photographs dramatically in front of Kaplan.

"What are these?" Kaplan asked.

"Your daughter was found tied to a bed, bound and gagged. And Allyn was one of two men apprehended at the scene. This is what is left of the squad car that was taking him to the station." Maddox pulled out another picture and dropped it on top of the rest. Officer Grimes was hardly recognizable. His skin was blistered and red; his hair, singed and burnt. The upper half of his uniform was missing, and its frayed edges were black. "This is Officer Grimes," Maddox said, pointing to a picture of the fallen officer. "The officer who had your son in custody."

"I'm telling you," Kaplan said, looking up from the pictures, "Allyn isn't capable of this."

"How would you know?" Maddox asked. "You haven't seen him in thirteen years."

Kaplan glared at him.

"A lot can change in that kind of time, especially for a man with such a traumatic childhood."

"Leaving was the best thing that I could do for them," Kaplan said. "Children follow their parents' footsteps. I didn't want my children to end up like me."

"You don't believe that," Nolan said. "If you believed that children grow up to be their parents, you would have become the person you wanted them to be. But you left instead."

"Addiction is a powerful villain," Kaplan said helplessly.

Maddox wanted to backhand the man. He hated people like Joseph Kaplan. People who hid behind excuses, refusing to take responsibility for their choices. Regardless of what Kaplan believed, addiction was just another choice. He had chosen to drink every night. He had chosen to leave his family behind. Addiction was just the convenient way out.

"And maybe that's what I'm doing now," Kaplan continued. "I wasn't as clearheaded then as I am today. I have to fix myself before I can fix the lives I've broken."

Maddox slid the pictures back into his folder. "Why are you in here, Mr. Kaplan?" He took an exaggerated look around the visiting room. "Why are you incarcerated?"

Kaplan glared at Maddox, fury burning in his eyes.

*Yes, your anger burns hot. Just like your son's.* Maddox made a show of shuffling through his paperwork and finding Kaplan's information. "Vehicular manslaughter. Killed a father on his way to pick up his daughter from dance practice, correct?"

"What's your point?"

"Maybe your son ended up like you, after all."

Kaplan stood abruptly, making the chair squeak across the floor. "Don't give me that self-righteous attitude, you son of a bitch!" Kaplan leaned over the table, pointing his finger in Maddox's face. "Buried somewhere inside you is regret. Guilt. I can see it! I can feel it!"

The guard was on Kaplan in an instant, and two more poured into the visiting area.

"Maybe you're a terrible father," Kaplan raged, "a terrible husband. I don't know, but it's in there, and instead of accepting it, you take it out on the world around you!"

The guards wrestled Kaplan to the ground, wrenching his arms behind his back and cuffing him. Kaplan screamed in pain.

Maddox closed the folder, stood, then strode over to where Kaplan was lying facedown against the dirty tiled floor. "Someday soon, I'm going to put your son away. Maybe he'll be a few cells down, and you two can make up for lost time. Have a good day, Mr. Kaplan."

Maddox turned to Nolan and nodded. They were done. Kaplan hadn't answered the questions, but he'd given him answers of a sort. Regardless of what Kaplan believed, anger raged through their veins. Hot, uncontrollable anger. The elder Kaplan kept his in check through deep remorse and guilt, but the younger Kaplan, the man who'd lost his father at a young age and his mother only a few years later, didn't have those safeguards. If pushed hard enough, he would snap. He had snapped.

"I hope he kills *you*, you worthless piece of—" Kaplan's voice ended in a scream as one of the guards buried a knee in his back.

"What the hell was that?" Nolan asked, turning on Maddox the moment they were out of the visiting area. Kaplan's screams and groans were still audible.

"Don't."

"No," Nolan said heatedly. "You baited him. Taunted him. Rubbed his nose in it. And where did it get us? We're no closer to solving this case now than we were an hour ago."

"He didn't know anything," Maddox said. "He said so himself."

"We'll never know what he knows," Nolan said. "You never gave him an opportunity to talk."

Maddox shook his head and started down the hallway. The door buzzed in front of him, and he passed into the control room, Nolan on his heels. Two guards sat in the center of a circular desk, monitors and controls around them.

"You don't have to like the man," Nolan said, "but you do have to respect him."

Maddox turned on him, pulling close, his face inches from Nolan's. "The man's blood-alcohol level was *three times* the legal limit the day he killed that girl's father." He spat the words with such intensity that Nolan recoiled. "Until the day he's paid his debts and walks through these doors as a free man, I don't have to respect shit. No amount of remorse can *ever* undo the damage he's done."

Nolan scowled, but before he could answer, the door behind Maddox buzzed. He turned from the younger agent, opened it, and walked into another long white hallway.

"If you believe that," Nolan said, "then why are you in the bureau? Our entire institution is based around the idea that men can change, that they can learn from their mistakes and become better people. If they can't, then what's the point of their incarceration?"

"It's not about that—it's about protecting everyone else. What happens when Kaplan gets out and can't resist temptation? What happens when his *addiction* kills one of *your* loved ones?"

"Who's to say he will?"

"Who's to say he won't?"

"You can't keep someone locked up because of what they *might* do."

"Of course you can. Every person in here is locked away because we consider them a danger to society."

They walked through the door into the main lobby. The two uniformed officers sitting behind the enclosed, half-moon desk nodded to them as they passed.

"That's different," Nolan said, stepping outside.

"How?" Maddox squinted in the sun. Puddles of rainwater still dotted the parking lot, but the pavement was drying out, returning to a muted gray that matched the color of the prison.

"It sidesteps the notion of intent. Kaplan wasn't looking to hurt someone that night, and responsibility aside, it was an accident. The real dangers to society—the murderers and rapists—intended to do what they did."

"Then you believe him when he says he's going to stay sober?"

"I believe that he believes he's going to stay sober. That's enough for me."

"It's not for me."

Nolan sniffed. "You're a tough man to please, Agent Maddox. Remind me never to get on your bad side."

Maddox had to smirk at that. He knew he could be a hard ass—it was perhaps a byproduct of growing up in a family of career military men—and his black-or-white view of the world had been at the center of his marital problems. But within the bureau, he'd found more people like him, more who shared his worldview. Men like Agent Nolan, the young and idealistic, were rare and didn't usually last long. They were too soft and were better off as social workers or counselors.

"Do you know what I hate most in this world?" Maddox opened the door to their new Impala and climbed in, breathing in the new-car smell. "Failure. If everyone just did what they were supposed to do, the world would be a much better place."

"I suppose you want to be the one who decides what everyone else is supposed to do," Nolan said sarcastically, sliding into the passenger seat.

"You like to talk, don't you, Agent Nolan?"

"It's one of my few character flaws."

Maddox bit back a smile. "You know, somehow, despite your liberal, pretentious, self-righteous bullshit, I think I'm beginning to like you."

"I think, somewhere, a criminal just pissed himself."

"Let's hope it was Allyn Kaplan."

# CHAPTER 11

The door was closed. Allyn raised a hand to knock then hesitated. *Is he sleeping or working?* Liam had worked in the quiet solitude of the manor's library, maybe he was trying to recreate an inkling of privacy—the room was, after all, Jaxon's. Allyn couldn't blame Liam; with almost two dozen people living in the small cabin, privacy was a thing of the past. Finding the time to think, let alone work, was difficult.

Allyn knocked softly. No response. He knocked a little harder. Still no answer, though he thought he heard an annoyed sigh from inside the room. He scowled. It was already midafternoon, and he wanted to know if Liam had made any progress in recovering the files. He considered opening the door slightly, just to see if he was sleeping, but thought that might skirt too closely to invading the privacy he obviously longed for.

Before Allyn could try, the door swung open, and Liam glared at him.

"What?" Liam asked sharply.

Allyn took a step back. "I just wanted to see how things were coming along."

"You're the third person to ask me that in the last ten

minutes," Liam said. "The transfer is in progress. That's all I know. I don't know how far along it is, and I don't know how much longer. Okay?"

"Okay..." Allyn said. "I wasn't trying to rush you. I just hadn't heard anything."

"I'll let you know when I have something."

"All right," Allyn said as Liam closed the door. He started down the hallway then stopped. The exchange had left him unnerved. Liam had been just as excited about the computer's prospects as Allyn had. It was their first solid clue, and it was something Liam could take the lead in. *What's changed? Why is he so agitated?*

*The library,* Allyn realized.

Jaxon had led them back to the manor, and Liam had been forced to confront everything he was trying to avoid. People had a way of taking things out on those closest to them, and as Liam's friend, Allyn knew suffering the blows was his responsibility. He would let Liam vent so he could heal.

Allyn turned and knocked again. The door swung open immediately.

If Liam could have wielded fire, Allyn might have been worried. Liam's dark eyes were ablaze, irate. *"What?"* Liam snapped.

"I just want to help."

"I don't want your help," Liam said. "Please leave me alone. I'll find you when I have something."

"I don't have anything else to do."

"Then go enjoy it," Liam said. "Most people would call that a vacation."

"Most people don't have to spend their vacations in a four-bedroom cabin with twenty other people." Allyn leaned against the doorframe. "Or have to share a single bathroom with all of them."

Liam's mouth tightened. *Was that the beginnings of a smile?*

"It could be worse, I guess," Allyn said.

"How?"

"We could all be in prison cells."

Liam turned back into the room, the tiny smile retreating from his face. Though Allyn didn't have much to do, Liam's list of responsibilities was growing by the day. He wasn't used to it. If he and Jaxon weren't careful, they would bury Liam under the new weight, and the lively, sarcastic teenager that they'd all grown to love would be replaced by this tortured, angry substitute.

"Let me help."

"There's really nothing to do," Liam said, gesturing toward the computer. "Once I got it set up, it just kind of does its thing."

The two computers sat side by side on a makeshift workbench Liam had constructed under the window. Pieces of the broken computer were stacked neatly on the sill, and a cable connected the hard drive to Liam's computer. Allyn didn't see a status bar or any other sign that the transfer was in progress.

"How will you know when it's done if it doesn't have a status bar?"

"Files will stop appearing in the folder I created."

"It's that easy?"

"It's that easy."

"What about the stuff that's already in there? Can we look at that?"

Liam shrugged and looked away.

*You sly little punk.* "You already did, didn't you?"

Liam bit back a mischievous grin.

"Why didn't you say anything?"

"I just peeked around a little bit," Liam said, blushing. "And I didn't find much. The transfer doesn't go in order.

Instead of getting one folder and then the next, we get fragments of this one, and fragments of that one. It's like looking at a painting through a straw. Until the transfer is complete, we only get to see part of the picture."

"Can I see?"

"You're not going to leave me alone, are you?"

"Not now."

"Fine." Liam might still be annoyed, but the heat in his voice had disappeared. "But close the door behind you."

Allyn stepped inside and closed the door behind him. The sparsely decorated room was roughly the same size as the others, and since it had always been the spare one, it held none of the childhood belongings that furnished Allyn's and Kendyl's. Liam had closed the blinds, but cold air still blew into the room through the drafty window. Even the bulb above was bare. The fixture had fallen a long time ago and had never been replaced.

Liam sat at the workbench, watching as random files continued to pop up on his desktop. Allyn stood beside him.

"What do you want to see first?" Liam asked.

"The file with my name on it."

Liam opened it. He was right—some of the contents were missing. Allyn couldn't pinpoint *what* exactly, but he knew he had seen more files inside the folder at his condo.

"Can I see that?" Allyn gestured to the computer mouse.

Liam hesitated. It was like asking to borrow another man's tools; there was just something personal about it. "Sure."

Allyn took the mouse and cycled through a series of files: his birth certificate, birth announcement, an article about his state-winning basketball team, and a picture of his graduating class. Seeing his childhood displayed like a dissected frog in a junior high biology class was unnerving. He felt violated. Exposed.

"Someone has been following you for a long time."

"I'm not sure about that."

"Why?" Liam asked. "Your whole life's in there. Every notable achievement."

"I think they worked backward. Look at this." Allyn pulled up another folder with only a single article inside. "Something got their attention, and they built a profile as they went along. Most of this stuff is in the public record."

"Public record?"

"Yeah."

"As in anyone has access to it?"

"Most of it." Allyn sometimes forgot how little Liam knew of the outside world. He wasn't as naïve as he'd once been, and his knowledge grew by the day, but there were still gaps. Allyn reopened his folder and clicked on another file. It was a list of graduates who had passed the bar exam, part of a quarterly review the board put out.

"Even your birth certificate?"

"Probably not that."

"Who would?" Liam asked.

"As far as I know," Allyn said, "only government officials or immediate family."

"Well, I think we can rule out family," Liam said. "What about the FBI?"

"Definitely," Allyn said. "I know what you're thinking, but I don't think this was the FBI. They would have had that place surrounded. The moment we arrived, the moment we stepped out of that car, they would have taken us down."

Liam didn't look convinced, but he didn't push the issue.

"What do you think would happen if all of this stuff disappeared?"

"What do you mean?" Allyn asked.

"You know," Liam said. "If all of the stuff about someone in the public record vanished."

"Not much. The information would still exist as hard copies. Newspapers, official records, that sort of stuff."

"Yeah, but who actually references that sort of thing?"

"I don't know."

"I think it would be like the video. Remove the digital information and the rest will slowly disappear, too, or at least make finding it a lot more difficult. The world might even forget that you ever existed."

"That's kind of sad, though, don't you think?"

"I guess." Liam's eyes grew distant.

"What's going on in that head of yours?" Allyn asked.

"I'm not sure yet," Liam said thoughtfully. "I just got the kernel of an idea."

"You mind sharing?"

"Not yet."

Allyn glanced at Liam out of the corner of his eye. Liam wasn't usually so coy, not when it came to computers. Allyn closed the folder. He hadn't found anything he hadn't already seen, and the lack of privacy disturbed him. He opened another folder. This one was nearly empty, only two files inside, both newspaper articles.

"This is what I mean," Allyn said, opening the first article. "Something like this caught their eye, and then they built a history around the person in question."

"What is it?"

"It's a newspaper article about a fire at a construction site," Allyn said. "The authorities believed a disgruntled ex-employee was behind it."

"What's so interesting about that?"

"I'm not sure."

"There might be other files that haven't transferred yet," Liam said.

"It's possible," Allyn said. "But I remember some of the folders were pretty bare. It's almost as if they came across a strange story and bookmarked it so that they could look into it later."

"What do you think they're looking for?"

"I'm still trying to figure that out."

Allyn closed the article and the folder. The next one bore a name he couldn't pronounce, spelled with letters he'd never seen. *Russian maybe? Eastern European, at least.* He moved on to the next. Allyn would have laughed if he'd seen the headline in the supermarket checkout, but it was from a reputable magazine, and he'd recently been exposed to a world he'd never known existed before. The outlandish didn't seem as ridiculous anymore. *Mother of Two Has Music Playlist in Her Head.*

"Look at this." Allyn sat up, scanning the article.

"What is it?"

"It looks like a journal article about a woman who claims to hear radio broadcasts in her head." Allyn continued to read. "Look here." He pointed to the screen.

"Have you ever had the annoying experience of having a song stuck in your head for more than a day? More than two? Imagine being unable to ever get it out," Liam said, reading the article aloud. "Charlotte Vegen, a thirty-five-year-old mother of two suffers from such intense audio hallucinations that she fears she's losing her mind. Vegen has what her psychiatrist refers to as 'musical ear syndrome'—a neurological disorder that causes her to hear the same handful of songs repeat in her head in a constant loop. But although the mixture of childhood favorites sound as if they are real, they're actually being produced by her brain."

"This is what I find interesting," Allyn said, scrolling down to the next paragraph. "She developed the condition after taking anti-depressant medication."

"It looks like they have a medical diagnosis for it," Liam said. "Auditory hallucinations."

"That's just the official way of saying 'you're hearing things,'" Allyn said.

"What are you suggesting?"

"I don't know how it works with normal magi," Allyn said. "But for someone like me, whose ability was blocked, something has to force it out of them. When Kendyl died inside Lukas's compound, I *snapped*. I knew what I had to do, and I did it almost instinctively. What if whatever caused her to take the medication in the first place made her snap?"

"What are you suggesting?" Liam asked. "You think she's a magi? A machinist?"

Allyn grimaced. "Actually, no. She probably is suffering from some sort of illness. It says here that one in ten thousand people over the age of sixty-five suffer from auditory hallucinations, and that's obviously not in line with the number of magi in the world."

"I'm not following you, Allyn. You say she might be a magi, and then you say she's not."

"It's not about what I think. It's what the person who made these files thinks." Allyn opened another folder. "Another folder. Another mystery." He opened the next then the one after that. "Here's another. And another. And think about the stories in my folder. A manor burned to the ground hours after a host of officers stormed the house and found it largely unoccupied. Dozens of bodies with no positive IDs litter the grounds. The suspects vanished into thin air. It's more than mysterious. It's damn near paranormal. This person is searching for magi, Liam."

"Searching for magi." Liam said the words as if he were trying them on. "If that were true, why?"

"Because they're a magi, too."

Liam took in a sharp breath. "You think they're like you! Someone who developed abilities outside the Families."

Allyn nodded. "Except I didn't develop my ability *outside* the Families. I'd seen Jaxon and Graeme in action, and even though I had a hard time believing it at first, I knew wielding was possible. I knew what your father was telling me was the truth. Imagine, Liam, this person developing abilities alone. No answers, no guidance. Imagine how terrifying that would be. What would be the first thing you'd do?"

"Find others like me."

"Exactly," Allyn said. "Fortunately for them, the Internet is the great equalizer. Whatever the ailment, whatever you're suffering from, you can find someone else who's suffering from the same thing."

"Except this," Liam said.

"Except this." Allyn scrolled through the folders, up and down, up and down. It was a habit he'd developed while working behind the desk. He wasn't searching for anything; the movement on the screen just helped him think. "So they searched them out, finding other people who might be living with similar abilities in secret, but the magi are too well hidden, so all they stumbled across were fragments or rumors."

"Until they found you." Liam stood and started to pace behind Allyn. "Do you think they're local to our area?"

Allyn raised an eyebrow. "Maybe. Probably. How else would they get their computer into my old condo?"

"Good point," Liam said. "But I meant, do they live here, or did they come here specifically to find you?"

"Why?" Allyn asked. "What's the difference?"

"If they're here specifically to find you," Liam said, "they won't leave until they do."

The hair on Allyn's arms and neck stood on end, sending a chill down his spine. He'd spent so much time arguing that the person behind the video wasn't the police that he hadn't spent enough time thinking about who it really was. Even though the police and the FBI hadn't been waiting for them at the condo, someone else could have been. Jaxon had been worried about bringing the computer back to the cabin, afraid that someone could track it. *But what if someone simply followed us?*

"We need to tell Jaxon," Allyn said. "We could have led them straight to us."

"What if we try and contact them?" Liam asked, ignoring the subject.

"Contact them?"

"Yeah."

"How?"

"We can leave a comment on the video."

"We took the video down," Allyn said. "Remember?"

"Oh," Liam said. "That's right."

*How much stress is he under? He's doesn't remember something he did yesterday.*

"We can do a response video then," Liam said.

"I'm not sure that's a good idea. We could accidentally give them a clue and lead them here."

"Then we go to them," Liam said. "Safely."

Allyn shook his head. He didn't like that, either. "Is there a way to contact them through their YouTube page?"

"Probably." Liam returned to his seat and pulled the computer back toward him, bringing up the Internet browser. With the transfer in progress, the computer was sluggish. The hard drive spun loudly and vibrated against the windowsill. Liam tapped the side of the computer as he waited. The low-hanging sun broke through the overcast sky, and sunlight streaked into the room, reflecting off the dust floating in the air. Liam squinted, shielding his eyes, then stood and closed the curtains, returning the room to darkness.

By the time he sat back down, the page had finally loaded. Liam searched for the user and eventually found J.P. Niall on the fourth page between a video about a skiing squirrel and another about a disoriented kitten. It seemed the user hadn't attempted to re-upload the video, likely believing that Allyn had removed it after seeing it.

"What happens if we click on the box in the discussion tab?" Allyn asked.

Liam clicked on it, and the site redirected them to a Google accounts page. "Do you have a login?"

"Yeah," Allyn said.

Liam slid the computer over so Allyn could type in his information.

Allyn hesitated, his fingers over the keyboard. They could be kicking the hornet's nest or stepping into another trap. What happened if the person behind the video wanted to meet face to face?

"We really should talk to Jaxon before we do this," Allyn said.

Liam waved a dismissive hand. "We're not agreeing to anything. We don't even know if this is going to work. If they respond, then we can talk to Jaxon about it, but for now, we don't have anything to talk about."

Allyn sighed. It felt reckless. Jaxon was still the leader of their Family. *But for how long?* That distinction would soon be Liam's—a responsibility that Allyn was sure he would have to help Liam shoulder. *Why shouldn't I listen to him now?*

He tapped the keys nervously then punched in his information. He stood abruptly and began to pace behind Liam, rubbing his prickly jaw.

"What do you think we should say?" Liam asked.

"Something short and to the point."

Liam thought for a second, then typed, *You have my attention.* "What do you think?"

Allyn looked over Liam's shoulder and gave him a nod of approval. Before Allyn could blink, Liam clicked Post, and the comment appeared. He exhaled. It was done.

*No turning back now.*

# CHAPTER 12

C ANARY'S EYES WERE OPEN, BUT they held little life. She stared at the naked bulb hanging from the ceiling, blinking on occasion, seemingly unaware of the other two occupants in the room. Her pale skin glistened with sweat, and her hair was tangled in a knot so intricate that Jaxon thought they would sooner cut it off than attempt to brush through it.

Jaxon watched her with his arms crossed, his expression firm. At his side, Joyce teetered on edge, as if she were about to rush to Canary's side. *But how do you help someone when you don't know what they're suffering from?*

"He's never going to win reelection turning the ball over," Canary said.

Jaxon pursed his lips. She'd been babbling incoherently since he'd arrived. Her tone was flat and emotionless, as if she were simply repeating things she heard. And she never stopped.

"Twenty-seven degrees at Government Camp before the cowboy got a little drunk."

"She hasn't slept for more than fifteen minutes in a single stretch," Joyce said. "And even then... she never stops. Her body might be getting rest, but her mind is not."

Jaxon wasn't even sure if her body was resting. Canary's eyes were bloodshot, and her face had the gaunt look of someone fighting a losing battle with cancer.

"It's wearing on her," Joyce said. Her voice was soft, not as if she were afraid of waking Canary, but soft with the sound of exhaustion. "It's wearing on *us*."

Jaxon looked at the older woman as if for the first time. In her late thirties, she wasn't much older than Jaxon, but she might as well have been decades older. Beyond her frazzled hair and dark eyes, there was a deep weariness in her demeanor. Her shoulders were hunched, her head drooped, and her every move was done with sluggish execution.

"Does she have any moments of clarity?" Jaxon asked.

"Early on, she did. Not anymore. You're the only person who's come to see her, and I think that weighs on her, too. Canary was always a very social girl. Now the rest avoid her as if she has the pox."

Jaxon kept his expression steady. He wouldn't admit it to Joyce, but he'd played a part in Canary's isolation. He might not have ordered the others away, but he'd made his intentions clear—she was to be left alone.

"If she could get out of her room and get some fresh air, see some of her old friends, she might start on her road to recovery."

"No," Jaxon said.

"She's not contagious, Jaxon."

"I know. But we can't afford to have her bring the Family's morale down any further."

"Jaxon—"

"No."

"So you're going to isolate her from everyone she cares about?"

"It's best for the Family."

Joyce's eyes narrowed. He couldn't tell if it was from

anger or disbelief. It didn't matter—it had to be done. But he could, perhaps, give her a little more.

"The Family is in a fragile place, Joyce. And we need symbols of strength to lead us through these dark times."

"And Canary isn't that symbol."

"No."

"True Families grow stronger during the toughest times, Jaxon. They don't cast their own aside."

Jaxon didn't know what to say. On one hand, he understood. Adversity builds strength in character. People never knew what they were truly capable of until they were faced with a seemingly insurmountable problem. On the other, he wasn't sure if there *was* a McCollum Family any longer. When word spread that the Forum had fundamentally disbanded their Family, would they hold together, or would that be the ax that split them apart?

Before that ax came down, they needed something to rally around. Something to remind them who they were. Why they were stronger together. They couldn't do that while they were distracted.

"I don't know how much longer I can do this." The edge was gone from Joyce's tone, replaced again by exhaustion. She couldn't even muster up the energy to fight anymore.

"You don't have to," Jaxon said. "I'll send Vincent in. He'll keep her under."

"For how long?"

"Until it's safe to bring her back."

———— •••• ————

Jaxon wanted to hide. He wanted to slip out of the cabin and run deep into the forest, away from the knowing eyes, the whispers, and his own guilt. Instead, he watched as Mason led a small group of magi through their first training session. Mason had them formed up in ranks on the deck that extended out of the living room. Shirtless and exposed to the elements, they shivered but were still barely able to contain their excitement and focus on Mason's direction. That inability to concentrate was the reason Jaxon preferred to hold those sessions individually.

*Had preferred,* Jaxon corrected himself. As grand mage, the responsibility of training new magi fell to someone else. He missed it, though.

The emotion surprised him. Training was arduous and frustrating—for both the trainer and the trainee. Wielding was an intimate experience that required years of training and a deep understanding of oneself, which made it problematic to teach. But if they succeeded, the young magi discovered parts of themselves that they never knew existed, and *that* was a powerful experience.

Jaxon turned back inside. His presence unnerved some of the young magi.

*True Families grow stronger during the toughest times.*

Joyce's backhanded swipe at his leadership hurt. Jaxon had often questioned Graeme's authority, jumping upon his mistakes as if they were an opportunity. He'd never done it publicly of course, but he'd voiced his discontent to Graeme himself. Or Leira. Sometimes Mason. Other times, Trevin. He'd done it more times than he remembered. And now Joyce was doing it to him.

*This is my punishment.* He was like the rebellious child who had grown up to become the exasperated parent, a victim of his own circumstance. Somewhere, Graeme was laughing.

*They don't cast their own aside.*

*How did Graeme do it?* He had made large-scale mistakes and suffered the consequences—often publically—in stride, while handling rumblings of discontent in the Family.

*He didn't run from it.* He'd faced it and either waited for the decision to work itself out or adjusted. When Lukas splintered the McCollum Family, Graeme remained firm, refusing to bend to Lukas's will if that meant violating his own beliefs.

But when confronted with Liam's new-age abilities, Graeme had accepted them, even though it had meant turning his back on the anti-technology philosophy he'd enforced for years. Graeme had been firm yet flexible, always gathering information and, when necessary, making adjustments.

Jaxon's father led with a different kind philosophy. Wesley Green was an unflinching leader. The words *bending* and *adjusting* weren't in his vocabulary. He made a decision, and he stuck to it. And he didn't tolerate derision. If the members of the Green Family believed he was making a mistake, they knew better than to voice it. Jaxon never would have gotten away with openly criticizing his father in the same way he'd been able to with Graeme.

Still, his father had sent him to study under Graeme. Was that because he had learned as he had grown older that being staunch and unwavering was sometimes counterproductive? Or was it so Jaxon could see other forms of leadership and make his own decisions?

Canary could be harmful to their movement. Jaxon would hold firm to that belief, but he also recognized that his actions could be equally harmful. When followers lost trust in their leader, it threatened the stability of the entire movement. How long would it be before Canary's friends began asking questions in earnest? Could he expect Joyce and Vincent to keep the secret? If the truth ever came out, he was finished.

The question was: did he embrace the firm yet flexible style of leadership and adapt as Graeme would have, or did he lead with a strong fist and clamp down on divisive whispers as his father would?

*Vincent already forced her under. It's done.*

Perhaps he'd already adopted his father's authoritarian leadership. Canary was a danger to the McCollum Family— Jaxon *knew* that, and he refused to bend on that point. But was there a way to adapt, to negate the potential danger he'd created by doing it in secret? A way that didn't threaten to splinter the Family further?

The truth was, Jaxon cared for those he led. He wasn't just a leader; he was a friend, confidant, mentor, and member, just as the other members of the Family were. He *wanted* their approval, and he would listen to their concerns. However, that didn't mean he was going to take a vote and decide what to do based on the Family's will—he was still responsible for setting the Family on the right path. It was a narrow path to traverse, and he would fail at times, but it was the necessary one.

Vincent had forced Canary under, but she wouldn't stay unconscious forever. He contemplated allowing her to wake up so he could explain her condition to Liam and Leira. Joyce might be unwilling to care for her anymore, but surely someone else would—and they might have a better idea of how to treat her. He didn't have to act unilaterally; he could slowly expand his circle of confidants and gauge the Family's opinion. He had options.

Jaxon was crossing through the living room, making for the front of the cabin, when he spotted something through the kitchen window.

*Is that—?*

The sentries positioned at the front of the cabin shouted with alarm.

Jaxon crossed the cabin in a blink, dashing past puzzled onlookers. Without his order, magi formed up behind him, and by the time he flung open the door, Ren, Rory, and Mason were on his heels.

A group of at least a dozen men, women, and children straggled up the driveway, huddled together in a defensive formation. Their soaked clothing was frozen, and they each wore the same grim expression. The frightened children wailed, clinging to their parents, urging them backward.

Jaxon heard the distinct sound of a match igniting, and

he felt the warmth of a fireball on his back. He heard the sound several more times, and Jaxon turned to see that each magi behind him was wielding, ready to strike at his order.

The disheveled group stopped abruptly, seemingly unsurprised to see men and women holding fire. They watched silently, only the children's wails interrupting the standoff.

"What are you doing here?" Jaxon asked.

The leader, a man of average height and build with thinning dark hair and deep-set eyes, cocked his head to the side, looking confused. He pushed the boy at his leg behind him. "We're accepting your invitation."

*Our invitation?*

Jaxon had sent out a blanket appeal to the local Families, stating the parameters that he had discussed with Allyn. The McCollum Family had appealed to the dregs of the other Families—the young, the weak, and those unable to wield, offering a fresh start, free from prior reputations and prejudices. Like all sales propositions, its pitch was vague and idealistic, and he hadn't thought any Families would take him up on the offer, especially so soon. It had only been little more than a day since he'd sent out the message.

The cabin door crashed open, slamming into the side of the cabin. Allyn rushed out, jumped down the steps, and raced toward Jaxon. "Wait!" he yelled. "Stop!" Allyn positioned himself between the group and Jaxon's squad, almost as if he were protecting the disheveled crowd.

"They're from the Hyland Family," Mason said, light from his fireball dancing in his eyes.

"I know."

"They tried to kill us!"

"No," Allyn said, glancing at the group. "Not them. They're refugees."

Jaxon studied the group with renewed interest. Many wore bulky, overstuffed packs, and their half-closed zippers exposed the belongings inside. Others carried jugs of water or umbrellas. Dust, dirt, and mud stained shirts and pants and covered shoes. They certainly looked like refugees. The Hyland Estate was seven or eight hours by car. *How long is that by foot?* Could they have made it in the time since he'd sent out the message?

"Stand down," Jaxon said.

The refugees relaxed.

"They're from the Hyland Family," Mason repeated. "The *Hyland Family.*"

"They weren't involved in the ambush," Allyn said. "Or the attack at the manor."

"How do you know?" Mason asked, incredulous.

"Because half of them are children!"

Mason sneered at Allyn, hostility burning as hot as the fireball that raged in his hands.

"I said to stand down, Mason," Jaxon said firmly.

Mason met his gaze and waited for a split-second longer than Jaxon would have liked before letting the fireball dissipate. Mason hadn't been involved in the ambush at the Hyland Estate when Darian Hyland had tried to abduct Allyn, but he had been an essential member of the strike force that had fought to reclaim the manor. In fact, his squad had suffered the most casualties. So Jaxon understood his apprehension, but those were different men in a different time, and it was no excuse to disobey orders.

"Get them some food and dry clothes, Allyn," Jaxon said, nodding to the leader of the refugees.

Nobody moved.

"It's okay," Allyn said, his voice compassionate. "Nobody will harm you. Come on." He walked past Jaxon's squad, beckoning the refugees to follow him into the cabin.

They lingered for a moment then followed, giving Mason and his open hostility a wide berth.

"Head inside and help how you can," Jaxon ordered his squad. They obeyed. "Mason." The man stopped and turned to face Jaxon, who closed the distance between them. He leaned in, keeping his voice quiet and firm. "If you have something to say, say it now."

Mason set his jaw and remained silent.

"Out with it."

"We can't trust them," Mason said. "We have nowhere to house them, and our food stocks are already depleted. Even if they are as harmless as you believe, they're looking for help that we can't provide. We can't even help ourselves."

"You're not wrong," Jaxon said. "But housing and food are temporary problems. What's more important is that the McCollum Family just nearly doubled in size."

"With magi we can't trust."

"Trust has to begin somewhere," Jaxon said. "These people ventured all the way from the Hyland Estate to find us. And as Allyn said, they weren't involved in either conflict."

Mason sniffed, shaking his head. "Why do you trust him, Jaxon?"

"Allyn?"

"He isn't one of us. Neither is his sister. I don't care what kind of abilities they have, they didn't grow up as one of us. They don't understand what it means to be a magi."

"They understand more than you think."

"Jaxon—"

"No," Jaxon said. "We're not going to single out members of this Family. Allyn and Kendyl gave up everything to be here. They are part of this Family. And in the future, if you wish to question my leadership or question my orders, you will do so privately. Do you understand?"

Mason clenched his jaw. "Yes."

"Good," Jaxon said. *Firm.* "Understand that I am open to discussing the intent of my orders, but I will not be questioned in front of the Family."

"Understood."

"Now," Jaxon said, allowing his tone to soften. *But flexible.*

"I have a task for you. I trust Allyn's judgment, but in the event he's wrong, I want you to select two or three magi and keep an eye on the Hyland refugees. If this is another of Darian's ploys, I want to be prepared."

---

The leader of the Hyland refugees was a magi by the name of Brandt Hyland. He was older than Allyn, perhaps in his late forties, with gray streaks at his temples and the beginnings of a beard. He scratched at it, likely unused to it, annoyed by the itchiness. Once inside, Allyn had worked quickly to get them dry clothes and something warm to drink, and already, Brandt looked like a new man—the color was returning to his face, and his hollow, deep-set eyes were more alert.

"Thank you," Brandt said, taking a fresh cup of tea from Liam. Steam rose from the rim of the cup, but it didn't stop Brandt from taking a sip. He licked his lips, grabbed two squares of sugar off the silver platter on the coffee table, and dropped them into the tea. "Thank you for taking us in. I don't know what we would have done if you hadn't."

Allyn gave Brandt a sympathetic smile. Brandt's wife, Juniette, sat beside him and gave Allyn a sharp smile of her own. Shorter than her husband by half a head, she had fair skin and long auburn hair. She had thin pink lips, high cheekbones, and perfect posture—the latter likely an old-world formality. They looked like a couple who had fallen hard in recent times. The remaining refugees were showering, changing into fresh clothes, or lying down in one of the bedrooms.

Liam sat down next to Allyn. The fire crackled behind Brandt, shooting embers up the brick fireplace. Its warmth was the only heat source in the cabin, and Brandt couldn't seem to get close enough.

"You said you came all the way from the Hyland Estate?" Allyn asked.

Brandt took a sip of his tea and nodded. "Yes. We left just after we received Jaxon's offer."

"That was yesterday," Allyn said.

"We..." Brandt paused to look at his wife. "We had been looking for a way out. It's a dangerous time to live among the Hyland Family. We didn't know where to turn until..."

"Until Jaxon's offer."

Brandt nodded.

"So you walked?"

"And hitched," Brandt said, the hollow look returning to his face. "Strangers can be compassionate when children are involved." He looked over his shoulder to where a sandy-blond-haired kid sat at the table, drinking hot cocoa. His resemblance to his parents was unmistakable. "We had to get him away. Darian has become fixated on you, Allyn. It isn't about Lukas's movement any longer. It's about exacting personal revenge. You humiliated him, and he's driven by a singular sociopathic desire—killing you."

Allyn shifted in his seat. "Then Darian survived." He'd been a distant threat, something in the back of Allyn's mind while they dealt with the other issues. But this was confirmation. "How many still follow him?"

"Not many," Brandt said. "Most died with Lukas. But those that do remain are the cruelest leftovers of Lukas's movement, and their defeat has only soured their mood further. It became dangerous to remain at the Estate. There were... accidents." Brandt patted his wife's leg. Her face had grown haunted. "Darian allows his vile members to do as they wish. We were set to run when I overheard Darian mentioning Jaxon's offer to another of his followers. It was what we needed—we had a place to go. And that's when we left."

"He knows where we are?" Liam asked, suddenly alarmed.

"I..." Brandt looked troubled. "I suppose."

Allyn and Liam exchanged a look. Darian knew where

they were, and he thirsted for Allyn's blood. How long would it be before he made a move?

Allyn spotted Jaxon leaning against the wall beside the newly constructed bunks, a silent observer to their conversation. He showed so little expression that Allyn wasn't sure if he'd heard the last bit. He would have to talk to him about increasing the number of sentries.

"Did you ever hear anything about a video?" Liam asked.

"A video?" Brandt scratched his beard. "What kind of video?"

"Something taken from the assault at the manor."

Brandt looked to Juniette, who shook her head.

"No," Brandt said. "I'm sorry. Why?"

"Are you sure?" Liam asked. "Anything at all?"

"Nothing."

Liam nodded grimly. They were still as much in the dark as they had ever been.

"Is it true that you can help non-wielding magi learn to wield?" Juniette asked.

"Hmm?"

"In Jaxon's offer," Juniette said, "he mentioned helping those who can't wield to learn. Is that true?"

"Uh..." Allyn said. He didn't know what to say. He wasn't sure how much Jaxon had said in his invitation. *Best to keep it vague then.* "We have some ideas."

"Oh." Juniette's posture slumped slightly.

Allyn gave Brandt a questioning look.

"It's our son," Brandt said. "He can't..."

"We just want him to be normal," Juniette said.

"There are others, too," Brandt said.

"How many?"

"Half of us."

"We'll help you," Liam said.

"But I thought..." Brandt said hesitantly, obviously afraid of offending Liam. "I thought, you couldn't..."

"Couldn't wield?" Liam asked with a grin. "We'll get to that."

This seemed to confuse Brandt and his wife even more.

*Hope drove them here,* Allyn thought, *and we're taking it away.*

"Like I said," Allyn said. "We have some ideas. We can't guarantee anything, but"—he turned to look at Liam, hoping Brandt and Juniette would follow—"we do have something of a track record."

Still confused, Brandt and Juniette seemed to sit a little straighter.

"If there's anything you can do," Brandt said, "we would appreciate it."

"We'll do everything we can," Liam said. "Welcome to the McCollum Family."

# CHAPTER 13

MADDOX FELT AS IF HIS eyes had been bathed in battery acid. The LCD computer monitor six inches in front of his face didn't help, nor did the pair of glasses sitting beside the keyboard. He'd taken those off an hour ago because the earpieces were too tight against the sides of his head, and it gave him a headache. Instead, he'd thought it better to move closer to the screen and squint. That had been a bad idea.

Maddox blinked, and his eyelids felt like sandpaper scraping across his corneas. He sat back with a frustrated sigh. He had reviewed the traffic videos supplied by the Oregon Department of Transportation. He didn't distrust Nolan; he just didn't trust him as much as he trusted himself. Part of him wanted to find an oversight, something he could use to place the blame of their fruitless investigation at the feet of the new agent, but Nolan had been right. There were too many cars over too large an area and not enough functioning cameras. If Nolan had missed something, Maddox hadn't found it.

Nolan was reviewing the details of the investigation from the night the manor burned. He and Maddox hadn't been involved then, and he wanted to be sure the investigators hadn't overlooked anything, but so far, he hadn't come up with anything new. There was only one thing to do when investigations reached this point.

Standing, Maddox grabbed his black suit jacket and stepped around his desk toward Nolan, who was hunched over his keyboard, chin resting in his hand, staring at a blinking cursor. He was on some kind of social media website. When he saw Maddox approaching, he sat up and quickly minimized the screen.

A flicker of frustration shot through Maddox. Young agents were easily distracted. A generation of kids who all thought they suffered from attention disorders. *As if there is such a thing.* Focus, discipline, and attention to detail had never been skills people came by naturally. Like all things, they had to be learned and practiced before perfected. But this lazy and undisciplined generation wasn't willing to put in the work. Their absent parents hadn't forced them. And anytime someone smacked them in the back of the head and told them to get to work, they played the victim card.

Maddox shuddered at the thought of what his father would have done to him if he'd tried that. He probably would have laughed before he proceeded to whip Maddox's ass. His father hadn't been a nice man. He hadn't been a friend; he'd been a parent—just like his father before him. And that was something far more difficult and profoundly more important. To this day, there wasn't another man in the world who terrified Maddox more than his own father, and every day, Maddox thanked him for it. His father had made him strong. Made him dependable. Made him a man.

"Calling it a night?" Nolan asked, glancing at the jacket slung over Maddox's arm. He looked much like Maddox felt. His eyes were red and swollen. His baby face was peppered with the patchy beginnings of a beard, and his starched white shirt was unbuttoned at the neck, his tie loosened.

"No," Maddox said, checking is wristwatch. "It's only nine thirty. Grab your jacket and come with me."

Nolan lingered for a moment, as if he didn't believe Maddox would keep him working later into the night. Then when Maddox leveled his expecting expression on Nolan, the younger agent stood and grabbed his jacket. "Where to?"

"You'll see."

Maddox pulled his arm through his jacket sleeve and buttoned the top button, making sure his black tie was tucked neatly inside as he and Nolan exited the field office. The wind whipped through downtown, howling through four-lane streets and alleyways alike. It was always windy in the city, perhaps a byproduct of following the river, though Maddox supposed an east wind could have been blowing in from the Gorge.

Mist hung heavy in the air. Rainwater dripped from rooflines and street signs and splashed from cars passing through puddles and over TriMet tracks. Shoppers and businessmen on the sidewalks shielded themselves or ducked their heads in an attempt to hide from the rain, but very few carried umbrellas. Rainy weather was a way of life in the Northwest. It was always wet, but it was also always green. Residents had to take the good with the bad. Beauty took work, just as success took tenacity.

Nolan pulled his jacket tight, letting his tie flap in the wind behind him. Maddox led him a few blocks to the north, into a nondescript building with a sign that the owner had forgotten to illuminate.

"What are we doing?" Nolan asked as they entered.

"Taking a break," Maddox said. "And grabbing a drink."

"I thought drinking on duty was against regulation."

"It is." Maddox left the confused agent behind and walked toward a vacant table near the back of the narrow building. He passed patrons sitting quietly at the bar, watching a muted TV that was bolted to the wall between shelves stocked with alcohol. The picture was fuzzy and overly saturated. This wasn't the type of place people went to watch the game and socialize. It was a place for a quiet drink and collecting one's thoughts.

Maddox sat down with his back to the wall, making sure he had a clear view of the entrance. The cracked-leather booth creaked under his weight. Nolan unbuttoned his jacket and sat across from Maddox.

"Fortunately for us," Maddox continued, "we're on break."

"Aren't you the one who told me that a good agent acts as though they're always on duty?"

"Does everyone under twenty-five have to be a smartass?" Maddox asked. "Can't a grown man buy his partner a drink without being called a hypocrite?"

"I'm twenty-six," Nolan said. "But you're right. I'm sorry. It feels good to get away."

The bartender was a man in his middle years, with stringy black hair that hung down to his shoulders. He approached, carrying a menu. Pock marks and deep wrinkles covered his weathered face, likely a sign of years of smoking and repeated drug use. "Happy hour is from nine 'til close." He dropped the menu on the table. "You guys know what you want to drink?"

"I'll take a Bud," Maddox said.

"Same here," Nolan added.

"Two Buds," the bartender said before returning to the bar.

"Why this place?" Nolan asked. "Why not the Gathering Place? That's where the other agents go."

"Nobody bothers me here."

"You're an interesting man, Agent Maddox." Amusement sparkled in Nolan's eyes. "You go to a public place to be alone."

Maddox shrugged.

"A guarded man, too, I've noticed," Nolan added. "You don't like it when people make observations about you."

"My father taught me never to call attention to myself."

"He must have been a hard man."

"He was."

"Military?"

"Career," Maddox said. "Like his father before him."

Nolan smiled.

"What?" Maddox asked, growing defensive.

"It's just all beginning to make sense now. That's all."

The bartender returned with their drinks. Maddox nodded his appreciation and took a sip. The beer had a skunky taste, as if the keg had gotten too warm or the tap needed cleaned. Maddox loved it. It was the kind of flavor that only a true dive bar could provide.

Nolan frowned, holding the beer up to the dim light fixture hanging over the table. He didn't appear to appreciate the flavor the same way Maddox did. He took another tentative sip.

"Why not you then?" Nolan asked, biting back a grimace from the spoiled beer. "Why not follow in your family's footsteps? I assume it was some kind of tradition."

Maddox took another drink, stalling. *He's waiting for me to dodge the question.* He had a reputation for being callous and aloof, bordering on unapproachable. Sure, his superiors and the other agents respected him—that came with success—but that didn't stop the whispers or the nicknames. They might respect him, but they didn't like him. They didn't understand him.

But Nolan wasn't just another agent. He was the longest tenured partner Maddox had had in years. So he deserved answers. The realization struck Maddox like a fatherly slap to the back of his head. When had he started thinking of Nolan as his partner and not just another fresh Quantico graduate who would wilt under his pressure?

"I grew up without a home," Maddox said simply. "I lived on a lot of bases, in a lot of houses, but never in a *home*."

Maddox rubbed the condensation off the side of his glass with his thumb. "Every time we moved, I had to say goodbye to my school and my friends. At first, it was fun. I got to see the country and meet a lot of new people. But by the time I was in middle school, I stopped trying. Why build new friendships when I knew I'd have to say goodbye? I promised myself then that I would never put my family through that. My children would have friends. They would have a home. So I decided that my father's life wasn't for me."

"I didn't know you had kids."

"I don't."

"But you're married?"

"Divorced," Maddox said. He held up two fingers. "Twice."

"What happened?"

"It didn't work out."

"Obviously," Nolan said. "It must be frustrating to forsake the family tradition in the name of a family you never had."

"I've never thought about it like that."

Nolan gave him a skeptical look but didn't press the issue. "How'd your father take the news?"

"He never forgave me," Maddox said. He took another drink to quell the building emotion in his chest. His father's anger had never subsided, not even during his final days.

"That's unfortunate."

Maddox shrugged. "That's the way of it. There's nothing I can do about it."

"You might say that, but I know you don't believe it. I can hear the pain in your voice."

Maddox snorted. "Pain? I don't know about that."

"It's okay," Nolan said. "I know you're a guarded man, Maddox, and I don't mean to pry, but it's okay to be regretful. You still are, I think, a human being."

The conversation was quickly turning into one Maddox didn't want to have. Talking about the past, even his father, was okay. But talking about *feelings?* Men just didn't do that.

Fortunately, before Maddox had to answer, the door opened, and two boisterous men stepped into the bar. They were laughing and yelling obscenities at someone outside. Once they turned their attention inside, they froze. The few patrons sitting at the bar irritably eyed the two men who had invaded their peace and quiet. The bartender watched from behind the bar, scrubbing the inside of a pilsner glass with a dirty rag.

The two—more boys than men—gave each other a disapproving laugh. Neither could have been a year or two over twenty-one. Both wore oversized button-down shirts tucked loosely into a pair of baggy jeans, unbuttoned to show their bare chests. Large diamond earrings, matching necklaces, and gold wristwatches filled out their attire.

"Bro," the first man said with a thick, wannabe-urban accent, "I thought this was gonna be a titty bar. Let's bounce."

"Nah, bro," the other said, talking out of the side of his mouth. "It's legit." He made for a booth near the entrance, walking with his legs wide, one hand holding the front of his pants so that they didn't fall down around his ankles.

"Really, dawg? There ain't even no bitches here."

The second man sat down, his back to Maddox. A series of designs had been shaved into his dark cropped hair near the neckline. The first man, who could have been his brother, groaned and cursed under his breath before reluctantly sitting down. The bartender shuffled to their table, hesitant, obviously not wanting to help his new patrons.

Maddox ground his teeth. He came to bars like this specifically to avoid people like them. Young, dumb, and with a supposed chip on their shoulder, these kinds of kids were dangerous, if only because of their sheer stupidity. Their *hardness* was likely an act, but their boisterous attitudes were bound to rub somebody the wrong way.

Nolan looked uncomfortable. It was hard to believe that the two kids were only a few years younger than he was. *I*

145

*don't give him enough credit*, Maddox thought. Compared to others of his generation, Nolan was an adult among children.

"You ready?" Maddox asked.

Nolan nodded, taking a final drink of his beer with another amusing grimace.

Maddox downed his and pulled out his wallet. After throwing a twenty onto the table, he stood and buttoned his jacket. The bartender had returned with the new patrons' drinks. He glanced at Maddox and rolled his eyes. He wouldn't be happy about losing business to the obtrusive customers. Maddox nodded at him, his silent way of saying, "I understand, but I'll be back." He and Nolan made for the front of the bar, passing the booth where the young men sat.

"Yo, this beer tastes like shit, homie."

Maddox stopped at the door, turning to watch the situation play out.

"What are you doing?" Nolan asked quietly.

Maddox ignored him.

"It's a fresh keg," the bartender said from behind the bar.

"I ain't drinking this piss."

"Would you like a bottle instead?"

"I want my damn money back."

"You haven't paid for anything yet."

The man's lips turned into a crooked smile. "Damn right. Come on, Travis. We're bailing."

"Really, Anthony?" Travis said. "Sit down, homie."

"I'm bouncing."

Anthony stood and strode for the door. Travis shook his head but followed. The two men approached Maddox, confident, probably expecting him to move out of their way. Maddox caught the bartender's eye.

"Let them go," the bartender said.

"They didn't pay," Maddox said.

"It's fine."

The more boisterous of the two, Anthony, strode up to

Maddox, stopping when their faces were only inches apart. He smelled like a mixture of alcohol and smoke, masked by too much cologne. Nearly as tall as Maddox but not nearly as filled out, he wore an exaggerated scowl that was likely meant to intimidate.

"You heard him, old man." He talked out of the corner of his mouth.

"You didn't pay."

Anthony sneered, wiping the edge of his nose with his thumb. "What are you gonna do, old man?"

"Let 'em go," the bartender said again.

Anthony's hand went to his waistband.

"Maddox," Nolan said. He'd positioned himself between Maddox and the second man.

Maddox glanced at Nolan. The younger agent stood in a defensive posture, hesitant but firm. He'd unbuttoned his suit jacket in case he needed to go for his weapon.

Maddox turned to the man in front of him. "You think the thug act intimidates me?" Maddox asked quietly. "I'm not afraid of your costume jewelry or that small piece you inevitably have tucked inside your pants."

"You wanna go—"

Maddox drove his forehead into the man's face. Anthony's nose crunched, and he stumbled backward, hands to his face, blood spewing between his fingers. Grabbing him by his shirt, Maddox threw him through the doorway onto the sidewalk. Someone screamed, and the bartender shouted for them to take the fight outside. Maddox stepped outside, appeasing the bartender.

Anthony was already climbing to his feet, reaching for the gun in his waistband. Maddox could see the black pistol grip against its chrome casing. The streetlights reflected off it, and the cool air fogged the chamber. In a single fluid motion, Maddox brushed aside his jacket, reaching for the gun tucked in the holster under his armpit. He flicked off the safety, pulling the gun out of the holster just in time to see the nine-millimeter Glock begin sliding out of the thug's pants.

"Freeze!" Nolan stood in the doorway, his gun pointed at Anthony. Any trace of his previous hesitation had disappeared. His months of training had finally kicked in.

Anthony pulled his hand away from the gun's grip and held both hands in front of him. His sneer had been replaced by a look of irritation. Pedestrians watched from both sides of the street, some going so far as to take pictures or capture the situation on video.

Maddox returned his gun to the holster, snapping the safety back on, and reached for the pair of handcuffs he had hidden inside the other half of his jacket. The police would arrive any moment—downtown was teeming with them.

"Get on the ground," Nolan commanded. "Hands behind your head!"

Anthony dropped to his knees, hands still held out in front of him.

Before Maddox could move forward, Nolan was tackled from behind. His gun dropped to the pavement and bounced against the sidewalk, out of reach. It took Maddox a second to comprehend what had happened. Travis had blindsided Nolan, and the two were now rolling across the sidewalk, in the middle of a grappling match.

Cursing, Maddox watched as Anthony's hand went back to his waistband. He hadn't had time to rid the young assailant of his weapon. In a blink, the weapon would be out, and the kid just might be stupid enough to use it.

Maddox didn't have enough time to go for his own gun. He charged.

Before the gun was completely out of the young man's pants, Maddox was on him, driving his knee into the man's face. Anthony fell backward, and Maddox stumbled into the street. A pair of headlights barreled toward him then dipped as the driver slammed on the brakes. The car screeched to a stop inches from Maddox, blue smoke billowing from the tires.

Maddox turned back to the fight. Nolan and Travis continued to roll back and forth, throwing wild blows. Nolan's suit was torn and ripped, dirt covered his back, and blood stained his starched shirt. He fought a trained fight, controlled and precise, and would eventually subdue the assailant, unless Travis landed a lucky strike.

Anthony rose to his feet. His nose was already swollen, and dark bruises were forming around his eyes. His gaze darted across the sidewalk, looking for something. The bulge from the gun was gone—the gun must have fallen out when Maddox tackled him.

Anthony raced forward. Maddox saw the gun lying with the butt of the grip pointed toward the sky, resting between the curb and a parked car. Choosing to go for it instead of his own weapon, Maddox got there a moment after Anthony did. He lunged, intending to tackle the man, but Anthony ducked at the last second. Maddox grazed his shoulders and landed on the concrete with a slap. Pain shot up his shoulder, and his right arm went numb.

Anthony was on his knees, turning to face him, gun in hand. *He really is stupid enough to use it.* Horrified, Maddox rolled onto his back. Anthony approached, holding the gun sideways. The sneer had disappeared from his face.

"Put it down," Maddox said.

Anthony adjusted his grip. Sirens rang in the distance, but they wouldn't make it in time.

"Don't do something you'll regret over a two-dollar beer."

"It's not about money, old man." Anthony's finger tightened around the trigger. "It's about respect."

Shots split the night.

Maddox flinched, squeezing his eyes shut. The muzzle flash was brighter than usual, illuminating the insides of his eyelids. Half a beat later, Maddox heard a *smack* and the sound of metal falling on stone. He opened his eyes.

Anthony was down. He lay on his back, the gun inches from his hand. Nolan was on his side, gun pointed at where Anthony had been. Travis was unconscious at his feet.

Maddox scrambled and rose. Rushing toward Anthony, he kicked the gun out of his reach and wrenched his arms behind his back to cuff him. The kid didn't give any resistance. Maddox rolled him onto his back and checked the wound.

"Where'd you hit him?" Maddox asked.

Nolan secured his firearm inside his holster. "Torso." His voice was shaky. He produced a second pair of cuffs and turned to secure the second assailant.

Maddox ran his hands across Anthony's chest and stomach then over his back. Other than a bloodied face and a few cuts and scrapes, the kid was unharmed.

"You sure?"

"He went down, didn't he?"

He had, but it hadn't been from a bullet wound. *He must have stumbled and hit his head on the pavement.* They would have to monitor him for a concussion. Most importantly, they were both safe, and the assailants, secure.

Maddox exhaled, laughing wearily. The sirens drew closer. He could see the flashing blue lights of approaching squad cars several blocks away.

"What's wrong with you?" Nolan leaned against the bar, exhausted. "You told the kid not to do anything stupid, but what do you call that? You almost got us killed over a beer."

"They didn't pay."

"You came here looking for a fight."

"You need to cool it."

"You did, didn't you?"

Maddox shook his head. "I don't have to listen to this."

"You can't take your frustration out on the world around

you," Nolan continued. "It's your responsibility to uphold the law, not enforce it. The bartender was happy to let them go."

"But it isn't *right*." Maddox pierced the air with an outstretched finger for effect. "The law isn't something that can be followed sometimes and not followed others. The law is the law *because* it's the law. It needs to be upheld all the time. Otherwise, it ceases to have meaning. And they broke it."

Nolan sighed. "Why did I have to get partnered up with Team America?"

"I won't stop you from putting in a transfer request."

"Are you that eager to be rid of me?" Nolan asked.

Maddox hesitated, sensing hurt in Nolan's eyes.

Nolan took his silence as confirmation and turned away.

Maddox groaned. He hated what he was about to say. Not because it wasn't true, but because he shouldn't have to say it. "No," he began. "I... *like* working with you. I won't stop you from putting in for a transfer, but I hope you don't. You're my partner—the first one I've had in a very long time."

Nolan eyed him for a moment and nodded, an understanding growing between them.

Maddox's pinched his forehead. Opening up was the most painful thing he'd had to do all night. He just wished Nolan had understood how difficult it truly was.

# CHAPTER 14

S NOW FELL STEADILY AROUND ALLYN and Kendyl. Already more than a foot deep, it had been walked on and trudged through so much over the last hour that it was packed hard, making it slick and dangerous. They were amid a small forest clearing, where they could move around, circled by pine trees heavy with ice and snow. Every so often, one of the thick branches snapped under the accumulating weight, dumping a fresh load of snow onto the layer that already covered the forest floor.

The training session had gone about as well as Allyn had expected. Inexperienced, he didn't have an overarching lesson plan, and without Jaxon's or Liam's deep understanding of magi tradition, he hadn't known where to begin. It made the session clunky and frustrating. Fortunately, Kendyl's positive attitude was contagious, and her encouragement gave him hope.

"You did good," Allyn said. He rested against a rough pine, taking shelter under its thick limbs. "Better than I did during my first lesson." He'd copied Jaxon's first lesson, giving Kendyl a puzzle to solve in a less-than-ideal setting. He'd even gone so far as to find an old tangled necklace and had her work the knot out of it. It was a mental exercise meant to help magi separate their mind from their body. Pain, as Allyn had learned firsthand, could block an undisciplined magi from wielding, and one needed to be able to separate oneself from pain and discomfort to avoid being rendered inept. It could mean the difference between life and death, and it was an ability that Allyn himself hadn't yet mastered. Another reason he didn't feel qualified to train Kendyl.

"Thank you." She breathed warm breath into her hands. Her slender fingers trembled and were a deep red; their tips, white. He'd meant it when he'd said she'd done better than he had. What had taken him hours had taken her less than one, and she was working under worse conditions.

*The knot wasn't as intricate,* Allyn told himself then had to stifle a laugh. Measuring his proficiency through competition was an old habit, and for some reason, it had always extended further with Kendyl. He didn't know if it was a sibling thing or a twins thing, but he'd always found himself competing with her over even the smallest of things.

"Do you understand why I had you do that?"

"It's like you said," Kendyl said, "if you're overcome with pain or anxiety, you can't wield. You have to separate yourself from it. You can't let it cloud your ability."

"Exactly." Allyn copied Kendyl's gesture, blowing warm air into his own hands. Like Kendyl, he was wearing only a thin layer of clothing. He didn't feel right exposing her to the elements if he didn't share in her discomfort. He thought back to that day when Jaxon had taken him into the forest that surrounded the manor. Jaxon had worn a sleeveless shirt, letting the rain cascade down his face, paying it no attention, while Allyn shivered and struggled to keep his teeth from chattering. He'd done better as the teacher, showing a modicum of control, but he had a long way to go before he was at Jaxon's level. He couldn't even keep his nose from dripping.

"How do you think you did?" he asked.

"It was hard at first, and after a while, my fingers were so numb that I didn't think I was going to be able to finish, but it eventually got easier. I don't know when. But it did."

"That's good. Do you know what changed? Why it got easier?"

Kendyl shook her head. "No."

"It might be different for every magi, but I find it easier to accept the discomfort than to ignore it."

"Accept it?" Kendyl furrowed her eyebrows in confusion.

"Yeah," Allyn said. "Have you ever been in the middle of something—painting or sculpting or anything—and gotten hungry or thirsty or had to pee, but you didn't want to stop?"

Kendyl laughed. "Of course."

"What did you do?"

"I finished what I was working on."

"How?"

"I don't know. I just pushed it to the back of my mind, I guess."

"You ignored it."

"Yeah."

"I don't work like that," Allyn said. "I can't just ignore it. If I was at the office and I was hungry or something, I'd just tell myself that I'd eat when I finished what I was working on. I'd recognize the hunger, accept it, and move on."

"It doesn't sound like it's that different."

"No," Allyn said. "The only difference is how we think about it. So figure out what your process is and apply it to this, and I bet it will get easier."

Kendyl played with the ends of her hair, giving him an appraising look. The glow from the freshly fallen snow bathed her in a soft white light, and a warm-brown sheen glowed within her dark locks. Her hair was one of the few striking differences between Kendyl and Allyn. His hair was dark, bordering on black, while Kendyl had inherited a trace of their mother's auburn hair.

"What?" Allyn asked, growing uncomfortable under her gaze.

"You're good at this."

Allyn laughed. "I don't know about that. I'm just making it up as I go along."

"Then you hide it well."

"I'm a lawyer, Kendyl. It's my job to bluff and fill you full of bullshit."

"Now you're just being modest. You don't see the way they look at you, do you? They follow you, Allyn. Liam, Leira, Nyla, even Jaxon. You're a natural leader."

He shrugged. "I'm not trying to be. I just want to be helpful."

"I follow you, too," she said softly.

Allyn's lips parted. He felt as if he should say something, but he had no idea what.

"You held it together after Mom died," Kendyl continued. Her eyes were growing moist. "I don't know what would have happened if you didn't, but you were strong. You told me it was going to be okay. And it was."

Allyn swallowed the lump in his throat. "I said that as much for me as I did for you."

"But you said it, and I believed it." Kendyl met his eye. "I don't think I ever said thank you."

"You didn't have to."

"Thank you, Allyn."

"Kendyl..."

"*Thank you*, Allyn."

"We got each other through that." Allyn's voice was quiet and tight with emotion. "I couldn't have done it without you, either."

"I don't know how much help I could have been."

"You were there," Allyn said. "I knew that whatever I was going through, you were, too. I wasn't alone—and on my toughest days, I had you to lean on."

Kendyl smiled, and it stirred old memories inside him. Their features and expressions were so much like their father's, but that smile—the way the right side of her face went a little higher than the left, her perfect teeth, and the sparkle in her eyes—was their mother's. It was times like that when Theresa Kaplan still lived, and in a way, it gave him strength and reassured him that everything was going to be all right.

"We gave each other strength," Kendyl said.

"And we still do."

---

By the time they began the short hike back to the cabin, Allyn felt as though something had changed between them. The uncomfortable tension that had been so prevalent over the recent weeks had vanished. They weren't what they were before—they'd been through too much to go back to that— but they were something new. And Allyn looked forward to finding out what.

When the cabin finally came into view, Allyn was quickly reminded of the previous days' events. He'd grown used to the quiet activity of the McCollum Family. With the addition of the Hyland refugees, the number of magi had doubled, and within the already bulging confines of the cabin walls, the activity seemed to have tripled. Kids ran and played, screaming as little kids do, having imaginary magi battles where snowballs replaced both fireballs and ice blasts. Erik and his small team of carpenters had felled another tree and were in the process of blasting it into small blocks for firewood. A steady hum of conversation ventured outside through the cabin walls.

Amid it all, Joyce sat on the porch, quiet and contemplative. She didn't notice Allyn and Kendyl approaching until Allyn spoke.

"Morning, Joyce."

She blinked, awareness returning to her eyes. "Allyn." The word lacked any emotion, as if she were simply pointing at something and naming it. "Kendyl."

"Everything all right?" Allyn asked. "You seem... troubled."

She gave him an appraising look, as if judging whether or not she could trust him. "It's not right," she said.

Allyn cocked his head to the side, confused. "What's not right?"

"She's only a kid."

"Joyce, I—"

"Allyn!" The voice was followed by a series of quick footsteps echoing across the wooden porch.

He turned to find Liam rushing toward him. He wore the same too-big smile he always had when he was truly excited, the one that looked less and less likely that he would ever grow into.

"I've been looking for you everywhere," Liam said, coming to a stop in front of Allyn.

"What's going on?"

"He responded."

"Who responded?" Allyn asked.

Liam's eyes flickered from Kendyl to Joyce then back to Allyn, as if he didn't want to share what he was about to say with the women. *"He* responded," Liam said.

*J.P. Niall! The person behind the videos.*

"When?"

"Earlier this morning." Liam glanced at Kendyl. "I didn't know where to find you."

"What did they say?"

"I'll show you."

Allyn apologized to Joyce, telling her they could talk later, then headed inside. When they were halfway through the hallway near the bedrooms, he finally realized Kendyl had no idea what they were talking about.

They hadn't told anyone else. But that was before he

and Kendyl had come to their understanding. Before their relationship had changed.

"We contacted the person behind the video," Allyn said.

Kendyl's eyes grew wide. "When?"

"Yesterday."

"What did you say?"

"That he had my attention."

Kendyl glanced at Liam, who was watching the two of them out of the corners of his eyes. "I take it not very many people know about this?"

"No," Allyn said.

"Then I won't say anything."

Liam relaxed and opened the door into Jaxon's room.

Allyn and Kendyl stood over Liam's shoulders as he brought up Niall's YouTube page. Under their comment was a response from the user: *You're a hard man to find, Allyn Kaplan.*

"Do we write back?" Liam asked.

Allyn leaned forward, taking the back of Liam's chair in his hands. The wood creaked under his grip. "I don't know."

"What are you guys trying to do?" Kendyl asked.

"I want to know who's behind these videos." Allyn proceeded to tell her about his theory that Niall was a magi who'd come to power outside the Families.

Kendyl chewed her bottom lip. "If that's the case, then they're not going to tell you who they are any more than you're going to tell them where you're hiding." She sounded as though she were thinking aloud. "So what are you trying to accomplish?"

*Accomplish?*

Kendyl must have read the confusion on Allyn's face, because she pressed forward. "Are you trying to get them to meet you somewhere?"

"I..." Allyn said. "I guess that makes the most sense."

"Then we need to gently nudge the conversation in that direction," Kendyl said.

"What do you suggest?"

"How about this?" She leaned over Liam and typed in the discussion box. *I could say the same thing about you.*

"I like it," Allyn said. "It's short and simple. Puts the focus back on them."

"That's what I was thinking," Kendyl said.

"You want me to post it?" Liam asked.

Allyn took a deep breath and nodded. Before he had time to second-guess himself, Liam clicked the Post button.

"And now we wait," Liam said.

"And now we wait," Allyn repeated, taking a step backward and sitting on the side of the bed. He pointed at the disconnected hard drive next to Liam's computer. "I take it the transfer is complete?"

"Yeah," Liam said.

"Have you begun searching the computer for other information?"

"It's clean," Liam said. "Whoever wiped the hard drive knew what they were doing."

Allyn cursed under his breath. It wasn't that he was surprised—he had known the person who'd left the computer wouldn't leave compromising information on it, not after going to such lengths to delete it, but Allyn had hoped that Liam's ability would prove more powerful than the person's expertise. Even a machinist's magic, it seemed, had its limits.

"How'd the first session go?" Liam asked, turning to Kendyl. He and Kendyl hadn't spent a lot of time together, but there was a certain understanding between the two. Kendyl was struggling to find her place, and that was a situation Liam knew all too well.

Kendyl smiled, glancing at Allyn. "It went well."

"Good," Liam said. "We'll make a magi out of you in no—"

The computer chimed. The corners of Liam's mouth

turned up as he spun back to the computer. Niall had already written back.

Allyn stood. "We both have reasons to hide," he read aloud.

"What are they hiding from?" Kendyl asked.

"Type this," Allyn said. "I'm hiding from false accusations. You?"

Liam tapped the keyboard.

The response came back seconds later: *I didn't say I was hiding from anything.*

"What does that mean?" Liam asked.

"It's a riddle," Kendyl said, running her fingers through her hair. "They're hiding, but not from anything in particular. So..." She tapped a finger against her lips. "They're hiding from *everything*."

"Because the people around him don't know he exists," Allyn said, picking up on Kendyl's train of thought. "He's hiding in plain sight."

"Just like we would if we returned to society," Kendyl said.

"And he's afraid to say too much in case the account is traced back to him," Allyn said. "But who is he afraid of? What does he have to lose if someone learns the truth?"

"What would you be afraid of losing the most?" Kendyl asked.

It was a simple question, but one Allyn struggled to answer. He'd already lost his career, his home, and his future. What else was he afraid of losing? Why was *he* hiding?

*You haven't lost your future. It just changed. The future you wanted became something different, and you're afraid of losing that.* But what was *that*? Was it the future he had in mind or the prospect of a future in general?

"He's afraid of losing his *choice*," Allyn said. "If he's caught, he'll be jailed or experimented on or worse."

160

"What are you thinking?" Kendyl asked. "She's in the military or government?"

"That would explain how he got your birth certificate," Liam said.

"If *she's* afraid," Kendyl asked slowly, "then shouldn't we be terrified?"

The conversation stopped, and a silent dread filled the air.

"I don't see how it makes much of a difference," Allyn said. "We're already being pursued."

"By the people Niall is afraid of?"

"If not now, we will be eventually," Allyn said. "And there's only one way to find out."

"Do you want me to write back?" Liam asked.

"Yeah," Allyn said, thinking. "Tell him we found the computer."

Liam typed the message, and again, the response came back within seconds, almost as if they were communicating through an instant messenger.

*What did you think?*

"I think you're searching for something." The steady rhythm of tapping keys accompanied Allyn's voice as Liam transcribed.

*Have I found it?*

"What do you think?"

The response came slower this time—Allyn could almost see the person sitting in front of the computer, thinking.

*I think so. Your coyness nearly confirms it.*

"He knows," Allyn said. "Ask if he's found any others."

*Only rumors. Until recently, I hadn't had the opportunity to investigate as deeply as I would like.*

"What's changed?"

*We're venturing too closely to exposing too much in a public forum.*

"He wants to meet," Allyn said. He took a deep breath,

looking to Kendyl and Liam for advice. They watched him, expecting him to make the decision.

"Are you local?"

*That depends where you're hiding, doesn't it?*

Allyn cursed. Niall was fishing for information. Exposing too much about himself and his whereabouts wouldn't endanger only him, but also the entire McCollum Family and its recent refugees. "I can be local."

*Then so can I.*

Allyn mulled over the words. He was reluctant to go much further without consulting Jaxon, who didn't even know they were in communication with the video's creator. He sighed. "And now we're venturing into an area where *I'm* concerned about exposing too much."

*I can understand that. Think on it, and when you have an answer, contact me again. In the meantime, know that I'm happy to have found you. Just knowing you exist answers many of the questions I've struggled with for years.*

Allyn remained silent for a time, watching the monitor, almost expecting another post to appear. One never did, and eventually, Liam turned to him.

"What now?" Liam asked.

"Now," Allyn said, "we find Jaxon."

# CHAPTER 15

"WHERE'S JAXON?" ALLYN ASKED.

Leira sat in front of the fireplace, resting against the red brick. Her legs were pulled tight to her chest. Her arms were draped over her knees, and without looking away from the book she held, she answered, "He'll return soon."

"We need to see him," Allyn said.

"Obviously," Leira said sarcastically, brushing a strand of black hair behind her ear. "Otherwise, you wouldn't be looking for him."

Allyn looked to Liam for support. He'd never known Leira to be sarcastic—she was usually quiet and direct, similar to her father. Liam was the sarcastic one.

Liam shook his head, seeming just as confused as Allyn was.

"Leira—"

"Allyn."

"It's important."

She looked up from her book, noticing for the first time that her younger brother and Kendyl accompanied Allyn. "I don't know where he is. He does this every day for an hour or two."

"Does what?"

"Something to clear his head," Leira said.

"And you have no idea where he goes?"

"Outside somewhere," Leira said. "He always tracks snow through the cabin when he returns."

Allyn turned to Liam and Kendyl. "He wouldn't have gone too far—he wouldn't risk leaving the property."

Leira grabbed her bookmark off the mantle and stuck it inside the book. "What are you going to do?"

"We're going to find him."

Leira sighed and rose to her feet. She was an inch or two taller than Liam was—though Allyn didn't know how much longer that was going to last—with a firm frame that she held with confidence. "He won't like that. He's entitled to his privacy."

"This is important," Allyn said.

"Can it wait an hour?" Kendyl asked.

"No," Allyn said. "I'm tired of waiting. Tired of dreading that door crashing down. Every hour we remain here is another hour the FBI has to find us."

Kendyl didn't argue—Allyn already knew she wasn't as concerned about the police as he was.

"Come on," Allyn said, turning and striding through the cabin. He stopped on the front porch, suddenly feeling very stupid. The cabin backed up to thousands of acres of dense forest that covered the hillsides to the north and south. Out front, the lonely, two-lane mountain road ran perpendicular to the cabin, over one hundred feet away and hidden behind a thicket of pine trees. If Jaxon wanted to hide, truly hide, he wouldn't have a problem doing so.

Allyn stepped off the porch onto the snow-packed gravel driveway. He stopped, waiting silently. Keeping still, he strained his ears for anything beyond the muffled murmur of activity inside the cabin. The others mimicked his stillness, peering into the tangle of branches around them as if expecting to see Jaxon's dark figure among the frosty landscape.

There was something different about mountain calm. Everything was quieter. The gentle wind, ever constant, brushed up against trees, unable to sway the heavy, snow-laden branches. And in the vast open space, the wind didn't howl, either. An occasional car passed, and it was quieter, too, as if the car were moving slowly, the sound of its tires muffled on the packed snow. People even seemed to talk quieter, perhaps uneasy about disturbing the odd tranquility. So when Allyn heard the peculiar *crack*, even as faint as it was, he immediately knew it had to be Jaxon.

"Did you hear that?" Allyn turned toward the distant sound. It wasn't the sound of a branch splitting and falling or of a boulder tumbling down the hillside. It was short. Sharp. Violent. He heard it again. He couldn't place it, but he knew he'd heard it before, and it made him uneasy.

The sound led him to a trail into the forest—the same trail Mason and Ren had led him through to his Branding. With each step, the noises grew louder, and the uneasiness in Allyn's chest grew with it. Nearly panicking, Allyn crested the hillside then darted off the trail, following a set of tracks.

Jaxon stood alone in a small clearing, his chest bare and his body slick with sweat. The bottoms of his loose-fitting trousers were caked in snow, and they rippled in the wind as his bare feet moved with a careful, almost choreographed rhythm. Allyn watched, mouth agape.

Jaxon's knees were bent, and he moved gracefully on the balls of his feet. He struck at the air in short, sharp movements, his arms coiled with muscle and sinew. Then he turned and kicked. It was some kind of kata, but it was unlike any Allyn had ever seen.

"What *is* that?" Allyn whispered, sliding behind a tree to hide from Jaxon's view.

"The *Mahari*," Leira said almost reverently. Allyn hadn't even known Leira had followed them into the forest.

Jaxon's kata built in intensity. He kicked, punched, jabbed, hooked, spun, and jumped in a complex series of moves as if he were battling foes from all sides. Then, with a final powerful strike, Jaxon returned to a resting stance, bowing his head and breathing heavily.

Afraid to interrupt, Allyn lingered, waiting for Jaxon to move. Leira laid a gentle hand on his shoulder, holding him in place. Then, like a snake snapping at its prey, Jaxon sprang into motion again, this time hurling a blast of ice toward a dead tree. The hollow limbs exploded, and a chunk of the decaying trunk sheared off. The wood cracked as the tree swayed ominously. Allyn waited for it to fall, but Jaxon was already spinning, forming another ice blast in his hands. He flung it at the tree, and it struck to the side of the initial blast. Teetering for only a moment, the tree groaned, seemingly falling slowly, then crashed into the earth.

Jaxon danced between the branches, three balls of ice already in his hands. He threw them straight into the air then wielded again, and before Allyn could blink, three baseball-sized fireballs sailed through the air. The fireballs struck, and the ice blasts exploded in a shower of mist. Jaxon hadn't missed a single one.

Spinning in the opposite direction, Jaxon launched another blast of ice. He ran, jumped off the fallen tree, and cast another, smaller ice blast. As it left his fingers, the air warped, popping as Jaxon hit the smaller blast with a concussion of air. It flashed through the forest, striking and shattering the larger blast. Bits of icy shrapnel struck the nearby trees, clipping off branches and imbedding into trunks.

Jaxon leaped onto the fallen tree, gained his balance quickly, and threw an ice blast. He spun then threw another in the opposite direction. Fire in his hands, he twisted, striking the first ice blast, and turned back to destroy the second. He repeated the moves, moving like a gymnast on a balance beam, spinning but never teetering.

The Mahari culminated in a crescendo of activity. Jaxon planted his feet firmly on the trunk then launched his volleys straight into the air, alternating between hands: ice, fire, ice, fire. He was so fast that Allyn could barely keep up. More ice. More fire. Every blast connecting. Every blast exploding.

Ice rained down like sleet, dusting Jaxon's exposed shoulders with white. The air was alive. Warping. Popping. Shimmering. Transparent blue ice and orange fireballs zipped into the sky, colliding below the canopy of branches. Then, bellowing a final roar as the last few blasts left his hands, Jaxon finished the display and stood alone, the hollow trunk cradling his bare feet. He breathed heavily as steam rose from his body. He lowered his head and whispered something then turned to the nearby tree, where his compression top hung from a low branch.

Jaxon started back toward the path, pulling his shirt over his head. He froze when he saw Allyn, his eyes growing wide with concern.

"What's wrong?" Jaxon asked, firm. Not angry, but alarmed.

Allyn wondered how they must look, four magi spying behind thick trees, and his face grew hot with embarrassment.

"It's okay," Leira said calmly. She walked toward Jaxon. "They said they have urgent news."

Jaxon pushed his arms through the sleeves and turned his gaze from Leira to the rest of them.

Allyn approached, feeling the weight of Jaxon's eyes. They had intruded on Jaxon's peace, overstepping a sacred boundary and violating his trust.

"I... we..." Allyn said. "Jaxon, I'm sorry, but that was *incredible*. I've never seen anything like it."

Jaxon sniffed and rubbed the sweat from his brow. "What's so urgent, Allyn?"

Allyn sucked in a deep breath—the cold air burned his lungs. "We've been in contact with Niall."

Jaxon blinked. "When?"

"Twenty minutes ago."

"How?"

"Through his YouTube profile," Allyn said. "It's all there if you want to read it, but there's nothing incriminating. Just a lot of implied information."

"Such as?"

"Such as," Allyn repeated, "he's a magi. Someone who came into his power outside the Families."

Jaxon's lips parted. He appeared genuinely surprised. "What do they want?"

"To meet."

Jaxon grimaced. He rubbed his forehead with his thumb and forefingers, smearing the beading sweat across his dark face.

"He's searching for us, Jaxon," Allyn said. "He's searching for answers. Imagine how terrifying it would be to develop magi abilities without the proper guidance."

"It's a bad time," Jaxon said.

"A bad time?" Allyn asked. "There couldn't be a better time! Don't you understand what we have? It's a list of other magi. And based on the information we have, it could be a list of potential machinists. We need this, Jaxon."

"I don't disagree that it's important."

"Then what's with the hesitance?" Allyn asked, incredulous. It offered them a way to rebuild their Family through a fresh mix of new blood and new abilities. Jaxon wanted the McCollum Family to become the first machinist Family, and this gave that dream potential. More than that, it provided them with a way to integrate back into the Forum.

Lukas had believed that by finding magi who could wield,

even ones who'd grown up outside the magi community, he could unite the Families and strengthen them through common purpose. The same opportunity had been bestowed upon Jaxon. They could prove that Allyn wasn't a fluke. He wasn't the exception. Magi lived, existed, and grew into power outside the magical community—and they had done so since the Fracture. But still, Jaxon was reticent.

"The manor's been locked down since we left," Jaxon said. "An order handed down by the FBI agent in charge, Special Agent Richard Maddox."

"How do you know all of this?" Kendyl asked.

"Liam's not the only one who knows how to use a computer."

It was official then—they weren't dealing with local PD anymore. They were running from federal agents.

"What do we know about him?" Allyn asked.

"He's one of the best." Jaxon said, leaning against a nearby tree. "He's a thirteen-year veteran of the bureau, with a ruthless reputation. He's received the FBI's Medal of Valor, Meritorious Achievement, and Shield of Bravery. He's a legend."

Allyn cursed, closing his eyes and pinching the bridge of his nose. He wanted to be sick. "And he was called in to find me."

"Actually," Jaxon said, "that appears to have been a stroke of bad luck. Agent Maddox transferred to the Portland field office two years ago."

"Why?" Liam asked. "What happened?"

"His second divorce."

Allyn shook his head. It was too much. Their involvement should have been avoided. If he'd just gone to the police the moment his sister had disappeared, he never would have incriminated himself. Or if he'd taken her in as soon as she'd been found, they could have ended the police pursuit. Now it was a tangled mess that Allyn had no idea how to unravel.

"What about his partner?" Allyn asked.

"I don't know much about him," Jaxon said. "Special Agent Gary Nolan is a first-year agent, but he graduated near the top of his class at Quantico. Most of these men are cut from the same cloth, so it's unlikely he's too much different from Maddox. He just lacks experience."

Allyn cursed.

"What were you hoping for?" Kendyl asked.

"Something we could exploit," Allyn said.

"Like what?"

"I don't know."

"This is why it's bad timing," Jaxon said. "We have the best of the FBI on our tails, and we have no way of shaking them."

"We need to run," Allyn said.

"And go where?" Liam asked.

"Anywhere," Allyn said, unable to think of somewhere specific. "It's only a matter of time until they find us here."

"They've already been to the cabin," Kendyl said. "Remember the tire tracks or the boot prints?"

"Those could have been from anyone," Allyn said. "You were up here with a realtor a few weeks ago. They could have been from you."

"Me? A size-twelve boot?" Kendyl laughed. "No. And we weren't the ones that smeared the windows like we were trying to look inside, either. The tire marks and the footsteps were fresh. I'm telling you, they've already been here, and they didn't find anything. They won't be back."

"Even if it was them," Allyn said, "and the police have been here, the moment their investigation hits a dead end, they're going to retrace their steps. They'll come looking again, I guarantee it."

"How do you know?" Liam asked

"Because that's what I would do." Allyn turned to Jaxon. "Have we heard from any of the other Families?"

"No," Jaxon said.

"Then we have nowhere to run and no one to help." Allyn rubbed the scruff on his chin. His throat grew tight in preparation for what he was about to say. "Just say the words, Jaxon, and I'll leave. I'll take the heat off you."

"No," Jaxon said.

"It's me they're after."

"We'll find a way," Jaxon said. "I'm not going to splinter this Family further."

Allyn exhaled. His arms and legs felt light.

"It's too bad we can't get to someone inside the FBI," Liam said.

Jaxon raised an eyebrow. "Why?"

"If we could get access to the FBI database," Liam said, "we could erase the files pertaining to Allyn and Kendyl—or at least fill it with bad information. It wouldn't destroy the evidence, but it would cut their legs out from under them."

"Would that work?" Jaxon asked, turning to Allyn.

"Maybe," Allyn said. "But it wouldn't be that easy. The FBI has too much information to store on one system. They probably have hundreds of databases, each with their own usernames and passwords. If someone was going to remove us from the system, they'd have to do it from each one."

"But it's possible," Jaxon said.

"Sure," Allyn said. "As long as that person knew what he was doing."

"Why would we need to get someone inside?" Kendyl asked. "Agents need access to those databases around the clock. There has to be some kind of remote access."

"We would still need someone who has access to those databases," Allyn said.

"We do," Kendyl said. "We have Liam."

"You're talking about hacking into the FBI's computer database," Allyn said. "One of the world's most encrypted, well-protected sites in the world."

"It's been done," Kendyl said, "by others without his ability. You're always saying that we don't know the full extent of Liam's capabilities. Maybe it's time we found out."

Liam was sweating and looking terror stricken. Kendyl had a point, and they all knew it. His abilities were still the largest variable they faced with the machinist movement. A power play of such magnitude would go a long way to proving their legitimacy.

"This might be the show of strength we need," Allyn said. "If you cut the FBI's legs out from under them and slow their investigation, it'll give us time to get the help we need and restore the McCollum Family to its rightful place. What do you think, Liam? Is it possible?"

"I don't know," Liam said slowly. "If you're correct and there are multiple databases, then we're not talking about just hacking into one, but several, and each one has its own set of unique challenges. It would take days, weeks even, and the entire time, someone might notice me tampering with their system and shut it down—or worse, trace us back here." Liam rubbed his face with the sleeve of his shirt. "And even then, say we succeed and erase you from the FBI databases—you're not removed from the grid. You'd still have records in the DMV, Social Security office, hospitals, schools..." Liam took a sharp breath, no doubt overwhelmed by the weight of the task.

Allyn laid a hand on Liam's shoulder. "Can it be done?"

"The FBI Database?" Liam asked. "Yes. The rest... I don't know."

Jaxon folded his arms, focusing a steady gaze on Liam. "Start looking into it."

Liam nodded.

"Hey," Jaxon said. When Liam met his gaze, he continued. "Don't dwell on the size of the task. Break it into manageable chunks and save the most difficult for last. If you can accomplish a little every day, you're going to do great. Okay?"

"Okay," Liam said softly, almost a whisper.

"Let me know when you get started."

It wasn't until they were headed back to the trail that Allyn realized the matter with J.P. Niall was still unresolved. He pulled Jaxon aside, letting the rest of their group file forward.

"Yes?"

"We still didn't decide what to do about the video."

Jaxon rubbed his swollen eyes. Minutes before, Jaxon was the epitome of strength, but he'd let down his guard, and fatigue had quickly won over.

"You said they want to meet?"

"Yeah."

"What do you propose?"

"I think we have to see it through," Allyn said. "If we choose the right location and position our magi around it, then we minimize the risk."

"And if it is the police?"

"Then I guess you won't have to worry about breaking into their system."

Jaxon barked a laugh, the tension disappearing from his face. "Put it together."

# CHAPTER 16

ALLYN REREAD THE MESSAGE FOR the last time: *I'm ready*, it said, and went on to provide the date, time, and location for the meeting. Allyn was more than a little nervous about putting that kind of information where anyone could see it, but he didn't have a choice. The best he could do was hope the account wasn't being watched. He'd picked an out-of-the-way diner on the outskirts of the city, and since it was open all night, he'd chosen a time in the late evening, hoping the diner would be slow. He'd toyed with the idea of picking an empty parking lot, vacant quarry, or some other isolated location, but he'd decided against it. Those locations allowed for too many unforeseen variables and too many places to hide. Most of them had one entrance and one exit. If it were a trap, there would be no way to escape.

Meeting in a public place had potential complications, too—mainly, he might be recognized by someone who would call the police—but the watchful eyes might also prevent a desperate man from doing something reckless. Allyn didn't know what to expect, and that made him nervous.

He shifted in his seat, his backside tingling from falling asleep. The weathered wood of the old patio chair scratched the backs of his legs through his jeans, and he had to be careful not to get a splinter when resting his arms on the armrests. An identical chair sat vacant on the patio beside him. The cold night was quiet and still, with only a gentle intermittent breeze. The thick clouds that had blanketed the region for the past several weeks had thinned considerably, exposing patches of dark sky and dozens of stars, which provided more light than he would have expected. Part of him longed to see them in their full glory again, as he had when he was a child, but the clouds wouldn't dissipate entirely until summer, and the McCollum Family would be long gone by then.

Allyn's breath caught in his throat as he clicked Post. Save for not showing up to the meeting, he couldn't back out now. Not that he would have ever done that—his curiosity outweighed his apprehension. Allyn watched the screen for several moments, almost expecting an immediate response. He hadn't needed much time to come up with a plan or put it into action. When Allyn had gone to borrow Liam's laptop, the young magi had retreated to the loft without showing any desire to help. Liam had made great strides since Allyn had first met him, becoming more sociable and confident, but he still had a bad habit of hiding in a dark corner anytime he was stressed.

They would soon have to break that pattern of behavior. As someone expected to lead, Liam couldn't hide every time the situation grew dire. He needed to be a symbol of strength. Of consistency. Never wavering. Allyn just hoped they could fix the problem in time because cultivating his new reputation would take months.

*Do we have that long?*

Jaxon had never given a solid indication of *when* he was leaving the McCollum Family, only that it was an eventuality. The open-endedness of the decision grated on Allyn. He feared the day, but the undefined date didn't allow for them to plan adequately. Without a date, they lacked urgency. Life and everything along with it continued at its steady pace. Sometimes a ticking clock was the most effective motivation.

Allyn clicked Refresh, and the discussions page reloaded.

"Damn." His message was still the only one on the *Discussions* tab. Their previous conversation had disappeared, likely having been deleted by the other user. Niall had insinuated that he was at great risk of being discovered, so he wasn't likely to leave a trail of evidence straight back to himself.

The front door opened with a squeak, and Kendyl's slender outline, lit from behind by the soft orange light of the cabin, stepped onto the patio.

"There you are," she said, closing the door. "What are you doing out here?"

"Working." Allyn closed the computer monitor. "Jaxon agreed to setting up the meeting."

Kendyl sat down in the empty seat beside him. She wore a surprised expression. "When?"

"Tomorrow," Allyn said. "If he agrees to it."

"Wow," Kendyl said. "So soon?"

"I'm tired of waiting." He set the computer down next to his feet and instantly regretted it. The computer had been warm, and its absence left a cold void on his lap.

Kendyl looked away for a moment, surveying the landscape in front of them. The light inside the kitchen shut off, plunging the patio into darkness. *What time is it?* If the others were turning in, he'd been outside longer than he thought.

*No wonder I'm so damn cold.*

"What do you think about Jaxon's plan?" Kendyl asked.

Allyn blinked. His vision still hadn't adjusted to the darkness, and he couldn't read Kendyl's expression, but there was a sadness to her voice. "I'm not convinced it's going to work. Why?"

Kendyl took a strained breath. "I hope it doesn't."

"What? Why?" Allyn asked. "You were so intent on it before. Wasn't part of it your idea?"

"I know." Kendyl turned back to him. "I was so captivated on whether we *could* do it that I didn't stop to think if we *should*."

"Why shouldn't we?" Allyn said. "I may not think it's going to succeed, but the prospect of getting the police off our backs sounds pretty enticing."

"It's not about the police. What happens when we disappear? What does it *mean* if we vanish?"

"I'm confused."

"We're all that's left, Allyn. We've become so fixated on saving the McCollum Family that we've forgotten our own. If we disappear, if we vanish from all record, then our family vanishes with us."

Allyn traced his bottom lip with his thumb and index finger. Kendyl continued to hold him with a steady gaze, waiting for his response. He hadn't thought about the implications of disappearing from the system, but he didn't agree that their family would die with the act. If anything, their family, as Kendyl defined it, had died with their mother. He and Kendyl had kept their father's name, and legally—even if they hadn't had any communication with him in a decade—they were more a part of that family than their mother's. But something still gnawed at his insides.

"You have nothing to say?"

"I guess I hadn't thought about it," Allyn said slowly, "because in my head, I'd already been through it. I used to think that I honored Mom through my career. Her money got me through school, and I got a job that I thought she would be proud of. Turning my back on that to join the Family felt like I was turning my back on her. And then I had to do it again when you told me you wanted to stay.

"But I did it," Allyn continued. "Because I realized that protecting you was the best way to honor Mom's memory.

She wouldn't care about a job or money. She cared about us. So I guess I don't see it the same way you do. To me, vanishing isn't tarnishing her memory. It's commemorating it by taking the final step to save the little family I have left."

"I never knew you felt that way." Kendyl bit her bottom lip. "It kind of makes me feel guilty for giving you so much crap about your job for all those years."

Allyn snickered. "You should." He smiled to let her know he was playing. It had been an important couple of days between him and Kendyl. First, she *thanked* him for being there when their mother had passed, and now she was apologizing for the way she had treated him. He didn't know what was going on, but he hoped it continued.

"I just wish there was another way."

"Me, too," Allyn said. "But I think Liam is beginning to understand the complexity of the assignment. You should see him right now. He could barely look at me. He's overwhelmed because he knows Jaxon ordered him to do the impossible."

"That was me," Kendyl said, guilt in her eyes. "I did that to him. I set him up for failure."

"How?"

"It was my suggestion."

"No. No, Liam said he could do it, and Jaxon ordered it. They made the decision—and who knows? Liam might find a way to do it. He's already done the impossible."

Kendyl frowned. "I'm so conflicted. I don't want him to fail, but I don't want him to succeed, either. I'm sorry, I'm not trying to lay this all on you. I just needed to vent. Needed to try and make sense of what I'm feeling."

"It's okay. I probably just made it worse anyway."

"No," Kendyl said. "No, you didn't."

"Good."

The front door opened, cutting the moment short. A dark frame stepped onto the porch, slow and shuffling like someone trying not to wake up a sleeping companion. It was Riordan, one of the Hyland refugees. He closed the door behind him and hesitated when he saw Allyn. Taller by almost half a head, with spindly arms, bony hands, and narrow shoulders, Riordan looked sickly. His eyes were sunken; and his face, hollow.

Allyn nodded to him. The man returned the gesture slowly then turned away and leaned against the railing near the stairs.

"Come on," Allyn said to Kendyl, standing. Riordan obviously wanted to be alone.

Kendyl stood then followed Allyn down the porch toward the door. Riordan watched them approach. Something about his demeanor made Allyn uncomfortable. His breaths were quick and shallow, and his eyes darted about nervously. Riordan's fingers drummed against the railing, his long fingernails tapping the wood. Instinctively, Allyn positioned himself between Riordan and Kendyl when he opened the door for her to enter.

The dry hinge squealed, almost hiding the noise, but after weeks of being on the run and having to fight for his life, Allyn's senses had become attuned to perceiving that sort of thing. A sharp, scratching noise accompanied by a *whoosh*. Fire igniting. Someone wielding. The interior of the cabin was dark, save for the crackling fire in the living room. The mess of sleeping bodies was alive with the hum of collective breathing. The noise had to have come from one of the bedrooms.

*Kendyl's with me, and Liam is in the loft—Jaxon's room then.*

Riordan's boot scraped the dry porch behind him. Kendyl stopped, perhaps also sensing something amiss, and glanced at him over Allyn's shoulder. Somewhere deep inside the cabin, something creaked.

*Riordan wasn't looking for privacy*, Allyn thought. *He was looking for me.*

Another creak.

Riordan took a step toward Allyn.

"Awake! Awake!" Allyn shouted. "Enemies in the cabin! Enemies in the cabin!"

Wielding, he turned to Riordan.

# CHAPTER 17

Red coils of electricity sprang to life around Allyn's arms. They writhed, colliding with each other, crackling and sparking. The red glow made Riordan's hollow face appear sinister.

"Awake! Awake!" Allyn continued to shout. "Jaxon! Mason!"

Riordan sprang into action, a pair of orange fireballs igniting in his hands. In the close proximity, Allyn wouldn't be able to dodge those, and as far as he knew, electricity did nothing to combat fire. So he charged, driving his shoulder into Riordan's chest and slamming the slender man into the porch railing. The wood cracked and swayed.

Riordan cried out, letting the fireballs dissipate. Allyn struck him in the face with a fist. The coils singed, turning from red to white on contact, and the air filled with the scent of burnt flesh as the side of Riordan's face bubbled.

The sour taste of nausea filled Allyn's mouth. *Not again. Not again.* But instinct won the battle with his conscience, squelching the guilt and filling Allyn with nothing but the need to survive and protect those he loved.

Riordan staggered, hiding his face in his arms, roaring in agony. Allyn kept him against the railing, punching and kicking him in the torso. The railing groaned against each blow, but the rotten wood held.

The air warped and cracked, and a concussion of air threw Allyn backward. Prepared, he planted a foot into the siding of the cabin, halting his backward momentum. There was a hole in the railing where Riordan had been, and the man had disappeared. Allyn took the brief lapse in the battle to assess the situation.

Kendyl remained where she'd been—crouching inside the doorway to the cabin, shielding her head with her arms. She was unhurt, but the inside of the cabin was in pandemonium. The throng of people shouted for loved ones and rushed for the exit. Some had fire or ice at the ready, but it was impossible to tell friend from foe.

"Kendyl," Allyn said. "I need you to get these people out."

She looked at him in horror. Her fear shook him—and made him think about his own.

*Don't think about that.* "Kendyl!"

She flinched at his command but met his gaze and nodded. She stood and turned her attention to the cabin.

"This way!" Kendyl shouted, her voice cracking in fear. "This way! Come on!"

The mass of people heeded her command, rushing toward the exit as a collective wave of bodies. Allyn hoped that only the allies would follow her command. Their enemies had another mission. He turned back to where Riordan had been and leaped off the porch, soaring over overgrown flowerbeds and the broken railing to land in the snow with a crunch.

Riordan was on his feet a few paces to Allyn's right. He'd been in the process of rushing toward the stairs to re-enter the fray. The left side of his face was blackened with burn marks, and his left eye was watery and nearly swollen shut. He squared on Allyn and hissed, unleashing a volley of attacks.

Riordan didn't seem to know about Allyn's inability to

counter fire and attacked with a series of ice blasts. They appeared in the air as fast Riordan could wield them. Allyn *reached* for them, and the coils of electricity burst from his hands, snaring the blasts out of the air. The ice exploded into a shower of mist. Allyn countered two this way then dove out of the way of the third.

Riordan strode toward Allyn confidently. Allyn rolled onto his feet in a crouch. Watching. Waiting.

Magi streamed out of the cabin, McCollum and Hyland Family members alike. Allyn didn't know whether to be pleased or outraged. A small number of magi, not the refugees as a whole, had orchestrated the attack. Allyn hoped Brandt and Juniette were as surprised by the attack as he was.

Riordan slapped his chest then lunged forward, slapping his hands together in an exaggerated clap. The air distorted, and the concussion threw Allyn backward, end over end. Fortunately, the coils didn't dissipate. They seemed more stable and to require less concentration than some of the other magi elements. But by the time Allyn dug his face out of the snow, Riordan had thrown an angry fireball at him.

Half on instinct and half in desperation, Allyn shot a static charge at the oncoming fireball. The charge, a series of tiny bands of electricity wrapped tightly around each other in a flattened disc shape, disbanded, and dozens of individual strands shot in all directions. One struck the ground near Allyn, burning through the snow with a hiss. Another struck Riordan in the leg.

Riordan cursed and wielded another fireball. Hobbling, he threw it at the ground as if it were a grenade, and it erupted into a wall of flame. Allyn heard the *crack* of a concussion of air, and the wall of fire raced across the landscape. Allyn sent a series of static charges into it, but they flew through the flames harmlessly.

Remembering a previous training session with Jaxon, Allyn threw an arm out to the side, casting coils of electricity at a nearby tree. They struck the battered trunk, and the air split, echoing like a gunshot. The tree became an anchor, and the electricity, the gunpowder. Allyn was shot away from the tree with such force that blackness crept in at the edges of his vision. He struck the ground on his side and rolled several feet before stopping, only narrowly avoiding the firewall.

Ears ringing and seeing stars, Allyn struggled to get his bearings. Every part of him hurt. His chest felt as if he'd been struck with a cannonball. Steam rose from his hands and arms, which were buried in the snow, red from irritation or burns, or both. His head throbbed, and pulses of agony rippled through his body with every beat of his heart. He blinked, focusing. *Where's Riordan?*

*There.*

Riordan hadn't moved, but Allyn's perspective had changed. He watched Allyn, hesitant. *Why? Doesn't he realize he has me dead to rights?*

Behind him, Kendyl ushered the last of the fleeing magi into the woods. Many of them could wield but were more concerned about their loved ones than assisting Allyn. Kendyl lingered behind, watching. Allyn tried to call out for her to go, but he couldn't get the words past the pain. He waved her on. She remained at the forest's edge for another second, and then after Allyn waved her on again, this time more urgently, she disappeared into the trees.

Allyn returned his attention to Riordan. The man seemed to have gathered himself and was wielding another attack. Allyn harnessed the pain rushing through his veins and wielded again. He didn't have to look down to know the red coils had returned. He could feel their heat. Their power. It made his hands tremble.

Just as he was about to launch them at Riordan, he caught movement behind the man. Dressed entirely in black compression armor, a slender figure darted around the cabin, using the shadows for stealth, descending on Riordan. Only a few paces behind him, the slender figure cast a blast of ice, and the blue glow illuminated her face. Ren.

Riordan spun on her just as she unleashed the blast. Fire met ice in midair, stalling the attack. But Allyn used her distraction and projected his electricity toward the man. The coils streaked through the air in a continuous, growing band of electricity that lassoed Riordan and engulfed him in burning tendrils of power. His body went rigid then shook violently as the electricity took him.

Allyn cut power to the coils, and they disappeared, but the damage had been done. Riordan fell to the ground. Smoke curled into the air above him, and the putrid smell of death already tinged the air.

Allyn staggered. *I've done it again.* He doubled over, emptying his stomach onto the untouched snow. Even his vomit tasted like death. His legs grew weak, and he fell onto all fours. Eyes closed, he could still see Riordan's lifeless body and the way it resembled Lukas when he had died. Angry-red, blistered skin. Eyes liquefied. Face unrecognizable. It didn't matter that these men deserved death. He could be the judge, but he couldn't be the executioner, too.

Ren grabbed him by his armpits and dragged him to his feet. "Good work," she said.

"Where are the rest?" Allyn asked, his voice quiet and strained.

"Mason chased one off the deck," Ren said. "The others went for Jaxon. They're still inside."

"Liam?"

"He's fine. Nyla has him."

Nyla was a cleric and lacked the offensive arsenal of other magi, but she was trained in hand-to-hand combat and had other battle skills. Allyn trusted her more than anyone. Maybe even more than Jaxon. She would protect Liam—or anyone else in the McCollum Family—with her life.

"Let's go," Allyn said, taking a labored step forward. His body was sluggish, not acting on command, and his steps were more of a shuffle than a run. "They would have made their strongest play for Jaxon."

Ren took the lead, darting up the stairs onto the porch, and threw her back to the wall beside the door. Allyn labored to keep up. Each step sent needles through his veins. After he'd settled in beside her, Ren gave him half a second to collect himself then raised three fingers and silently counted down. On zero, she rounded into the cabin with fire in both hands. Allyn stormed in behind her, wielding again.

The red coils and orange firelight lit the inside of the empty cabin. Chairs, blankets, and pillows mixed with other personal belongings, littering the floor in a chaotic mess. The sliding-glass door that led onto the back deck was open, and winter air blew inside, making the flames that still burned in the brick hearth flicker. Ren and Allyn crept forward, quick but silent.

Ren checked for assailants hidden behind an overturned couch, while Allyn focused his attention to the loft. He didn't see anyone, but someone crouching could hide behind that half-wall. Ren circled the couch, apparently finding nothing, and locked eyes with Allyn. He pointed toward the loft, but Ren shook her head, evidently content that nobody was up there.

With the living area secure, they made for the hallway to the bedrooms. Scorch marks marred the hallway, and wet carpet squished under their feet. A few tiny lingering ice crystals refracted the firelight onto the walls.

As they passed the first two bedrooms, Allyn heard a distinct thump. His eyes darted to Ren, but the slender woman had already rushed forward. He quickly scanned the insides of each bedroom. The last thing they needed was someone coming up from behind to flank them. Both rooms were empty, and by the time he emerged from the second, Ren was already in position outside Jaxon's room.

Allyn stood at Ren's side and waited for the order. Ren paused. *For what?* The door to Jaxon's room was cracked, and a dim light was visible inside, but Allyn couldn't make anything out. He heard labored breathing. And...voices. *How did I miss that?* Allyn struggled to hear more, but the voices were too faint. All he could hear was the tone. Angry. Sharp. To the point.

"Jaxon?" Allyn mouthed to Ren.

"I think so," she mouthed back.

Allyn took a deep breath. If they didn't let Jaxon know they were outside the room and ready to storm in, he might attack before thinking and injure one of them. But if they gave away their location and Jaxon wasn't in control, they would lose the advantage.

He had to risk it.

"Jaxon?" Allyn said, hesitantly. "It's Allyn. I'm coming in."

The door swung open before Allyn could move, and Jaxon's bulky frame filled the doorway. His face was hard. Allyn could almost feel the fury radiating from him. He saw Allyn and Ren, and his posture relaxed. Slightly.

"Report."

"There were five that I know of," Ren said without missing a beat. "Allyn killed one, I killed another, and Mason prevented a third from assassinating Liam. He pursued them into the forest. As for the other two..." Ren peeked inside Jaxon's room. Sitting with his back against the wall was another of the Hyland refugees. His face was a charred mess of burnt flesh, and blood stained the front of his compression armor.

"Casualties?"

"Not that I know of," Ren said. "Thanks to Allyn's quick thinking."

Jaxon nodded his gratitude. "Who?"

"Riordan," Allyn said.

"And Tomas," Ren said.

"The third?" Jaxon asked.

"William, I think," Ren said. "But I can't be sure."

"Could it have been Brandt?"

"No."

"I think this was a splinter group," Allyn said. "Probably sent here by Darian himself to assassinate the leaders of our Family."

"I agree." Jaxon turned back inside the bedroom.

Allyn followed, nearly overwhelmed by the coppery scent of blood. What he saw reminded him of a gruesome crime scene. Blood puddled on the floor, and a large crimson stain had soaked into the mattress. Even more dripped from the box spring, tapping onto the floor with an unsettling rhythm. There was too much for a single person, and Allyn scanned the room for a second assailant. He found him lying facedown on the far end of the room.

Leira sat in a chair beside the first assailant, clutching her side. She wasn't wearing compression armor, only a thin cotton top with a matching pair of bottoms. Her shirt was stained, but otherwise undisturbed. Allyn hadn't noticed at first, but Jaxon's side was also injured, so her wounds had likely come from healing him.

The assailant leaning against the wall was a man named Aric. His pasty skin had gone as white as cream, and sweat beaded on his brow. The labored breathing Allyn had heard a few moments ago was his, and he clearly didn't have long. Allyn cursed under his breath. The man had kept largely to himself, and Allyn had only spoken a few words to him. In hindsight, Allyn realized, neither Riordan nor Tomas had worked to integrate themselves into the Family. Their mission wasn't to make friends. It wasn't reconnaissance. It was to infiltrate and assassinate. Straight forward.

*I should have known something was amiss. I should have seen this coming. I shouldn't have trusted them so blindly!*

"This isn't over," Aric said through blood-stained lips.

"It is for you," Jaxon said, crouching in front of Aric. He placed his hand on the man's chest, and before Aric could cry or plead, Jaxon wielded an ice blast through his heart. Recognition flashed in Aric's eyes for a brief moment, then his head drooped to the side.

"You didn't ask him anything," Allyn said.

Jaxon pulled back his hand and stood. The tip of the ice blast was barely visible in Aric's chest. "Would you have believed anything he said?"

"No."

"Me either."

———————•◦•————————

"Are you sure you're okay?" Allyn asked, pointedly ignoring Riordan's remains.

Leira walked with one hand against her side. Her face had lost much of its color, and she was hunched over, wearing a perpetual grimace. "I'll be fine," she said.

Allyn wanted to say something but held his tongue. She didn't look fine. In fact, she looked downright awful, but her word had been enough for Jaxon, so it would have to be enough for him.

The tracks made by the fleeing magi led into the forest, and Allyn followed their trail with his small group in pursuit. Kendyl hadn't taken them far. They were waiting atop the first rise, huddled together, looking cold, wet, tired, and scared. Kendyl stood with her back to the host of magi, watching the head of the trail intently. She saw Allyn and rushed toward him.

"You're hurt," Kendyl said, looking him over.

"I'm fine. How are they?"

"They're in shock, but nobody's injured. The Hyland refugees are nervous, afraid of retaliation, I think, but other than that..." She turned to observe the group. The Hyland refugees had formed a tight circle on the other side of the trail. There were only seven of them, three of which were children, and they watched the rest anxiously. Brandt was already striding up to Jaxon.

"Good job," Allyn said to Kendyl. "You did really good."

"I didn't do much."

"I don't know about that," Allyn said, smiling his approval, and then he made his way toward Jaxon and Brandt.

Brandt, always a man of perfect posture, slouched as he approached Jaxon. He reminded Allyn of a dog that knew it had done something wrong and was about to be punished. He had shaved his beard, revealing a face that was quickly losing its battle with age. Sleep deprived and anxious, his deep-set eyes were wary; his wrinkles, deeper and more pronounced.

"Jaxon," Brandt said, "I... I had no idea..."

Jaxon remained silent, watching Brandt with cold eyes, judging him.

"They joined us when we fled the Hyland Estate," Brandt continued. "I had no way of knowing... surely, you know I couldn't... I wouldn't..."

"How is your family, Brandt?" Jaxon asked.

"My family?" Brandt's face lost all of its remaining color. "They're..." He turned to face them. Juniette held their son in front of her, watching her husband. Her auburn hair was tied back in a ponytail, and even in the dead of night, she was stately. Proper. The boy in her arms, Devon, couldn't have been older than nine or ten, and his shaggy, sandy-blond hair had bangs down to his eyebrows. He'd inherited his mother's fair skin and his father's deep-set eyes, but his face mirrored both parents' worried expression. "They're shaken."

"We're all shaken."

Allyn couldn't read Jaxon. Never a man of many words, Jaxon grew even terser when he was tense or anxious. His face was hard, jaw set, eyes drilling into Brandt.

"Jaxon, you have to believe me. I knew nothing about

this. We fled the estate to avoid violence, not to find it. I'm just as outraged as you."

"I know."

"If... if you need us to go..."

Jaxon's eyes narrowed. Allyn wanted to say something, to side with Brandt and help Jaxon see reason. Brandt had fled the Hyland Family because Darian had grown into a sociopath and because the McCollum Family afforded new opportunities for Devon. Brandt hadn't selected who had fled with him. This man had been duped, just as they had been.

"No," Jaxon said, his voice growing soft. "That won't be necessary. I believe you. I just struggle with the idea that nearly half of your group was sent here to assassinate me, and you had no idea."

"We didn't ask questions," Brandt said. "I figured we all left for different reasons, and their reasons were their own. If they didn't want to talk about it, I wasn't going to pry."

"And it never got brought up?" Allyn asked. The question was out of his mouth before he realized it. He didn't know why he asked it; Brandt already had his trust.

"Never," Brandt said.

Jaxon turned to Allyn. "It's late," he said. "Get everyone back inside."

Allyn couldn't tell if Jaxon was angry that he'd worked his way into the conversation or if it was simply time to try to return life to a level of normalcy. Either way, he complied.

Allyn located Kendyl again, and the two of them quickly rounded up the disorganized magi and led them back to the cabin. The remaining Hyland refugees lagged behind the others, heads down and quiet. Allyn tried to calm their nerves by offering a kind smile and walking with them, but it did little good. They were just as nervous of the McCollum Family as the McCollums were of them. Allyn didn't know how they would be able to integrate the Hylands into the Family now. The distrust ran too deep. It would be like healing a splinter, and in Allyn's limited time with the Family, he'd never seen or heard of it being done.

"They should take our rooms for the night," Kendyl said, slowing from the group to fall into step with Allyn.

"I agree," Allyn said. It would separate the two Families, giving each a level of privacy while allowing their emotions to settle. "Take the Hylands inside and get them comfortable."

Kendyl dropped back to speak to Juniette, then ushered them inside. Allyn sought out Ren and soon found her on the front porch, peering uneasily into the forest.

"Mason is still out there," Ren said as he approached.

"So are Liam and Nyla."

"Liam and Nyla are safe."

"How can you be sure?"

"Who do you think prevented Liam's assassination?" Ren asked, giving Allyn a knowing look. "I don't like it, Allyn. He should have been back by now."

"You want to go look for him."

"We don't leave magi behind."

Allyn thought back to the assault on Lukas's compound and the battle of the manor, wondering how much truth there was to that statement. "It'll have to wait," he said.

"I'm not a young magi just coming into my abilities, Allyn," Ren said. "I don't need to be told to do my duty. Until the last assailant is captured or otherwise taken care of, they are still a threat to this Family. We'll set up a watch tonight and hope Mason returns by morning. If he hasn't, I'm leaving at first light."

Allyn's face grew hot, and for once, he was thankful for the late hour. If Ren noticed his discomfort, she didn't say anything. "I want to go with you," he said.

"You don't even like Mason."

"That doesn't mean I don't want to help him."

Ren's eyes narrowed, distrustful. Allyn cursed under his breath. He needed to do a better job of hiding his feelings.

"I want to help," he said with as much conviction as he could muster.

Ren pursed her lips but nodded.

# CHAPTER 18

A LLYN STEPPED OUTSIDE AS THE first rays of sunlight appeared on the horizon. The muscles in his legs, back, and core screamed at him—every step a separate plea for him to stop and rest. His very bones hurt, and he'd been only marginally successful in pushing the constant dull ache to the back of his mind. His body had every right to be angry with him—he'd damn near electrocuted himself when he'd used the tree as an anchor. He wanted to listen to it. He wanted to stop. He wanted to curl into a ball and wait for the pain to end, but he'd made a commitment, and he would see it through. So it was pure will that propelled him onto the deck, where Ren was already waiting for him.

She had remained on watch through the night, even though Jaxon had relieved her hours ago. Perhaps realizing Ren wouldn't stand down, Jaxon had set himself to circling the grounds, sometimes venturing into the forest but always remaining within view. Nyla had returned with Liam shortly after Allyn returned to the cabin, but Mason had vanished— and Allyn feared the worst.

Mason was one of the strongest magi within the McCollum Family, but in battle, life always danced on the blade of a knife. One mistake or one mental error could turn the battle ugly. And chasing an unnamed aggressor into the forest during the dead of night offered plenty of inopportune possibilities. Mason could have simply slipped, tripped, or stumbled, giving the attacker the advantage.

Ren appraised Allyn with a steady expression as he stepped onto the deck. If she was surprised to see him follow through with his word, she didn't show it.

"This is the last place I saw him," she said. "He leaped off the deck in pursuit."

Allyn stepped up to the railing and leaned over, peering down. He gulped. The twelve-foot drop was made worse by the sharply sloping ground at the bottom. He didn't know how Mason had jumped and not broken a leg.

In the dim morning light, he could see a large crater in the snow where Mason and the attacker had landed, as well as the tracks that led from there down the hillside and into the forest.

"At least we know where to start," Allyn said. "You ready?"

Ren nodded then cleared the top of the railing of snow and hopped on top of it.

"What are you—?"

Ren leaped off the railing. She landed in a crouch, stood, and looked up at Allyn expectantly. "You coming?"

"I'll walk."

"I'll catch you," Ren said patronizingly.

Allyn laughed. "I'll be right down." He turned back to the door and walked inside, careful not to wake the sleeping members.

Nyla was waiting for him on the front porch, dressed in her navy compression armor. Her silver hair was tied back in a ponytail extenuating her long neck. "I thought I missed you," she said.

"Almost," Allyn said. "You coming along, too?"

"That's the plan."

A wave of relief flooded through him. Ren didn't make him

feel uncomfortable, but he wasn't as close to her as he was to Nyla. The woman standing in front of him had confided in him, telling him her deepest secret, and she'd been there when he'd needed her most. They shared a bond. Besides, it made sense to have a cleric in their party. If Mason was injured, Allyn and Ren weren't capable of giving it to him the same way Nyla was.

"Good," Allyn said. "Ren's already out back."

Ren had descended the hillside and stopped at the tree line by the time Allyn and Nyla rounded the cabin. She crouched, observing the tracks that led into the forest. Allyn pulled his dark coat tight and the zipper a little higher.

"The tracks are deep," Ren said, turning back to Allyn, stumbling on her words when she noticed Nyla. "We shouldn't have a problem following them, but we still need to be ready. We don't know what waits for us in there."

Ten or fifteen paces into the forest, they entered a different world. The dense fir and hemlock trees towered over them. Pines blocked the morning light, plunging the forest floor into darkness. The little light that did pierce the blanket of ice-laden pine branches streamed through in sheets, cutting the darkness like a razor.

Thick, fragrant sap seeped from tree bark, making the trunks look wet. Birds fluttered from tree to tree, darting among the branches as if they were dancing, chirping and squawking playfully. The forest floor was largely untouched, making the tracks simple to follow.

Their biggest difficulty was keeping their footing on the increasingly steep hillside. The powdered snow made each step more difficult. Though if they did fall, Allyn supposed it would prevent them from tumbling uncontrollably down the hillside.

Allyn lumbered along in silent agony. The snow had already soaked through his boots, and the cold was slowly creeping up his legs, chilling him, leaving numbness in its wake. Staring at his feet, he counted his steps.

*One hundred seventy-two. One hundred seventy-three. One hundred seventy-four.*

He couldn't remember how many times he'd lost count and had to start over. And even now he couldn't tell if the numbers matched up with his steps, or if they followed their own rhythm.

*One hundred seventy-nine. One hundred eighty.*

They continued steadily down the hillside, until at last, the ground leveled out into a deep valley. Towering hills of stone and evergreen trees surrounded them on three sides, and the land stretched out in front of them as far as Allyn could see.

There was no sign of Mason.

Allyn sighed. He'd hoped this would be quick. Follow the tracks. Find the man. Bring him back to the cabin. Simple. He wasn't prepared for a trek, mentally or physically. And he sure as hell wasn't dressed for it. *Stupid. What were you expecting? You have to prepare for the worst. Always.*

"Are you all right?" Nyla stepped up beside him. Her head was cocked to the side. "You're suddenly as pale as Liam."

The thought of Liam's "library tan" brought a smile to Allyn's face.

"It's cold," Allyn said.

"And you're not dressed for—"

"Shhh!" Ren said, scanning their surroundings. Her eyes were narrow, alert, darting from tree to tree. She cocked her head and leaned to the side as if she were straining to hear something in the distance. Her attention was focused on a fallen tree a few dozen paces in front of them. A tangled thicket of bushes strangled the rotten trunk. Ren turned back to them. "Nyla?"

She took one step forward and extended a hand in front of her. She closed her eyes. The seconds ticked by, turning into minutes, until Nyla finally opened her eyes and dropped her hand. "I don't know," she said quietly. "I'm not as strong as Leira, and there's too much energy in these hills. But I think I can feel something."

Ren nodded and bounded forward, throwing snow from the bottoms of her boots, fire ready in her palms. Allyn follow her, his body raging again, but he gathered the pain into the void, and the electricity sprang to life half a second later. The lemony taste of nausea was only a minor annoyance this time. His body was too tired to care.

Approaching the fallen tree, Ren pointed to the right then the left, and Allyn and Nyla flanked the tree on either side. The ancient fir had landed atop younger timbers, giving Allyn a space to crawl under. He waited, however, for Ren's command. Once Nyla was in position at the base of the trunk, Ren nodded, and they pushed forward.

Ren leaped onto the trunk as Nyla dashed around the base. Allyn scuttled through the small opening, and he and Nyla appeared on the other side simultaneously, coming to an abrupt stop. The pristine snow was stained a deep crimson.

The space under the trunk had been dug out, and three walls of snow and ice had been constructed. Mason lay inside, slumped against one of the walls, his chin on his chest.

Nyla placed a hand on his chest as Ren jumped from the tree. From her perspective, only the blood would have been visible.

Mason's skin was ashen, and he didn't appear to be breathing. A tourniquet made from his torn shirt had been tied around his thigh, and below it, the meat of his leg was shredded, the bone visible but unbroken. Even if Mason was alive and Nyla could bring him back to consciousness, he wouldn't be walking anytime soon.

"He's alive," Nyla said. "But he's suffering from severe hypothermia and has lost a lot of blood. We'll have to splint the leg. There's nothing else I can do for it."

"Is he going to lose it?" Allyn asked.

"I don't know," Nyla said. "The snow slowed the degradation, but until we get him back to the cabin, I have no idea. I could try and heal part of the wound, but then you'd have *two* people to carry back."

"Do what you can," Ren said. "Get him ready to move as quickly as possible. I want to be back by midday. We can't get stranded out here." She turned to Allyn and leaned in close. "Remain here with them and stay alert. I'm going to circle the area."

"They're still out there, aren't they?" Allyn asked.

Ren nodded. "I didn't see any tracks leading away."

"They could have brushed them away."

"Undoubtedly," Ren said. "But only to mask where they're hiding, not where they were going."

"Then what are they waiting for?"

"An advantage."

"Don't you think we should stick together then?"

Ren gave him a bemused look.

"You're *trying* to lure them out," Allyn said.

Ren gave him a slight nod and darted off.

Allyn positioned himself with his back against the tree, keeping his eyes on landscape. The stillness mixed with his anxiety and played tricks on his eyes. The dark patches jutting out of the snow resembled hulking human shapes, ready to bound up and attack, and the sporadic breeze tickled the hairs on the back of his neck, sending shivers down his spine.

He wanted to ask Nyla to help him keep watch—there was too much ground to oversee—but she was busy.

A twig snapped in the distance.

Allyn whipped his head in its direction, but the same stillness that had pervaded the last several minutes lingered. He stared at the same patch of forest, almost willing someone to appear. And just as he was about to move on, another twig snapped—this time, accompanied by a moving black mass. Broad-shouldered, with a large head that looked larger because of a receding hairline, William slid out from behind a thick cedar tree. He stepped to the side, watching Allyn, a six-foot mass of bristling confidence and bravado.

Allyn held his arms wide, displaying the coils of electricity, and took a few steps forward in his own show of swagger. He hoped he looked stronger than he felt. *How many more times am I going to be in a kill-or-be-killed situation before I lose my mind?*

William squared up on him, menace in his eyes. William—like Riordan, Tomas, and the other would-be assassins—had infiltrated the McCollum Family for one purpose, and it wasn't to negotiate. Ren had been correct. These people wouldn't flee. They would regroup and try again. That's why William hadn't killed Mason—he'd used him as bait.

"How close is he?" Allyn asked Nyla.

"He's stable," Nyla said.

"Can he walk?"

"No."

"Then why don't you come out here and give me a hand."

Nyla looked up. Noticing William, she started, hitting her head on the bottom of the trunk. She cursed then ducked out from the shelter and circled wide, giving William two targets instead of one. Nyla would be ineffective at that distance, but if she could get close enough to touch him, she could force William under—if she didn't kill him first.

Air concussed in the distance. Allyn flinched and nearly missed the object streaking through the air in William's direction. Roughly the length of his arm and as thin as a finger, the clear object was filed to a point. William saw the ice blast too late. It took him in the chest, throwing him backward and impaling him against a tree with a solid *thunk*.

Ren emerged from a tangle of blackberry bushes. The air warped again, and Ren's second blast took William in the chest, mere inches from the first. Allyn watched in sickened awe. Ren was like a sniper—silent, accurate, and above all, effective. She nodded in Allyn's direction then made for William. Allyn followed.

William's head hung limply, and blood streaked down from the corners of his mouth, already drying in the cool air. Allyn hadn't noticed from the distance, but William had a nasty gash across his side. He'd tried to cauterize it but had done a sloppy job, and drops of blood still seeped from the burned flesh.

Ren grabbed William by his hair and yanked his head up. His face was pallid, his dark eyes devoid of life. Allyn's gut twisted, and his face grew hot as nausea washed over him.

*Another dead.* Not by his hands, but he'd still played a role. *It was him or you,* a distant voice said. But did that make it okay? Did that make it *right*? He was here to protect his family, not to fight. Not to kill. *Protection sometimes requires violence,* the voice said. Allyn didn't like it. *You don't need to,* the voice replied.

"You okay?" Ren asked. "You hurt?"

"No," Allyn said. "I'm fine." *I'm just having a silent argument with a voice inside my head. That's all. Nothing to worry about.*

"Good. Let's go." Ren started back toward Nyla and Mason.

"Are we just going to leave him here?" Allyn shouted after her.

"Yes."

Allyn looked over William. The two ice blasts that lanced through him would eventually melt, and his limp body would fall to the forest floor, to be picked apart by coyotes and wolves. Allyn had a hard time explaining why, but he felt the man deserved better.

"Allyn!" Ren's voice cut through him, bringing him back to the present. She and Nyla had pulled Mason from his shelter and were in the process of splinting his leg.

With a sigh, Allyn turned from William and started for the two women. They still had a lot of work to do. They would need to construct a litter for Mason, then drag him—uphill and through the forest, dense with snow and thick with underbrush.

Allyn's body began wailing again.

———————•••———————

Allyn felt as though a very large man were standing on his chest. His breathing came in short, agonizing breaths, and he found himself holding it in fear of the pain. But even then, the pain didn't go away. It had started as a dull ache he could ignore. But as they towed Mason's makeshift litter up the mountainside, Allyn's breathing had become more ragged; the pain nearly debilitating. And it was only getting worse.

*It's the air. It's freezing my lungs.* But he couldn't stop— they were almost there. He could see the top of the hill only a couple hundred feet above them.

He adjusted the rope over his shoulder and took another painful breath, continuing the trek upward. The rope was little more than braided vines that had been sheared clean of barbs and brambles. It stretched behind him, taut, attaching to the front of Mason's litter. Ren was a few paces to Allyn's side, pulling a second rope.

They'd begun in unison, pulling in a similar step and cadence, but as the ground had grown steeper and more treacherous, their stamina had waned and their cadence had become disjointed. Now they pulled as ragged individuals, each jockeying for the lead like a pair of thoroughbreds coming around the bend.

Nyla continued to monitor Mason, periodically calling for Allyn and Ren to rest. Mason had grown worse. His skin burned hot with fever, and he'd grown restless, tossing about in the litter and making Allyn and Ren's task more difficult. Nyla had retied the tourniquet around Mason's thigh and continued to clean his leg by having Ren use fire to melt snow and drip warm water across the wound. She occasionally took over the pulling duties for Ren or Allyn, but Allyn preferred her to stay with Mason. Nyla might have been able to do his job, but he couldn't do hers.

Allyn kept his head down, focusing on his individual steps and not the number he had left. He didn't want to look up. It was like looking down from something very high; it just made him uncomfortable. Even the short distance felt overwhelming.

So, focused on his feet, Allyn didn't see the magi assembling at the top of the hill until Ren and Nyla hooted in relief. He followed their gaze until he saw the party waiting for them. Brandt and Rory had already broken from the group and were dashing down the hillside to give them a hand. Allyn and Ren stopped and let the ropes drop. Allyn knew instantly that it was a mistake. He'd given in to his fatigue, and the powerful wave of exhaustion nearly dropped him.

"You found him," Brandt said as he neared. "How is he?"

Allyn was too exhausted to speak.

"We need to get him inside," Ren said.

"Let's get him home then," Brandt said. Allyn couldn't tell if the man was relieved or angry. Probably a mixture of both—he and the remaining refugees had a stake in Mason's well-being.

Brandt and Rory took the ropes and started up the hill. Allyn watched Mason pass by before taking his first step.

By the time Allyn reached the peak, Jaxon had arrived with Liam and Kendyl. Each wore a relieved expression and hit Allyn with an avalanche of questions. He ignored them, lumbering through the mass of people toward the cabin. His job was done—Leira, Vincent, and another cleric from the Hyland refugees were working with Nyla and seeing to Mason's wounds.

Allyn's body felt slow and unresponsive, and his vision

had narrowed to a tight tunnel. Someone took his arm and slung it over their shoulder, and together, they circled the cabin. Kendyl. Once inside, she let Allyn crash onto the nearest bunk. *I should take my boots off,* he thought, but decided against it—*too much work.*

"Onto your back," Kendyl said, lifting his leg onto the bunk.

He groaned and rolled away from her.

She slapped him.

Allyn blinked and rolled back to face her, consciousness coalescing around his anger. His skin burned where she'd slapped him.

"I said roll onto your back."

"You hit me." It was equal parts question, statement, and accusation.

"You weren't listening," Kendyl said. "You still aren't, so don't make me do it again. Now roll onto your back."

She slid off his boots and wet socks. They dropped to the floor with a solid *thud.* She pulled off his pants next then covered him with a blanket. "I'm going to get you something warm to drink. Whatever you do, don't let yourself fall asleep. I think you're suffering from hypothermia."

As Kendyl disappeared into the kitchen, the cabin door opened, and a chill blew through the room, halting any progress he had made in regulating his body temperature.

"How is he doing?" Liam asked.

"We need to keep him awake."

"I've got something for that."

Liam appeared beside Allyn's bunk a second later, computer in hand. His unsettling smile was too much teeth and not much else. "You better get well fast, Allyn."

Allyn grunted something that might have been construed as a question.

"You've got a meeting with J.P. Niall tonight."

# CHAPTER 19

AGENT MADDOX SLAMMED THE CASE file closed, feeling suddenly invigorated. He leaned back, contemplating the case. Had he really done it? Had Kaplan's location been in front of his face the entire time? It all seemed to make sense. Most criminals were caught with family or friends, and since Kaplan was short on both, he'd resort to different methods. But that didn't mean he hadn't followed the pattern. He'd returned somewhere familiar, a place he felt was safe. And that might have been his critical mistake.

Maddox grabbed the case file and stepped out of the quiet office. He'd left the main floor of the field office to get away from Nolan's incessant talking and commandeered one of the handful of vacant offices on the sixth floor. He enjoyed a little white noise while he worked, but he valued silence while he read.

As he stepped off the elevator on the third floor, Maddox quickly spotted Nolan huddled with a group of agents around Abernathy's computer. When Nolan saw Maddox approach, his smile faded quickly, and he broke away from the group to meet him at his desk.

"You look satisfied," Nolan said.

Maddox threw the case file onto his desk. "I found them."

"You... what?" Nolan glanced at the case file then back to Maddox. "Where?"

"Kaplan has a family cabin on Mount Hood."

"Maddox," Nolan said mournfully, "we've already been over this. The police have already searched the cabin. Remember? Twice. And they didn't find anything either time."

"That was before we found Kaplan at the manor." Maddox opened the case file and pulled out a history report. "Look at this. They sent officers to the cabin on the fourteenth and then again ten days later. But Kaplan wasn't found until the twenty-ninth. It's safe to assume that when the officers searched the cabin, Kaplan was at the manor, but after it burned, where did he go?"

Nolan sifted through the file. "It sounds too reckless," he said. "He commits a serious crime and then hides in a family cabin that he knows we'll search? It doesn't add up."

"You're the one who always said that Kaplan doesn't fit the profile."

"That's different. Kaplan is a highly educated man with a thriving career and an understanding of procedure. If he wanted to hide, he wouldn't do so in a place that's so vulnerable."

"Not unless he had to," Maddox said. "Where else would he go? He has no friends, no family, and we have his picture on every TV screen and computer monitor from Washington to Arizona. The cabin is familiar and isolated, two things our perp values."

"I suppose," Nolan said. "May I?" He gestured toward the computer.

"Go for it."

Nolan sat down and pulled the keyboard close, then cursed when it prompted him to log in. He turned to Maddox. "You mind?"

Maddox typed in his information.

"You really should think about changing your password," Nolan said.

"What do you mean?"

"Your ex-wife's name combined with your birthday isn't very secure."

"You watched me type in my password?"

"I couldn't help it," Nolan said. "You type like a gorilla." He made an exaggerated motion of someone typing with one finger.

"My fingers are too big for the keyboard."

"Said no man, ever." Nolan laughed and turned back to the computer. "What's the cabin's address?"

Maddox flipped through the file then set the information beside the keyboard so Nolan could see. Nolan's fingers were a blur on the keyboard, his eyes on the Internet browser.

*How can someone type without watching their fingers?*

"You might be onto something," Nolan pointed at the screen. The monitor displayed a topographical view of Portland and its surrounding areas, and a colored line traced a path from one point to another. "This is Kaplan's condo." Nolan indicated the first point. "His last known whereabouts. And this"—Nolan followed the path to the second point—"is the cabin. When you had me trace the traffic footage backward, we lost them somewhere around the I84, I205 intersection." He circled that area on the map.

"That's on the path," Maddox said.

"Yes, it is." Nolan leaned back, rubbing the stubble on his face. "If Kaplan had come from the cabin, he would have followed this path and hit every junction we've already connected him to."

Maddox slapped the back of Nolan's chair triumphantly. "Grab your coat."

"You're not really thinking of going out there tonight?"

"Of course I am."

"Maddox, it's nearly three hours away," Nolan said. "Send the local PD."

"They've already had their opportunity."

"I'm not saying for them to apprehend them. Just drive by and see if the lights are on."

Maddox hesitated. He was getting ahead of himself. Someone had helped Kaplan at the manor, and Maddox himself had spotted him with unknown associates. Kaplan had also shown he wasn't afraid to use violence or risk innocent lives. Maddox would have been entering a potentially hot situation without a proper team. Not to mention, their evidence was little more than circumstantial. They needed something more concrete before the higher-ups would allow him to assemble the proper strike team. Even then, it would take hours.

"You're right," Maddox said. "Make the call. Have local PD drive by. But do not, I repeat, do not allow them to initiate contact. They are to remain in their car, on the road, as far from the cabin as possible. This may be our last chance to apprehend him, and I will not see it botched because of shoddy work."

"What are you going to do?"

"I'm going to make sure we don't fuck this up."

# CHAPTER 20

THE REMAINDER OF THE EVENING inched by in a crawl. As soon as Nyla had said it was okay, Allyn fell into a fitful sleep, only to be woken by pain returning slowly to his body. His feet and calves had taken the worst abuse. What Allyn had thought were blisters on the bottoms of his feet were really just patches of raw, bloody skin. He walked tenderly on the sides of his feet, only to find that that put more stress on his cramping legs. His stomach rolled on itself, simultaneously hungry and tight, and the headache made it impossible to eat and keep it down. The little restless sleep he had gotten left him feeling worse.

Once, he'd woken to Nyla kneeling beside his bunk. She'd had her hand on him, but when she noticed he was awake, she promptly put him back under. When he awoke the next time, he thought that the pain had become a little more manageable, and it left him wanting to chastise Nyla. She was pushing herself too hard. They needed her more than they needed him. But he had a hard time criticizing someone for trying to help, especially when it left him feeling better.

Allyn still hadn't returned to full health by the time he got up. But the day was quickly fading, and lying down hurt more than standing did.

Allyn found a pair of clean pants folded and tucked under his bunk, along with a compression top and dry socks. Once dressed, Allyn walked gingerly through the great room, stretching the knots in his feet and legs, trying to regain some flexibility in the rest of his body. Fortunately, the pressure in his chest had eased significantly, and breathing was no longer painful. He nodded to a pair of magi who sat at the table, sharing a cup of tea and a quiet conversation. They returned the gesture and went back to their private discussion.

It wasn't until he walked into the kitchen that Allyn noticed the light in Jaxon's room was on. Allyn filled a glass of water and went to check on him.

Jaxon's door was pulled so only a crack of light escaped between the door and frame. Allyn heard the faint, rhythmic breathing of someone sleeping inside. He was about to turn back when the floor creaked. There was more than one person in the room. Allyn knocked quietly and, without waiting for a response, entered.

Jaxon sat on a chair beside the bed, his elbows on his knees, hands clasped in front of his mouth. He looked at Allyn and straightened before turning his attention back on the man lying on his bed.

Mason was unconscious, his chest rising and falling softly. His milky-white skin glistened in the dim light. Makeshift straps made of belts and rope hung from the edges of the bed where they'd been tied to the frame, and Mason's wrists and ankles were red where they'd been rubbed raw from fighting the binds. A bloody bandage covered the stump of his right leg.

Allyn's face grew hot. Cold sweat sent a chill through his body. They hadn't been fast enough. Allyn suddenly felt ashamed. His minor injuries were an irritant, nothing more than bumps and bruises. Mason had lost a *leg*. He would never be the same, never again able to do the things he'd done for nearly his entire life.

"They did everything they could." Jaxon's voice was soft. Somber. Allyn could hear the emotion that must be churning inside him.

"Does he know?"

Jaxon rubbed his forehead. "The pain was too intense for Leira to keep him under, and he was in and out of consciousness. There's no telling what he knows."

Allyn forced himself to look at the stump, swallowing the tightness in his throat. He'd seen too many wounds to be bothered by that anymore, but the thought of a man waking to find himself forever changed disturbed Allyn. Mason already had a chip larger than a continent on his shoulder. *What will become of him now?*

"He nearly killed me in the process." Jaxon held up his arms. His dark skin was freckled with large patches of pink and white skin—burns that had already been healed. Somewhere, a cleric was suffering from the pain and discomfort of treating the injury.

"Will he make it?" Allyn asked.

Jaxon stood with a sigh. "He should. Mason is the most stubborn man I've ever met. He may be slowed by the injury, but he won't be stopped."

"Is there any way I can help?"

"Mason will have to heal in his own way," Jaxon said. "He'll let us know what we can do."

Allyn pinched his forehead between his thumb and index finger.

"I know that look," Jaxon said.

"How's that?"

"Because I see it every day in the mirror. It's the look of guilt. And I'll tell you the same thing everyone tells me—it's not your fault."

*Does anyone else see his stress?* Allyn wondered. *The exhaustion? Do they even care?*

Allyn pursed his lips. He knew he shouldn't feel responsible for someone else's actions, but he'd told Jaxon they could trust the Hyland refugees, and if it weren't for that, Mason wouldn't have been fighting for his life.

"It doesn't make you feel any better, does it?"

"No," Allyn said. "I learned at an early age that the things I do and say have repercussions. That if I wanted to take credit when things went right, I have to be willing to accept the blame when they don't."

"My father taught me the same thing," Jaxon said. "The fact is, I wasn't entirely comfortable with the refuges, either. I had Mason shadow them for any suspicious activity. If it hadn't been for him, I'd probably be dead. So if you're responsible for Mason's injury, then so am I—and so is he, for agreeing to it."

"That doesn't bring back his leg."

"No, it doesn't," Jaxon said. "But either Mason accepts his new reality, or he doesn't. At this point, there's not much else he can do."

Leira entered the room, looking well rested but walking with a slight limp. Her arms were covered with bandages. She regarded Allyn for a moment before focusing on Mason.

"Has he woken up yet?" she asked.

"No," Jaxon said.

"Good." Leira sat on the edge of the bed and probed Mason. Ripples of light shot through his ashen skin, making it almost translucent. As they dissipated, Leira turned to Jaxon. "He'll be out for a while still. I'll take over if you want to go rest."

"Thank you," Jaxon said softly. He kissed Leira on the forehead then withdrew.

Allyn nodded his appreciation to Leira and followed Jaxon.

"Are you prepared for your meeting?" Jaxon asked once they were out of the room.

"I haven't had a lot of time to think about it," Allyn admitted.

"I have," Jaxon said. "And I want you to know that you won't be going alone. I'm coming with you, along with Nyla, Leira, Rory, and Ren. If this is some kind of trap, we will be prepared."

"Thank you."

"Prepare yourself," Jaxon said. "You've got a big night ahead of you."

———————

The compression armor sometimes felt like a straightjacket. Snug and warm, it didn't breathe particularly well, making him hot indoors, while doing little to keep him warm in the cool air outside. Worse, the top liked to ride up, creeping above his belt line to expose the soft pink skin underneath. Despite that, he'd grown used to the compression armor top—it was the bottoms hidden under a pair of jeans that were bugging him.

Like the top, they were restrictive and resisted movement, almost as if he were wearing a sports brace on his knees and elbows, making walking and running awkward. They pinched the inside of his legs and caused his sweaty areas to chafe. Part of him wondered if the light armor was worth the uncomfortable distraction. They were, after all, only good for a glancing blow, but like a soldier wearing Kevlar on the front lines, Allyn figured a little protection could be the difference between life and death.

"You didn't hear me, did you?" Liam asked.

Allyn looked up. "Hmmm?"

Liam's face flushed, and Allyn quickly realized he had probably been talking for several minutes without realizing no one was paying attention.

"I said I made a couple modifications to your phone," Liam repeated.

"Oh," Allyn said. "Sorry. What kind?"

Liam shook his head—whether he was amused or annoyed, Allyn couldn't tell—and handed Allyn his phone. At a quick glance, it didn't appear any different.

"I tapped into your GPS," Liam said, "so that it sends me a continuous signal. I should be able to track you wherever you go."

"Assuming I have my phone."

"Are you planning on losing it somewhere?"

"No."

"Didn't think so," Liam chided. "Short of implanting a transmitter under your skin, this is the best we've got."

"I'll go with this."

"I figured you would."

Allyn slipped the phone into his jeans pocket. "Thank you."

"No problem. Just get us some answers."

The sun had fallen low on the horizon by the time Allyn made it outside. The low-hanging clouds glowed with violent colors. *Not a sign of things to come, I hope*, Allyn thought, pulling at the tight collar of his compression armor.

Kendyl waited for him with Jaxon and the rest of the squad. Her face was tight, nervousness hidden behind a façade of strength. It made her look angry and filled him with a grim sense of determination.

"Time to go," Allyn said. He tried to keep his voice warm and playful as if he was going to meet up with an old friend for a drink.

"Be safe," Kendyl said.

"I will."

She didn't need to say anything more. They all understood the risks and rewards.

*Time to go.*

"Someone is definitely living up there," Agent Maddox said, hanging up his phone. He leaned back in his chair, turning to face Nolan, who sat across the aisle. The rest of the floor was largely vacant, since most of the agents had left for the night. For an investigative unit, it was strange how many of its agents clung to normal business hours.

"The power's on?" Nolan asked then glanced at the clock on the wall.

Maddox nodded. "Can you believe it? They go through so much trouble to disappear, and they're undone by something as simple as the electricity bill."

"When was it turned on?"

"Two days ago."

Nolan raised an eyebrow. "So much for coincidences then."

"Has local PD put any eyes on the residence yet?"

"Not yet."

Maddox cursed. "What's taking so long?"

"It's a large county, and they're understaffed."

"You told them who we're dealing with, right?"

"I did," Nolan said. "But local emergencies take priority."

"Call them again, and this time, make it clear that we expect an answer within the hour. I'm putting in the paperwork—we already have enough to go on. Kaplan's going down."

# CHAPTER 21

THREE HOURS AFTER LEAVING THE cabin, Allyn walked into the diner. It had a retro feel, with black-and-white-tiled floors and red leather booths that circled a kitchen at the center of the restaurant. A jukebox played an oldies station across the PA, and it smelled of chocolate shakes and freshly cooked fries.

Allyn picked a booth at the back of the restaurant, near the emergency exit that overlooked the empty parking lot. His waitress, a bubbly high school girl with a blond ponytail wrapped with a red ribbon, came to take his order. Early for the meeting, Allyn stalled by asking for a few more minutes to go over the menu.

He breathed a sigh of relief when she smiled and bobbed away without seeming to recognize him. It was one of the reasons he'd chosen this particular restaurant—its workforce was made up almost entirely of high school kids. Allyn doubted they would make the connection between the man coming in for a late bite and the fugitive he really was.

Allyn, along with Jaxon, Leira, Nyla, Rory, and Ren had arrived early enough to patrol the surrounding area. Finding nothing amiss, Jaxon positioned Leira and Rory near the front of the restaurant—far enough away not to be conspicuous, but close enough to quickly respond—and Nyla at the back, where she stalked the shadows between the emergency exit and the kitchen entrance. If anyone entered the restaurant, the McCollums would know. Ren remained in the car, listening to an online police scanner.

Jaxon entered after Allyn and chose a booth a few tables behind him, with a clear view of him and the front door. He gave Allyn a slight nod then looked down at the menu.

The minutes crawled by, and Allyn had difficulty watching anything but the front door. He'd finally had to order the third time the waitress came to the table, lest he look like a transient seeking the warm, dry confines of the building. He wasn't hungry, but the menu made him salivate. His diet since joining the McCollum Family had been far different than he was accustomed to. High in protein with plenty of greens, it lacked the grease, salt, and saturated fat he craved. Looking at the menu was like coming across a picture of his old college friends. He missed the reckless good times they'd had together.

Allyn's phone vibrated, announcing the meeting time. He straightened in the booth, eyes fixated on the entrance, and waited.

Five minutes past the set meeting time, Allyn tore his eyes away from the entrance. The street and parking lot were quiet, not another car or pedestrian. *Where is he?*

His food arrived—a bacon cheeseburger on a toasted bun, all the fixings except mayonnaise, and a plate of hand-cut fries. It glistened under the florescent light. Jaxon gave him a crooked smile and shook his head.

The bell above the door jingled.

Allyn stood abruptly. The man who entered the diner was roughly his age, though taller by at least a few inches, with broad shoulders and a square face. His blond hair was cut short and styled meticulously, matching the sharp lines of his dark suit. He was a man among boys and walked with a swagger that knew it. Confident. Assertive. Authoritative. It was the walk of a cop.

Special Agent Gary Nolan.

Agent Nolan saw Allyn from across the diner and stopped short, as if surprised to see him. Was this J.P. Niall, or was it an unlucky coincidence?

Allyn turned to Jaxon. He remained seated, though his eyes were wide with surprise. He recognized the man, too.

Allyn didn't move. He wasn't sure why. Everything in him told him to run.

Agent Nolan glanced behind him—he was alone—and made for Allyn, holding his hands in front of him submissively. "It's me," he said. "Please don't run." Nolan glanced at Jaxon as he approached, assessing the threat. "I'm here to talk. Nothing more."

"You?" Allyn asked.

The blond waitress emerged from the server station, her warm smile at odds with the tense situation, and arrived as Nolan slipped into Allyn's booth.

"Sit," Nolan said. "Please." The sincerity in his voice did little to ease Allyn's nerves.

Allyn sat reluctantly, his sweaty palms on top of the table.

"Hi there," the waitress said, placing a napkin and a glass of water in front of Agent Nolan. "Can I get something for you, too?"

Agent Nolan undid the top button of his jacket and placed an arm across the back of the booth, feigning nonchalance. "I'll take a coffee," he said. "Black. And... that actually looks pretty good, too. I'll have what he's having."

The waitress flashed a perfect smile and left to fill the order.

Nolan leaned over the table and clasped his hands together. He spoke in a quiet tone as if he were sharing secrets among adversaries. "I apologize for being late. Getting away from the office was... difficult."

"I'm confused," Allyn said. "Are you here to arrest me?"

"Arrest you?" Nolan asked. "Allyn, it's *me*. You have my computer. We've been in communication for the past twenty-four hours."

Allyn couldn't help it—he glanced around the diner and strained to get a better view of the parking lot, which was still quiet.

"I assure you, nobody but me knows you're here."

"But...why?"

"For the same reason you're here, I assume." Nolan leaned in a little closer. "For answers."

"But you're a cop."

"A federal agent, actually," Nolan corrected. "But that doesn't mean I have all the answers, especially for what I'm looking for."

Allyn shifted in his seat.

"If it makes you more comfortable," Nolan said, "your friend over there is welcome to join us."

Allyn glanced at Jaxon. He remained in his seat but had given up all pretense of being a casual observer. He stared at Allyn and Nolan, appearing not to have heard Nolan's invitation.

"It's okay," Allyn said, steeling himself. "I'm good."

Though Jaxon's presence would have calmed Allyn's anxiety, Jaxon would have dictated the direction of the conversation, and Allyn wasn't ready to give up control. They were here because of his curiosity. For better or worse, this was Allyn's play, and it was his responsibility to see it through.

"What are you looking for?" Allyn asked.

"For you, of course," Nolan said. "Haven't I made that clear?"

"But *why*?"

"You intrigue me, Allyn," Nolan said. "What makes a man who has it all suddenly throw it all away?"

*This is it,* Allyn realized. *This is my opportunity to clear my name.*

"Whatever you think I did, I'm innocent." Allyn winced at the words. He remembered saying something similar to Michael Clarke, the partner at his old law firm. They had sounded like a cliché then, and they still did.

"I have no doubt," Nolan said. "So why don't you tell me what really happened?"

Allyn licked his lips. *Could it really be so simple?* Allyn paused. He didn't have anything to lose, but something didn't feel right. This conversation wasn't supposed to be about him.

"What do you really want to know?" Allyn asked.

"The truth, Allyn."

"The truth about what?" Allyn asked. "You're not here for me. Your computer was filled with dozens of folders about other people. What are you really searching for?"

Agent Nolan transformed in front of Allyn. It was a subtle thing, but Allyn spotted it. Nolan's posture slumped; the air of confidence, bravado, and superiority wilted. Nolan was no longer a federal agent. He was a man who was as lost and confused as any other.

"I'm not lying when I say that I've been looking for you, Allyn," Nolan said. Even his voice sounded different. "I've been searching for you long before you were on the FBI's radar. Maybe not you specifically, but someone *like* you. Someone like me."

*My God,* Allyn thought. *It's true.* "You can wield."

Nolan met his eye and set his jaw. "Is that what you call it?"

"It's what *they* call it," Allyn said, nodding toward Jaxon.

"They?" Nolan asked. "There are more?"

Allyn nodded.

"How many?"

Allyn opened his mouth to speak but hesitated. The

conversation felt too much like an interrogation for his liking. He needed to be the one asking the questions.

The waitress returned with Nolan's coffee.

"How long have you been able to wield?" Allyn asked, as the waitress disappeared into the kitchen.

"Since I was a teenager," Nolan said.

"What happened?"

"My older brother," Nolan said. "He was a real piece of shit. He used to beat me up for fun. Out of boredom. One day, things got a little too heated, and he had me pinned to the ground with a knee in my chest. I couldn't breathe. He was going to kill me—I knew it—and I *snapped*. One moment, he was on top of me. The next... he wasn't."

"You killed him?"

"No. But he never messed with me again." Nolan took a sip of coffee. "What about you? When did you start... wielding?" The word sounded awkward coming out of his mouth.

Allyn shrugged. "I don't know. A month, maybe?"

"A month?" Nolan repeated, arching an eyebrow. "That's after your sister disappeared."

Allyn nodded. "You said you wanted to know why someone who had it all was willing to give it all up. Well, there you go."

"What happened?"

Allyn took a sip of water, deciding how much he was willing to divulge. Whether Nolan was a magi or not, he was still one of the men charged with bringing him into custody.

*He confided in* you.

Allyn began telling his story. It was rough, and he often had to backtrack to fill Nolan in on a detail he'd forgotten, but he got it out. He began with the attack at his condo and ended with the manor burning to the ground. Allyn wasn't about to give him their current whereabouts.

"That explains why you didn't go to the police," Nolan said.

"They wouldn't have done any good. I knew who had Kendyl, and I knew who'd help me get her back."

"She's well then, I take it?" Nolan asked.

"Yes."

"And she'd be willing to corroborate your story?"

"Of course."

"I'm not sure how much I can help you," Nolan said. "My partner isn't one who cares about guilt or innocence. That's not our job, he says. Our superiors put a name in front of him, and he finds them—it's as simple as that."

A sinking feeling crept into Allyn's gut—no matter what he did, no matter where he went, someone like Agent Maddox would always be searching for him. *Impossible as it may be, disappearing may be our only option.*

"I'll do what the magi have always done then," Allyn said. "I'll hide."

Nolan stirred anxiously. His eyes flicked away from Allyn's.

"What?" Allyn asked. "Do you know something?"

Nolan gave him a sidelong glance, his face troubled.

"Tell me."

"Maddox knows about the cabin."

The sinking feeling in Allyn's stomach became full-blown terror. Adrenaline pumped through his veins, mixing with the panic, making him feel light and unsteady. "The cabin?" he asked, doing his best to feign confusion. "I don't know what you're talking about."

"The Kaplan family cabin," Nolan said. "Surely you knew you couldn't hide there forever."

*I've been trying to convince Jaxon of that since the moment we arrived. It was only supposed to be temporary.*

"I've tried to stall him," Nolan continued. "Hiding information, sabotaging leads—I had to be sure about you. But I can only stall him for so long. He's coming, Allyn, and there's nothing I can do to stop him."

"How long do we have?"

"Not long," Nolan said. "He's assembling a team as we speak. I don't think I can hold him back beyond tomorrow."

Allyn pinched his forehead. He'd known this moment would come ever since he'd suggested hiding in the cabin, but he'd hoped they would have other possibilities before that time came. Instead, it was just like that night in the woods. They were alone with nowhere to go and no one to turn to.

"There's nothing you can do?" Allyn asked.

"I've already done all I can," Nolan said. "Warning you is the best I can do at this point."

"Then come with us." The words slipped out of Allyn's mouth before he knew what he was saying.

"What?"

"You're one of us," Allyn said. "You belong with the magi."

"Allyn—"

"No," Allyn continued. He was finally putting words to the feeling that had been building inside him since the first time he realized he could wield. "I know it's terrifying, but this *thing* that separates us makes us special. It doesn't set us apart—it brings us together. You're already breaking the law by just meeting with me. What do you have to lose?"

"You think you have a lot of heat on you now, Allyn?" Nolan asked. "You think you have nowhere to hide? Well, imagine the attention I'd receive if I fled with a wanted man. It would blow into a nationwide manhunt. Every agent, every bureau, every state and local cop would be searching for the two of us. As tempting as the offer is, it's just not possible."

"You know how the system works," Allyn said, refusing to give up. "You could anticipate their moves. With your help, we could lay low until it blew over."

Nolan shook his head. "It would never blow over. The search never stops, Allyn. The case never closes. I'm sorry, but there's nothing more I can do. Get yourself to safety."

Nolan stood from the table, his eyes darting around the room. "I've already been here for too long. Thank you for the offer, Allyn. It means more than you will ever know. I'll be in touch when I can."

With that, Nolan gave him a curt nod and rushed for the door, nearly crashing into the waitress, who was just appearing out of the kitchen with his food.

Jaxon approached. "He left in a hurry."

"He took a great risk by coming here," Allyn said.

"What did you learn?'

"He said they know about the cabin. They're coming for us."

"Can we trust him?"

"I think so," Allyn said. "He's one of us, Jaxon. He doesn't know it yet, but he is."

"Then we need to go," Jaxon said. "We don't have much time."

Allyn left his half-eaten dinner behind. It had sounded better than it tasted, and the meal had settled like a brick in his stomach. The waitress called for them to have a good evening as they exited the restaurant.

Their car was parked under a burnt-out street lamp in the far corner of the parking lot, Ren's silhouette barely visible inside.

Jaxon stopped.

Allyn noticed too late and bounced off Jaxon's powerful frame with a grunt. The blow knocked the wind out of him—it was like running into a boulder. Collecting himself, Allyn followed Jaxon's gaze.

Nolan was standing outside the window of a new Chevy Impala, talking to the driver. The car was running. Nolan's nervous body language made Allyn uncomfortable. He tapped his fingers against the roof of the car, making as little eye contact with the driver as possible. He glanced over his shoulder, noticing Allyn and Jaxon, his eyes growing wide. The driver peered around Nolan, following his gaze.

He was a behemoth of a man whose head nearly touched the roof of the car. Completely bald, he wore a dark suit much like Nolan's that seemed somehow stiffer, with straighter lines, as if it had been cut from cardboard.

Allyn cursed. He'd seen the man before.

Special Agent Richard Maddox.

# CHAPTER 22

AGENT MADDOX KICKED OPEN THE door, slamming it into Agent Nolan's shoulder and knocking him out of the way. He was out of the car in an instant, his hand going to the inside of his jacket for his sidearm.

Allyn shoved Jaxon forward then bolted across the empty parking lot. He raced toward their car—there was nothing but open blacktop between him and it. Nowhere to hide. Nowhere to take cover. He thought he heard Jaxon's footsteps behind him, but he wasn't sure. It might have been the deep booming noise of his blood pulsing through his ears. *Where's Nyla? Where were Leira and Rory?*

Gunshots ripped through the night.

Allyn stumbled, covering his head, waiting for the inevitable searing pain that accompanied a gunshot wound.

"Freeze!"

It might have been years of societal influences or his fear of being shot, but Allyn froze. No sooner had he slid to a halt than a powerful force slammed into him. Allyn hit the ground hard, slapping onto the blacktop. Jaxon landed on him, pushing the air from his lungs. The black mass of muscle and might rolled off him, landing in a crouch. Allyn struggled to his side, blinking away pain.

Gun raised, Maddox advanced, shouting instructions into his radio.

Nolan remained still, eyes darting between Allyn and Maddox, watching the scene play out.

*Where the hell are the other magi?*

"Stay on the ground!" Maddox was only a couple of parking spaces away, his voice booming. "Hands on top of your heads. Do it now!"

Allyn leaned on an elbow, placing his off hand on his head. The power raged inside him, mixing with adrenaline. Most times, he had to pull it out of him, to *project* it, but the power boiled through him like expanding gases within a canister, ready to explode. Allyn fought to wrestle it under control. Maddox would accurately see the magic as a threat and react accordingly, and Allyn wasn't willing to kill the agent just so he could save his own skin.

"I said, put your fucking hands on your fucking head!"

Jaxon had remained crouching on the balls of his feet, hands at his sides, fingers splayed. Maddox recognized the threat but not the extent. Jaxon rose slowly. He was steady and cautious yet confident.

"Last chance," Maddox said coldly. "Get on the ground with your hands on your head, or I will bury a bullet in your chest."

Jaxon rose and squared on Maddox.

Maddox fired.

Jaxon cried out and dropped to the ground, clutching his thigh.

"No!" Rory and Leira rounded the corner of the restaurant at a full sprint.

Maddox turned on them, gun at the ready. Blue light enveloped Rory's hands as shards of ice formed in his palms. He hurled them forward. More shots split the night, and Leira and Rory dove for cover. The ice blast narrowly missed Maddox, whipping at his suit jacket as it zipped past.

Vague comprehension formed on his face, and his expression hardened.

"Stop!" Nolan bellowed.

Nobody complied.

Rory was on his knees, wielding fire. Unlike the ice, which could disappear in the darkness, the fire burned bright, streaking across the empty parking lot like a meteor entering the atmosphere. Maddox dove to the side, avoiding the fireball.

Allyn checked on Jaxon. He was on the ground, a few feet away, still clutching his leg. The blacktop beneath it was dark with blood. "How bad?" Allyn asked.

"I'm fine," Jaxon grumbled, gritting his teeth. "Help me up."

Allyn took his hand and pulled. Jaxon's injured leg was like a deep root that wasn't ready to be unearthed, and it took nearly everything Allyn had, but he got Jaxon on his feet. Rory and Leira's entering the fray left Allyn and Jaxon on the outskirts of the battle, and nothing was between them and the car. Ren was still waiting there, taking cover behind an opened door, watching. Maddox had his back to them. Occupied with Leira and Rory, he would never notice Allyn and Jaxon slipping away, but Jaxon didn't show any signs of wanting to flee.

Leira and Rory cut the distance between them and Maddox in half then split to flank him. Maddox followed Rory with his eyes, clearly considering him the greater threat.

Another shot echoed through the empty streets. The battle froze. Attention turned to Nolan. He stood with his gun in the air, his other hand outstretched as if he were preparing to wield. He leveled the pistol on Rory. "Stop," he commanded. "And place your hands behind your head. Make one move, and I pull this trigger."

Rory didn't have a chance to obey. Maddox fired, and Rory crumpled to the ground, writhing in pain.

Allyn felt the heat before he saw the flame wrap around Jaxon's arm.

"Jaxon!" he screamed.

But there was no stopping the man. Maddox turned just as Jaxon threw the blast. It didn't take the shape of a fireball. Pure flame erupted from Jaxon's hands. It sped toward Maddox, tendrils of fire stretching forward like a living creature seeking Maddox's flesh.

"No!"

A flash of light sparked in the distance, and a white orb collided with the flame. It exploded, and a violent shockwave hurled everyone away from the blast.

Allyn found himself on the ground, his hands raw and clothing torn from sliding across the blacktop. His face was singed, and he tentatively brought a hand to it. Hot but not bloody. A minor burn. Jaxon was beside him, groaning as he rolled onto his back.

A figure stepped forward, his hands glowing with white light. Nolan. With one glowing hand pointed toward Allyn and Jaxon, he held out the other to help Maddox to his feet. The older agent cowered, shielding himself as if he were afraid his partner was about to strike him.

"Come on." Nolan waved Maddox up. "On your feet."

Maddox found his gun and stood, keeping his distance from the younger agent. He remained silent, but there was fury in his eyes.

"Cuff them," Nolan said.

Maddox shook himself out of his stupor, bringing his gun back up to point it at Jaxon. He approached cautiously, though any pretense of fighting seemed to have drained from Jaxon. Nolan's attack had left more than just Maddox wary.

"What are you doing?" Allyn asked. "You're not one of *them*."

Nolan gave him a quizzical expression but said nothing, instead covering his partner as he rolled Jaxon onto his stomach to cuff his hands behind his back. Leira was tending to Rory several paces away, while Nyla was—

*Nyla!*

As silent and nimble as a lioness, she dashed forward, using her dark compression armor to blend into the shadows. Her silver hair was pulled back into a tight bun and covered with a hood.

"I'm sorry, Allyn," Nolan said. Then quieter, he added, "This wasn't how this was supposed to go." He never noticed Nyla sneaking up behind him.

Her hands snaked forward, taking Nolan by the sides of his face. A bright light flared on contact, illuminating the insides of Nolan's eyes as if he were a jack-o'-lantern. He went limp then fell to the ground, unconscious. Before Maddox had a chance to turn, Nyla was on him, too. She struck hard, kicking Maddox's wrist as he pulled Jaxon's arms behind his back. Maddox cried out in pain and turned just as Nyla drove her knee into his face. He fell onto his back, and Nyla landed on top of him, pinning his arms to the ground with her knees. Just as she'd done Nolan, she gripped Maddox's face and forced him under. She rose, looking over her shoulder at Allyn and Jaxon.

Allyn jumped to his feet, biting back pain. The shockwave had hurled him a good ten feet, and his chest felt as if it had been kicked in. He and Nyla pulled Jaxon up, and Allyn shouldered the injured man.

"You're hurt," Nyla said, gesturing toward Jaxon's bleeding leg.

"I'll be fine," Jaxon said. "Check on Rory."

Nyla dashed across the parking lot, sliding to a stop beside Rory. The young man was flat on his back, arms and legs spread to the sides. His breathing was quick and shallow. Leira had ripped open his shirt at the shoulder. Using the torn cloth to keep the wound clean, she worked in quick bursts to heal him. Gunshots were difficult to treat. The entry wound was the least of their concern—the shockwave the bullet created when it punctured the body caused all sorts of tissue damage, and if the bullet had ricocheted off a bone... *They know what they're doing.*

"What do we do with them?" Allyn asked, looking at the unconscious men in front of him.

"Leave them," Jaxon said.

"Nolan is one of us."

"He might be able to wield," Jaxon said. "But he's not one of us. You don't believe this was a coincidence, do you?"

*I don't know what I believe.* Nolan's actions seemed at odds with his words.

"You're too trusting, Allyn," Jaxon continued. "This is the same situation as the Hyland refugees. If you don't learn, people will continue to use your credulity against you."

Allyn took a deep breath. Jaxon was right. His decisions continued to lead to his friends getting hurt.

"We need to get your leg looked at," Allyn said, thinking of Mason. "We can't lose you, too."

"Later," Jaxon said. "Right now, we need to get back to the cabin."

Jaxon raised his hand into the air and beckoned Ren forward. The sedan roared as Ren raced across the parking lot like a teenager driving for the first time without her parents. She skidded to a halt, car tires squealing and filling the air with the scent of burnt rubber.

Allyn helped Jaxon hobble to the car. Allyn threw open the back door, and Jaxon fell into the backseat.

"Scoot over," Allyn said, opening the driver's door.

Ren frowned but complied, and Allyn moved the car alongside Rory and the two clerics. They lifted the injured magi, and Allyn jumped out of the car to open the back door so they could slide him inside. Rory was still conscious and obviously in pain. The left side of his shirt was soaked with blood, but the bullet seemed to have missed any vital organs.

Rory gave Allyn a small smile—his teeth were stained red. The magi took pride in their injuries, like boys showing off their scars to impress a girl.

Shaking his head, Allyn returned to the driver's door, stopping with one leg inside the vehicle. Sirens rang in the distance.

Allyn cursed, sliding inside the vehicle. He stomped on the gas pedal, and the car lurched forward. Tires howled as he tried to put distance between them and the restaurant. The injured magi groaned and cursed at him from the backseat. Allyn apologized, and once they were several blocks away, he slowed down.

He used the side streets to bypass major intersections, and by the time they'd driven several miles, he felt safe enough to make for the interstate.

When the city proper was in their rearview, everyone breathed a sigh of relief. It was to be short lived, however, because within a matter of hours, the cabin would be swarming with feds. And if they had any chance of surviving, they needed to be long gone by the time that happened.

---

Special Agent Gary Nolan awoke to find himself in handcuffs. He was groggy and disoriented, as if he'd woken from a long night of heavy drinking. His head throbbed, pounding with the beat of his heart, and was made worse by his sudden sensitivity to light. His body ached, and his left leg was asleep. The handcuffs, which pinched his wrists and dug into his lower back, had been put on too tightly.

*Maddox*, Nolan thought.

He was in the back of a squad car. Red and blue lights flashed in a steady rhythm that could have sent an epileptic into a seizure. The black leather backseat was cold and sticky. Steel bars covered the windows and separated the front seat from the back, creating a small cage that resembled a prison cell. It made Nolan claustrophobic. He shut his eyes, trying to work through his calming exercise and slow his accelerating heartbeat. The space wasn't too confining, but he had an irrational fear that he would never get out. That he was stuck. Confined. Caged. His chest grew tight, and he began to hyperventilate. His face felt flushed as the hot flash took him.

*Steady*, Nolan told himself. *Breath through it.* He kept his eyes closed, forcing himself to take a series of exaggerated breaths. He imagined an expansive blue sky. Freedom.

*It's temporary*, he thought, filling his lungs.

*You'll get out,* he told himself, exhaling.

*It's temporary.*

The actions gave him something to focus on other than the mounting panic attack, and he felt his nerves relax with each breath. Eventually, the symptoms retreated enough that he was able to open his eyes. He would never be cured of claustrophobia—he still felt lightheaded—and the rest of the symptoms could flare up again at any moment. For the moment, though, he had it under control.

The squad car was parked at the edge of the diner parking lot, and a mass of cops and detectives swarmed the area cordoned off by yellow police tape. From his obscured vantage, Nolan could make out detectives taking pictures of chalk tracings and yellow identifier tags, which likely marked bloodstains, bullet casings, or other small forms of evidence. Other officers had pulled aside the restaurant staff, to take statements and information, while even more were inside the diner, dusting for prints or viewing the surveillance footage.

Nolan cursed under his breath, shifting uncomfortably. *They have me. There's no getting out of this one.* The surveillance footage alone would show him arriving at the scene a full hour before Maddox and meeting with a fugitive alone. It would also show him leaving him behind un-apprehended.

*But will it show the shootout in the parking lot where*

*I...*Nolan stopped short. That line of thinking would lead nowhere. *What's done is done.* He couldn't do anything about it now. Besides, he wasn't sure he would have done anything differently. He had to know who he was. He had to know if he was alone. *It was worth the risk.* Still, he still had to be prepared with a story to justify his actions. Something that would, at the very least, give Maddox and the other detectives pause until he was able to come up with something cleaner.

*You're in cuffs, moron. There is no giving them pause. They have you—but I saved Maddox's life. That has to count for something, doesn't it?* The cold steel biting into his wrists suggested otherwise.

Maddox came into view a short time later, walking with a pudgy detective wearing a tan trench coat that went down to his shins.

*He's giving a statement*, Nolan thought. He wished he could hear what Maddox was saying. Loyalty was everything to the man. He wouldn't stab Nolan in the back, would he? *He also believes in order.* What ran deeper—Maddox's sense of loyalty or his dedication to order?

The car rocked to the side as Maddox climbed into the driver's seat. He sat silently for a moment, refusing to look at Nolan, then finally took a deep breath and started the engine.

"Maddox—" Nolan started.

"Not now," Maddox said sharply.

"But—"

"I said *not now*."

Pushing the issue wouldn't get him anywhere with a man like Maddox. Better to remain quiet and let him direct the conversation when he was ready. That time came when Maddox pulled into an empty parking lot in the industrial district under the Freemont Bridge. A series of grimy warehouses with flaking paint and boarded-up windows covered the landscape. Graffitied railcars lined the tracks behind them, and the air was thick with the smell of diesel fumes, coal, and blue-collar labor.

Maddox shut off the engine and turned slightly, so that one half of his face was hidden in shadow. "You lied to me."

"Maddox—"

"Let me talk," Maddox snapped. "I never should have trusted you. I should have seen it from the beginning—a fresh recruit with a spotty past, your infatuation with the library, the leak. I don't know who you are, but you're *not* my partner."

"I saved your life."

"You're one of *them.*"

"Maddox," Nolan said. "I don't know what you're talking about."

"Damn it, Nolan!" Maddox barked. "I *saw* you. I saw them. I saw..." Maddox pinched the bridge of his nose and closed his eyes as if he were unwilling to believe what he'd seen.

Nolan knew the feeling well. The confusion. The fear of going mad. The fear of being a freak. Differences didn't bring people together. They drove them apart. They made the world think in terms of "us versus them." And Nolan was *one of them.* Regardless of what Maddox believed, though, Nolan respected him.

He thought briefly about telling him the truth. He'd met with Allyn because they were different—outcasts. Nobody knew what it was like to be truly alone, always hiding, but Allyn did. Something had made him leave behind a successful career, and Nolan believed it had to do with his abilities. In that, they were similar. And it meant neither was forced to live in isolation anymore.

*You're one of us.*

*Us.* The word had a strange meaning, and it stirred a deep longing inside Nolan. The bureau was a tight community of like-minded men and women, and they often used words like *us* or *we,* but Nolan had never felt fully part of that brotherhood. When Allyn had said it, he'd meant it *because* of their shared abilities, not in spite of them.

But how could he explain all of that to Maddox? He was far from a sentimental man, and his belief system didn't allow for emotional weakness. In Maddox's eyes, Nolan had broken the law and needed to be disciplined accordingly. Nolan couldn't escape imprisonment by catering to Maddox's supposed sentimental side.

"How long have you been working against me, Nolan?"

"What?"

"You're working with them."

Nolan cursed under his breath. The improbable task had just become impossible.

"Maddox," Nolan said, "I'm not working with anyone but you."

"Bullshit!" Maddox slapped the steering wheel. "You thought you could sneak behind my back? You've been leaking information through this entire investigation, always keeping Kaplan one step ahead."

"You don't know everything you think you know."

"Really?" Maddox turned to face him. "I spoke with the Hood River Police Department. They said they never received a call from the FBI to look into Kaplan's cabin."

"Maddox—"

"You never called them, Nolan, because you knew Kaplan was hiding up there. You purposely sabotaged my investigation."

"It's not what you think," Nolan said.

"I had you followed," Maddox said. "You were at that diner for nearly an hour with the very man we were supposed to catch, and you really expect me to believe you're not working together?"

"If I was working with them," Nolan said, "then why didn't I run with them? Why stay behind?"

"Maybe they were done with you." Maddox's expression

turned hard. "I know *I am*. I'm going to bury you, Nolan. I hope you like those bars back there, because you're going to be seeing a lot more of them."

"Maddox," Nolan said. "He reached out to me. I was going to call you in once I knew it was him!" It wasn't entirely true, but that really didn't matter.

Maddox remained silent, putting the car in gear.

"He's afraid," Nolan continued. "He's looking to make a deal, to come in. He just needed to be pushed in the right direction—he couldn't be forced. That's why I didn't tell you." Now he was flat-out lying, but he was growing desperate. "Maddox? Maddox! Answer me!"

Maddox pulled the car back onto the road and continued toward the Steel Bridge. That would lead them into downtown, to the detention center. Maddox had made up his mind.

"No," Nolan said. The walls closed in again. Heart racing, he slammed his eyes closed, but instead of quiet solitude, he was somewhere else. Another tight space. A cage. He heard Sam's high-pitched, maniacal laugh, muffled by the pale-gray walls of the cage. Slits had been cut into the side, allowing for slivers of light to pour through. A dark shadow paced outside.

*Not again.*

The cage smelled of dog and urine. His urine. He imagined himself sliding to the back of the plastic kennel, hugging his knees, bending his head awkwardly under the low ceiling. Sam beat on the outside of the cage as he ran circles around it, shouting curses at Nolan, telling him he would never let him out. It was a game to Sam. Make Nolan a pet. Command him. Make him obey.

Shadow, their old dog, was supposed to help Sam, calm him by giving him something that depended on him. It had only turned him into a full-blown psychopath. And after Sam had been caught throwing firecrackers at the dog, Shadow

237

had gone to better owners, and Sam's wrath had been redirected twofold on Nolan.

Nolan opened his eyes. He was back in the police car. Maddox watched him from the rearview mirror, smiling, taking pleasure in seeing Nolan trapped. The air disappeared from Nolan's lungs, and he slammed his eyes shut again, trying to recall his calming exercise.

Sam sat on his chest. Nolan fought, trying to roll his brother off him, but he was too strong. Sam hadn't been a big kid—in fact, he had been long and skinny, with sharp elbows and exposed ribs—but he was older than Nolan by four years and stronger with age. Sam wriggled, driving his tailbone into Nolan's sternum. Nolan tried to yell for his mom's help, but Sam covered his mouth with his hand. Nolan's weak cry barely reached his own ears. His eyes burned. Tears streamed down his face. He was going to die.

Sam laughed, encouraged by Nolan's silent pleas, and raised a fist. Nolan barely saw the blow coming before his vision went white. The blows continued. More pain. Blood mixed with tears.

Desperation swelled inside Nolan, cultivating something along with it. A buried instinct. His need to survive. His desire to fight. He wasn't a cornered animal anymore—he was alone in a vast vacuum. It was dark, and Nolan struggled to orient himself. Sam wasn't the problem. Nolan was. He was too willing to roll over. To hide. To cry. Not anymore. Sam wouldn't be stopped by a pet or responsibility. He wouldn't be stopped until someone made *him* the victim.

The blows continued to rain down. Nolan barely felt them anymore, as if his newfound inner strength made him immune to them. Holding onto his tether of desperation, he knew what to do.

Nolan let the desperation fill him, strengthening him. He arched his back, heaving Sam off. His eyes snapped open—

The car lurched. The seatbelt snapped taut, digging into

Nolan's chest as the momentum carried him forward. His head narrowly missed slamming into the Plexiglas barrier. The car came to a rest in the middle of the street, in a haze of blue smoke. Gravel from the center lane rattled against the undercarriage.

Maddox turned to Nolan, his eyes wide with terror. A car barreled toward them from behind, its headlights painting the inside of their car with white light. Maddox reached for something—a black object that seemed to absorb the light rather than reflect it.

A gun. He shouted something that Nolan couldn't make out.

The light grew blinding as the car approached. *No*, Nolan realized. *There is no car.* He tore his eyes off the gun. His hands, still cuffed behind his back, glowed up to his elbows, clearly visible under his starched white shirt. It pulsed, matching the speed of his heartbeat. A haze almost like vapor distorted the air around his arms, creating shimmering light.

*The light hasn't been this bright since—*

"Stop!" Maddox had the gun leveled at him.

Nolan looked down the barrel of the gun, unflinching. The tool scared him less than the confinement did. Besides, the three-inch glass was bulletproof. The worst a gunshot would do inside the car was deafen each of them. If Maddox truly wanted to shoot Nolan, he would have to get out of the car. Maddox seemed to realize this, met Nolan's eye, and flung open his door.

Nolan turned his back to the door as Maddox approached, sliding as far to the other side of the car as he could get. He knew that look in Maddox's eye. He'd seen it too many times before in Sam's. He'd stood up to him once—he could do so again. The door popped open, and Nolan *released*.

His hands, pointed at the door, grew so bright that they seemed to suck in the light around them. The light that had crept up his arms disappeared, pooling into his hands, then exploded.

The release of energy sounded like a freight truck rumbling down a cavernous tunnel. Deep. Vast. Powerful. A split second later, the window to the door Maddox was opening shattered. The door shrieked in a terrible symphony of metal on metal as it was ripped off the hinge. Like the recoil of a large-caliber gun, the release of power should have propelled Nolan in the opposite direction, but it didn't—it had never worked like that. The energy went one way, like a flashlight, never affecting him.

By the time Nolan turned to look, Maddox was on the ground, still clutching the handle of the driver's side door resting on top of him. The older agent was unconscious, and blood streaked from a small cut on his forehead.

Nolan looked on, half expecting the man to rise, the other half fearing he was dead. It had happened so fast. One moment, he'd been trying to calm himself, and the next... *I won't be caged again.* Feeling suddenly confident, Nolan inched his way out of the car and made for Maddox. He found the keys to the cuffs on Maddox's belt and made quick use of them. Dropping the cuffs to the ground, he massaged his wrists, quickly surveying his surroundings.

Across the street was a MAX station—a covered pavilion similar to a bus stop with benches and kiosks to buy tickets. Light-rail tracks wrapped around the station, making it into a concrete island of public transportation that extended for nearly a full city block. This particular stop was a hub for MAX transit and would have normally been teeming with riders, but it was, save for a homeless man sleeping on one of the benches, empty during the odd hour.

The cut on Maddox's brow was superficial and already beginning to clot. His breathing was strong, and Nolan couldn't find anything else wrong with the man. Nolan took the gun and the second revolver that Maddox kept hidden in his ankle holster and tossed them into the car. He took Maddox's cell phone, looked at the fallen man one last time, and returned to the car.

Once he was several miles away, he called it in. *Officer down. Suspect fled. Send medical.* Nolan hoped Maddox would understand, but he was doubtful. Still, knowing he'd done everything he could eased the knot in Nolan's stomach.

He merged onto I84, heading east, praying a squad car driving down the interstate with a missing door wouldn't draw too much attention.

*You're one of us*, Allyn had said.

It was time to find out what that really meant.

# CHAPTER 23

THE CABIN WAS IN A state of organized chaos. Chaotic because the McCollum Family was once again forced to flee the place they called home, but organized because they had been through it before. Liam supposed it helped that nearly everything they had ever owned had burned with the manor—they had very little to pack.

Jaxon's word had come down hard and fast, and with very little information. All Liam knew was that they'd run into some kind of trouble and were en route back to the cabin. He was to prepare the Family to run. That hadn't stopped the rest of the Family from bombarding him with questions and constant requests for updates—well after he'd made it clear that he hadn't been given any.

Finally tired of the repeated distractions, Liam had activated the GPS on Allyn's phone and broadcasted it through his computer on the dining room table. The blue circle on the colorful topographical map drew ever closer to the densely wooded area around the cabin, acting as a visual countdown. It had all but ended the questions. The closer Allyn's signal came, the closer their answers were.

During his efforts to organize the Family's remaining unpacked contents, he saw Vincent and Joyce sneak away into the garage. The way Vincent held the door open for Joyce while surveying the grounds to make sure no one was watching told Liam they were hiding something. *But what? And of all times, why now?*

Liam had enough to do without digging into their secrets—and he was more than a little afraid that he'd walk in on something he would rather not see—but he needed all hands assisting him with the preparations. So despite his better judgment, he followed.

He entered through the side door, sneaking into the dusty confines of the seldom-used garage. When the Hyland refugees had arrived, there had been brief discussion of housing them in the garage, but its thin, un-insulated walls did little to keep out the bite of winter. It was better to be uncomfortable in the house than dead in the garage.

A few boxes of old belongings lined the shelves, while rusted tools, loose nails, and scraps of molded wood littered an old workbench at the head of the garage. The room was dark, and dust tickled the back of his throat. Liam had to swallow then breathe through his nose to keep from coughing. The air smelled of sweat and spoiled gasoline.

Liam made for a room adjacent to the main space, and he was halfway across the room when he heard a sharp gasp. He stopped, his heart suddenly pounding in his throat.

"It's okay," Joyce said. "It's okay. It's me."

Heavy breathing. Rustling.

Liam crept forward.

"It's me," Joyce repeated. "Look at me. Can you hear me? Relax."

The door to the room was only halfway closed. Liam leaned into it with his shoulder, peeking inside. Joyce stood beside an old metal bedframe, a pale, slender hand in hers. Two feet, hidden under a thick comforter, wrestled aimlessly, and with her other hand, Joyce patted the person's leg in what he assumed was supposed to be a calming gesture. He couldn't see the person's face.

Liam pushed the door open a little more.

"Canary," Joyce continued. "Canary, can you hear me?"

The door squeaked.

Liam froze.

Joyce looked up from the bed, locking eyes with him. Before Liam could utter a word, the door handle was ripped out of his hands, and Vincent appeared on the other side of the door. The soft man wasn't much taller than Liam, and he'd gone completely bald in recent years. His eyes, magnified by thick prescription glasses, were full of shock and fear. He looked from Liam to the bed.

Liam followed his gaze. He knew the girl in the bed. Yellow and black streaked hair. A heart-shaped face. Creamy tan skin.

Canary mumbled so quickly that Liam couldn't pick up more than one word in five—but her deep, emerald-colored eyes told him everything he needed to hear. *Help me.*

"What in the name of our First Families is going on here?"

---

The trip back to the cabin was the longest commute of Allyn's life. Jaxon held Rory down against the backseat by his shoulders while Leira and Nyla operated. They couldn't heal the wound until the bullet was removed, and without the proper medical equipment, they'd been forced to use more barbaric methods. Leira, with the slenderest fingers, had dug through the wound, tearing Rory's skin like a hole in a pair of denim jeans as she searched for the slug.

Nyla had pushed Rory under, but the pain was too great, her pool of exhaustion too shallow to keep him there. He awoke with every attempt, screaming, kicking, thrashing, and tearing his wound even more. And each time, they had to start over. Blood stained each of their hands and was soaking into the backseat. The metallic stench was so strong that Allyn could taste it.

It took them nearly an hour to find and remove the bullet, and by then, a nervous energy filled the car. Nyla and Leira shared the burden, taking on Rory's injuries equally. They didn't heal him completely; doing so would have incapacitated the two of them, but they went far enough to stop the bleeding and close the wound. Rory wouldn't have use of his arm for a while, but he wouldn't bleed to death, either.

In an effort to escape the procedure in the backseat, Allyn had coached himself through the night's events. Nolan had all but confirmed he was a magi, and then in the melee, he'd proven it. What had that light been? Not fire, ice, or electricity. *Some kind of energy maybe?*

The one thing Allyn did know: Nolan was powerful. He only wished he knew whose side the man was on.

The look of genuine surprise on Maddox's face when he'd seen Allyn exiting the diner had been enough to convince him that Maddox hadn't expected to see him. Or Maddox was the best actor Allyn had ever seen. *Not likely.* But that didn't rule out the idea that it all could have been a ruse, with Nolan acting as the bait and calling Maddox in to apprehend him. However, that didn't make much sense, either. Why not surround the diner with undercover officers? Call in the cavalry once they identified him or after Nolan's informal questioning? If Nolan had truly intended to capture him, he'd had plenty of opportunities.

*Then why side with Maddox?*

The questions gnawed at Allyn's insides, tickling his brain like an elusive word on the tip of his tongue. It was right *there*. He just couldn't connect the dots, and he ran out of road before he solved the puzzle.

He didn't know what he'd expected to see in the cabin, but he hadn't expected the scene to be so methodical. The McCollum magi teemed about the cabin, organized, loading their few belongings onto the porch. As it stood, Allyn didn't know how they were going to transport the entire Family and the Hyland refugees, let alone their belongings. And where were they headed? Jaxon hadn't given him any indication.

*One thing at a time. You can't worry about tomorrow until you take care of today.*

Liam rushed out of the cabin just as Jaxon pulled Rory from the backseat and handed him off to Leira and Nyla. Liam didn't slow—he hit Jaxon square in the midsection, throwing the injured man to the ground. It wasn't until then that Allyn saw the tears in Liam's eyes.

"Liam!" Allyn shouted.

"How could you?" Liam asked, his voice shaking. He kicked at Jaxon wildly, missing as often as he connected.

"Liam!" Allyn grabbed him from behind and dragged him away from Jaxon, catching an elbow in the ribs for his efforts. "Liam, stop! What's gotten into you?"

"He betrayed us!"

"What?"

Leira and Nyla stopped, turned, and faced the commotion.

"You ordered her isolation," Liam yelled. "You forced her under." He kicked again but was too far away. All it did was fling snow across Jaxon's dark face. "How could you? How *could* you?"

"Liam," Allyn said. "Liam, slow down. Back up. I don't understand what you're saying." He felt Liam's body relax then let go of the boy.

Liam turned to face him. "Canary is sick," he said softly. "And they didn't know how to treat her, so Jaxon isolated her from the Family and kept her unconscious."

Allyn blinked. Liam might as well have hit him. Allyn was dazed. He looked from Liam to Jaxon, hoping to see confusion and bewilderment on Jaxon's face, but the man's expression remained blank. He stood, using the car for leverage.

"Is that true?" Allyn asked.

246

Jaxon didn't look at him.

"Jaxon?" Allyn said. "Is that true?" He said each word slowly, drawing them out for effect.

"She's unstable," Jaxon said. "We had to do something."

The world suddenly shrank, as if he were looking at it through a straw. Everything in his peripheral vision dissolved into nothingness. Jaxon and Liam were all that remained.

"You knowingly divided this Family?" Allyn asked.

Jaxon met Allyn's eye. His expression had gone cold. "I did what I had to do to hold the Family together."

Allyn harnessed the anger inside him, ready to wield if needed. He'd never seen this kind of fury in Jaxon. He was worried the man might strike.

"It was for the best," Jaxon continued.

"The best for what?" Allyn said. "Because it certainly isn't the best for this Family."

"The other Families won't help us because we appear weak. We need symbols of strength, Allyn. And she is not it."

"That doesn't make it right," Allyn said.

"I didn't say it was right," Jaxon said. "I said it was necessary. How do you expect us to attract other Families when we can't even hold ourselves together?"

"You don't see it, do you?" Liam asked. "You're just like *them*. The other Families won't help us because they're worried about what the other Families will think, or that we'll somehow drag them down. Now, we won't even help our own because we're concerned about what *they* think? That's not the Family my father died to protect."

Jaxon exhaled. He seemed to deflate, becoming less intimidating. Less menacing. More human. For the first time since Allyn had known him, he saw Jaxon as an equal. Magi or not, born leader or not, Jaxon was capable of making mistakes.

It might have been the weight of responsibility or the difference between their two cultures, but Jaxon had always

247

seemed older than Allyn. It made him easy to look up to, easier to follow. Surprisingly, his mistakes made him easy to relate to, easier to empathize with. Allyn felt his anger dissipating. It was quickly replaced by embarrassment for having been, in some way, a part of Jaxon's decision. He should have seen it. He should have said something. Allyn had seen Canary's deteriorating mental state—they all had—but he'd kept his distance. If he'd been more proactive, or if he'd worked with her... but he hadn't. And something dark had happened under his watch.

Resolve crystalized inside him—the need to fix the mistake and make sure it never happened again.

"We'll make it right, Liam," Allyn said. "But right now, we have the whole Family to think about. The FBI is coming, and they don't want to play."

---

"Agent Nolan is J.P. Niall?" Kendyl asked.

Allyn nodded, stifling a yawn. Dawn was only a few hours off, and already, the black sky was closer to a dark shade of purple. He sat with Kendyl and Liam on the front porch, happy to be away from Jaxon but struggling to keep warm. A worthy sacrifice. The man had crawled inside himself, ignoring Allyn and Liam as if they, too, were having nervous breakdowns. The cabin's activity had slowed to a crawl as most of the inhabitants were resting, but Allyn couldn't sleep. Not after the night he'd had.

Allyn didn't know how many of the Family would continue to follow Jaxon, but for the moment, Jaxon continued issuing orders, and they kept following them. Brandt, Juniette, and the rest of the Hyland refugees were on their way with Jaxon to pick up a fleet of cargo vans. Allyn hadn't asked what they were for, and Jaxon hadn't offered the information.

Nolan had said they had less than a day before Maddox would arrive at the cabin with an assault team, but that was before Maddox had arrived at the diner. *Who knows how long we have now?* Chances were, it was a lot less time.

The impulsive thing to do would be to flee into the forest, but Allyn was still recovering from the day he had spent in its wintery embrace. That was at the bottom of the list of last resorts. Whatever Jaxon was planning, it still seemed to be their best option.

"I should have seen it," Liam said.

"How?" Allyn asked.

"I didn't realize it at first," Liam said. "But it's a code. J.P. Niall is a name in one of the diaries I transcribed—one of the diaries still in the library."

"He wanted us to know it was him," Allyn said.

"Yeah," Liam said. "But why?"

"Maybe he wanted us to trust him," Kendyl said.

"To what end?" Liam asked. "What did he want?"

"He's searching for answers," Allyn said. "He's like me—a man stuck between two worlds."

"He's trying to find out where he belongs," Kendyl said.

"Or find out what he is," Allyn agreed.

"And now that he knows," Liam said, "what's he going to do?"

"That's what confuses me the most," Allyn said. "He wasn't going to arrest me. He let me go, but his partner showed up right as we were leaving, and *he* had other ideas. Jaxon was going to killed him, but Nolan revealed himself and saved Maddox's life."

"Maddox saw him?" Liam asked.

Allyn nodded. "Yeah, and I don't know what kind of ability he has, Liam, but he's more than a magi. Nolan is one of us—a machinist."

Liam shook his head in apparent disbelief. They'd been thinking about other machinists since Allyn and Liam had realized what was happening with the magi numbers, but they hadn't actually found any. The idea that the FBI agent tasked with finding them was one would be enough to rattle the entire magi community to its core. Not only were magi living among normal people, but there was also a new breed of magi.

"You're sure Maddox saw him?" Kendyl asked.

"Positive."

Kendyl and Liam exchanged a look.

"What?" Allyn asked.

"That's not going to be good," Kendyl said.

"No, it's not," Liam agreed.

"You think Nolan's in trouble?" Allyn asked.

"You said it yourself," Kendyl said. "He let you go. Then he revealed himself as a magi. Whether he saved his partner's life or not, Agent Nolan just became a suspect."

*Of course!* Based on the little information Allyn had, Agent Maddox was an overzealous agent. His dedication to law and order pushed him to the extremes of what his position allowed. Someone like Maddox would ride the line of what was morally justified, always staying just within the confines of the law. There was no room for sentimentality. Actions were lawful, or they weren't.

Agent Nolan had broken the law then compounded the mistake by outing himself. Maddox would certainly book him for his crimes, then the revelation would call into question every interaction, discussion, and situation they'd been through. In revealing himself, Nolan had buried his own career. And his own partner would see it done.

*No wonder he was so reluctant to get involved in the fray. And why he'd been so secretive online.* He understood the stakes. Allyn suddenly felt a strong connection to the man. Nolan's situation was even more complex than his had been. He had more to lose and less to gain. Allyn's decision to leave his life behind had been an easy one on the surface—Kendyl was more important than anything else in his life—but Nolan didn't have that. What drove him was something much less tangible.

Answers.

And those were a lot easier to take away.

———————— ••• ————————

Finding the story was simple. It was listed under the breaking news at the top of the *Oregonian* website. Local diner. Shots fired. Officer injured. Suspects on the loose. Inside was a cryptic message about an FBI agent being sought for information. They didn't name him, and they didn't imply he was a suspect, but his mention in the story told Allyn everything he needed to know. Nolan was going to take the fall.

If Nolan was "being sought for information," then the authorities didn't have him in custody. Allyn found himself cheering for the man. If Nolan, an FBI agent on the run from every law enforcement agency in the country, could escape, then so could the McCollums. Allyn wished he had a way to contact Nolan, to help him learn from the mistakes he'd made. Fixing Nolan's life, helping him find what he was looking for, would be like fixing his own.

Allyn had Liam set up a Google alert for Agent Nolan. Any time his name was mentioned online, it would be flagged and Google would send an alert to Liam's e-mail. Allyn suspected the activity would spike early then slow to a trickle as the story grew older. In time, Nolan's name, much like Allyn's, would be buried by other, more pressing issues. And they would be forgotten—or so Allyn hoped.

*The search never stops.* Nolan's words floated in the back of Allyn's head like an annoying insect on a muggy summer day. He couldn't get away from them. The idea went against common wisdom. His case would surely remain open, and there would always be automated alerts set up any time he used a credit card, accessed bank information, or attempted to travel overseas, but nobody would be actively searching for him. Concern for the investigation would be replaced by interest in true conspiracies, terrorists, and federal emergencies.

*The case never closes.*

Allyn sighed. He was going in circles, and none of it mattered. *You can't worry about what you can't control.* He left the computer and his thoughts behind, seeking out Jaxon. The man had returned a short time ago with a host of white cargo vans, which they were loading with the last of the Family's belongings. Jaxon hadn't made it clear where they were headed, only that he would decide and that he had a plan.

*At least one of us does.* Ever since Lukas had attacked him in his condo, Allyn felt as though he'd been *re*acting instead of acting. Waiting for the other guy to move so he knew how to respond. Playing defense. But that was a losing strategy. At some point, the other guy would make a move he didn't see coming, and he wouldn't respond quickly enough. Success was the gift of proactivity, and the time had come to be proactive.

Allyn stepped outside just as the squad car with a missing door pulled into the driveway.

The cabin grounds went still as a dozen magi froze in their steps. They watched the squad car the same way a spooked dog might an intruder—alert and ready to strike. From Allyn's vantage on the raised porch, he had a good view over the top of the cargo vans. The squad car's lights weren't flashing, and other than the missing door, the car appeared unmarred.

The driver was but a shadow inside and as still as the magi who looked on.

*Where are the rest? Where are the other officers?* Allyn wondered, trying to see through the foliage on either side of the driveway. No lights. No sounds. Something was off.

252

Maddox wouldn't have sent only a single squad car. He would have come with a full team of heavily armored, heavily armed professionals.

Allyn took the steps slowly, keeping his eyes locked on the car, weaving through the cargo vans and magi. "Get inside," he told them. They didn't listen. The cabin didn't offer any safety that they didn't already have in numbers.

The squad car continued to run, humming softly. Allyn slipped through the throng of magi, and as he came to the forefront, the shadow inside the car shifted. The driver's door popped open.

The air cracked behind Allyn—the sound of someone wielding—and a flurry of activity happened all at once. Voices rose as panic finally became more powerful than inaction, and magi rushed inside to warn the rest and gather support. Others formed up behind Allyn, fireballs and ice blasts at the ready. Allyn glanced over his shoulder, surprised to find Brandt and a number of the Hyland refugees standing with him.

The figure rose from the car.

"Nolan?"

"Allyn," Nolan said, his voice tight. He surveyed the force behind Allyn, trained eyes assessing the threat. He must not have liked the conclusion he came to, because a moment later, his hands and wrists glowed white with energy. The glow gathered in his palms as if he were holding it, and it pulsed with intensity, almost like the waves of energy a cleric used when healing. It grew brighter, then fainter, with a steady rhythm. The air distorted around it, like steam rising from wet blacktop during a hot day.

Allyn resisted the urge to wield, afraid doing so would incite an attack. "What are you doing here?"

"Is there a way we could talk... privately?"

"We're a Family here, Nolan. We don't keep any secrets." Allyn wasn't sure where Jaxon was—he should have been outside, overseeing the operation—but he hoped the man had heard him.

Nolan met his eyes. He didn't have the same intensity as his partner did, but he was obviously used to others doing as he said.

The pause in their conversation was filled by a series of heavy footsteps. Allyn didn't have to turn to know it was Jaxon approaching. He stopped at Allyn's shoulder, glancing between him and Nolan.

Nolan blinked first, exhaling a long, deep breath. The light in his hands dimmed, and though it didn't dissipate entirely, it did grow less threatening. Allyn turned to the magi behind him, motioning for them to also stand down. They complied.

"What happened?" Allyn asked, returning his attention back to Nolan.

"They tried to arrest me." Nolan's voice took on a softer tone, somewhere between sullen and honest. "My *partner* tried to arrest me. He's afraid of me, I suppose. Thinks because I'm like you that I've been working with you to undermine his case."

"Haven't you?"

Guilt washed over Nolan's expression, and he looked at his feet.

"What was your plan?" Allyn pressed. "You posted the video to find me, but what were you going to do when you did? Were you ever really going to arrest the man who could give you answers? Who could help you understand who you are?"

Nolan radiated a defiant silence.

"I didn't think so," Allyn said. "You never intended to do anything. You just hadn't realized it yet."

Nolan's head dipped, and he blinked rapidly. He looked at Jaxon then back at Allyn. "Is your offer still good? Will you still take me in as one of you?"

Jaxon shot Allyn a nervous look. He hadn't heard Allyn's

offer, and his body language suggested he didn't approve. A murmur swelled through the watching magi crowd.

Allyn met Jaxon's gaze. The man was apprehensive, though since he hadn't spoken up, the clues were likely noticeable only to Allyn. Eyes slightly narrowed. Jaw clamped down. Chin tilted toward his chest.

*He's waiting to see what I do. And he knows he can still overrule me.*

Nolan stirred, his words hanging in the air. His appearance of authority had vanished and been replaced by a terrified man looking for help.

A realization bloomed in Allyn's chest—Nolan had inside knowledge of FBI tactics and procedures. He had access to their databases, files, and records. He was the person they needed to undercut the FBI investigation and get a head start. But would Nolan do it?

He had rejected Allyn's original offer, choosing instead to try to arrest them. Then he showed up, hoping the offer was still good. Nolan didn't know what he wanted, and that made him a hard man to trust.

Allyn glanced at the crowd behind him. All eyes were on him. The McCollum Family, Jaxon, Nolan... the Hyland refugees.

He'd stood in the same spot, having the same discussion with Brandt and the rest of them, and he had chosen to trust them. He'd brought them in because he sympathized with their struggle, and Jaxon and Liam had nearly been assassinated because of it. Mason had suffered a life-altering injury. Four magi were dead. Allyn had vowed to learn from that mistake. But there he was, prepared to make it again.

*No. This is different.* The situation might have been similar, but the circumstances were different. Nolan wasn't Brandt, Riordan, or William. He was his own man, with his own intentions. The assassination attempts had been prevented, and the Hylands who truly needed their help had received it.

That wasn't a mistake. Trust *wasn't* a mistake. He'd made a mistake when he'd accepted them as their own and let down his guard. The insurgents had exploited that, driven a wedge between the two Families, and made Allyn second-guess his instincts. He wasn't going to let them win.

"Yes," Allyn said. "The offer is still good."

# CHAPTER 24

"**B**UT UNDER ONE CONDITION," ALLYN continued. "You're one of us. That means if we go up against the police, the FBI, or your partner, you fight with us. No hesitation. No second guessing."

"If you're asking me to kill..." Nolan swallowed hard.

"Nobody is saying that," Allyn said. "But you said they're coming, and when they do, I'm sure they're coming with force. If that happens, I can't be concerned about your allegiances."

"I understand," Nolan said.

"I need an answer."

"I'll do what needs to be done."

"Good," Allyn said. "Second—"

"I thought you said you had one condition?"

"I was a lawyer not an accountant. Numbers aren't my thing," Allyn said.

"Fair enough."

"Then second, you have access to FBI databases and case files. I need you to delete, alter, or submit fake information. Anything you can do to slow the investigation down, I need you to do it."

"I'm sure my access has been restricted by now."

Allyn cursed. He should have thought of that. "We'll

have to try anyway. The last condition—unless I think of something else—is that you stay with me. Always. Period. No exceptions."

"I can do that."

"Good." Allyn turned to Jaxon. He spoke quietly and firmly, having a private conversation among a dozen onlookers. "You can overrule me if you need to, but know that if you agree, he's my responsibility."

"He pointed a gun at me," Jaxon said, still focused on Nolan.

"Yep."

"And he tried to arrest us."

"He did."

"And still, you want to bring him in."

"He didn't have a choice." Allyn inched closer to Jaxon's ear. He didn't want Nolan to overhear the argument.

"You always have a choice."

"And he's making his," Allyn said. "I know what you're afraid of, but he let us go. He never intended to arrest us."

"I don't trust him."

"You don't have to," Allyn said. "But trust me."

Jaxon finally turned to Allyn. "We've been down this path before, Allyn. And it hasn't ended well. Why will this time be any different?"

"He's a machinist," Allyn said. "Isn't that worth the risk?"

"That doesn't mean he's one of us."

"Neither was I," Allyn said. "But give him time, and he can be."

Jaxon took a slow breath. "This is your last chance, Allyn. If this goes wrong..."

"I understand," he said. "I accept the risk."

Jaxon's eyes expressed little emotion, but he nodded slightly then bellowed in his deep voice for all to hear, "Back to work!"

The crowd of onlookers dissipated, making for the cabin at their own pace.

"Ditch the car," Jaxon said to Allyn. "And find me when you're done."

———————————————

Allyn and Nolan ditched the car on an overgrown logging road a little more than a mile from the cabin. It would eventually be found, but it wouldn't be found at the cabin when Maddox arrived with his strike team. He might suspect Nolan was with the McCollum Family, but he would have no way to prove it—not until he found the car, and Allyn hoped to be in the clear by then.

They took the pair of handguns Nolan had taken from Maddox, extra magazines, a shotgun with extra shells, the first-aid kit, emergency blankets, a radio, a scanner, and other miscellaneous equipment before ditching the car then made their way back to the cabin.

"Why did you do it?" Nolan asked once they'd returned to the main road. The mountain road had little traffic and was never plowed, but the snow was still packed and easier to traverse. "Why did you take me in?"

"Because you tried to help," Allyn said. "And we're a little short on trust these days. Plus... well, I don't have time to get into all of it now, but know this: not all magi are friendly. As a whole, they're secretive and distrustful. They've been through horrors you and I can't begin to imagine, and that's left scars. For some, those scars have made them hostile. This is a transformative time for the magi community, and believe it or not, you're an integral part of that."

"How?"

"Until very recently, magi were capable of only two things: wielding elemental-style magic—fire, water, and air—or healing. But about the same time I was introduced to their world, we learned about a new kind of magi. People like us, whose abilities extend beyond those limitations. We're different. And this Family believes magi like us are the future of the magi race."

Nolan took in the information with the cold expression only a cop with years of training could. Allyn yearned to know what he was thinking. He'd been on the opposite end of this conversation and knew firsthand how confusing it could be. He liked to think he had taken it in stride, but really, he had lived in shock for days. Even though he'd witnessed magi wielding firsthand, even had it used to hurt him, he hadn't truly believed until he uncovered the ability within himself. Nolan had an advantage in already knowing he could wield. Where the magi world was forced on Allyn, Nolan was actively seeking it.

"What does your magic look like?" Nolan asked.

Some things are better shown than explained. On command, the red coils of electricity sprung to life around Allyn's arms, humming in the early morning air.

Nolan stopped, his eyes wide. "What is that?" he whispered.

"Electricity," Allyn said. "Produced by the electrical system inside my heart."

"In your heart?"

"Yeah," Allyn said. "All magic has costs. When a magi wields fire, they're using the heat from their body to create combustion. When they wield air, they're pulling it out of their bloodstream. Water, from their body. Pull too much, and it will kill them. Our magic is different. It still has its limits, but it's also sustainable."

Something clicked inside Nolan; Allyn could see it in the way the corners of his mouth turned up into a small, satisfied grin. Answers to a lifelong question sparkled in his eyes. "That makes sense," he said. "But your heart doesn't produce that much electricity. Where does it all come from?"

"We don't know," Allyn said. "It's almost like fire where a spark ignites flame, and it grows from there. My body doesn't produce this much electricity, but once the current is created, maybe it's able to expand. The truth is, we're a new breed of magi, and we have more questions than answers. But we do know this: all magic has limits, and this isn't any different." He let the coils dissipate.

As if to show his own since Allyn had displayed his, Nolan's arms began to glow. The white light extended out from his hands and wrists. The air distorted around it, as if he were pulling the energy into himself. Allyn thought he could almost feel heat radiating from it.

"What is it?" Allyn asked.

"It doesn't sound much different from yours," Nolan said.

When he looked at it directly, the white light burned an afterimage in Allyn's eyes, but it lacked the sinister quality of Allyn's electricity.

"It just manifests differently."

"As what?"

"My best guess?" Nolan said. "Raw energy."

"Kinetic or thermal?"

"I don't know the difference."

"Is it stored or absorbed?" Allyn asked.

Nolan shook his head. "No idea."

"Where does it come from? Do you have to spend hours resting in order to build a reservoir of energy, or does it come from another source?"

"I..." Nolan looked confused.

"How do you feel afterward? Drained? Does it replenish quickly?"

"A little of both, maybe," Nolan said, wincing. "I'm sorry. I don't know."

"It's okay," Allyn said. "We'll figure it out later. But right now, we need to get back."

Jaxon was waiting for them at the mouth of the driveway when they returned. He watched as they approached, distrust painted on his face. The cabin grounds had gone still. The swarm of magi was back inside.

"It's done," Allyn said then held up the guns and other police equipment they'd taken from the car. "We took everything we thought might be useful."

"Good," Jaxon said.

"What's the plan?" Allyn asked. "Where are we running? Who's taking us in?"

"We're not running."

"But—" Allyn started.

"They're coming," Nolan said, interrupting. "Soon. And you don't want to be here when they arrive."

"I have no intention of doing so," Jaxon said. "This is our opportunity. They think they know where we are, and they're coming in hot and strong. But we're going to take the fight to them."

"I don't understand," Allyn said.

"The library," Jaxon said. "We need that information. It's the only thing of value we can offer another Family. Nobody will take us in unless we have it."

"You'll have to contend with local PD," Nolan said. "It's under twenty-four-hour security."

"Can we get by?" Allyn asked.

"If you know what you're doing," Nolan said.

"It's a good thing we've got a guy on the inside then, isn't it?" Allyn said. He turned to Jaxon. "What's the play?"

"We take everyone," Jaxon said. "Sneak in, secure the manor, begin moving the library, and be out before anyone on the outside ever knows we were there."

Allyn mulled it over. Jaxon made it sound as if they would be strolling through the booths at the Portland Saturday Market, but they were assaulting a highly sought-after piece of property, guarded by at least half a dozen armed and trained police officers with reinforcements only one call away. The

McCollums had the strength. Allyn wasn't concerned about that, but these things never went according to plan.

If they disabled security. If they got into the library. And if they succeeded. What then? There were thousands of books with another hundred or so pieces of incredibly fragile artwork. Allyn wasn't sure they would have enough time to move everything before the radio silence from the manor tipped Maddox off to their new whereabouts.

*And yet, Jaxon's right.* The library was the key to everything. To unraveling the mysteries of Liam's book. To rebuilding the image of the McCollum Family. To finding someone to take them in. They needed leverage.

"It's not going to be that easy," Allyn said.

"It never is."

"We'll need eyes on the ground," Allyn said. "Someone scouting the area, watching patrols and crew shifts."

"It's already been done."

*Was that triumph in Jaxon's expression? Gratification? Relief?*

"When?" Allyn scanned the driveway, counting the cars. Each of the cargo vans was accounted for.

"When we picked up the cargo vans," Jaxon said.

"Who?" Allyn asked.

"Nyla and Ren. They'll have the grounds scouted with a plan in place by the time we get there."

Allyn was growing excited—he couldn't help it. It was the same action-versus-inaction dilemma he'd had before. The prospect of actively doing something, even if it was risky, was enticing.

"Say this succeeds," Allyn said. "Where do we go?"

"The Green Manor."

"Your Family will take us in?"

"They will if they want their son back," Jaxon said.

They could scout, plan, and move against the library when they were ready, but seeking asylum with Jaxon's Family meant Wesley and Talisa Green were the decision makers. The McCollum Family would be powerless.

"That's not a lot to go on," Allyn said.

"You asked me to trust you," Jaxon said. "Now I'm asking you to do the same. Let me worry about my Family."

He wanted to say that trusting Jaxon would have been easier had he not knowingly isolated the one member of the Family who needed the most help, but he left it alone—calling that to attention would get them nowhere.

"I just don't like stepping into a situation where I have no control," Allyn said. "You know how it is."

"I do," Jaxon said. "And I really wish we had that luxury. Instead, we need to focus on what we can control. Right now, that's staying cohesive and alert. By this time tomorrow, we should be free of police pursuit."

———

"We're doing it," Liam said. "We're finally going after the library." He bounced about, excited and giddy, talking to himself as much as anyone else. He was like an over-excited puppy seeing its family after they returned from a vacation without him.

The remaining McCollum and Hyland magi organized themselves into teams to make sure nobody was left behind.

"I'll finally be able to get back to work," Liam continued as the magi headed outside to load up. "Isn't it going to be great?" Something else mixed with his excitement. Relief. *Relief!* The rest of the magi were feeling the building anxiety that came before a battle, and Liam looked as though he felt better than he had in weeks.

Allyn shook his head and stifled a laugh. He didn't want others to think he was celebrating their impending battle.

Kendyl appeared out of the hallway that led to the bedrooms. Slung over her shoulder was a duffel bag she'd found at the top of one of the closets. The black bag was cracked and weathered, and it smelled of mildew and sweaty gym socks. Light on supplies, the Family was even lighter on ways to transport them—they used what they had.

"Hey," Allyn said as she neared. "You ready?"

She took in a heavy breath. "Yeah." Then with a long look, she scanned the inside of the cabin for what would likely be the last time.

Allyn wrapped his arm around her shoulder and gave her a small hug, sharing in her silent goodbye. It was a sad way to leave the cabin behind. It had always been a place of peace and solitude, where they could escape the summer heat and crowds, to enjoy in the spring when the trees and wild flowers were in bloom. It had been a place to find oneself.

*And I did*, Allyn realized. *One last time.*

"Come on." He turned for the door.

Kendyl resisted slightly, taking in one last image of the cabin as if she were snapping a mental picture, then she stepped outside.

Allyn pulled the door closed.

# CHAPTER 25

THEY ARRIVED TIRED, STIFF, AND sore—hardly the way Allyn would have wanted to begin the risky operation. They parked half a mile south of the manor at an abandoned forestry site and proceeded on foot into the dense wood, using only memory to guide them.

Unfamiliar with the woods, Allyn stumbled through the underbrush, snapping twigs and fallen branches, tripping over vines and exposed roots like a drunken bear. It drew irritated looks from some, amused grins from others, and indifference from most. Allyn didn't understand the irritation. By the time they made it to the manor, the sun would be high enough that they would lose their greatest advantage. Besides, even the quietest among them were far from silent, and with nearly two-dozen of them hiking through the forest, the noise had swollen into something far louder than a nocturnal predator seeking sleep.

A handful of magi had remained with the children and vans, ready to bring them to the manor once it was secure. Nolan was at Allyn's side, the only one among them who was louder and clumsier than he was. Instead of donning the magi compression armor that the rest of them wore, Nolan had opted for a bulletproof vest, which he wore over his starched white shirt. It made the dark outline of his torso unnaturally bulky and disproportionate, as if he were a body builder who'd skipped too many leg days. Kendyl was at Allyn's other side, and she slipped through the underbrush with a grace that Allyn could only yearn for. She had always been more comfortable in the forest than he was.

*I don't care what she thinks. She belongs among the magi every bit as much as I do. Maybe more.*

Their force trudged down the hillside, coming to the bottom of a shallow valley, where a creek overflowed with mountain runoff. Atop the next hillside, and probably another quarter mile to the north, would be the manor. Allyn pictured the top of the hill as an enormous plateau buffeted on three sides by the creek. After using a fallen tree as a bridge to cross the roaring waters, they spent another hour ascending the hillside. Even then, the manor was another quarter mile off.

Allyn's breath caught in his throat at the sight of it. Stadium lights surrounded the perimeter of the manor, so that even in the dead of night, it was well lit. The bodies had long since been taken to the morgue, but much of the manor appeared as it had the night they had fled. A few of the exterior stone walls stood a few feet above the ground, gray stone black with soot and ash. Rising from the ashes like a gravestone was a section of the grand staircase that had once been the entrance of the manor.

The library, though, had been dug out, and a mound of fresh soil circled the structure, forming a ridge and obscuring it from view. Unable to see the library, Allyn could imagine it: a long rectangular concrete building excavated from the ground as if it were an ancient city on an archeological dig, with ladders leading down from the ridge.

The rest of the magi had stretched out to either side of Allyn in a long line parallel to the tree line. They breathed a collective breath as one people, one Family, witnessing the destruction of all they knew. It was the conscious, rhythmic breathing of someone holding back emotion. Allyn didn't need to ask how they felt. He knew because he'd been through something similar when he'd returned to his condo.

A home is more than a series of rooms connected by hallways and held under one roof. It's a collection of memories and emotions. A testament created between the house itself and those who lived inside it. A relationship. The McCollum Family wasn't looking at the charred remains of brick, stone, and wood; they were looking at the corpse of a loved one, someone most of them had known their entire lives.

Mourning with the Family felt wrong, as if he were a *plus one* at a funeral. He withdrew and found Jaxon with his back to him, peering into the forest. The early morning darkness always played games with Allyn's eyes. Strange shadows. Movement. Noise. A forest was never truly quiet or still, and the long shadows cast by the rising sun made it worse.

"Where are the rest?" Allyn asked, stopping at Jaxon's side.

"They'll be here," Jaxon said.

And he was right. A few minutes later, a pair of shadows broke from the rest, and Nyla and Ren emerged. The two women couldn't have been any more different. Nyla was elegant. She walked confidently, with her head up, as if she already had it all—or had nothing to lose. She wasn't the same moody, cold-hearted woman in mourning that he had first met, but he didn't believe the quiet, methodical, duty-driven woman before him was the real Nyla, either. Whether he would ever meet the real Nyla was still to be determined.

Ren, on the other hand, was a viper. Sleek. Slender. Silent. Her eyes quickly assessed the pair of men in front of her, and to Allyn's surprise, she didn't relax.

"You're late," Ren said. "Daylight is only an hour off."

"We had an unexpected visitor," Jaxon said. "Give me your report."

"Three patrol vehicles," Nyla said. "Six officers. They form

268

a triangle around the grounds. Two at the front. Another with the library."

"Any communication?"

"Between the vehicles?" Ren asked.

Jaxon nodded.

"Not that we've seen."

Frowning, Jaxon looked to Nyla, perhaps hoping for a different answer. She shook her head.

"What about patrols?" Jaxon asked. "Shift changes?"

"None," Ren said. "The only movement we've seen out of any of them is to take a piss—nothing of note."

"Their entire operation is running off a generator," Nyla said.

"Where?" Jaxon asked.

"South side of the manor."

"That's one of our first objectives, then," Jaxon said. "We lose it, and we lose the library."

"You think they'll sabotage the generator?" Allyn asked.

"I don't know what to expect," Jaxon said. "But I know if I wanted to stop someone from getting into something, I'd have a plan to lock it down. Form up into your squads. We're moving forward."

---

Allyn watched as Nolan strode down the gravel driveway, toward the two police vehicles that barricaded the front entrance to the manor. Unlike traditional squad cars, these were large black SUVs with tinted windows and reinforced bumpers. Aggressive assault vehicles. Nolan disappeared behind the stone fountain at the center of the driveway, and for the split second it took him to reappear, Allyn saw their entire plan unraveling. He was putting a lot of trust in Nolan—alone and striding up to men who used to be his comrades, nothing prevented Nolan from alerting them to the McCollum Family's presence.

But they'd needed a distraction, and Nolan seemed the most logical.

Nolan buttoned the top button of his jacket and quickly wiped away the dried dirt. It was probably some kind of nervous habit. Allyn sucked in a sharp breath as he saw movement inside the vehicles. For all his reservations about sending Nolan in alone to distract the officers, he would know if he'd been betrayed rather quickly.

The officers jumped out of the vehicles, using the open doors for cover, guns drawn and pointed at Nolan. The deep bass of the officer's voice didn't carry well across the grounds to the tree line where Allyn and the more than half a dozen others were hiding, but his commanding tone did. The officers knew Nolan was a suspect.

"We move on my mark," Leira said.

Nolan stopped abruptly and threw his hands in the air. The two officers on the edge of the line advanced. More commands. Nolan dropped to his knees.

"Go!"

Allyn dashed across the manor grounds. The plan was for Nolan to distract the officers while Allyn and the rest of the squad snuck up behind them. It worked flawlessly.

The two remaining officers didn't hear their approach until the squad was nearly upon them. They turned, guns swiveling, but Leira and Nyla were too fast. In a blink, the two officers were on the ground, and the clerics were already moving to the next.

The advancing officers were nearly upon Nolan, guns still drawn and barking for him to put his face to the ground.

Nolan complied but not before his eyes flickered over the officers' shoulders and toward the advancing squad. A squat, balding officer, nearly wider than he was tall, followed Nolan's gaze.

"Shit," Allyn said as the officer spun on him. The officer's expression cycled through surprise, alarm, and finally, recognition.

Allyn wielded, and at the sight of the red tendrils, the officer's face snapped back to alarm. Allyn knocked the gun out of his hand with a static charge then jumped and used his forward momentum to drive his heels into the man's soft chest. The officer grunted as he stumbled and fell onto his back. Allyn hit the ground, rolled, and continued forward—but Ren was already there. The air concussed in front of her, throwing the final officer away from Nolan and sliding him across the gravel driveway.

Leira was on him half a beat later, forcing him under.

The magi squad went still, listening for the sounds of alarm. Jaxon had said there was a third police vehicle behind the library—if any of the four officers had called for backup or had alerted the remaining officers of Nolan's surprise appearance...

The grounds remained silent. They breathed a collective sigh of relief. The first part of the assault was over.

"Good work," Allyn said.

Ren and Leira made short work of using the officers' own cuffs to lock their hands behind their backs then stashed them inside the police assault vehicles. Once done, the squad gathered at the base of the stairs. Liam's eyes were alive with excitement. Allyn could almost feel it exuding from him, and it was contagious. They were so close.

The manor had been built atop a small rise, which hid the magi from the remaining officers on the other side.

"We need to move," Leira said. "We've already been here for too long."

Allyn, Nyla, Ren, and Liam nodded in silent agreement, and Leira quickly led their squad into the remains of the manor. Since the grounds surrounding it were well lit and offered little in the way of cover, they had decided that sneaking through the interior of the manor was their best chance of moving unseen.

The air was thick with the smell of smoke, which intensified as each step kicked up more ash. They passed through room after room, stepping over half walls and rubble.

Allyn returned to the night it had burned. Tiled floors slick with blood, sweat, and urine. Paint bubbling under the intense heat. Screams. Cries. Agony.

He saw the faces and lifeless eyes of those who had burned with the manor. Trevin. Griffin. Ari. Nobody would ever see them again, but like so many other things about that night, Allyn would never forget them.

Leira cursed and quickly dropped behind what remained of a wall for cover. Without command, the rest of the squad followed, hiding behind whatever they could or dropping to the ashy ground.

Allyn leaned against something protruding through the ash. It hummed with the dull echo of something hollow. "Have we been seen?"

Leira shook her head. "I don't think so—but I can see the library."

Allyn resisted the urge to see for himself. "What do we do?"

"Small groups," she said. "Get Liam and Nolan to the library. Ren and I will make sure you aren't seen."

Allyn nodded and waved Liam and Nolan over. "We're making for the library."

"There's a ladder in the northeast corner," Nolan said. "It's the only way down."

"Okay," Allyn said. "We make for the ladder then. Stay low and stay close. Wait for my mark."

Allyn stood, surveying the scene. The library was maybe fifty feet away, marked only by a ridge of ash and soil that rose four or five feet above the ground. The police SUV was parked behind it, the tops of the tinted windows barely visible above the ridge. Allyn traced a path that would lead them through the former dining room—recognizable only by the crystal chandelier on the ground, caked so thick in soot that only one or two crystals still sparkled—and into the dead zone, where all of the debris had been cleared. There, they would be entirely in the open. Thirty feet without cover. They would have to rely solely on speed and luck.

"We go one at a time," Allyn said, turning to Nolan.

"I don't think I like that idea."

"One person might be able to slip through," Allyn said, "but three? And what happens when we make it to the ladder? Two of us wait while the other climbs down? No. We go one at a time."

Nolan took an irritated breath but nodded. "I'll go first. Once down, I'll move the ladder so it's along this side of the ridge. Should save you some time searching."

"Good thinking," Allyn said.

Nolan replaced Allyn at the edge of the wall, waiting, ready to break for the ridge. Allyn and Liam found separate holes in the wall to watch through. Though the police vehicle remained still, Allyn couldn't help but think that the odds of them all crossing the barren ground without being seen were slim. Fortunately, he didn't have time to second-guess himself before Nolan broke into a run.

Allyn pressed his face close to the wall—the bubbled paint and blackened timber were rough against his skin—and watched Nolan's dark figure dash across the uneven ground. He'd taken his black suit jacket off again, but the white starched shirt was largely hidden under the tactical vest. The SUV remained lifeless. In a matter of seconds, Nolan was more than halfway across the dead zone, and Allyn still hadn't seen any movement inside the vehicle.

Nolan slid to a stop at the base of the ridge and scrambled up, stopping near the top and dropping onto his stomach to peer over the crest. He must have been content with what he saw, because he scrambled over the debris and disappeared onto the other side.

Allyn's blood pounded through his veins so hard he could feel his pulse in the tips of his fingers. He realized that he was holding his breath, expecting at any moment to hear the wild wail of sirens. When they didn't come, he turned to Liam.

"Looks like it's your turn."

Liam's eyes went wide with fear. "You want me to go next?"

"Yes," Allyn said. He didn't think Liam had the courage to follow if he and Nolan weren't there to push him.

If Liam understood that, he didn't say anything. He took a couple sharp breaths and moved into position at the edge of the wall where Nolan had been. Still a head taller than Liam, Allyn was easily able to see over him. The distance between them and the ridge seemed longer than it had a moment before, the odds of success slimmer. But they were committed.

"Ready?" Allyn whispered.

"Yeah." Liam's voice was stronger than Allyn had anticipated, filled with a nervous excitement.

"Okay," Allyn said. "Pick a spot and go. Keep your eyes locked on that spot. Don't look back. Don't look to see if anyone notices. Just run."

"Allyn," Liam said, determination in his eyes. "I've got this."

Taking a step back, Allyn measured the kid who stood in front of him. He seemed taller and broader, more of a man than he'd been before. Circumstance and responsibility had forced Liam to grow up.

"All right then," Allyn said. "Whenever you're ready."

Liam scanned the area in front of him one final time and took three sharp breaths, a silent countdown. Then he broke into a run.

Liam had never been a graceful runner, lacking the

coordination of most boys his age, but in that moment, he looked like something else. Head level. Legs driving. Hands relaxed. He reminded Allyn of a well-trained athlete running a forty-yard dash. Allyn watched the surroundings, ready to shout an order for him to drop, but the world remained calm. Something didn't feel right about that, but he chalked it up to the fact that their plans always seemed to be fraught with unexpected complications.

Liam dropped to his knees, sliding the final few feet to the base of the ridge, then, breathing heavy, he turned to give Allyn an enthusiastic smile and waved him forward.

Not wanting to tempt fate—and perhaps worried he might lose his nerve—Allyn pushed himself from the wall then sprinted into the dead area between him and Liam. It was a strange feeling, running while expecting to be seen or have your head blown off at any second. Not that he expected the cops to shoot without being provoked. Then again, the Portland Police Bureau didn't exactly have a stellar reputation.

He did precisely what he'd told Liam not to do—succumb to the temptation to watch the black SUV in the distance. For the first time, he thought he could see movement behind the tinted windows.

He strained his eyes, willing himself to see beyond the barrier, and lost focus, stumbling and tripping. He hit the ground hard, cracking his head on a rock. Darkness crept in from the edges of his vision, and he found himself looking up at the pink sky, where stars peeked through the thin layer of clouds, saying goodbye for the day. Allyn rolled onto his knees, rubbing the side of his head. The rock wasn't a rock at all, but a hand-blown vase, somehow untouched by the fire that had claimed everything else.

Allyn rose to his feet, his head still ringing, his steps sluggish and uneven as if he were walking drunkenly through sand. Liam was on the ladder now, his back to the SUV, only his head visible above the ridge. He waved Allyn on emphatically.

By the time Allyn made it to the ridge, he'd regained a level of normalcy. He crawled up the ashy mound, which coated his hands in the dry residue. Liam had finished crawling down the ladder and was waiting with Nolan at the base of the library. Keeping as low as possible, he whipped a leg over onto the ladder. And that's when he heard it—the distinct sound of a door opening.

Allyn snapped his head around. The driver's door was open. The officer kicked his legs out, a cigarette hanging from his lips. He laughed and said something to his partner then moved farther out of the vehicle.

Allyn acted without thought, pulling his leg back off the ladder. He didn't jump, so much as he dropped. He'd never given much thought to how far down a single story was. Fifteen, twenty feet maybe, from the top of the roof to the ground. Far enough to break bones. To experience free fall. To understand true terror.

His stomach lurched into his chest as the wind roared past his ears. The light disappeared around him, and the ash gave way to dark soil as the ground rose to grab him. He heard a distant scream. It might have been his.

He hit the dark soil as if he'd hit concrete. His legs buckled under his weight, and he folded up like one of Liam's laptops. His kneecaps drove into his chest, and his chin bounced off the earth. Pain shot through him, from his feet, to his chest, to his head, and a high-pitched squeal filled the air. Allyn blinked. Rolled. More pain. *What is that noise?* Coughing, he struggled to regain clarity—and failed.

His chest in agony, he struggled for breath. The squeal grew louder. *It's me. The squeal is me.* He stopped fighting and let the pain wash over him.

He didn't know how long he lay there, likely only a few seconds, but long enough for his mind to catch up to what his body had just done. *Stupid. You're no good to anyone dead.*

Liam and Nolan appeared a moment later. They were talking. Concerned.

"Allyn... Allyn... can you hear me?" Nolan whispered, crouching down over him. His eyes flickered to the ridge above. "Allyn, blink if you can hear me."

"I'm fine," Allyn said, surprised by how much speaking hurt. He planted an elbow under him and rolled onto his side. The cool earth felt good against his exposed skin, helping him focus on something other than the pain.

"I don't think that's a good idea," Nolan said, watching as Allyn rose to his feet.

Allyn stifled a cry of pain. His whole body ached, but as far as he could tell, nothing was broken.

"I'm fine," Allyn repeated. "Let's go."

They shuffled down a narrow pathway, the concrete exterior of the library on one side and a wall of earth on the other. The library had been excavated like an ancient tomb. The narrow path of dark, wet soil circling the outside was squishy under their feet, and in places, long sheets of plywood had been laid over standing water. Everywhere, the smell of living earth was heavy—a welcomed retreat from the suffocating scent of smoke, ash, and death.

At the front of the library, they waited. It was the closest point to the officers. Only fifteen or so feet above and a few yards behind the ridge, they could hear the thick coughs of a lifetime smoker and muffled conversations between partners. Allyn couldn't make out the words, but the conversation was lively and jovial.

When they finally heard the solid *thunk* of the door closing, they made for the library's glass door. The interior was dark, and a red light shone on the electronic keypad, indicating it was locked. Allyn placed a hand on the wall for support as Nolan punched in the new passcode.

The door hissed and slid open, and the interior lights flickered on. It might as well have been a gunshot in the deep silence of the night. Allyn waited, expecting shouts of surprise and alarm from above, but they never came. So, without wasting another second, they moved inside.

Under the McCollum Family's care, the library had proudly displayed rare magi artifacts, art, and armor, but it seemed as the FBI had taken over, they had turned the library into an extension of their evidence room. Already boxed, organized, and prepared for transport, the artifacts were grouped together by type, stacked, organized, and catalogued in a grid. The majestic display that Allyn had fallen in love with had been replaced by the cold efficiency of law enforcement and bureaucracy.

Liam's face was a mix of relief and disapproval. Allyn thought back to the trip to his condo and the feelings that had brought up. He hadn't known if Liam's reaction would be as strong or stronger. He'd held it together in the manor, but the library had been his. It very obviously no longer was. The door hissed closed behind them.

"At least they did half the work for us," Allyn said lightly. "I'll let Jaxon know we're in."

Nolan strolled past Liam, lightly slapping him on the back. "Let's get to it."

Allyn texted Jaxon. *We're in.* The first two parts of their plan had come together with only minimal complications. Allyn breathed a sigh of relief.

It was punctuated by a distant boom that sounded much like a low note from a bass guitar. Nolan stopped abruptly, box in hand, his eyes going wide.

"What was that?" Liam asked.

Another boom.

Then another.

Allyn peered skyward out the glass door in time to see the last of the stadium lights shut off. The final boom echoed across the grounds, vibrating the library like an exclamation point.

And a half-second later, the library went dark.

# CHAPTER 26

"**T**HERE'S NO POWER," LIAM SAID. "It won't open."

Allyn refused to listen. He held his palms flat against the glass, trying to force the door open. Nothing happened, but he tried again anyway.

The interior of the library had gone dark, and Liam was little more than a shadow behind Allyn. Allyn's palms slipped, screeching across the glass as he tumbled.

Nolan caught him under his armpits. "Let me help."

"The entire manor collapsed around it," Liam said, "and you really think you can open it with your hands?"

Ignoring Liam, Allyn counted down from three, and together, he and Nolan tried their combined efforts. Allyn's face went hot with exertion, and his breath rushed out as he gave up.

Nolan studied the door as if it were a puzzle he could solve. "Back up."

"What are you going to do?" Allyn asked.

"Just get behind me." Nolan's hands began to glow. The light was a welcome sight within the darkness.

"What are you doing?" Liam asked. "Don't! It won't do any good!"

"We have to try something." The energy pulsed through

Nolan's arms, growing brighter with every beat of his heart. "Get back."

Allyn moved deeper into the library, finding a place near the empty bookshelves. Most of the books had been individually bagged inside what looked like large freezer bags then placed inside green plastic totes that snapped shut. The totes were then stacked in front of the shelf. Peeking around from behind one of these stacks, Allyn watched as Liam tried to talk Nolan out of blasting the door.

"You're just going to hurt yourself," Liam said. "Or damage the artifacts we have in here."

Nolan turned on Liam. "That door is our only way out. And in case you haven't noticed, it's sealed shut. That means we're not getting out until it's open. It also means that unless you have some sort of backup system pumping air into this room, the only air we have to breathe is in here right now. So if we don't get it open soon, the three of us are going to die in here."

It might have been the white light radiating from Nolan's hands, but Liam appeared to suddenly go very pale. "I hadn't thought about that."

"I know," Nolan said. "Now, please, step back and find some cover."

Liam moved next to Allyn and watched as Nolan's arms grew brighter. The light poured back and forth from his hands to his elbows like water in a tube. As the wave rushed back toward his hands, Nolan threw his arms forward, his palms outstretched. The light erupted from his hands in a streak that reverberated through the chamber. Allyn threw his hands over his ears, barely covering them before the energy struck the glass barrier. A brilliant, violent light exploded on contact.

Allyn slammed his eyes shut—too late. The afterimage burned in his vision. He felt the energy rebound through the room like a ripple in water. The stack of totes shuddered, and across the library, something crashed to the ground. Glass shattered and plastic scraped across the rough floor. When the wave returned from the opposite direction, it was little more than a casual breeze. The concrete wall had absorbed much of the energy.

Allyn opened his eyes. They were wet, and he tried to blink away the white afterimage, but it didn't help. Rubbing them didn't help, either.

"I can't see," Liam said.

"Me neither."

"I'm blind!" Liam said.

"It'll pass," Nolan said from across the room. "Give it a few minutes."

Fortunately, it took less time than Nolan had suggested. When Allyn's vision returned, he found Nolan in the same place he'd been before—his attention still consumed by the door in front of him. It remained closed, and the only damage was a small dark blemish in the center of the glass.

"I told you," Liam said. "You can't force it open."

"What do we do?" Nolan asked, half to himself.

"We get the library ready for transport," Allyn said. "And hope to fucking God that somebody can get the power back on."

---

"Sabotaged?" Jaxon said, reading the message for the second time. He looked up from his phone, only moderately aware of the gathering group around him. He remained along the tree line, surveying the battlefield as an ancient commander would. However, instead of music and flags to relay messages and orders, Jaxon had the best of modern technology.

It had only taken them a few moments to realize something was wrong after the stadium lights flared out. The steady rumble of the generator powering the site had gone quiet, replaced by an ominous silence. If Allyn's squad had entered the library, they would be trapped—so it was with growing apprehension that he'd sent Brandt and Andrew out to power up the generator.

*How?* Jaxon wrote back.

*Wires ripped free.*

Jaxon frowned. Why would the police sabotage their own generator? Had they purposely trapped Allyn inside? Though the idea was a little convoluted, it wasn't entirely out of the question.

The next message came. *I don't think we're alone.*

*Elaborate,* Jaxon wrote back.

*Hasty job. Irreversible. No power without another generator. The added darkness does nothing but give us the advantage.*

Jaxon closed his eyes. Brandt's conclusions validated the growing sense of unease in his stomach. They were mid-operation, with one unit likely trapped inside a concrete cell, while at least one active police force was still on-site. If there was an unknown force, he needed to know about it before they proceeded.

*All units hold,* Jaxon wrote. Then to Brandt: *Return on the double.*

An explosion shook the ground.

Jaxon whipped his head up to see an orange ball of flame erupt under one of the SUVs at the manor's entrance, sending hulking mass of metal soaring into the sky. Jaxon's first thought was that one of the units hadn't received his orders in time—or that they had ignored him altogether. But none of the McCollum magi would have acted like that. And besides, those SUVs and the police inside had already been subdued.

As the first SUV landed in a crunch of screaming metal and shattering glass, the second SUV was attacked. Alert this time, Jaxon caught the orange fireball as it streaked down the gravel driveway. It pummeled the side of the SUV, wedging it against the concrete partition of the elevated gardens.

Jaxon traced its trajectory back to about a dozen shadows hustling toward the manor. They moved with undisciplined chaos, descending upon the SUVs, ripping off the doors, and launching more fire at the helpless officers inside.

*Pop! Pop! Pop!*

The third SUV, the one that had been guarding the library, sped toward the battle. The officer in the passenger seat leaned out of his window, shooting at the mysterious group.

All but one of the enemy magi took cover. They moved as if they intended to intercept the SUV then launched a third fireball, which struck one of the front tires. The SUV lurched and spun. Driven by forward momentum, it flipped, rolling once, twice, three times, before coming to a rest on the cab, the tires pointed to the sky.

The battlefield went quiet, save for the crackling of the distant fires. The unknown magi force formed back up into their undisciplined line and stepped into the manor. Their course would take them to the library.

"I knew it."

Jaxon nearly jumped out of his skin then relaxed as he realized the two figures that had appeared in front of him were Brandt and Andrew.

"I knew we weren't alone," Brandt continued. A lather of sweat covered his face, wetting the tips of his gray hair. "Do you think they had time to call for backup?"

"There's no way to know."

"Who is it?"

Jaxon shook his head. "I can't be sure, but I don't know many magi who would openly attack a human police force."

"No," Brandt said, his voice trembling in anger and fear. "I suppose there's only one I can think of, too."

Inside the library, the sounds of explosions were muffled, yet unmistakable. The concrete rumbled under Allyn's feet, and the dark florescent lights swayed, squeaking softly. Allyn imagined dust falling off shelves and from the ceiling, but that would never happen in Graeme's library. The microscopic dust particles would savage the artifacts. The police, however, hadn't been so precious, and Allyn thought he felt dust tickling his nose and the back of his throat.

Moisture hung in the room, clinging to the walls, books, and art, creating condensation that clung to the edges of shelves, tables, and chairs. The glass encasements that had once housed artifacts were fogged and wet to the touch. Allyn thought he could almost smell the scent of moldy decay of everything Liam held dear. The damage would be irreversible. He just hoped Liam would be able to preserve the contents in a digital form before their stories were lost.

Liam was across the library, stacking plastic totes and using the flashlight application on his phone for light. The tiny single light source left him alternating between an elongated shadow and a silhouette. He froze as a second explosion vibrated the library, his wide eyes following the invisible sound as if he were attempting to spot a plane on the horizon.

"They're on their way," Allyn said.

"You said it wouldn't come to this," Nolan said. He was behind Allyn, in the bowels of the library, and his voice echoed across the bare chamber. The pinprick of his flashlight moved toward Allyn like a ping on a radar detector.

"We don't know what happened up there," Allyn said. "If Jaxon attacked, it was provoked. I can promise you that. Regardless of what your partner believes, we're not in the habit of killing cops."

"Old partner," Nolan said. He came closer, carrying a tote, his phone resting on top. The light pointed upward into his face so that dark shadows circled his eyes, giving him a sinister appearance.

*This is how they see us—as monsters.*

"Even so," Allyn said. "That's not what we're about." He bagged up the last of the books from the shelf then placed them in the green tote and snapped it shut. "How much is left?" Allyn asked when it became apparent Nolan wasn't going to force the issue.

"Just a couple more." Nolan dropped the tote near the door.

Liam didn't answer. He picked up a book from the floor. The dry leather spine creaked as Liam opened it, and a loose page fell from the binding and stuck to the damp floor. Liam's expression soured as if he had just opened a present he'd been dreaming about for weeks, only to find it broken and unusable.

Allyn started to say something, but movement near the door caught his attention. He winced as he set the tote on the ground—the dull ache in his body was growing worse—and gingerly took a couple steps toward the door. Light from Nolan's and Liam's flashlights reflected off the thick glass.

"Turn your lights off," Allyn said.

"Why?" Liam asked, keeping his eyes on the book.

"I think someone's here."

Liam looked up and followed Allyn's gaze to the door. A moment later, the library went dark, and Allyn heard Nolan's shuffling steps draw closer.

"I don't see anything," Liam said.

"Give it a moment," Allyn said. "Let your eyes adjust." Even as he said it, his own self-doubt grew stronger. There wasn't much room between the door and the wall of soil. The darkness was deep and the dim reflections of Nolan and Liam on the glass played games with his eyes.

Nolan passed Allyn, walking toward the door in a slight crouch, his legs taut, ready to spring into action. His hands were at his sides, palms facing out and ready to wield. Something had spooked him. And that made Allyn nervous.

Something cracked against the door, exploding with a flash of blue light. Allyn started as Nolan's silhouette stumbled backward. The library went dark again.

"What the hell was that?" Nolan shouted.

*Crack!* Two more mini-explosions briefly illuminated the area around the door, like fireworks in a summer sky. Standing several paces behind the door and partially hidden from view was a group of dark figures, half a dozen in all, and evenly split so three flanked either side of the door. They were dressed in black, with dark hoods and masks that concealed the lower halves of their faces. And they were wielding again.

In unison, the magi at the end of each line unleashed their new creation. Still solid, the blue ice glowed from within with a flickering orange light. Allyn recognized it as a volatile concoction of ice and fire meant to combust on impact. They struck the glass door with enough force to rattle the empty bookcases against the bare walls.

For a brief moment, Allyn thought it would be enough to bring down the door, but as the flash dimmed, there wasn't so much as a chip in the glass. The two units, once again nearly invisible in the darkness, waited.

Allyn slid forward beside Nolan, a sudden rush of adrenaline easing his aching muscles. He harnessed it, using the adrenaline to stoke the power inside him, and almost immediately, his magic sprang to life. Nolan followed his lead, and a moment later, the strange white glow of energy emitted from his palms.

Outside, a slender figure roughly Allyn's height broke from the units and approached the glass door. The man's piercing blue eyes narrowed as he saw Allyn, burning with an intense hatred. He didn't have to pull down his mask—Allyn already knew who he was. Darian Hyland.

"Do you know that man?" Nolan asked.

"Yeah," Allyn said. "He tried to kill me."

"He looks like he wants to try again."

"Yep." Allyn stretched the word into two syllables, never breaking eye contact with Darian. They were two predators, each trying to establish superiority, and Allyn wasn't about to lose.

Darian took two steps back so that he rested against the excavated earth. The others fell in beside him, extending out in a line that paralleled the door.

"What are they doing?" Nolan asked.

"They're going to try and blow our house down," Allyn said.

"Will it work?"

"No." Liam's face didn't reflect the confidence in his voice. "That door is made of dual-paned bulletproof glass, nearly seven inches thick. You could hit it with a tank, and it wouldn't buckle."

"That doesn't look like it's going to stop them from trying," Nolan said.

Weapons of magical destruction glowed in the hands of the Hyland magi, and on Darian's command, they released their destructive creations, wielding again, and again, and again. It sounded like a war zone. The attacks echoed like mortar rounds. Allyn's irrational self fought with Liam's logical explanation, and he had to restrain himself from diving for the nearest cover.

When the assault finally subsided, a cloudy haze lingered outside the door. Darian strode through it confidently. His lips parted for a second, then his expression turned into something vile. He pounded his fists on the unbroken glass, screaming at Allyn.

Allyn strode to the door, stopping only inches from it. He met Darian's eye, his stony expression matching the younger grand mage.

They stared each other down for moment, their breathing fogging the glass between them.

A sudden muffled *crack* broke the tension, and Darian whipped his head around to bark an order. His units disappeared from view, likely headed toward the ladder, which Nolan had placed on the backside of the library. Alone, Darian looked over his shoulder, a silent promise in his eyes.

*This isn't over.*

"Where'd they go?" Liam asked.

"I think our boys just arrived," Nolan said.

# CHAPTER 27

THE CACOPHONY OF EXPLOSIONS ECHOED through the manor rubble as Leira's squad advanced. She took point—an odd position for someone who didn't have the magical ability to deflect attacks. But this was her charge. Her call. Since she'd received Jaxon's order to hold, enough time had passed for the situation to evolve.

A rogue magi force had replaced the police, and by the sound of things, they were trying to break into the library. She wasn't sure if Jaxon knew the situation on the ground. But that was her brother in there, and she wasn't about to wait for Jaxon to get up to speed. She wouldn't lose Liam, too. Besides, Jaxon trusted her judgment, and it wasn't as if she was acting in secret. The moment she had decided to proceed, she'd sent word back to Jaxon, and he hadn't reaffirmed his order.

Ren was at her shoulder. Leira felt more comfortable having her there, not only because she was one of the most powerful magi in the McCollum Family, and thus, able to protect Leira in ways she couldn't protect herself, but also because she had been one of Leira's staunchest detractors. She'd argued so vehemently that they should remain and follow Jaxon's orders that Leira had almost expected her to stay behind alone. Ren running point did more than keep Liera safe; it kept their squad whole.

The rest of their squad had formed two columns behind them and followed at a moderate pace. Though they didn't purposely seek cover, they remained in the thick of the manor rubble, where the half walls and piles of debris obscured them from view. And since the stadium lights remained off, the rubble was more than enough to keep them hidden.

The *crack* of magical explosions stopped, and an eerie silence fell over the grounds. Leira slowed and held up a fist. Her unit stopped behind her. Even if they were hidden from view, the sound of eight pairs of feet trampling across the manor ruins would alert the others to their presence.

White smoke—or perhaps a thick mist—rose from the far end of the library. *They were trying to break in.* Did the silence mean they had succeeded?

Movement caught her eye. Shadows on the horizon. Two. Four. She hadn't seen them before. They wore black on black and blended into the dark horizon. Even their faces were obscured from view, either in shadow or by masks—she couldn't be sure. They walked along the ridge that circled the library, backs to the structure, eyes surveying the grounds.

"A rear guard," Ren said, appearing again at Leira's shoulder. "I suppose that settles the friend-or-foe dispute."

"They might still be ours," Leira said, though the knot in her stomach told her she didn't believe it.

"There's little cover between us and them," Ren said. "How much are you willing to risk by that statement?"

Leira ignored the question. Ren was right, and she knew it, so she was trying to rankle Leira as she had when they were teenagers. When they'd been friends. Before Jaxon. Before the accident.

The expanse of shin-deep ash and soot stretched out in front of them. The moment they moved forward, they would be seen.

"What do you think?" Leira asked. "What happens if this turns sour? Do we have the numbers?"

"There's four on the ridge," Ren said, sounding as if she were thinking aloud. "And I can't be sure, but maybe another six or eight below. If we take care of those four and hold the ridge, then I like our odds. But if they break into the library, that can throw a kink in things."

"Okay," Leira said. "Wait for my signal and have the others focus concussions of air on the magi on the ridge. If it comes to a fight, blow them into the pit. That should take most of them out and keep our advantage of having the high ground."

"I'll let the others know."

A minute later, Leira and Ren emerged from the manor rubble into the open stretch. Their squad—a mix of six magi from the McCollum Family and Hyland refugees—formed a wedge behind them. They weren't a quarter of the way through the gray expanse before the first guard spotted them. He raised the alarm, blasting a three-foot-wide fireball into the early-morning sky then turned toward them, flames continuing to kiss the skin of both arms.

Leira stopped and held up a fist, halting her unit behind her. They shifted into a line that stretched out from her shoulders.

"He doesn't look like he wants to talk," Ren said.

The remaining rogue guards rounded the ridge and took up positions beside the first guard, mirroring the McCollum squad. One barked something to those below then strode in front of the magi line. He wore a mask that obscured the lower half of his face.

"And that one must be in charge." Leira flexed her hands nervously and rocked her shoulders back, willing herself to appear confident. "I am Leira McCollum. This is my home, and we are in the process of retrieving that which is rightfully ours. Who are you? And what business do you have?"

The leader stopped and pulled down his mask, revealing his face.

Leira didn't believe it. "Cason?" she asked, her disbelief clearly audible. "I thought you were..."

"Dead?" His wicked smile split his face. His sandy-blond hair had been cropped short, and his face bore half-healed scars. But there was something more, something that twisted Leira's insides. The structure of his face was off. Like a shattered vase that could never be repaired to its original beauty, Cason's appearance revealed the traces of an extensive healing process. His face was no longer his—instead, his features were a combination of his and another's.

In a sudden and absolute wave of anger, Leira found herself clenching her fists and grinding her teeth. The adrenaline coursing through her veins willed her forward, encouraging her to strangle the breath out of the vile man in front of her. That kind of healing would never be done consensually. Like Cason, whoever had performed the healing would bear the scars and a misshapen face for a lifetime—if the cleric had lived through the process. It was an abuse of power. A violation. A perversion. A forbidden magi act, as equally offensive as developing an echo.

"You're a monster," Leira said.

"I'm necessary."

"Did she live?"

Cason's smile grew wider. "Leira, Leira, Leira. You're a cleric. You exist solely to serve the more powerful. Don't you understand? You're my plaything, and I'll do what I want with you and your kind, because that's what you're made for."

Leira set her jaw and turned toward Ren. The shorter woman met her eye and nodded.

"Then play with this," Leira said. "Now!"

Ren and the rest of their magi took a single step forward. The air distorted in front of them, and half a second later, the concussion rocked the landscape. Under the combined force, the unit of Hyland magi flew backward into the hole where the library had been dug out—everyone but Cason. Two separate concussions of air hit him squarely in the chest, and he flew backward over the hole, landing on top of the library in a heap. He rolled and slid until he finally came to a stop more than halfway across the roof.

"Bring him back to me," Leira growled, then turned to the rest. "Advance and hold the ridge. Do not let them up. And if they so much as sneeze a spark, kill them all."

Ren led the force forward to hold the ridge. She approached at a dead sprint, leaped, and launched a blast of air at the ground below her. The concussion propelled her higher into the air, and she easily cleared the gap, landing on the roof of the library in a crouch.

Cason wasn't yet standing when Ren unleashed her first attack.

---

*Ready the trucks*, Jaxon wrote. *Wait for my command.* He turned to Brandt, who was busy watching the flashes of battle in the distance.

"How'd he know we were here?" Brandt asked. He sounded exhausted.

"We have another spy," Jaxon said.

Brandt sighed and looked at the ground. He wasn't exhausted; he was beaten down. Defeated. The bags under his eyes were growing bigger; the wrinkles in his face, deeper. His shoulders were stooped, and there seemed to be more gray in his hair. He had thought fleeing Darian Hyland meant escaping the psychopath. Instead, Darian had exploited him, using Brandt and the McCollum's collective desperation to his advantage.

"I didn't want to believe it."

"I need you to pull your family back," Jaxon said. "I can't have a spy undermining my operation."

"I understand."

Jaxon turned to leave.

"And Jaxon?"

Jaxon stopped.

"It isn't me."

Without a word, Jaxon left the older man behind and returned to the forest, where the rest of his unit lingered. "Form up! We're going in!"

---

"Stand back," Allyn said, red coils of electricity already around his arms.

"Allyn—"

"Stop!"

Allyn barely heard Liam and Nolan before he unleashed the energy. It struck the glass like a wave crashing against the shore, spraying uncontrolled tendrils of electricity about the room. One strand slapped against a loose stack of books and parchment, immediately engulfing them in flame.

"Damn it!" Liam screamed. He rushed toward the spreading fire and quickly snuffed out the flames using a thick woolen blanket that had been tossed over a stack of green totes. Liam took a piece of blackened parchment between his fingers and held it up delicately, glaring at Allyn.

"What did you think was going to happen?" Liam bellowed. "Darian couldn't break in here with an army of magi. What did you think you could do?"

"I had to try something," Allyn said, matching Liam's intensity.

"You could have killed us!"

Allyn pointed a finger at the ceiling. The muffled booms of battle sounded distant, but Allyn knew it was only an illusion created by the well-insulated walls. "Listen to that. That's your sister, Liam. That's your Family."

Liam's face grew red with anger, and he strode toward Allyn purposefully. "You think I don't know that? You think—"

Nolan grabbed Liam from behind. "Easy, Liam."

Liam fought against his grip. "Let me go!"

"Cool it!" Nolan shouted.

Liam slipped an arm free and flailed wildly, catching Nolan on the side of the head with his elbow.

Nolan's expression hardened, and any pretense of empathy or compassion disappeared. "Get control of yourself, or I will."

"No," Liam growled. The weeks of building frustration had finally caught up with him. Allyn and Jaxon had each had separate meltdowns at different times, but through it all, Liam had held it together. His turn had come.

Nolan hurled Liam backward and spun on him, finally placing himself between the two men. He held Liam back with a hand to his chest. "Knock it off! This isn't helping things." Nolan pointed a finger at Allyn. "You're supposed to the adult here. Get it together."

"He's—" Allyn started.

"Stop!" Nolan bellowed. "You're being irrational. Stop doing and *think*."

"There's nothing to—"

"No," Nolan cut in. "*Think*. What is the problem?"

"We can't get out."

"Why?"

"Are we really going to do this?"

"Why can't we get out?" Nolan repeated slowly, stressing every word.

"Because the door won't open."

"And why won't the door open?"

"Because there's no fucking power, Nolan."

Nolan hummed calmly in agreement. "Because there's no power."

Allyn shook his head. "We don't have time for this."

"The computer," Liam said wistfully.

Allyn stopped. Liam's softly spoken words pulled at something inside him, prodding at reason buried under his emotion.

"The computer," Liam repeated more firmly.

"What computer?" Allyn asked.

"Nolan's computer. The one you found at your condo and tried to power with your magic."

"Stop dancing around the edges, Liam, and come out with it," Allyn said, annoyed. "What are you saying?"

"You can power the door open."

Allyn barked a humorless laugh. "You remember what happened to the computer, right? I nearly melted it."

"Fortunately for us, that door requires a lot more power than a computer does."

Allyn licked his lips nervously. "I wouldn't even know where to start."

"I do." Liam rushed toward the door. "The walls are solid concrete, so unlike a normal room where the electrical wires are strung through the walls, the wires in here are encased in this." He kicked a small, insulated tube that stretched along the wall near the floor. "If we expose the wires, and you can feed them with enough electricity, the door should power up and allow us to enter the code to get it open."

"And if I feed it with too much electricity?" Allyn asked, thinking back to his mistake with the computer.

"Then you'll arc the circuit, and we'll never get out."

"Why did I even ask?"

"I doubt that'll be a problem, though," Liam said. "Those electrical wires feed everything in here. You'd sooner overtax yourself than you would arc the circuit."

"That's not making me feel any better."

Liam didn't seem to hear him. He raced across the room and leaped onto the table near Allyn. With his head only inches below the dark florescent light, Liam grabbed the wires connecting it to the ceiling and yanked them free. The light swung gently as the wires fell onto the table, their ends fileted. Liam brought the wires to his mouth and bit then grabbed the jagged piece of rubber insulation and pulled it back to expose more of the copper interior. He did this with both sets of wires that connected to the ballast of the light fixture.

"We can practice with this," Liam said, holding up both electrical wires. "Wield only a trickle and project it into these. Then slowly amp it up until the light glows consistently."

Allyn took the wires, watching as Liam jumped off the table. When he landed, he turned to Allyn anxiously.

Allyn felt foolish under the weight of the young man's expectations. Sure, he enjoyed being underestimated—hell, he relished it—but he loathed blind faith and the idea that success was something other than the culmination of years of hard work. Still... the sounds of battle continued to ring outside, and for a second, he was able to take a mental step back. For that brief moment, he didn't care about the pair of anxious eyes waiting for him to succeed or fail. He was transfixed with the continued sounds of fighting. His friends were dying, and his ability to stop it began with the wires in his hand. Foolish as he felt, he had to try. He had to succeed.

"Stand back." Allyn closed his eyes, so he couldn't be sure if they stepped back or not, but he *felt* as though they had. The void was easy to find and was already pulsed with energy. Grasping the bare wires, he imagined the void was a sponge soaked with water, and instead of twisting it, he gave it a gentle squeeze.

He felt the energy spring forward and opened his eyes as the coils of electricity connected with the copper wiring in his hands. For a brief moment, the wiring glowed, and Allyn's hope swelled.

And then the light exploded.

Jaxon rushed across the grounds, favoring speed over concealment. Something tugged at him like a rope tied around his midsection, compelling him forward, pleading with him to move faster. The feeling terrified him, and he wanted to stop and retreat back into the forest, but the compulsion intensified, snapping at him like a switch to his backside. He kept his eyes alert, scanning the landscape for unseen assailants. Part of him wondered if the unnatural feeling was a new ability found by an enemy machinist. One thing was certain—it was pulling him toward the battle.

His squad, splintered and only numbering five in all, followed in his steps. He could hear the crunching of their boots and their labored breathing growing more distant behind him. But he didn't care—he had to get into the battle.

The battle itself was contained to the flat ground in front of the library, where the ankle-deep ash made moving slow and laborious. Jaxon stumbled as he stepped into it. The sudden resistance felt as though he'd been lassoed around his ankles. Running through it was like running through sand, but unlike sand, the ash hung in the air like a dense fog, obscuring his vision and making breathing difficult.

The first magi appeared out of the fog, lost and alarmed, wide-eyed like a frightened doe. Jaxon started, hesitated, realized the magi wasn't one of his, and struck. He booted the man with an air-aided foot, sending him skidding through the ash and disappearing into the haze. He waited, watching as dark figures punctuated by flashes of red, orange, and blue streaked chaotically through the white smog.

He was fighting a battle unlike any he had ever fought before. Without cover, the magi units had dissolved into multiple one-on-one battles. It had become a free-for-all, where being struck by friendly fire was as likely as being struck by an enemy, the kind where luck won as often as superior tactics or numbers did.

The rest of his unit caught up to him, skidding to a halt as they suddenly came upon him.

Someone coughed. Another cursed.

Jaxon barely heard any of it. The compulsion was stronger than ever, willing him toward the edge of the battle near the library. *No. It's pulling me toward the library itself.*

"Continue forward," Jaxon said. "Rally our magi into a cohesive unit and fall back into the rubble, where there's cover. Restore order. Chaos favors Darian."

"Where are you going?" Andrew asked.

"Toward the library," Jaxon said. "Go."

His unit streaked past him, entering the fray, and Jaxon veered off toward the library. As he drew closer, the air grew less hazy, and two figures appeared atop the roof.

Jaxon recognized Ren's effortless movements. She fought with a deadly grace that was in contrast to her short and slender frame. Her opponent was taller than she was by almost a full head, with sandy-blond hair and pale, shining skin.

*Cason. He's supposed to be dead.*

He struck with reckless abandon, moving from one attack to the next, making up for his lack of efficiency with persistence. It kept Ren on the defensive. She backed across the library, countering fire with water and meeting ice blasts in midair with blasts of her own. She neared the edge but didn't appear to notice. She took a final step, and her foot came down on nothing but air. She teetered, arms flailing wildly as she worked to regain her balance.

Cason exploited her lapse in concentration and hurled a volley of fireballs in her direction.

With nothing else to do, Ren dropped. She fell off the library, the fireballs narrowly missing the top of her head. At the last possible second, she caught the edge of the roof.

Cason advanced. Ren dangled off the side of the library, kicking the walls, searching for a foothold or rough patch of concrete she could use for leverage. As Cason neared, Ren stopped, peering upward at him, calm and resolute.

Charging forward but still more than twenty feet away, Jaxon knew he wouldn't get there in time. Frustration gripped him. His hands balled into fists as he ran, and he threw his arms forward, sweeping the air as if he were charging through water. His scream tore across the distance.

Cason looked up.

Ren let go of the edge and launched herself backward. The air near her feet warped and cracked, and the wall fractured. Chunks of concrete fell to the wet ground below as Ren was propelled backward with unnatural speed. Something thin and blue formed in her hands then shot across the void. It took Cason in the neck just as Ren struck the ridge. Her head snapped back, and she did a backward somersault, landing on her stomach, her feet and hands sinking into the ash.

Cason gripped his neck. The blue shard of ice was red with blood, and more poured across his compression armor. He fell to his knees then his side, and his body shook as he took his last ragged breaths.

Jaxon came to stop atop the ridge. Ren was on her feet again and moving away from him.

"We lost the ridge," she said over her shoulder. "We need it back."

The compulsion willed Jaxon into the pit with such intensity that he nearly leaped into it. His logic won out, though, and he kept to the high ground, circling the pit, moving in the opposite direction as Ren. He hadn't heard it before. They had been muffled within the depths of the pit and overshadowed by the sounds of Ren's battle, but Jaxon could hear them now.

Labored breathing. Gasps. Curses.

He moved with a renewed sense of urgency. He knew who

was down there. Crystal clear amid the static of battle, her voice cut through the rest.

*Leira.*

Jaxon froze. He understood the feeling now. The distance. The compulsion. And the reason it resembled fear and pain mixed with hope and determination.

A contradiction in two parts. In two people.

The echo.

Jaxon cursed.

# CHAPTER 28

"**W**E ONLY GET ONE SHOT at this," Liam said, sliding the table beneath another set of florescent lights.

"I know," Allyn said.

"And if we fail—"

"I understand the consequences," Allyn interrupted. "But the fact remains that I can *practice* until I've blown out every light in here, and I still won't be any closer to being ready."

Liam stopped and took a sharp breath. His shoulders dipped in resignation. "What do you want me to do?"

"I want you to trust me."

Liam squirmed under Allyn's gaze, and his eyes slid away, turning to the bare walls instead.

"I..." Allyn began, "I can't explain it, but I've never been as good at practicing something as I was when I was under pressure. I remember rehearsing my opening and closing statements. My words were always jumbled and forgotten, but when I stepped in front of that jury..." Allyn smiled, cocking his head to try and catch Liam's attention. "I thrived, Liam. I don't know why, but I need the external pressure. Practicing with these lights isn't going to help."

Liam met Allyn's eye, his face a furious mix of logical fear and desire to believe in the irrational.

"Not to interrupt," Nolan said slowly. "But shouldn't I have a say in this, too?"

Allyn remained quiet, refusing to turn away from Liam.

"Because if I do," Nolan continued. "I say we trust him. If Allyn thinks he can do it, then I believe he can." When nobody responded, Nolan added, "Just thought you'd want to know."

Allyn thought he could hear a tinge of embarrassment in Nolan's voice, but he kept his eyes on Liam. It wasn't that he felt he had to convince the young magi; he just wanted his blessing. When Liam finally met Allyn's gaze, Allyn offered him a small shrug. *What do you think?* it asked.

Liam gave him a small nod, grabbed something off the table beside him, and tossed it at Allyn. A glint of silver soared through the air. Allyn instinctively slid out of the way and caught the object by its leather hilt. It was heavier than he'd expected, and it threw him off balance, twisting him about. Once steady, he held the object in front of him. Three feet long, with a polished double-edged blade and intricate carvings of the magi symbols for fire, water, and air on its hilt, the broadsword had to weigh close to five pounds. On the pommel was a symbol he'd never seen before—a shield with tarnished red, blue, and white paint, decorated with more elemental symbols. A family crest perhaps.

Allyn held the sword reverently, his dark shadow barely visible in the gleaming blade. He turned to Liam. "Did you just throw a *sword* at me?"

Liam blushed. "Sorry about that."

"I'm glad I caught it," Allyn said sarcastically. He turned to the wall and drove the sword between it and the wire housing that ran down its edge. It made a rough scraping noise across the concrete, likely tarnishing the blade. Allyn winced. The damage already done, he took the hilt and pommel in both hands and, using the point against the wall as leverage, pulled back. The black housing ripped free. Allyn then sliced through the wires as easily as if they were flesh. From there, he quickly cut away more of the rubber insulation, exposing enough wire for him to grasp.

Outside, the booms of battle were growing more distant. Was it drawing to an end? *Who's winning?* He had to find out. He had to find Darian.

Oozing feigned confidence, Allyn took the wire in his hand and wielded. He followed Liam's earlier advice and began with a trickle of energy—roughly the same amount he had used when the light had exploded. The copper wires glowed and—

Nothing happened.

*More*, Allyn thought. He projected more energy into the wire, willing the keypad to glow to life.

Still nothing happened.

*More.* Allyn took the cable in his other hand, and dueling coils of electricity poured into the wires. They sparked and clashed as the raw tendrils of energy touched each other, but still, the keypad remained dark.

"It's not working," Allyn bellowed over the crackle of exposed electricity.

Liam rushed forward, careful not to step too close. He followed the insulated housing up the wall, tracing the wires back to the pad itself. Halfway up, he stopped.

"Stop!" he yelled.

Allyn released, and the library went dark again.

As the coils dissipated, Liam set to work. He grabbed the sword from the ground and pried the metal housing away from the wall. A portion of housing was glowing, and the concrete wall was black behind it.

"There," Liam said, fishing the thin wires out of the metal housing. The color-coated wires were black where the rubber insulation had melted away. "They were arcing inside. Give me a minute." Liam licked his fingers then ripped back the rubber insulation, trimmed the wires, and reattached them to the main circuit by twisting them around each other. "It won't be perfect, but it should do the trick."

The red coils sprang back to life as Allyn took the cables back in his hands. He watched as the energy coursed through the hastily reattached wires, sparking intermittently, but continuing to blaze with power.

The keypad glowed to life.

Liam was on it in a flash, typing in the FBI's four-digit code. The chime was lost in the crackling of electricity, but the red light quickly turned green. Gears inside the wall let out a deep groan, and the door shuddered open an inch.

"More!" Liam shouted.

Allyn squeezed the void, wringing out all the energy he could. Light flooded the room as the florescent bulbs sprang to life, then popped with a flash and shattered. Sparks and glass rained from the ceiling. Liam and Nolan took cover, but Allyn continued to hold onto the cable as if his life depended on it.

*It's not enough*, Allyn thought. *How?* He'd seen less power accomplish more. *There's another bad connection somewhere.* They didn't have time to track it down. He had to get that door open.

"Aaaahhhh!" Allyn screamed, willing more power into the cable.

*Magic has limits*, Jaxon had said. *We don't know what yours are.*

Allyn was again caught between two likely deaths. One had two people he cared about dying with him. The other had him sacrificing himself to save them. Liam was more important to the Family than he was. Liam was their future. He was the future of the entire magi race. Allyn could die for less.

Allyn squeezed the void dry, willing every bit of energy he had into the cable. The power raged through him, searing at his insides like a torn stomach spilling acid and bacteria into his bloodstream.

Something tore, and pain shrieked through his chest. He collapsed, dropping the cable. *No,* he thought. *No!*

Nolan caught him before his head slapped against the floor and laid him down gently.

"I'm sorry," Allyn said, weak and gripping his chest. His heart thumped sporadically like a child hitting a drum for the first time. "I failed."

"No," Nolan said. "No, you didn't."

Allyn followed his eyes. Liam stood in front of the door. Allyn blinked. *No.* Liam was on the *other* side—outside.

A cool breeze blew into the library, carrying with it a scent of soil and smoke. Allyn smiled in spite of the erratic thumping in his chest.

---

Halfway down the ladder, Jaxon jumped. The sheet of plywood cracked under his weight, and muddy water splashed up from the edges.

A single magi lay on his stomach a few feet away. Jaxon hesitated, peering into the shadows around him. The sun had risen above the ridge, but half of the corridors were still bathed in darkness. When no one attacked, Jaxon rushed forward and rolled the magi onto his back. It was Gerek, one of Leira's squad. Mud caked the side of his face, and a deep gash cut across his temple toward the back of his head. Jaxon placed two fingers on his neck, checking his pulse.

A muffled scream.

Jaxon dove into the muddy water as something sliced through the air where he'd just been and struck the dirt wall with a solid *thwack.*

*Ice,* Jaxon thought. It had to be ice.

He jumped to his feet, fire burning in each of his hands. Water, thick with mud, dripped from his elbows onto the moist ground, sounding like muffled footsteps. Whoever had attacked was using ice to avoid giving up their position. Still, only so many places could conceal him from Jaxon's direct line of sight. The trajectory of the attack limited the possibilities even more.

The next attack was little more than a ripple in the night, a moving shadow that shouldn't have been possible. Jaxon met the ice blast in midair with a fireball, and half-melted ice pebbles peppered him harmlessly. Jaxon hurled a fireball into the corner of the corridor. It struck against the wall, briefly illuminating two figures.

It was all he needed to recognize Leira—then again, he'd already known she was down there.

Darian emerged from the shadows, using Leira as a human shield. One hand covered her mouth. The other was outstretched beside her head. The threat was clear—Darian could kill her before Jaxon could kill him.

The two men scowled at each other. They didn't say anything—there was nothing to say. Darian wasn't going to let Leira go, and Jaxon wasn't going to leave without her.

Leira remained silent and alert. She moved with Darian, her steps only half a beat behind his. Her eyes never left Jaxon's, and behind them was a storm of emotions that Jaxon struggled to make sense of. Anger. Frustration. Determination. Even embarrassment. The last one surprised him.

"Jaxon!"

Darian's eyes shot from Jaxon searching for the voice.

Jaxon launched a fireball, propelling it forward with air. Darian leaped to the side. He dragged Leira with him, and the two of them splashed into the mud. The fireball exploded against the wall with such force that it rippled the ground. Loose chunks of mud fell from the wall, landing with sloppy *slaps*.

Leira scrambled to her feet and dashed across the slick ground toward Jaxon.

Jaxon stepped closer to the wall to get a better angle on Darian. The blond man was wielding fire. Jaxon didn't pause. Ice was in his hands in a heartbeat, and he blasted it forward indiscriminately. The first three ice blasts shot through the air, sticking into the muddy wall behind Darian, but the fourth collided with Darian's fireball in midair. They exploded, sending chunks of ice and wisps of fire into the narrow corridor.

Jaxon didn't let up. He launched another volley. Darian rolled, rose to his feet, and dove behind the corner of the library.

Jaxon caught Leira in his arm and spun her so that he was between her and Darian's cover. "You okay?"

"Yeah."

"You sure?"

She didn't respond. Embarrassment swelled inside him. It was so powerful, he almost thought it was his.

He turned toward her. Even wet, muddy, and sporting a deep bruise across her cheek, she was the most beautiful woman he'd ever seen. He longed for her. He wanted to hold her. Be with her. Tell her he understood. And he could sense the same feelings in her.

"I..." He didn't know where to start. His eyes searched hers. Did she know? Could she feel it, too?

"Something's wrong." Liam stood a dozen steps behind Leira.

*He's the one who called out*, Jaxon thought, replaying the confrontation in his mind.

"It's Allyn," Liam continued. "He... I think he pushed himself too far."

"I've got it," Leira said. "Find Darian—he's been gone for too long already."

"Get them inside the library and wait for me," Jaxon said.

Leira lingered for half a breath then moved away without word. Jaxon watched her go, though he ached to follow her.

A sudden *crack* from the other side of the library saved him from dwelling on it further. Leira stopped, shooting him a curious expression.

Jaxon's torment bent itself into a smile.

"Ren," he said.

---

Ren took sadistic pleasure in tormenting Darian. She was a lioness playing with her prey. He put up a fight, but somewhere deep down, he had to know it was over.

Atop the ridge, she had the high ground and, with it, a clear vantage of their battlefield. More than that, she had cover and leverage. She kept Darian moving, breaking his will a little more with every attack. It wasn't as though she could kill him at any time, but the advantage was clearly on her side.

The final blow came when Jaxon rounded the edge of the library behind Darian. He stopped when he saw Ren, and she halted her game.

Darian froze. His eyes slid to his feet, and he let out a defeated breath. "And so it ends."

"And so it ends," Jaxon agreed.

Darian turned to face his would-be executioner, and before Ren could blink, desperation replaced defeat. He threw his hands forward, and a steady stream of white-hot flame burst forth.

Jaxon retreated behind the wall. Darian pursued, the fire pouring out of his hands like water from a fire hydrant. Constant. Steady. Powerful. The gray wall turned black, and fire sizzled against the damp ground. And still, Darian pursued.

Ren shot a pair of ice blasts, which took Darian the back of the legs, driving through his hamstrings and into his thighs. Letting out a strangled cry, Darian fell to his knees. But the flames did not stop. He raised his hands to the sky and screamed. The flames extended well beyond the pit, and even ten feet away, Ren had to shield her eyes from the heat.

She prepared another blast of ice.

The fire disappeared.

Darian collapsed. He kicked and thrashed, his arms and legs shaking violently. His chest arched toward the sky, and his head snapped back as a pained groan left his lips.

Jaxon reemerged, stopping a few paces in front of Darian. He dropped into a crouch, watching as the man died. He said something that Ren couldn't hear. But she knew what she would have said.

"Magic has consequences."

---

Allyn felt as though his heart were running away. It beat so fast, it hurt. And then every so often, it would trip up like a sprinter in the last leg of a race and crash to a dead stop. In those moments, a split second lasted an eternity, and Allyn feared his heart wouldn't start back up again. Fortunately, so far, it had.

He heard a woman's voice, distant and quiet, but the world took a backseat when he wasn't sure if his heart was going to explode or not. Whoever she was, her presence soothed him.

He opened his eyes, expecting to see Kendyl or Nyla, but the room spun, and he felt as though he might pass out. He closed them again, but it was all he needed.

Leira knelt beside him, her cold hand pressed against his arm. Even through his eyelids, he could see the soft glow as she probed him.

"Arrhythmia," she said.

"What's that?" Liam asked.

"An irregular heartbeat."

"Will he be okay?"

"Yes," Leira said. "He'll need rest, and he probably shouldn't wield again until it returns to normal, but he should be fine."

Allyn felt her withdraw her hand and move away.

"You hear that?" Nolan asked. "Quit milking it and get up." He pulled Allyn into a sitting position.

Allyn opened his eyes. Gravity played games with him, pulling him one way, then the other, then backward. He swayed, fell, and caught himself, all just in time for it to shift again. "Give me a moment," he said, his throat tight.

It was some time before he was able to get up, and even longer before he'd worked himself into a chair. He was sitting doubled over with his elbows on his knees, hands in his sweat-slick hair when Jaxon and Ren entered the library. Cuts, scrapes, bruises, and burns covered them from neck to foot, all partially hidden under layers of mud and ash. Their tired expressions were hardly the looks of victory.

"What happened?" Allyn asked.

"It's over," Jaxon said.

"Who won?"

Jaxon wore a haunted expression. "Nobody."

A steady stream of magi appeared in the doorway behind him.

"Let's load up and be done with it."

# CHAPTER 29

THE MCCOLLUM FAMILY TOOK MORE than an hour to load the library's contents into the cargo vans. The sun had risen high enough to top the tips of the evergreen trees, and a thick fog still hovered a few feet above the ground, thickest in the grassy areas that surrounded the fallen manor. It gave Jaxon the impression that he was walking on clouds.

Liam oversaw the work, valuing caution over speed and occasionally barking out orders when he was displeased, more to prove a point and reaffirm his desire to finish without further damage than because anyone did anything wrong.

Leira worked with Nyla and Vincent to set up a medical triage station. Brandt's clerics, Galvin and Enova, joined them. All in all, there were four McCollum magi dead and three more injured, two of whom would likely suffer from lifelong disabilities. Jaxon had given the dead Hylands battlefield burials. So many fallen.

*It's not over yet,* Jaxon reminded himself. *There's still one more.*

Brandt kept his magi separated from the McCollum Family and gave Jaxon an apprehensive look as he approached. He broke away from the group to meet Jaxon before he reached them.

"I need to speak with them," Jaxon said.

"Of course," Brandt agreed, a slight quiver in his voice.

The Hyland magi watched him warily, some even with open contempt. Many had likely seen this as an opportunity to right previous wrongs and impose justice on their old Family. They weren't content being ordered to the sidelines.

The person Jaxon was looking for stood near the back of the group, her face expressionless. Blond hair, frazzled by the damp air, framed her round face. She licked her red lips, showing no signs that she knew what was coming.

"I appreciate your patience as we've regained control of the situation," Jaxon said. "It's no doubt been a very difficult night for you." He hoped his voice sounded kinder to them than it did to his own ears.

Most of the magi in front of him were good people who would have risked their lives to stop Darian if given the chance. But before he'd had an opportunity to speak with Liam, he hadn't known whom he could trust. Even then, he had no way to be sure he'd rooted out the last of the spies. He prayed the movement had died with Darian, but as he'd seen when Darian had picked up Lukas's mantle, there was never any way to know where it would truly end.

"We're nearly finished," Jaxon continued. "So if you'll make your way to the vans, we'll be moving shortly."

The magi groaned and grumbled among themselves, but moved as a sheepish unit toward the vans parked around the perimeter of the manor.

Brandt remained behind with Jaxon, watching as they shuffled away.

"Did you find the mole?" Brandt asked quietly.

"Blond hair," Jaxon said. "Bringing up the rear."

"Roselie?" Brandt's expression went from surprise to dismay then finally rested on cold anger. "And you're just going to let her go?"

"No. But they're not my family, and my hands are already stained with enough blood."

Brant licked his lips nervously. "I assume you have proof?"

"It'll be in her phone."

Brandt's face twitched as he struggled to bite back a scowl. He didn't question why she had a phone. Unlike the McCollum Family, which had, at Graeme's order, largely disavowed technology, the Hyland Family had embraced it. Each of Darian's magi carried one.

"Roselie!" Brandt shouted.

The blond-haired girl stiffened.

"A minute, *please*."

Roselie turned, and Jaxon and Brandt approached.

"I need to see your phone," Brandt said.

"Of course," Roselie said. Her eyes flickered to Jaxon then back to Brandt. "What are you looking for?"

Brandt handed the phone to Jaxon. "We fear there's another mole among us. It wasn't a coincidence that Darian was here tonight. Someone told him to be."

Jaxon brought up the text messages and wasn't surprised to see that it had been wiped clean. He scrolled through the recent calls. And again, there was nothing incriminating. He sighed. She wasn't going to make it easy.

"And you think it was me?"

"Was it?" Brandt asked.

Roselie met Brandt's eye. "I shouldn't have to answer that."

"You don't have to," Jaxon said. "You can delete messages, but data is never lost. And fortunately for me, there are some in my Family who know how to access that information." He tapped the final button and brought up the cached data Liam had told him how to find. The message was short and simple. He held it up for Brandt to read.

*They're moving. McCollum Manor. Tonight.*

Roselie's lips parted as if she were going to say something, but nothing came out. Her face drained of color, and she swallowed.

Having been through enough desperate attacks recently, Jaxon was prepared for another. It never came. Instead, Roselie's shoulders slumped, and her head drooped to stare at the ground.

"He had my son." Her voice was almost a whisper. "He said... he said if I didn't..." She closed her eyes and exhaled a long, resigned breath.

Brandt looked pained, caught somewhere between anger and empathy. They had each made great sacrifices to protect their children.

"How many more were feeding Darian information?" Jaxon asked.

"I don't know," she said. "He never told us anything."

"If I find out you're lying or holding something back..." His implications were clear.

"I'm not," she said hurriedly.

"How many remain at the Estate?"

"Not many," Roselie said. "Only a handful."

"All loyal to Darian?"

Roselie's face curled with anger, and she looked up from the ground to meet Jaxon's eye. "No. Very few remain loyal to that maniac. The rest of us are prisoners of fear and circumstance."

Jaxon let his mind wander for a moment. The pieces in his head began clicking into place, but he wasn't certain how to proceed.

"What are you thinking?" Brandt asked.

"I'm not sure yet," Jaxon said honestly. "Bring her. If there's any punishment, we can figure it out later. Right now, I want to be gone from this place."

---

The motion of the car did little to help Allyn's loss of

equilibrium. He was thankful Kendyl had made sure he rode in the Cadillac—another bumping, swaying ride in the back of a cargo van might have thrown him over the edge. The car glided down the driveway, its air-ride suspension absorbing most of the ruts and potholes. The soft, worn-in leather seat felt like a feather pillow under him, caressing him like a mother's touch. He didn't feel *good*, but he certainly could have felt worse.

Quiet and concerned, Kendyl was riding in the back with him, completely oblivious to the small looks Nolan periodically shot her way from the front seat.

Jaxon turned off the driveway onto the old, two-lane mountain road, passing the stone pillars that had once held the steel gate that shielded the McCollum Family from the outside world. The stream of cargo vans followed, and Jaxon led them through the curvy pass, keeping his pace well below the speed limit. The wounded rode in one of those vans, packed in like the library contents, something else to be transported.

Allyn kept his eyes closed and his arm resting on the door, touching the cool, damp glass of the window. The rest of his body was burning, and he was covered in an uncomfortable sweat. Not the watery kind that followed an extraneous activity, this was the thick, sticky sweat that covered an ailing body. It was confining. And just thinking about it made Allyn's skin crawl.

He focused on two things: the coolness of the window and the steady rhythm in his chest. Leira had been right. His heartbeat had returned to normal, and the pain had subsided with it. He still felt weak, and even sitting down, his body was weary. But his heart felt as strong as ever. That didn't mean he didn't pay close attention to it.

Preoccupied with his inner thoughts, he barely heard Jaxon's curse. He was, however, greatly aware of the car's sudden lurch and the squeal of its tires. Allyn's eyes snapped open. A couple hundred feet in front of them, more than a dozen police vehicles blocked the their path to the highway. Squad cars and SUVs parked two deep formed a phalanx of metal and machine. Officers stood behind opened doors with their guns drawn. And at the head was a white Chevy Impala.

Special Agent Richard Maddox waited two steps in front of his hood, well beyond the line of cover. His dark suit was sharp and pristine, his head clean shaven, and his thick beard carefully sculpted. A series of shallow cuts and light bruises covered one half of his face, no doubt from his encounter with Nolan, and he held his wrist in one hand, the gun in the other, its barrel pointed toward the ground.

The car squealed to a halt some thirty yards from Maddox. A cacophony of locking brakes and howling tires sang behind them, quickly followed by the horrific banging sounds of metal crashing into metal. Allyn stiffened, flinching every time the dull *crash* thundered through it all, anxious that they would be hit next.

It ended as quickly as it began. Blue smoke hung in the air like a toxic haze, and its acrid smell stung the back of Allyn's throat. Shattered pebbles of glass littered the road, glittering under the morning sun like tiny diamonds. Allyn shook the cobwebs loose. Jaxon was as still as a mountain, his eyes wide, hard, and unblinking. He watched Maddox, his hands flexing on the steering wheel.

Maddox didn't seem to notice. He was fixed on Nolan.

"Is everyone all right?" Allyn asked, never taking his eyes off the agent.

"Yeah," they each said, in varying degrees of distress.

Allyn scanned the scene in front of them. The crescent shape of the police phalanx stretched from one shoulder of the road to the other, extending all the way to the guardrail. Behind Jaxon's lead car, the McCollum Family's cargo vans had come to a stop in a haphazard mess, blocking the road from ditch to ditch. They had nowhere to go. They were stuck.

"We're not getting out of this one," Allyn said.

The leather of the steering wheel creaked under Jaxon's flexing hands, and Allyn thought he could hear his grinding teeth.

Allyn was so angry, he could feel the tears of frustration welling in the backs of his eyes. They'd been so close. But instead of getting away, the entire McCollum Family and the Hyland refugees who'd trusted them were going to be taken in. Everything had been undone because of Darian Hyland's surprise attack. He was, for the first time, jealous that he hadn't been the one to kill the psychopath.

"Allyn," Kendyl said. "Allyn, look at me."

He couldn't do it. He was afraid she would throw him over the edge, that he would lose control of his swelling emotions. She grabbed him by the back of his head and pulled his forehead against hers. She looked at him from the tops of her eye sockets, her green eyes radiating with intensity. It was a game they used to play—smashing their foreheads together and waiting for the other to wilt under the pain. Their mother used to say they were trying to find out who was more stubborn. Kendyl always won.

Allyn set his jaw against the pain and closed his eyes. He was still afraid to look at her. He'd failed her. Again.

"We can do this, Allyn." Kendyl pressed harder. "I know we can. We've been through worse. I believe in you."

The pain grew so intense that Allyn barely heard her, and just as he was about to cry out, she released. Allyn's head drifted backward, the stars in his vision slowly disappearing as the pain and pressure subsided. Buried beneath it, a new feeling blossomed. A sense of hope. Optimism. Confidence. Worry disappeared under its weight like morning fog under the rising sun. He drew in a deep breath, coursing the positive energy through his veins until his entire body was alive with it. His vision grew sharper. The lines of worry in Jaxon's face seemed crisper, and the silence of their standoff sounded deeper. He suddenly felt as though the odds were in their favor.

Kendyl blinked, her eyelids drooping slowly, and shook her head, rubbing her temples, likely trying to shake away her own stars. When she looked at Allyn, her face was expressionless. His strong, confident sister had become a quiet, placid woman who looked as though she were on the verge of passing out.

"Kendyl..." Allyn said.

"I'm fine," Kendyl said. Her voice was soft and slightly confused.

"Are you with me?"

"Always."

Allyn unbuckled his seatbelt and popped open the door. Only then did Jaxon snap out of his stupor. He wheeled on Allyn, reaching for him.

"What are you doing?" he demanded.

Only a short time ago, Allyn would have wilted under such intensity, but now he was swimming with confidence. He met Jaxon's eye. "They're after me."

"Not anymore," Jaxon said. "They'll have us all now."

"I know," Allyn said. "But I have to talk to him."

"You're turning yourself in?"

"Not if I can help it."

Jaxon's expression softened. He looked at Agent Maddox then back at Allyn, no doubt coming to the same conclusion Allyn had. He gave Allyn a slight nod and pulled his arm back.

"It's been a ride." The words slipped out, coming from the deep recesses of Allyn's memory. They weren't his mother's final words but were near enough. Allyn smiled, more at the memory than anything else, but the corner of Jaxon's mouth arched into a grin.

Allyn stepped out of the car, and an immediate wave of clicks met him as the officers switched off safeties and chambered bullets. Allyn had never felt so alone. He'd been targeted, hunted, and attacked, but through it all, he'd had the help and support of people who cared about him. They had gone through it together. But as he took a series of uneasy steps toward the front of the car, he had to face down more than twenty black barrels, each holding a round with his name on it. If someone had a twitchy finger or had grown weary of chasing him, it would be all over.

Allyn stopped at the front of the car, mirroring Maddox's position. Maddox's cuts and bruises made him more menacing, more human. The boulder of a man could bleed. He could be hurt. He could feel.

A soft murmur traveled through the mass of cops, and Allyn turned to see Kendyl approaching. She walked confidently with her back straight and chin held high. Her long hair blew radiantly in the gentle breeze, displaying her uninjured face. She stopped at Allyn's shoulder and folded her arms. If Maddox was cool, Kendyl was ice, and her cold fury was directed squarely at the agent.

Maddox gaped. He uncrossed his arms and took a tentative step forward. His eyes narrowed as he fixed on Kendyl, obviously distrusting the truth of what he saw. Another door popped open, and Maddox's surprise grew into something far more intense. He set his jaw and squared himself into a powerful stance, his knuckles whitening around the butt of his pistol. Allyn didn't have to turn to know Nolan had stepped out.

The former agent joined Allyn and Kendyl, stopping at Allyn's other shoulder. Allyn nodded to him, silently wishing Nolan had remained in the car. They had definitively drawn a line in the sand, and Nolan's picking the side of the fugitive was a further slight to his former partner. If the growing rage on Maddox's face was any indication, the situation had just grown more dangerous.

Jaxon appeared half a beat later, extending their line

from three to four. And then to Allyn's surprise, more filled in around him. Leira. Liam. Nyla. Ren. They poured in so quickly that Allyn couldn't keep them all straight. Rory. Canary. Joyce. Andrew. Even Brandt, Juniette, and the other Hyland refugees. His friends. His Family. They had stood with him against Darian. They had defeated Lukas. And even in the certainty of defeat, at the end of their line, they remained together.

Not considering the unarmed people a threat, the police kept their guns raised but didn't fire.

More magi slipped into position. They walked, limped, and hopped forward. Full strength, and wounded, the magi stood with him. They stretched from ditch to ditch, a single line of strength and purpose. Allyn met each one of their eyes, nodding with a silent appreciation. Then, as he felt the guns move from him to the others and the tension build to a crescendo, he took a purposeful stride forward.

"You really thought she was dead, didn't you?" Allyn said. His words easily carried across the distance, cutting through the silence. "I know you've questioned my old coworkers and classmates and anyone else that might have had a passing knowledge of me, but if you knew anything about me, you'd know that there is nothing more important to me than family. What I did was for Kendyl. What I do now is for all of them."

What he was about to do next defied reason. But with the recent display of solidarity, he dared to hope. He separated himself from the group—if it went badly, he didn't want it causing death among those who'd bravely stood with him— and wielded.

# CHAPTER 30

TWENTY-FIVE GUNS WHIRLED TO FOCUS strictly on Allyn. He anchored his feet to the cracked pavement, steeling himself against the sudden flutter in his chest. The coils dimmed slightly, though they were still a wonder to the unknowing eyes.

"Hold!" Maddox held a fist in the air.

Allyn took hold of his words, using them to flame his will. His legs trembled, and he felt as though he were about to topple off a cliff into a deep canyon.

*Hold*, he repeated. *Hold.*

"This only ends one way, Allyn," Maddox bellowed over the crackling coils of electricity. "And that's you coming with me."

Allyn shook his head slowly. "I no longer believe that."

Maddox's eyebrows rose with surprise. "Really?" He held his arms out to his sides, gesturing to the tactical unit behind him. Most were outfitted in full riot gear comprised of Kevlar vests, thick padding over the arms and legs, and helmets with glass visors. The assortment of weapons drove the point home.

As if in a silent argument, the Family revealed their own powers. In a sharp contrast to the mechanical sounds of safeties and bullets being chambered, the magi call to action was organic. Fire sparking. Water gurgling. Air whooshing. And a new sound joined the others. Like a deep drum reverberating through a musical chorus, Nolan's power hummed violently. The light began in his palms, stretched up to his elbows, and disappeared under his sleeve.

Allyn studied the officers. He heard more than a few gasps and curses, and the ones he could see wore disbelieving expressions—mouths agape, eyes wide in shock, confusion, and terror. Guns lowered as many took uneasy steps backward, and for a brief moment, Allyn believed their display was enough to break the force. But the most hardened of officers held it together. They showed little reaction—only a slight dip in their gun barrels or a thin parting of their lips as they exhaled—and their strength was enough to keep the force from breaking. As quickly as the shaken officers lost their composure, they regained it and formed back up in rank.

"We are not your enemy," Allyn said. "But push us, and we can be."

"You," Maddox yelled back, "are a fugitive! A man who kidnapped his own sister. A man who killed too many of our finest." The officers stiffened at this. "You *are* our enemy."

"Listen to him, Maddox," Nolan said. "He's telling—"

"Do *not* speak to me!"

Nolan snapped his mouth shut and pursed his lips angrily. Allyn silently thanked him for it. Nolan's intentions, however heroic, would only instigate matters further.

"The only crime I've committed," Allyn said, "was that I didn't come to the police as soon as I should have. All of your other allegations are false. My sister stands here, unharmed, and she can verify everything I've said."

Maddox only shook his head. "I don't care if you're guilty or not—that's not my job. I exist to bring you in so others can decide. Of course, if it were up to me, I'd shoot you dead and be done with it. So tell your friends to back down before this thing turns ugly."

Allyn didn't know how much of Maddox's bluster was rooted in truth, but he didn't want to find out. He glanced uneasily at Jaxon. The enormous magi was the only person he'd ever met who was as stubborn as Maddox. He briefly met Allyn's eye and cocked his head to the side, indicating for him to return to the magi line. Allyn retook his position between Nolan and Kendyl.

"Air," Jaxon ordered in a voice that only his unit could hear. "Focus it on the front line. Nolan, I want you to hit the underside of the lead car. Wait for my order."

"They'll return fire," Allyn said. Those around him wielding fire and water quickly switched to air.

"Aim to injure. Do not kill. We're only trying to stall them."

"We'll be slaughtered," Allyn continued.

Jaxon ignored him. "For those of you who cannot wield, make for the nearby vehicles and clear a path. Leira, Kendyl, go with Nyla and Liam. As soon as there is an opening, I need you leading the caravan through it. Joyce, you, too."

"What's it going to be, Allyn?" Maddox asked.

"The rest of you," Jaxon said, "advance after the initial volley. As long as they have us at a distance, they hold the advantage. Close the gap. Fight together."

"So be it," Maddox bellowed. "Fi—"

"Now!"

The very air twisted around Allyn, and light *bent* as if he were seeing it through a glass. Before Jaxon finished sounding his order, the air exploded as every McCollum and Hyland magi acted as one.

Maddox was tossed off his feet and thrown backward into the windshield of one of the vehicles. Then as the second volley of air hit, like a muscle car with too much torque, the car flipped and tossed Maddox as if he were a boulder in a catapult. As the car crashed into the second row of vehicles, officers scrambled and dove to the pavement. Others watched in horror as the unseen force quickly savaged the front line of their unit.

Very few opened fire, and by the time they did, they were too late.

Maddox's car went up in flames. Nolan's energy charge ignited under the gas pan, throwing the vehicle fifteen feet into the air. It crashed to the asphalt, tires exploding, windows shattering, flames licking the undercarriage.

Jaxon led the magi unit forward, breaking for the first line of vehicles. A bullet zipped perilously close to Allyn's ear, snapping him into action. He rushed forward and leaped over the hood of a vehicle. The officer on the ground was just getting to his feet. Allyn kicked him in the chest savagely. It was like kicking stone. He cried out, grasping the mirror of a nearby SUV to keep from collapsing. The officer rose to his feet, pulling his baton off his belt.

The officer swung ruthlessly, aiming for the biceps of the arm that held the mirror. Allyn let go just as the baton struck, ripping the mirror off the car. The officer whirled. Allyn lunged, and the tip of the baton sang through the air, narrowly missing his chin. The officer advanced, his left forearm held in front of him, nightstick at the ready.

Allyn wielded. The trickle of energy formed as a single coil of electricity around each arm, but it was enough to make the officer freeze. Allyn sprang forward and slapped the officer's chest. The coils surged, wrapping around the officer like a whip. His knees buckled, and he fell to the ground, stunned. He didn't move as the coils withdrew.

Blinding light filled Allyn's vision, and he found himself curled on the ground, protecting his head. He hadn't seen the second officer approach. The blows continued to rain down with a ferocious rhythm, striking Allyn's arms, shoulders, and back. Allyn cried out and tried to roll away, but the space was too confined. He had nowhere to hide. The air cracked, and as quickly as the blows had begun, they ceased.

Allyn opened his eyes to find a powerful shadow standing over him. The second officer had fallen atop the first.

"Get up." Jaxon's gruff voice was pained and to the point, not one to be argued with.

Allyn winced as he uncurled, stretching beaten muscles against their will. By the time he rose to his feet, Jaxon was already gone. Allyn surveyed the scene. The first batch of police vehicles had already been moved, and the cargo vans screamed down the mountain road fast enough to bottom out as they hit the highway. Sparks flew out from the undercarriage of the lead van as it slid sideways onto smooth pavement. It teetered on two tires before crashing back down onto all four and jetting through the hole in the police defensive. The next two followed without the theatrics.

Allyn picked up the nearest baton. It was lighter than he would have imagined, balanced so that the tip was heavier, and made of aluminum. He wielded again, projecting the current into the nightstick. The coils snaked around the metal baton, and the grip grew warm in his hand.

The first officer he found was already in a heated battle with Rory. Allyn came from behind to strike a small swath of exposed skin under the base of the officer's helmet. The officer went rigid, his chest arching forward, and Rory hit him with a concussion of air that sent him hurling into the driver's-side door of a nearby SUV. Rory nodded his appreciation, and together, he and Allyn advanced.

They circled through the phalanx, overwhelming individual battles and gathering more magi into their rank. Slowly, the series of individual skirmishes became one large force picking off smaller ones. They were halfway through the phalanx when Allyn risked another glance toward the edge of the police presence. The hole in the police defensive was larger, and three more cargo vans zipped through. The rear van slowed, and four shadows broke from the battle and rushed for it. When the van sped away, the shadows were gone. The magi were fleeing. Risking another glance, Allyn saw why. Only a handful of the vans remained.

"We're fleeing," Allyn said.

Rory whipped his head around to watch the vans speed down the road. Less than a quarter mile away, brake lights flared, and two shadows emerged from the lead van to rush back toward the battle.

"They won't leave without us," Rory said. "We need to get the rest."

"To me!" Allyn bellowed. "To me!" He held his baton in the air. The glowing metal was hot to the touch, and the red coils continued to rush around it in a twisted mess of raw power. "To me!"

A series of gunshots popped. Allyn ducked instinctively as metal around him clanged and sparked. A ricocheting bullet grazed his arm, and another glanced off his hip. On his stomach, Allyn peered under the vehicles, searching for his assailant.

A pair of glossy black loafers approached from the hollow center of the crescent, where Maddox had originally been.

Allyn growled, jumping to his feet. He wielded again— the electricity had winked out when he'd ducked—and flew around the vehicle.

Maddox, startled by the sudden movement, hesitated. Then realizing it was Allyn, he brought his gun up to fire. Allyn heaved the glowing baton. It spun through the air and struck Maddox's gun hand.

A single shot rang off, fired harmlessly into the night.

Allyn was on him in less than a blink. He punched Maddox in the nose, then again just below the left eye. He brought a knee up, aiming for Maddox's midsection, but missed, catching the bottom of Maddox's hidden Kevlar vest.

Pain blossomed in Allyn's knee. He tried to steady himself, but his leg collapsed, and he fell to the asphalt.

Maddox rebounded quicker than Allyn could have imagined. He rolled onto Allyn, grabbing him by the front of his shirt, and threw a softball-sized first into his face.

The stars returned. Another blow broke something in Allyn's face.

Allyn went limp, no longer able to think, and coughed up copper-flavored blood.

Maddox let go of his shirt, and Allyn flopped to the ground. Maddox rose and didn't see the jagged piece of ice streaking through the air toward him.

"No!"

A bright ball of light flew toward it, colliding with the ice blast in midair. *Crack!* Tiny ice bits and harmless droplets of water sprayed Maddox across the back.

Maddox spun.

Nolan emerged from the line of cars. His starched shirt was cut in half a dozen places and soaked in blood. Sweat and dirt streaked his face, but he strode forward with purpose.

*Nolan saved Maddox.*

Maddox scanned the ground hurriedly. His eyes found the gun. He looked at it, then at Nolan, as if doing the math to see if he could get to it quickly enough.

"I wouldn't do that," Nolan said. His hands were glowing.

Rory appeared behind Nolan, another ice blast forming in his hands.

Maddox saw it and retreated.

Nolan noticed the ice blast in Rory's hands and rounded on the younger magi. "I said no!"

Rory looked at him, incredulous. "Why?"

"Because you don't need to be become the person he fears. The person he believes you are."

Rory's face soured. "He tried to kill us."

"And he likely succeeded with a few," Nolan said. "But he

329

didn't do it out of hate or spite. He did it because he believed he was protecting his people. Are there any among us who wouldn't have done the same?"

The remaining magi gathered in the hollowed space of the phalanx. *Is the battle over then?*

No one answered Nolan's question.

"I didn't think so." Nolan closed the gap between him and Maddox. He may have called for peace, but his arms continued to pulse with energy. "Allyn said that we are not his enemy. Let's not dishonor that sentiment."

"What do we do with him then?" Rory asked.

"We leave him."

"What?" Rory bellowed. "He'll come after us again."

"Perhaps." Nolan shrugged. "But if he does, the last memory he'll have is an act of mercy. And that's a powerful ally."

A final form appeared from the line of cars. Broad and powerful, Jaxon walked with a significant limp. His leg was a bloody mess of fabric and torn flesh. Welts covered his exposed arms, where he had no doubt blocked baton strikes, and his expression was the kind that attempted to mask the pain but failed to do so.

Rory took one look at Jaxon and immediately looked away. Even Nolan seemed to shrink. There was little doubt who would make the final decision.

"Leave him," Jaxon said in a tight voice.

---

Three hours removed from the battle, Allyn began to suspect that Jaxon wasn't taking them to the Green Manor. His face was a swollen mess, and the pain hadn't subsided in the least. He had a vague memory just before he'd lost consciousness of Jaxon ordering his clerics to heal the wounded police—but not his own force.

Allyn tried to blink the blurriness from his eyes for the

hundredth time, but all it did was crack the dried blood and reopen the cuts on his face. His vision was little more than a series of shapes and colors. Still, a sense of familiarity began to tickle the back of his mind. Something about the road. The trees. Their direction. His head pounded fiercely, making him groggy and slow of wit.

By his best estimation they were headed west, and judging by the neglected pavement, they weren't on any recognizable highway. They traversed a series of large hills, where roadside signs warned of snow and ice, and each time they crested a hill, another loomed larger in the distance. *Not hills,* Allyn eventually realized. *Mountains.* And the only mountains to the west were in the Cascade Mountain Range—not where the Green Family lived.

"Where are you taking us?" Allyn asked, surprised by how weak he sounded. They were the first words he'd spoken since waking in the car.

Jaxon ignored him. His lack of answer told Allyn what he needed to know. They weren't returning to the Green Manor. Had they been, Jaxon wouldn't have had any reason to hide it.

Allyn straightened in his seat, grimacing as his tight muscles quarreled with him, and attempted to focus on his surroundings. The sun was high behind them, creating long shadows among the thick foliage. Sunlight that cracked the canopy hit the forest floor in sheets of gold that somehow looked tangible, and it held a magical quality that marked the day as something more than just a new day. They had put an end to the Hyland nuisance and finally escaped the clutches of Agent Maddox and the FBI—the latter done without any casualties, a wonder Allyn had yet to fully comprehend.

A gentle hand took his. Kendyl was sitting in the seat next to him. She gave him a soft smile, and Allyn tried to smile back. The cuts on his lips split, and he tasted the bitterness of blood. The sight of her jogged something loose in his subconscious.

Was that why this all looked so familiar? Was it an old highway he and Kendyl had traveled in their youth? Or maybe the mountain pass reminded him of the one leading to the cabin. But neither of those felt right. There was something recent about his memory of this place.

When Jaxon turned off the two-lane mountain road onto another, the feeling intensified. This lane was narrower than the one before. More of a private driveway than a public road, it had no white or yellow lines, guardrails, or turnoffs. The foliage was thicker; wild branches and brambles competed with each other, creeping over the edges of the road like tentative fingers reaching to steal a cookie when nobody was watching.

Jaxon led the caravan down it for what seemed like several miles, until somewhere in the distance, Allyn heard the muffled rumble of surf. White seagulls flew overhead, and the air was thick with the smell of apprehension and seawater.

Allyn groaned, growing alert as Jaxon rounded a bend and the Hyland Estate came into view. "Jaxon," Allyn said.

He ignored Allyn again, parking on the unkempt lawn, only a stone's throw from the front entrance. The caravan followed his lead and parked behind them. Jaxon sighed deeply as if he were about to take a large test he was unprepared for then shut off the car and stepped outside.

Allyn moved to follow. His body protested, but his worry and curiosity proved stronger than his body's argument. The rest of the McCollum leaders stood beside Jaxon, and the Hyland refugees waited with them. Allyn limped through the gathering Family, struggling to get a better view.

Something about the Hyland Estate seemed off. It was still the grand two-story wonder of modern architecture built along the cliff overlooking the Pacific Ocean, but the pristine lines were gone. The flowers in the garden had been neglected and left to wilt; the windows, once clear and clean, were layered with dirt and dust. It looked like a beautiful girl after a heavy night of drinking. There was no doubt that she was still a beauty under her puffy eyes and tangled hair—seeing that just took a little imagination.

The extravagant double doors opened, grinding on their hinges, and a man whom Allyn didn't recognize emerged. He was in his late thirties and slightly overweight where old muscle had deteriorated into fat. A tinge of gray touched his otherwise-brown hair. He walked with the air of command of someone who was new to it—and exhausted by the work it had required to earn it. He stopped under the covered patio, and more Hyland magi joined him, suspiciously scanning the massing McCollum group.

Brandt stepped forward.

"Brandt?" The man's tired voice was surprised, yet affectionate. "You've returned. We thought... Darian said—"

"Darian is finished," Brandt interrupted.

"Finished?" The man raised an eyebrow.

"Gone, Parke," Brandt said. "Dead."

A soft murmur rose among the handful of Hyland magi. They exchanged curious glances, the smallest hint of smiles touching the corners of their mouths. The tension melted away into... Allyn couldn't tell what. *Relief?*

Parke kept his face expressionless. "I see," he said. "By your hand?"

"By his own," Brandt said.

"And the rest?"

"Gone, as well."

Parke nodded, his own smile finally creeping across his face. "Darian was always too ambitious for his own good." He turned to the group behind him. "This is good news. When he left, the majority of his followers went with him. We... *removed* the rest." The words hung in the air, their implications clear.

"Those who remain were never true to Lukas or Darian. We remain true to our *Family*."

Jaxon moved forward to stand beside Brandt. "Our two Families are splintered," he said. "Devastated by greed and violence. In an effort to rebuild our own, we seek asylum."

An eternal breath followed, and in that space, Allyn saw their future if the Hyland Family rejected their plea. The Family adrift. Groups of twos and threes being assimilated into existing Families. The rest faltering and splintering into oblivion. Bloodlines dying out. Confusion. Pain. Loss.

Parke's voice brought him back. "It would be an honor."

# EPILOGUE

LIAM DRAGGED HIS HAND ALONG the porous basement wall of the Hyland Estate. The scratchy concrete tickled his soft fingertips and left a faint white residue on his pink skin. He couldn't help but feel more than a little uneasy strolling through the dimly lit corridors. The last time he'd been here, he'd been forced to hide in a holding room after Darian Hyland's betrayal. Now it was supposed to be their asylum, their new home.

Liam chafed at that. Burned or not, McCollum Manor would always be his home. Everything else was little more than a shelter, a means to an end. And even though they were currently storing most of the library's artifacts at Hyland Estate, it would never be their permanent resting place.

The six-inch-thick double doors with reinforced-steel bindings loomed ahead. Rory appeared in the open doorway, striding purposely into the wide corridor. He smiled at the sight of Liam.

"Almost there," Rory said. "Just going up to get the last of it now."

"That's great," Liam said, putting on his best smile. "I appreciate your hard work."

Rory returned the gesture and passed Liam, disappearing into the network of corridors behind him.

Liam stopped at the doorway, taking in the sight in front of him. The furniture in the holding cell had been pushed to the edges of the room to make room for the green totes, and even stacked four or five high, they occupied most of the room. The existing furniture would have to go.

The holding cell lacked the scale of the library, and it didn't have the climate-controlled air or the purifying system, either. It was cozy. And without any natural light, he didn't have to worry about sun damage. It was a start. Something that would work until they found more permanent arrangements. The environment might not preserve the texts, but it wouldn't destroy them, either.

Allyn and Kendyl were in the corner of the room near the wall of built-in shelves, playing with what sounded like an old radio.

"What are you guys doing?" Liam asked, approaching.

"We're trying to get this old thing to work," Allyn said, adjusting the antennae. "We can't get any reception down here."

"I keep telling him it's broken," Kendyl said, turning the knob. "But he won't listen to me—he never listens to me."

"That's because you never say anything worth listening to," Allyn said sarcastically. He looked up at Liam with a wry smile. "You done already?"

"Yeah," Liam said. "It went smoother than I expected."

"That's always nice."

"I wouldn't have been able to do it without Nolan," Liam said. "They'd revoked his credentials, but he was able to sign on as Agent Maddox. Apparently, the man never changes his password. But it actually worked out better that way. By signing on as the lead investigator, it gave us privileges that Nolan wouldn't have had under his own user profile. We were able to alter the FBI's record of your Social Security number, your driver's license number, passport information, addresses—anything we could think of, really."

"Wait," Allyn said. "You could do all of that through the FBI?"

"No," Liam said. "It's just the information law enforcement has on you. It doesn't change the information at the Social Security Office or DMV. It just makes it so no other agency can cross-reference the FBI's information. Slows them down—that's all."

"Every little bit helps," Allyn said.

"Yeah," Liam said, growing irritated that Allyn wasn't more impressed. Even though the FBI had a single sign-on to the National Crime Information Center and the hundreds of FBI microsites, it was still a notable achievement. It wasn't all luck. "Plus, using Maddox's credentials, we were able to build a shadow user that we'll be able to use to continue to falsify documents. We plan to continue to be a thorn in the FBI's paw."

"I like it." Allyn let out a frustrated sigh and stepped away from the radio.

"I told you it was broken," Kendyl said.

Allyn ignored her and rubbed an irritated hand through his hair. "I'm telling you," he said. "I got something out of it earlier."

"You're imagining things," Kendyl said.

"You mind if I give it a try?" Liam asked.

"Be my guest," Allyn said. "I haven't listened to music in so long, I might even welcome some country." He said the last bit in an exaggerated Southern drawl.

"I'd rather it stay broken," Kendyl said.

Liam didn't have the slightest clue what they were talking about, so he set to inspecting the radio. The moment he touched it, the radio roared to life.

"Whoa!" Allyn said. "What did you do?"

"I didn't do anything," Liam said.

Allyn stepped forward and took hold of the tuner. Immediately, the radio went back to static.

"It doesn't like you," Kendyl said.

"Apparently." Allyn took a resigned step back, and the radio began to play again.

"Don't move," Liam said.

"I won't," Allyn said. The radio continued to play.

"What do you want to listen to?"

"Find some rock," Allyn said. "Some Nirvana or Pearl Jam or something."

"How old *are* you?" Kendyl teased. "Good luck finding *that*. How about some alternative? Some Mumford and Sons or Imagine Dragons?"

"I don't even know who that is," Allyn said.

"That's because you're still living in '92." Kendyl stuck her tongue out at Allyn for effect and turned to Liam. "Just see what you can find, Liam."

Liam didn't know who *any* of those bands were, so he cycled through the stations slowly, hoping Allyn or Kendyl would tell him to stop. When each station came into reception, he let it linger for a moment then kept going when neither Allyn nor Kendyl approved.

When he came to the end of the tuner spectrum, Liam turned the dial back to the only station he'd recognized. He scrolled faster than he had before, and the songs and stations went by in a blur, mixing talk radio with random melodies.

"Can you believe... so long, Astoria... I did it for... the rain on Tuesday."

He had trouble finding the station, and cycled back through in the opposite direction.

"Before their grandmamma buried treasure in the gridlocked senate."

"Wait," Kendyl said suddenly. "Stop!"

Liam froze. "What?"

"Do that again."

"Do what?"

"What you were just doing."

Liam cycled through the stations again.

"Faster," Kendyl said. Liam complied, and Kendyl's face grew contemplative. "I can't believe it," she said.

"Can't believe what?" Allyn asked.

"She was right there in front of us the whole time."

"Who?"

"Follow me."

―――――――――――――――

*How do you tell the woman you love that you're about to leave her?* Jaxon waited alone under the awning outside the double doors of the Hyland Estate, his hands clasped behind his back. He watched patiently as a steady drizzle fell, making the landscape look as if he were seeing it through a dirty window. The air was cold, and the erratic wind gusts coming off the ocean made it even more uncomfortable. It was a bad combination. The worst. *Why couldn't it be just a little colder so the rain would turn to snow?* At least that was pretty. Rain had a way of making things feel dirty.

The last of the McCollums' possessions had been brought into the estate over an hour ago, and Brandt and a small group of Hyland magi had left to return the cargo vans. They wouldn't be back until well into the night. Jaxon wanted to sigh in relief. They had done it. The McCollum Family was safe, they had their most important possessions back, and they had the Forum's attention. He'd accomplished everything he had set out to do.

*Then why do I feel like a failure?*

Was that how he was supposed to feel? Wasn't the good always tempered with the bad? They were safe for the short term, but the Hyland Estate didn't have a proper place to store the fragile McCollum artifacts, and the Forum could just as easily uphold their previous decision as they could reinstate the Family. He had accomplished everything he had intended, but it might not have been enough.

*And Leira. How could I have been so reckless?* The echo was forbidden, one of the deepest violations of their Order. And like the erratic wind making the cold winter drizzle more uncomfortable, their actions would be considered worse because they were each the children of respected grand mages. Their actions would not only reflect poorly on them, but would also largely discredit their Families. He could already feel his father's wrath and his mother's deep sense of disapproval. That scared him more than anything.

The great door opened with a deep groan and a squeal from the dry hinge, and Leira appeared in the doorway.

"Hi," she said, walking up to stand beside him.

"Hi."

"You're hiding from me."

The directness of her accusation threw him off. He hesitated for a second, then as he went to deny it, Leira placed her finger on his lips, silencing him before he began.

"I know it looks bad," Leira said. "And I know you're afraid, but I don't care. I think it's wonderful."

"Leira," Jaxon said, taking her hand in his and pulling it away from his face. "We developed an echo. An *echo*. It *is* bad. It's more than bad—it's profane."

"I refuse to believe that anything that brings us closer together is profane."

"You're not thinking clearly."

"On the contrary," Leira said. "I've never been so clearheaded. It saved my life."

"That's where you're not looking at the bigger picture," Jaxon said. "You don't understand the compulsion. I felt a hollow echo of your fear, but the compulsion to find you, to make that fear go away, was so strong I couldn't think clearly. I left my squad to find you, and I put myself *and* the entire Family at risk. That's unacceptable."

"That's because you weren't used to it," she said. "It'll get easier."

"I can't count on that." He took a deep breath. "I can't be around you, Leira."

"You can't be around..." she repeated slowly.

"As soon as the Forum hands down their decision, I'm returning to the Green Manor."

"No—"

"I'm sorry, Leira, but I've made my decision."

"Hiding from it isn't going to make it go away."

"Maybe not," Jaxon said. "But it'll keep me from acting on it. It'll keep you and the Family safe."

"Safe?" Leira said bitterly. "You're doing this because you're scared."

"That, too, I suppose."

"Who's going to lead the Family, Jaxon? We've been through too much change. To lose another grand mage... it'll break us. If you want to make a difference, a *real* difference, then you have to live up to your responsibilities. You've led this Family through the darkest times I've ever seen, and here we are, on the brink of rebirth. Don't undo everything you've fought for."

"Leira—"

"Set your feelings for me aside," Leira continued, "and think about Liam. About Nyla. Rory, Ren, and Mason. Think about Allyn and Kendyl. Think about my father."

"That's not fair."

"Remember Trevin and Griffin and Ari. Remember Baylis and Jarrell. Remember all of their sacrifices and the cost to their broken families. They *need* you Jaxon, just as I do."

"It's not that simple."

"Make it that simple, then. It's just like before. Focus on what you can fix and worry about the rest when you can get to it."

Jaxon stared into her eyes. He thought he'd seen conviction

before, but he'd never seen anything like what he was seeing in Leira now.

"What happens if I say no?" he asked.

"Then I'll come up with a better argument and keep fighting."

"You'll never give up, will you?"

"No."

"You'd make a better grand mage than you give yourself credit for."

"Maybe," Leira said. "But right now, you'd make a better one."

"What about Canary?" Jaxon asked, letting the implication hang in the air.

"That was a mistake," Leira agreed. "But one mistake doesn't turn a Family against you. The important thing is that you learn from it."

"You think they'll continue to follow me?"

"I know they will."

"Fine," Jaxon said. "Then I'll make you this promise: if the Forum reinstates the McCollum Family and gives me their blessing to remain as the McCollum Family's grand mage, then I'll stay."

Leira's face blossomed into a radiant smile.

"But if they don't—"

"It's a start." Leira stepped forward and wrapped her arms around him, squeezing him so tightly that Jaxon knew she was still afraid she might lose him. He hugged her back, breathing in the sweet smell of her hair. She looked up at him, love and victory dancing in her moist eyes. He would have done anything to stay there, in that moment, forever, but as soon as he drew his face close to hers to kiss her perfect lips, he heard a rush of feet on tile.

"Jaxon!" Liam shouted from inside. "Jaxon!" He appeared in the doorway a moment later. "Jaxon," he said, his face wild with excitement. "Come quick."

"I don't understand," Jaxon said. Canary was propped upright in her bed, her blankets wrapped tightly around her legs. Her eyes were open, but she didn't seem aware of any of her immediate surroundings. As always, she rambled a stream of incoherent thoughts.

"It's a bittersweet. I'm here, I'm here. Waking up is hard to do."

Allyn and Kendyl stood with Liam beside her bed. In Liam's hand was a retro radio.

"Watch." Liam turned on the radio, and warm music filled the room. Liam, Allyn, and Kendyl looked to Canary expectantly. It wasn't immediately obvious at first, but the tenor of her ramblings changed. They still had the same emotionless quality, but they felt more focused. More coherent.

Liam changed the radio station, and Canary's tone changed with it.

Jaxon took a step forward. He watched her lips. Listened to the radio. Watched closer.

"She's repeating the radio," Jaxon said.

Liam shook his head. "No."

Jaxon watched more closely. Liam was right. Canary wasn't simply repeating the radio—she was saying the same thing at the same time as the broadcast. Liam changed the station again for effect, and again, Canary changed with it.

"How is she doing that?" Jaxon asked.

"She's an antennae," Liam said. "She's not suffering a metal breakdown. She's being bombarded with information she can't filter. She's a machinist, Jaxon."

"Why now?" Jaxon asked, disbelieving. "Why wasn't she like this at the manor?"

"My jammer blocked all unwanted transmissions—which, because of my father, was pretty much all of them."

"And why is she suddenly so..." He struggled to find the word.

"Lucid?" Liam asked. "Because we're giving her something to focus on."

"She's like someone suffering from autism," Kendyl said. "Everything she hears is *loud*, and she can't tune any of it out or push it to the back of her mind. It's like she's in a room with a thousand conversations going on at once, and everyone is yelling. She can't distinguish between them."

"So her ramblings..." Jaxon started.

"Are her picking up bits of phone conversations or radio transmissions," Liam said. "Maybe TV or texts. I don't know how broad her spectrum is yet."

"Unbelievable." Jaxon shook his head—he couldn't help it. His first thought was that they could have used Canary's ability to pick up on radio transmissions and communications for the past week. They could have known what the police were going to do before the orders were even sent out. But that quickly morphed into something bigger. Something more important. "Three machinists..." Jaxon's quiet voice carried through the room.

"Four," Allyn said.

Liam shut off the radio. "Four?"

Allyn turned to Kendyl. "I'm sorry. I wanted to talk to you about it first, but I found it."

"Found what?" Kendyl glanced uncomfortably at the other occupants in the room.

"Your purpose," Allyn said. "In the car, right before the battle with Maddox, you did something to me. And I didn't realize it at the time, but I think I understand now."

"All I did was tell you that we were in this together," Kendyl said dismissively.

"No," Allyn said. "You gave me confidence."

"That's what I was trying to do."

"You gave me *your* confidence."

Kendyl went very still. Leira shifted in the corner of Jaxon's vision.

"How did you feel afterward?" Allyn asked. "Because I can't tell you how confident I was facing Maddox. I've never felt anything like that before. And you... you looked like you were going to pass out."

"I..."

"It's just like a cleric—only instead of healing me, you gave me your emotion. So I started thinking, and you know what I realized? You've been doing it for a long time. Remember how I said that we pulled each other through Mom's death? That we were there for each other, gave one another strength? Well, that was quite literally what was happening."

"Allyn," Kendyl said, smiling nervously, "I love you, but you don't have to make things up to make me feel better."

"I'm not making this up," Allyn said. "How many times have I joked about your personality being contagious? Or that I can feel your mood from across the room? Are you telling me that you didn't notice anything?"

"I... I'll have to think about it."

The room went uncomfortably quiet. Allyn looked frustrated, as if he'd expected Kendyl to agree with him right away. He should have known better. People with such strong doubts about themselves need something nearly supernatural to snap them out of their self-perceived limitations.

"She's not a machinist," Leira said. "She's an *empath*."

"A what?" Allyn asked.

"An empath," Leira repeated.

"That can't be," Jaxon said. "They died out."

"Not entirely," Leira said. "They're just extremely rare, only one born every couple generations or so, if that. Kendyl, you're brother's right. You're very special."

"Will someone please tell me what an empath is?" Allyn asked.

"They wield emotion," Leira said. "And what you've seen

345

is just the beginning. In time, Kendyl will be able to control it, manipulate it, and fill you with feelings of her choosing—as long as she has it inside to pull from. Empaths are very powerful—and very dangerous."

Kendyl took a tentative step away from the group and brought a hand up to cover her mouth.

"Kendyl?" Allyn said, worry thick in his voice.

She broke down in tears.

———————————

Allyn's room was on the backside of the estate, overlooking the ocean. It was a good size and reminded him of his room at the McCollum Manor, complete with a queen bed, bedside tables, a sitting chair, and floor-to-ceiling curtains. The sky was a majestic mural of warm colors as the last of the sun's rays clung to the horizon.

"I'm so embarrassed," Kendyl said from the sitting chair. She leaned against its arm, massaging her forehead with her hand, keeping her eyes closed. Since leaving Canary's room, she'd been quiet and contemplative. Part of Allyn thought to give her some space, let her work things out on her own, but if that was what she'd wanted she could have returned to her own room. Instead she was here with him, using his silent presence for support.

"You have nothing to be embarrassed about." Allyn turned from the window and sat on the edge of the bed. "It's a lot to take in. I know—I've been there."

"It's more than just being able to wield," she said. "It's…"

"Having something to do it for."

Kendyl bit her bottom lip and nodded. "I haven't felt this much at home since Mom died."

Allyn didn't know what to say. He stepped from the bed and sat on the arm of the chair, pulling Kendyl close. She melted into him.

"Me neither," he said. "Me neither."

A knock at the door interrupted the moment, and Liam popped his head into the room half a second later. The eager smile slipped from his face as he realized he had interrupted something special.

"It's okay," Allyn said, letting Kendyl out of the embrace. "Come in."

Liam's smile returned as he stepped into the room. "I brought you something," he said, handing Allyn and Kendyl each a rectangular object.

"What are these?" Allyn asked.

"What do they look like?"

Allyn flipped his over. He was looking at a picture of himself, an image taken five or six years ago when he'd renewed his driver's license. Beside it was the standard name, date of birth, height, weight, issue date, and other information found on an ID. None of it matched Allyn's.

"I figured if you can't be Allyn and Kendyl Kaplan anymore, you might as well be Allyn and Kendyl McCollum."

"Liam—" Allyn started. The lump in his throat made it hard to talk.

"This is wonderful," Kendyl finished.

"Thank you," they said together.

Liam's smile was radiant. "Welcome to the Family."

The story continues in...

# MARTYR

The Machinists Series, Book Three
**Coming Soon**

For exclusive content follow Craig
Andrews on Facebook or sign up
for the Mailing List.

https://www.facebook.com/craigandrewsauthor

http://eepurl.com/IEjIr

# ACKNOWLEDGMENTS

I KNEW THAT WRITING THE SECOND book to an ongoing series was going to be difficult. The story and conflict needed to get bigger, the characters and world needed to feel deeper, and there needed to be a sense of progression toward the larger story arc—even if it wasn't absolutely clear what that arc is. But I didn't know it was going to be *this* difficult. It wasn't until I was about halfway through the first draft that I realized the book I was writing was, in many ways, the opposite of what my preconceived notions of what a sequel should be.

The book you're holding in your hands is in many ways a more contained, more personal story than *Fracture*. Gone is the mystery, the clearly-defined villain, and overall sense of dark wonder. In its place is a story about people trying to hold their family together, about trying to find their place in a strange and terrifying new environment, and coping with the idea that they're capable of doing something truly awful in the name of love and survival.

All that said, *Splinter* is, without a doubt (and for better or worse), the book I set out to write. I tell you this, because I've had a lot of help over the last year, and while I can't mention *everyone*, I want to publically thank those that were there for me every day.

As always, it begins with my wife, Tiffany. We welcomed our second son into the world last November, so sleep and quiet time was replaced by chaos and stress; and somehow, even with two children and a dog all under four years old, she held it together and helped me find time to write. Sometimes I wonder why she sticks with me (I'm not the easiest person to live with), but she does, and I'm a better person because of it.

Thank you, Gary and Gala for spending so many weekends at my house playing with the boys, and helping Tiffany with whatever project she had going that week. Simply put, without your help I never would have found enough time to finish this book.

To my own parents, who this book is dedicated, words can never express the amount of pride I have to be your son. As a relatively new parent, I'm just beginning to understand the never-ending sacrifices you've made for your children, and I grow more and more thankful every day. You're heroes and role models in more ways than one.

For Ender, who points at my book anytime he sees it and shouts, "Dad, look! It's your book!" You're my inspiration, and I'm already a bigger fan of your accomplishments than you are of mine. And Callan... Your smile. Your laugh. Like your brother, you can turn a rough day into a magical one in the time it takes for me to walk through the door.

Thank you Lynn and Stefanie at Red Adept Publishing. It's been another year, with another book, and it's still a wonderful experience.

To Scott, Mary, and Megan, thank you for your early feedback and enthusiasm. You'll never know how important it is for me to have someone to talk to about sticky plot points or troublesome characters arcs. I couldn't ask for better friends, or more excited fans. You're awesome.

And of course, a huge thank you goes to every person who has joined me on this journey. You took a chance on an unknown author, and for that I'll be forever grateful. I hope you stick with me as we delve into the next adventure. Big things are coming!

—Craig Andrews

CRAIG ANDREWS GRADU-ATED FROM PORTLAND State University with a Bachelors of Arts in English. Growing up on a healthy diet of fantasy and science fiction, some of his favorite childhood memories include being  traumatized by the TV shows *Unsolved Mysteries* and *The X-Files*. He currently lives in a small, rural town outside of Portland, Oregon with his wife and two boys.

*Say "hi" at any of the following*:
craigandrewsauthor@yahoo.com
http://www.craigandrewsauthor.com
https://www.facebook.com/craigandrewsauthor
http://eepurl.com/IEjIr (mailing list)